The Ghost of
Silicon Valley

The Ghost of Silicon Valley

William D. Blankenship

Writer's Showcase
presented by *Writer's Digest*
San Jose New York Lincoln Shanghai

The Ghost of Silicon Valley

Writer's Showcase
presented by *Writer's Digest*
an imprint of iUniverse.com, Inc.

For information address:
iUniverse.com, Inc.
620 North 48th Street, Suite 201
Lincoln, NE 68504-3467
www.iuniverse.com

All characters and events in this work are fictional

ISBN: 0-595-13283-9

Printed in the United States of America

Other novels by William D. Blankenship:

The Helix File

The Programmed Man

The Leavenworth Irregulars

Yukon Gold

Tiger Ten

Brotherly Love

Blood Stripe

The Time Of The Cricket

The Time Of The Wolf

Dedicated to
Samson Nakamura Blankenship

CHAPTER 1

"You're Kevin Pierce? I'm Captain Patterson, San Francisco Police Department." He looked me up and down with distaste. No offer of a handshake. Without warning he grabbed my arm and put his face a few inches from mine. "Understand this. I don't want you here. Guys like you make me puke. Phonies and leaches, you always come out of the woodwork at a time like this."

I shook off his hand and reminded myself there's no way to stay out of jail if you punch a police captain in the mouth. "You don't want me here? That's fine. I don't want to *be* here. You sent a couple of detectives to my house at one o'clock in the morning. I was yanked out of my bed and brought into the city, they wouldn't even tell me why. *Police emergency* was all they'd say. So have your guys drive me back home right now, I can probably still knock off a couple hours sleep before the sun comes up."

"I just knew you'd be a smartass, too." Patterson jammed his hands in his pockets and paced around in a tight circle. He wasn't a big man, but his shoulders had bulk and his jaw reminded me of the scoop on one of those yellow Tonka dump trucks every toddler owns. His suit was better than you'd expect and his hair had been razor cut by someone with a sense of style. Captain Patterson had higher ambitions.

"I'm gonna send you home in a while. First there's a problem I have to finesse. It seems your *special expertise* has been requested and I'm not in a position right now to say no."

"What *expertise* are you talking about?"

"It's got to do with that." He waved at the crime scene behind him. A major crime, from the look of it. Portable lights had been set up to illuminate a fifty yard stretch of an otherwise dark street off 19th Avenue near San Francisco State University. The area was marked off with the inevitable yellow crime scene tape. Within the tape, about a dozen detectives and technicians and medical examiners were at work collecting evidence, shooting videotape, weighing possibilities. Uniformed officers were keeping the public and media behind the tape. The focus of everybody's attention seemed to be a mailbox, of all things.

"Who's been killed?"

"Nobody yet...I hope." Patterson lifted the tape and gave me an impatient nudge. My name was written in a crime scene log. The last thing I wanted to do at two a.m. on a chilly morning was to look at a crime scene, but Patterson was determined to show it to me. "What happened here is that an eight-year-old boy named Toby Hillyer was savagely beaten at approximately eight-thirty p.m. He was taken to the hospital, the doctors say he's going to be okay. He became conscious for awhile at the hospital, said *a big man* hit him. Everybody looks big to an eight-year-old, so that's no help. At least he could tell us his attacker was a male Caucasian, that's something. The frosting on the cake? Toby's five-year-old sister Tara was with him at the time and she's missing."

"You still haven't told me why I'm here." I was afraid of the answer.

"Not my idea, that's for damn sure. His parents asked for you, said they read a newspaper story that called you *The Psychic of Half Moon Bay*." Patterson glared at me. "One of those supermarket tabloids, was it? I wouldn't know, I never heard of you till the boy's father mentioned your name."

This was exactly what I'd feared. "Captain, let me tell you what this is about. Last year I helped the San Jose PD break a murder case. The victim was into satanism and I happened to run across some information that led the police to the killer, that's all. Nothing supernatural about it. End of story. Or so I thought. The San Francisco *Chronicle* did a follow-up piece, headlined me *The Psychic of Half Moon Bay*, which is pure bullshit. I'm not a psychic, I'm a portrait artist. That story has been a first-class pain in the ass to me. I still get crank calls, women asking me to make contact with their dead husbands, guys wanting me to pick winners for them at Golden Gate Fields, jerks looking for stock market tips, all sorts of weird shit. I can't be of any help to those people *or* to the Hillyers. This sort of thing is totally out of my realm."

Patterson rocked back in surprise. "You're not a psychic? That's a relief. Will you tell that to the parents of Toby and Tara Hillyer?"

There was more to my involvement in the San Jose murder than I'd admitted, but I wasn't about to share my history with Patterson. "Of course."

"Okay." He looked for a way to backtrack. "So maybe I was wrong about you." Patterson took me by the elbow, more gently this time, and escorted me back under the tape and into a darker spot on the street. In the moonlight, his eyes were as green as a cat's. "Here's the deal. The Hillyers live at the end of this street. Some time after eight o'clock they sent Toby down to the corner, that corner where the mailbox is, to mail a letter. They used to let him do that, this street has always been safe till now. This time they let Tara, Toby's little sister, go along with him. Big mistake. A few minutes later a woman who lives on the street heard screams. Did nothing about it at the time, the miserable bitch. A few minutes after that another neighbor was walking home. It's dusk, going dark fast, he sees something, somebody, in the gutter, turns out to be Toby. Kid's bleeding and unconscious. A car, old and American-made is all the neighbor can tell us, is roaring away. Toby's suffered multiple blows to the head, Tara's gone."

I got the gist. "Somebody grabbed the girl. Started to drag her into a car. Toby, her brother, tried to protect his little sister from the kidnapper, got himself beaten up."

"Bingo. Kidnapping and attempted murder." The green cat's eyes narrowed. "You see the tv cameras over there? The print guys yelling questions at my detectives? It's your Class A media feeding frenzy. I've got forty-five cops on the street. I'm pulling in every child molester we got on the computer, canvassing the neighborhood, supplying a picture of Tara to the newspapers and tv stations, got parole officers out of bed all over the city and started them digging into their pervert files. Like they say, I'm kickin' ass and takin' names. Meanwhile the parents are hysterical. Blame themselves, and between you and me the Hillyers were negligent to let an eight-year-old and a five-year-old walk out of the house alone at that hour, all the schizoid sleazebags running loose in this city."

Patterson's formidable jaw moved up and down. "They're not bad parents, I'm not saying that, but they're both school teachers, they should have known better. The Hillyers just got back from the hospital. Toby'll survive, we're all concentrating on finding Tara. The Hillyers appreciate everything we're doing, or so they say. But they want more. They want a *psychic* brought in to find Tara. Gave me your name. I sent two detectives to bring you to me. Here you are. Sorry if I came at you like a mad dog, foaming mouth and all, I just don't have time to make nice."

My groan gave Patterson further hope that I wasn't a fake mystic looking for personal publicity.

"Will you tell the Hillyers you can't help them, Mr. Pierce? Do that for me, five minutes of your time, I'll have you back in your bed forthwith."

"Don't worry, I'll tell them exactly that."

Like a lot of San Francisco houses, the Hillyer home was small and cramped but essentially charming. The furniture was bright and modern, oil paintings and Japanese woodblock prints on the walls. I recognized the work of Lewis Holland, a local artist. We'd taken a workshop together down at Carmel on the chemical elements of pigmentation. I liked Lewis better than I liked his paintings. I suppose some people say the same about me.

The police had made the house their headquarters, cops going back and forth and talking on the phone as if the Hillyers hardly existed. Every face looked grim, every voice was hushed. I don't know much about police work, but I read faces and body language as well as the next person. With every minute that passed, little Tara Hillyer's chance to stay alive diminished.

"John Hillyer...Emily Hillyer...this is Kevin Pierce."

We sat down across from each other. I'd only had time to throw on a sweatshirt, pants, and a pair of sneakers without socks. My hair was uncombed. I needed a shave. I worried that my attire might somehow look disrespectful to the Hillyers.

Emily Hillyer didn't seem to think so. "Thank you so much for coming." She grabbed my hand and actually kissed it. "God bless you." Her eyes were wild and she threw her head around like a mare being dragged from a burning stable. "Tara's still alive, I know she is, I can feel it right here." Tapping her own chest with an open palm. "If she were dead, I'd know that, too. Toby, he's going to be all right, they've got him sedated, but he has some awful wounds, they had to take stitches all down the side of his head. Now we've got to find Tara. She's alive somewhere and you must help us find her, she's so young, only five years old and so *little*, even for that age."

"Emily..." John Hillyer put a restraining arm around his wife's shoulder.

"Trusting, too," Emily Hillyer jabbered. "Tara's always been trusting. Oh God, why didn't I put more *fear* into her? She needed *fear*, I can see that now. I warned her never to go with strangers, John will tell you that, but she lacked real fear." She sobbed and rotated her head fiercely, as if trying to make it fly off her shoulders.

The Hillyers were probably in their mid-thirties but had aged ten years over the last few hours. She was thin and hollow-eyed, vaguely pretty, dressed in a solid blue pants suit she'd probably worn to work. John Hillyer, a heavy man with plain and grave features, was more in control than his wife, at least on the surface. I saw a lot of panic in his eyes, tremendous pain. He was holding himself together with hope and hot coffee.

"Yes, thanks for coming so quickly, Mr. Pierce," John Hillyer said. "Emily remembered that story in the *Chronicle*, how you helped the police in San Jose find a killer? Can you help us find Tara's kidnapper?"

The idea of calling me obviously came from the wife. Now that I was here, standing in front of them, the husband had become a believer. I didn't take that as a compliment. The poor guy was ready to believe in anything that fed his hope. I took a deep breath. They were looking at me with such fervor that I hated to crush their expectations. "Captain Patterson told me what happened to Toby. I'm terribly sorry for your troubles, but I'm glad Toby's going to be okay. He also told me about all the people he has out on the streets looking for your daughter, the other actions he's taken. Sounds to me like he's on the right track and I'd just be getting in his way."

"No!" Emily Hillyer twisted away from her husband. Her reddish hair flew like streaks of lightning. "You can find Tara! I know you can! They said in the newspaper you used psychic power to find a killer for the San Jose police!"

"The story was an exaggeration," I explained. Patterson watched me closely, eager to end this and get back to the real investigation. "I truly don't have any special powers, Mrs. Hillyer."

"They said in the newspaper!" She was weeping now, still tossing her head, her fingers twisting her husband's shirtsleeve so violently that he felt compelled to speak.

"We don't expect miracles. Insight. A special sensitivity to these things. Psychology. Whatever you brought to that case in San Jose might work here, too." John Hillyer's voice broke, he was on the verge of cracking up. "Tell us what you think, do that at least."

"I think you need to put your faith in Captain Patterson and his investigation, not in me." I cringed at the disappointment that greeted my words. "They're professionals, they know what they're doing." My voice sounded whiny to my own ears. "Really, there's no way I can be of help. I'd only be a hindrance, waste some police officer's valuable time with any ideas I might have. That story you saw wasn't accurate. Please believe me." I rose, hoping to escape without leaving any rancor in my wake. "I'd better go now."

"No!" Emily Hillyer cried out dramatically. "Wait!"

She ran from the living room to the back of the house, bumping into police officers along the way, bouncing off them like a pinball. In other circumstances it would have been funny. Her husband looked first at me and then at Patterson and shrugged wearily. With his wife out of the room, John Hillyer allowed himself to slump into outright despair. Moments later, when Emily's footsteps could be heard returning to the living room, Hillyer straightened his back and adopted a more positive pose.

"Here, Mr. Pierce, this is one of Tara's sweaters." She thrust a child's red woolen sweater at me. "Take it with you, please. You might pick up something from this, I don't know what exactly, a vision or something, from the sweater I mean."

A vision? I opened my hands reluctantly, took the sweater, made a vague show of running my fingers over the material. "Sure, I'll do that." What else could I say? I folded the tiny sweater neatly, put it under my arm. "Good luck to you, I hope you get Tara back very soon. And again, I'm awfully sorry about what happened to Toby. I'm glad he's going to recover."

Outside, Patterson squeezed my arm. "Thanks, Pierce. You did good."

"I did nothing."

"That's what I mean." He looked to his left and waved for a uniformed officer to come over. "Patrolman Lang will drive you back to Half Moon Bay."

"Good luck in finding the little girl."

"She may be dead already. That's the way these cases often play out." Patterson's face went red as he stoked his own anger. "Whatever's happened to her, we'll find this sicko, I guarantee you that. Lang, drive this gentleman home and then get right back here." He turned without saying good-bye and stalked off to see if his people had any good news for him.

I climbed into the back seat of the police car in total depression and with a host of questions rattling around in my head. Why did Toby Hillyer have to be a victim of some deranged psychopath? Pure bad luck, being in the wrong place at the wrong time? Or is there a design to tragedy as well as triumph? Where was Tara Hillyer? Who had her? How soon would Emily Hillyer collapse from strain and grief and how many years would this event take off her life? Would the Hillyers ever be able to go back into a classroom full of kids? Could I have done *something* to help those people?

Every time I start to feel comfortable in the world, good about myself and what I'm doing with my life, some ugly event like this seems to come along. The Hillyers' troubles made me question whether there was any reason at all for people to create beautiful and interesting things. In my case, paintings. The world had become such an ugly sewer on so many levels, why bother?

That was either a lousy attitude or a realistic assessment of the human condition, I was too upset just then to swing one way or another. Patrolman Lang must have sensed my mood because he didn't utter a word all the way down Highway 1. It was three a.m. before I crawled back into my bed. I laid the red child's sweater on a chair next to the bed, neatly folded as if waiting to be put on by Tara Hillyer.

When dawn came at a few minutes after six, I still hadn't found any sleep.

Since I couldn't sleep, I got out of bed shortly after sunup and elected to do some work. Moods are quirky things, they come and go depending on what you're doing at the time. Any black thoughts I have usually ease off when I have a brush in my hand, a canvas to work on, plenty of paints, an interesting face taking shape in front of me. A cold beer on the table next to the easel helps, too. Even at seven o'clock in the morning. There are those who say a serious painter should never drink while working, and I don't dispute their thinking. But I grew up in Blanco county, Texas where they have another word for beer. They call it breakfast.

So I was having a Carta Blanca breakfast, diddling along with my work, enjoying the stillness of the early morning and trying to put the Hillyer family way at the back of my mind. My house is up in the hills above Half Moon Bay, about thirty miles south of San Francisco. The deck overlooks the slope that runs down to Highway 1 and the Pacific ocean, a glistening and endless blue on this particular morning, no fog at all. Great place to work.

The ocean view is the best feature of the house, which is supposed to be a classic A-frame. The contractor must have been drunk because one leg of the A is slightly shorter than the other. A couple of years ago, after eight of my paintings sold in a single month, I felt flush enough to buy what realtors call a "fixer-upper." Unfortunately, those sales turned out to be a peak experience. Since then I've been lucky just to make my mortgage payments, so the "fixing up" hasn't happened. The roof still leaks. The exterior desperately needs a coat of redwood stain. The fireplace flu is broken. I can't get much water pressure. And I think the termites have finally punched through to the foundation. Or maybe those creaks and groans mean something else.

The face I was working on belonged to a carpenter who did some work on the house next door. Good carpenter, I wish I'd had enough money to hire him to reconstruct my roof, but as far as I was concerned his real asset was his face. The years of working outdoors had hardened every line. He had a perpetual two-day growth of beard (I can't imagine how you do that), straight sunburned nose, enormous creases in the corners of weathered eyes, a strong chin below a very straight mouth.

The individual features were only mildly interesting. Taken together they expressed decades of hard-bitten labor.

The carpenter let me take some Polaroids of him. I had shoved them into a bureau drawer with photos of other faces because I need to let an idea percolate for a while. Also because I'm too lazy to take quick action on anything. The other day, pawing through the Polaroids in the drawer, I came upon the carpenter's likeness again. Now I had two Polaroids of him clipped to the edge of my canvas and had done an outline of his head in charcoal and sketched in the features. I was out to paint him in oil. I wanted him drenched in sweat, concentrating mightily on his work, tired as hell, with sawdust and thin curls of wood caught in the hair on his powerful arms.

I worked steadily until about eleven o'clock. During that time I ate a banana and an English muffin with a second Carta Blanca on the theory that all the potassium in a banana offsets the effects of alcohol. Nobody ever told me that and I didn't read it in the *New England Journal of Medicine*, it's just a personal theory. My grasp of nutrition may be shaky, but it helps me work in some decent food around my beers.

The carpenter's face took shape fairly quickly. Maybe I took some liberties, gave his features somewhat more character than the Lord originally allowed him. If so, the carpenter should thank me. Not that he'd be likely ever to see this painting. With luck, my sales agent would place it in a gallery somewhere and it would end up on a wall in somebody's house or maybe even in a museum. Four of my paintings that I know of are in museums, and maybe others that I haven't yet heard about. Not major museums. I'm talking about small museums in places like Birmingham, Alabama and Woodstock, New York. At least they're museums.

A few minutes after eleven the phone rang. My agent, Marie Spector, calling from Los Angeles to discuss what we laughingly call my career.

"Kevin, I've got good news and bad news," Marie started off. "Which do you want first?"

"Tell me the good news and stick the bad in the mail. Don't bother to put a stamp on the envelope."

"Not businesslike," she chided. "I keep telling you, Kevin, that art is also a business. What's happened is this, the Lowen Gallery in Santa Barbara is returning all five paintings we sent them in March. They couldn't move even one of them."

I experienced the kind of sinking sensation you get on the Matterhorn ride in Disneyland. "The gallery owner said he loved my work."

"Franz Lowen still likes your work, he just can't move it off his walls. He's promised to give you another showing next year."

It wasn't lost on me that Franz Lowen now *liked* my work instead of *loved* it. I'd hoped those paintings would bring at least ten thousand dollars. I could hear the termites in my foundation laughing and telling each other they had nothing to fear from the pest control man this year. "So what's the good news?"

"The Peabody Gallery in Palm Beach did move one of your pieces, the portrait of the itinerant farm worker. It went for four thousand dollars and that's *very* good news indeed. You aren't selling as well as you should but the prices on the canvases you do sell are going up. You'll get a check this week for that sale, less my commission and the split from the gallery."

Some fast mental arithmetic told me I'd realize about twenty-two hundred dollars from that portrait (before taxes), enough to pay my mortgage and mollify the rapacious accountants at Visa. There might even be enough left over for more Carta Blanca and bananas. "Thanks, Marie. Look, I really appreciate the way you've stuck with me. I know I haven't made much money yet for either of us."

"Kevin, you're only...what...thirty-one? You've got a fine eye for portraiture. You're building a reputation, and that takes time. Just stay with it. What are you working on now?"

I told her about the carpenter and also described a portrait I'd finished of a pregnant woman sitting on a bench waiting for a bus.

Fortunately, the day I saw the woman in downtown San Francisco I had my small 35 millimeter Rollei in my pocket. I managed to snap off a couple of shots before the bus came along and took her away. I'd worked from those photos and was pleased with the result. "The woman wasn't young, early forties I'd say, obviously uncomfortable and maybe even in some pain. Her face had a stoicism that grabbed me. She was blissful in her discomfort. You could tell she was willing to put up with any amount of hardship for her unborn baby, even give her own life if it came down to it. I tried to capture that."

"Yes, that's the kind of face you do best. I don't see many big smiles in your portraits, Kevin. Sometime you'll have to tell me why that is. Hey, don't get depressed about Lowen returning your paintings. I'll find another gallery for them. The right gallery. May take some time, but we'll sell them. No doubt in my mind."

"No doubt in mine either." I spoke with an air of confidence I didn't feel.

Marie rang off a few minutes later and I went out on the deck to take another peek at my carpenter's face. The beginning of the face didn't look quite as impressive as it had when I walked away from my easel to answer Marie's call. When I come back to a piece of work, it seldom looks as good to me as when I left it. The fear of not being up to the subject I'm working on used to send me into a panic. Or even into depression. Franklin Delano Roosevelt said *The only thing we have to fear is fear itself*, which was better than average thinking for a politician. I took his words to heart and these days I don't scare as easily. The basic blocking on the carpenter looked okay and the beginnings of the face, shoulders and arms hinted at real character. The rest of the painting would unfold in its own good time. In a week or so, with luck and a lot of hard work, I'd probably have a canvas I could take some pride in.

Meanwhile, those lost hours of sleep in the middle of the night with Captain Patterson and the Hillyers, plus the two Carta Blancas for breakfast, had left me sleepy. I went inside, flopped on the couch, closed my eyes.

CHAPTER 2

I'd been asleep on the couch for three hours or more when I came partly awake feeling a chill. My hand went out looking for something to pull over my shoulders. Nothing there. The chill got worse. I pulled a cushion over myself but that didn't help.

As I struggled into a sitting position, I began to tremble from an insistent breeze moving through the room. I blinked away the residue of the nap and came to grips with what was going on in my house.

Yesterday I'd picked some wildflowers from the hill behind my deck and put them in a vase in the living room. The flowers were Mexican Hats, deep rusty orange in the center and bright yellow around the edges. Vivid colors. The half dozen wildflowers did a better job of brightening the room than a dozen hundred watt bulbs could ever do. Now, right before my eyes, the Mexican Hats were drooping down over the neck of the vase and beginning to die.

What was happening didn't scare me because I'd seen it before. "Go away!"

As if that would stop him.

The movement of air gradually localized in one corner of the room. Something resembling a small whirlwind, the kind you see zipping across the flat plains of Texas, gathered force. A nearby area rug shot across the room. One of my favorite pictures, an Ansel Adams black and white photo of Yosemite, fell to the floor and the frame shattered. I pressed back against the cushions and hoped nothing would come flying at my head.

The whirlwind became more visible as it took on a pale yellow color. In the eye of the miniature storm, something like red forks of lightning appeared accompanied by crackling sounds. I held onto the arm of the couch as my living room shuddered and bucked. Another picture hit the floor. Glasses on the kitchen counter were swept away, a few of them smashed when they hit the floor. The whirlwind grew to the size of a man. Then the wind died, the crackle of lightning subsided, the apparition took a human form and went through a medley of colors before consolidating into a pale green.

"Hiya, Kevin."

"Hello, Sport." I got up from the couch and went around the room picking up my pictures and carefully collecting pieces of broken glass. "After all this time, can't you make a less messy entrance?"

"I don't have much control over those things."

"Who does?"

"The fuck should I know? I'm in limbo here. L-I-M-B-O. You know what that means?"

"I think so."

"I ain't alive," Sport explained, as if to a child. "But I ain't totally dead, neither." His greenish form glowed white hot for just a moment, like a light bulb burning out. Then it went all red. "I ain't in heaven or hell, I'm in fucking limbo, get it?"

"You've explained this to me before, Sport."

"Yeah, but you always look surprised when I turn up, like you never seen me before."

"You're the only spirit I've ever met, so it still bothers me when you come barreling into my life in a blast of wind and colored lights."

"Get used to it."

"I don't want to get used to it. You annoy me, Sport."

"I ain't especially fond of you neither. But I got no control over where I go, or when. I'm your spirit guide, not your asshole buddy."

"You're my curse, is what you are."

"Fuck you, Kevin." The apparition that was Sport Sullivan began striding around my living room, peering here and there as if he'd never seen the place before. Actually, he hadn't been around for almost a year. I'd begun to hope I'd seen the last of the miserable creep.

"You oughtta take better care of this joint, it's falling apart. Nice view though. What is that, an ocean?"

"The Pacific ocean."

"So what is this, California?"

With a sigh. "The last time you were here I told you it was California. You don't remember?"

"I was never big on geography. My whole life, I never got farther west than Chicago, and that was a fucking disaster for me. You want to hear the story?"

I didn't want to hear it, but I knew Sport Sullivan would tell it to me again. He always did. I grabbed another Carta Blanca from the refrigerator and retreated to an easy chair on the opposite side of the room from where Sport was striding back and forth, talking in his tough New York accent as if the events that had turned him into a ghost, or a *spirit* as he preferred to be called, had happened just the day before instead of more than eighty years ago.

"It was September of 1919 when Arnold Rothstein sent me to Chicago with twenty-five grand in my kick. Arnold practically ran New York in those days, y'know. I ain't kidding about that. He was a gambler, a fixer, a loan shark, a real power guy. Arnold Rothstein knew every politician in New York, did favors for all of 'em, fixed 'em up with women, handled their payoffs. You name it, Arnold was into it." Sport noticed the bottle in my hand. "What's that you're drinking, pal?"

"Beer."

"What brand?"

"Carta Blanca, a Mexican beer."

Sport Sullivan made a face. "Mexican beer? All the good beer comes from Milwaukee or New York, everybody knows that."

"Times change, Sport."

"You're telling *me* times change?" He looked sour. "Can't even recognize the world I was born into, ain't that a fine fix?" Sport moped about his peculiar status for a few seconds, then returned to his story. "So I go to Chicago with twenty-five grand of Arnold Rothstein's money in my suitcase. Arnold's already paved the way, set the stage. I'm just the go-between, y'understand?"

"Today they'd call you a bag man."

"Bag man? The fuck's that supposed to mean?"

"Bag of money. You're carrying a bag of money to someone, that's a bag man."

"Dumb way to say it. Anyway, I meet with Joe Jackson of the Chicago White Sox in a little bar on the north side. Place where nobody would notice us. That year, 1919, the White Sox are a cinch to win the pennant and go on to the World Series. Arnold Rothstein, he's out to fix the Series. Fix the World Series!" The color behind Sport Sullivan's eyes glowed and went through several different shades of red as he laughed and rubbed his hands together. "Arnold Rothstein always thought big, y'know. Figured he could get away with anything, even fixing the goddam World Series. And he did! Joe Jackson, they called him Shoeless Joe Jackson because he came to the Major Leagues from some shithole down South where they don't wear shoes and screw each other's sisters, took the twenty-five grand. Joe was the heavy hitter on the White Sox. If he and a few other players had a bad Series, the White Sox didn't have a chance. Shoeless Joe promised to spread that dough among a few other players. It was supposed to be a down payment on a bigger payoff. Naturally, Arnold Rothstein planned to stiff the players for the rest of their dough."

"Naturally. But why would the players do it?" Sport had never been clear about that. "Throw a World Series?"

"The players hated the management of the White Sox, that's why. In 1919 they were the champion cheap bastards of the United States. Paid their players shit wages and kept the lion's share of any playoff money for himself. To save a few bucks the management only got the players' uniforms cleaned once a week . How'd you like to play six or seven games a week in a dirty, smelly baseball uniform? That kind'a treatment made some of the players ripe to throw a Series. Arnold could smell that the team was pissed all the way from New York, he was a master at sniffing out stuff like that. So I give Shoeless Joe the payoff, he's gonna spread it around to a few key players. I go back to New York and tell Arnold the fix is in."

I asked Sport how much money Shoeless Joe Jackson made as a Major League player.

"I don't remember exactly, two or three grand a year."

"These days the top Major League baseball players earn eight or ten million dollars a year."

"Bullshit."

I picked up that morning's San Francisco *Chronicle* and held the sports page up so Sport could read a story about the Giants catcher who was bitching because he'd only make four million this season.

"Holy shit! In my day a Major League player pulled down maybe twenty-five hundred bucks a year, didn't matter how good he was. The second stringers got maybe a thousand year, they were lucky." Sport shook his head, sending a shower of sparks flying around the room. I backed off and returned to my easy chair.

Sport asked: "So who's leading the National League this year?"

"The Colorado Rockies."

"There ain't no Major League team in Colorado. The Rockies are just a bunch of mountains!"

"These days the Rockies are also a National League team. An expansion team. There are a lot more teams in both leagues than there were in 1919. You've got teams in L.A. and San Francisco. Denver. San Diego. Florida. Phoenix. Seattle. All over the place."

"World's gone crazy." Sport's color faded as he let himself become depressed about some of the changes that had taken place since he died. "Almost makes me glad I'm not alive." His eyes flickered like torchlights. "Anyway, I paid off Shoeless Joe Jackson, he spread the money around the team, and half a dozen players agreed to throw the Series.

"The White Sox went against the Cincinnati Reds in that Series. The Sox lost, everybody was surprised. The Sox didn't get the hits or the pitching. Everybody says that's too bad, the Sox'll be back next year." Sport winked. "Arnold had big money bet on the Reds. He laid it off all over the country under different names, including mine. When 1920 rolls around, everybody's forgotten the Series. Or so I thought. But the guys who threw the game are talking about what they did, complaining to their wives and buddies they got stiffed on the big payoff. Of course Arnold stiffed them. Why wouldn't he? He's already got the milk, why feed the cow? Y'understand me?"

I nodded to indicate I was following Sport's story, just so he wouldn't get upset. When Sport gets upset, he tends to make things fly around the room and smash into walls.

"Once the players started to talk, the owners called in a guy named Judge Mountain Landis to clean up baseball. The whole story comes out, everybody starts calling them the Chicago Black Sox. Some players get kicked out of baseball for life. And everybody wants to nail the man who fixed the Series. They *know* Arnold Rothstein did it, he's the only guy with the juice to pull off a deal like that. But they don't have any proof." Sport Sullivan's eyes crackled with fire. "My name comes up in the investigation. Shoeless Joe fingers me as...what did you call me?...the *bagman*.

"So on the night of August 10, 1920, I'm sitting in a bar on 51st Street in New York trying to figure out where I should go. I have to lam it out of New York, get lost for a year or so, that's what Arnold tells me. He's sending a guy with ten grand in travel money. Pay me off, get me out of town." Sport shook his head in disgust. "Should'a seen it coming. I get paid off all right. Guy walks into the bar. Comes right up to me with a gun already drawn. Puts five bullets into me, I'm dead before I hit the floor. Not totally dead though. Like I say, I'm here in limbo."

"Better than burning in hell," I suggested.

"Yeah, so I hear. But what if hell comes next? What if this is just a warm-up for hell? I mean, *nobody* tells me *nothing*. I float around from one decade to the next. The world changes around me. I surfaced one time in the middle of a war, everybody around me's talking German! I scared hell out of a bunch of German soldiers, I can tell you that. Now the only person I get to talk with is you, I don't know why. And I don't even like you! Down-at-the-heels artist is all you are."

"So go see somebody else. I'm all for that."

"I can't go no place else! I don't know how! That damned Rothstein." Sport looked down at his suitfront. The bullet holes are still there. Five of them, neatly spaced, decorating a suit that may have been stylish in 1920 but looked ridiculous today. "I get sent down to hell some day, Arnold's bound to be there too. I'll tear his head off."

Sometimes I like to needle Sport. "If Arnold Rothstein is as smart as you say, he's probably running the place."

"Y'think so?" Sport's shoulders drooped and his neon faded. "Wouldn't that be a bitch?"

"Sport, can you tell me if there really is a hell?"

"The fuck should I know? I'm nothing but a peon around here. You probably got a better fix on why I'm in limbo than I do."

"Why do you say that?"

Sport replied with a nasty laugh. "You don't see it? Come on, Kevin. You gotta know I only come around when you send for me."

'That's crap. I've *never* sent for you."

"Sometimes you get a bug up your ass, you're upset about something, all of a sudden I get pulled down here. That's the way it seems to work. So what's bugging the great artist today?"

Sport strode over to the doorway and looked out at the easel sitting on my deck. He didn't step into the daylight. I'd noticed over the years that he seldom sets foot outside. His visits usually took place indoors and at night.

"Who's that guy you're painting?"

"A carpenter."

"Carpenter! No wonder you're all riled up. There's no dough in doing portraits of carpenters. Am I right about that?"

"I make a living."

"That's what every loser says. You should be doing portraits of millionaires, that's where the money is. Make 'em look better than they do in real life and they'll pay whatever you ask."

"The Sport Sullivan school of art." Talking with Sport often made me sarcastic. "Maybe you can get yourself reincarnated as the curator at the Louvre."

"What the hell is that?"

"A museum in France."

"You're pulling my dick, but you know I make sense. That what you called me down here for, jawbone with you about art?"

"I'll tell you one more time. I didn't *call you down here*." The words were out of my mouth before it hit me that Sport Sullivan might not be totally off base. "Or…maybe I did." I got up, went into the bedroom, returned carrying the red woolen sweater given to me by Emily Hillyer. "This sweater belongs to a little girl named Tara who lives in San Francisco. She was kidnapped last night, nobody knows where she is."

With a smirk, Sport said, "You artists get into some kinky stuff."

"This has nothing to do with me. The girl's mother gave me the sweater, thought it might tell me something. I tried to convince her I have no special powers, she wouldn't believe me."

"You think I can help?"

"You did once before."

Sport nodded. "You mean the time I fingered that killer? The one who was into voodoo?"

"Satanism. The killer was part of a satanic cult."

"I worried about that afterwards, wondered if I should have helped you. I mean, suppose one of these days I do get jolted loose from limbo and sent to hell. There's Satan himself. Asks me why I helped put one of his guys behind bars. I can't give him a good answer, he'll have me emptying the shit buckets down there in hell. How'd you like to spend eternity on your knees in hell's toilet? All because I did a favor for some artist I don't even like."

"Sport, this one has nothing to do with satanism. There's a five-year-old girl who may still have a chance to live if someone can get to her in time. Can you help her?"

The spirit's eyes flickered red and blue with deep thought. Finally he said, "I'll give it a shot. What'cha want me to do?"

"Just let me give you this sweater." I tossed it to Sport. The sweater sailed through him, falling to the floor within his aura. "Tell me if the sweater gives you any ideas about where she might be."

"You don't want much." Sport looked down at the garment, which lay within his greenish person. He frowned and closed his eyes. His form gradually began to shrink until it was about two-thirds its usual size. For the next five or six minutes nothing at all happened. No fireworks. No neon lights. Nothing to indicate Sport Sullivan was actually concentrating on Tara Hillyer's abduction. I didn't trust him at all, he could easily be playing with me.

After a very long interval, Sport's eyes opened and his form expanded to its usual size. "The kid's in real trouble."

I felt sick. "Is she still alive?"

"What do I look like, the ghost of Christmas past? I don't know everything that happens down here. I can't say for sure she's alive, but I think so. Look, I never been to San Francisco. Like I said, I never traveled farther west than Chicago, and look what that got me. You got a place in San Francisco called Mission?"

"Mission? We've got a Mission Street. A Mission District."

"Yeah, somewhere around Mission there's a joint like the ones we had in New York back in the old days, mostly down in the Bowery. A place where you can relax, have a nice rubdown. Once you're on the table, you can get yourself laid."

"A massage parlor?"

"I wouldn't know what those joints are called these days. All I can tell you, the kid's being held in a fuckhouse at a place called Mission. Guy who works there's got her."

"Are you sure?"

Sport gave a barking laugh. "I ain't even sure what century this is. Yeah, the kid's there. I may be in limbo, but I ain't lost my feel for the street." He winked at me. "We through with each other for now, Kevin?"

"I guess."

"Then don't be a stranger. I kind of like to get out in the world once in a while, even if it's only to see your ugly puss. So long…"

Sport telescoped down into a greenish ball about the size of my fist and disappeared. Half a second later I began to sweat as the temperature rose dramatically and the humidity leaped into the ninety percentiles. I felt too dizzy to stand. Groping my way to the couch, I leaned back with my eyes closed. My heart hammered at my ribcage and pain radiated out from there into my arms. When Sport makes one of his sudden exits, he usually leaves me fearing that I'm in cardiac arrest.

I think Sport does that deliberately.

When my heart stopped pounding and I returned to some sort of normalcy, I reached for the phone and called the San Francisco Police Department. I asked for Captain Joe Patterson and was told by a fellow detective that Patterson was too busy to come to the phone. "He has others taking calls for him today, including me. What can I do for you, sir?"

"I need to talk with Captain Patterson about Tara Hillyer. Break through to him right now. Tell him Kevin Pierce has some information about Tara."

"Captain Patterson is busy. I'll be glad to…"

"No! I need to talk with Patterson himself. He pulled me into the crime scene at two o'clock this morning to ask for my help. Doesn't that tell you he'd want to talk to me personally?"

After a pause loaded with indecision, the detective said he'd try to get Patterson on the phone.

I was put on hold for a long time, long enough to eat a banana and reload my Mr. Coffee. When Patterson did come on the line, he sounded as pleasant as an unleashed tiger.

"Pierce? What do you want?"

"I've got some information about Tara Hillyer."

"I thought you were out of this."

"So did I, but some information came to me. I didn't expect it, didn't look for it. I've been told Tara may be held on Mission Street, or somewhere in the Mission District at least, in a massage parlor. By someone who works in the massage parlor."

"Where'd this information come from?"

I knew I'd be asked that question and had an answer ready. A lousy answer, but the best I could do. "The info comes from a source you wouldn't believe in, wouldn't find credible in any way. But I believe it."

What are you telling me?" Patterson's teeth were grinding. "You got a flash from Elvis? From somebody else on *The Other Side*? You got a tip from Jacob Marley maybe?

"Something almost as bizarre. But I *believe* what I'm telling you."

"I was right the first time. You're one of those lowlife, scum-sucking leaches that always pops up in a case like this. You called Channel 4 yet, shared your big news? Got a tv interview set up?"

"You're the only person I've called, or will call." I had an idea. "Unless you blow me off. If you do that, I'll call Mrs. Hillyer. You can insult me, ignore me, hang up on me. You can't do that to her, can you? If I tell Mrs. Hillyer that Tara might be in a massage parlor in the Mission District, she'll be all over your ass to check it out."

"You do that, I'll have you arrested for impeding this investigation."

I was glad I hadn't taken my information to him in person. My head would be lying on his station house floor by now. "Captain Patterson, you've got people searching the city for Tara Hillyer anyway. Why don't you just assign a few men to check the massage parlors in the Mission District?"

"Because you're full of shit, that's why."

"How can you say that? You've got so many leads you don't need to follow up on this one, is that it?"

Cold silence.

"I'm not jerking you around. I think this is a genuine lead. I can't guarantee anything, but this is not a bid for self promotion. I promise you that."

"Assholes like you lie to me every day."

"So I have to call Mrs. Hillyer?"

"No, you don't have to do that." Patterson's voice was no less acid, but it did have a conciliatory side. "I'll send some men to check out the massage parlors in the Mission District. If they find nothing, the City of San Francisco will bill you for the time those detectives spent following up a worthless lead. You may also be sued for reckless endangerment to Tara Hillyer. Now, you still want me to have the parlors checked?"

I swallowed hard on that one. Sport had set me up real good. If he was wrong, I might lose everything. My reputation. My house. My measly bank account. Everything depended on the word of…well…let's face it…the word of a ghost. A ghost who didn't even like me, who might even enjoy watching me lose what little I possessed. Why was I betting everything on a ghost who was so dishonest he'd helped fix a World Series? Because I had no choice, I'd taken this too far. "I understand there could be consequences for me if this lead doesn't pan out. And I'm asking you to search those massage parlors."

"You got it." Patterson hung up on me.

The late afternoon light on Half Moon Bay is no good for my kind of work. When the sun begins to set on the Pacific ocean, those of us who live along the beach are hit straight in the eyes by light so intense you have to squint in order to see what you're doing. Nice excuse not to work. I use it all the time.

Instead of working, I walked the mile from my house down to the beach and shoved my shoes into my pockets so I could feel the sand between my toes. I walked slowly up and down the beach for about an hour. Usually I enjoy my time on the beach. Not today. I kept glancing at my watch. Wondering if Captain Patterson had done as he promised and sent some men to canvass the massage parlors in the Mission District. Wondering whether Sport Sullivan knew what he was talking about.

I found my right hand straying to the back of my head, my fingers probing under the hair, touching the round one-inch-in-diameter titanium plate a team of surgeons had imbedded in my skull. The plate was there simply to fill the space where I'd lost a chunk of my skull to a nine millimeter bullet that had done a lot of damage without actually killing me.

That was ten years ago, in my army days. When I was a kid who thought, as all kids do, that I was immortal. Or damn close to it.

I learned better in a place called Zaire, way over there in Africa, one of those places that has civil wars and ebola virus outbreaks instead of theme parks.

They had a civil war in Zaire about ten years ago that involved a bunch of rebels shooting down their fellow citizens with AK-47s, or when they ran out of ammo hacking them up with machete-type implements. By the thousands. They say forty thousand people were

murdered, men, women and children. Some sort of tribal dispute.
Animosities that went back hundreds of years.

The usual assortment of Americans lived in Zaire at the time—
diplomats and their families, corporate types bleeding the country for
whatever they could, Peace Corps workers with stars in their eyes, mis-
sionaries, potheads, dropouts from civilization, agricultural engineers,
manufacturers making zippers and watchbands and other stuff for pen-
nies to sell for dollars. They must have been crazy, the whole bunch, to
live in the middle of a killing field. They didn't even try to get out until
it was almost too late, which is always the case. Get yourself in deep shit,
then call for Uncle Sam. That's what people do.

So they put a battalion of infantry on the aircraft carrier Carl Vinson,
hauled us over to the coast of Africa, lifted us off in choppers to go pick
up whatever U.S. citizens in Zaire hadn't yet been shot or hacked to
death. We went into Kinshasa, the capital city of Zaire. Half the city was
on fire and the other half was being looted by roving bands of rebels.

I was a corporal and a squad leader. Ten man squad, most of the men
eager for a fight. I'd have to include myself in that bunch. I liked the
action in those days. Our choppers landed in a circular pattern in the
streets around the American embassy. Every U.S. citizen still alive in
Zaire had gotten to the embassy, where they were huddled behind the
protection of high walls and a single squad of U.S. Marine guards. The
street in the front of the embassy was littered with rebel dead, a testament to the accuracy of the Marine riflemen. But they couldn't hold out
forever. Not with the rebels out there making deals to buy rockets from
their friendly arms dealers.

We landed just in time, the bands of rebels had formed up into a
single unit under an officer who must have had some actual military
training. They were moving toward the embassy in company-strength
units, even laying down covering fire for each other.

My ten-man squad was attacked but not flanked by about sixty
rebels, at least two thirds armed with automatic weapons. They came at

us screaming, waving their weapons like swords, so close I could see the spittle on their lips.

"Fire low," was the only order I gave my guys. They didn't even need that much direction, they were pros.

I took out five screaming attackers with a single burst. If they hadn't bunched up, they'd have had a better chance at us. My squad laid into them with overlapping fields of fire, cut down men by the dozen. More screaming from the wounded on the ground. Lots of swearing. I didn't speak the language, but I know swearing when I hear it. Somebody lobbed a grenade.

"Heads down!" I yelled.

The grenade fell short, exploded and killed a couple of their own wounded men.

"Move into the embassy grounds," I ordered. "Two men at a time. Do it now."

We fell back in an orderly manner. I was aware of the smell of death hanging over the city. The twitching of the wounded. Gagging sounds. Cries for help in English and other languages. I wasn't moved by any of that. Instead I felt disgust about all the wasted life and the stupidity of people intent on destroying their own neighbors and property.

Inside the embassy grounds about three hundred American citizens were cringing along the walls, holding suitcases and backpacks close to them, flinching at the gunfire pocking the embassy walls.

"Nice work out there," one of the Marines said to me. "They'll think twice about comin' at us again."

"Yeah, but they must have got themselves a leader. Somebody formed them into units. Taught them to cover each other. Next they'll have rockets."

"We'll be outta here before that," the Marine said. "The choppers have started airliftin' the civilians already."

A chopper did lift off from the embassy roof at that moment. Two platoons from A Company were on the roof, firing down into the streets to cover the lift-off. They riddled the streets. Took out some rebels, from the fresh screams that penetrated the walls. Two of our guys on the roof were killed by small arms fire. Their bodies were put on the next chopper out. Our unit had a tradition of never leaving a body behind, we took care of our own.

It took an hour to get the rest of the civilians into the air and on their way to the Carl Vinson. Another of our guys was hit, only a wound this time. He went out with the civilians. The rebels had their rockets by then. They blew out a section of the wall and tried to come into the grounds. We popped them right and left until they got discouraged and backed off.

Then the choppers came back for us and for the Marine guard. It would take two flights to get everyone airborne. We didn't lose any choppers, thank God. My squad was set to leave on the second flight.

As my chopper lifted off, the rebels swarmed into the embassy grounds and fired skyward at us. That's when I learned for sure that I wasn't immortal. One of the rounds zipped up under my helmet and hit me in the back of the head, ripping off a piece of my skull.

Later they told me the bullet knocked me clean out of the chopper. A buddy, Big Sam Cody, grabbed my shirt and pulled me back inside. Two hours later, in a rough sea, surgeons on the aircraft carrier Carl Vinson stopped the bleeding and, despite the way the deck under their feet was pitching and yawing, successfully inserted the plate in my skull to fill the cavity.

I seldom think about the plate, it's been a part of me for so long. I only pay attention to it when Sport Sullivan makes one of his onerous appearances. That's because after the operation I came out of the anesthesia in a one-man sick bay to find Sport perched at my side. He introduced himself and started talking a mile a minute about how he'd helped Arnold Rothstein fix the World Series, only to be double-crossed and murdered by one of Rothstein's hoods.

I thought I was hallucinating. But he came back a few days later when Big Sam Cody was in the sick bay with me. And then Sport came back again. And again. And again.

I know there's some kind of connection between Sport Sullivan and the titanium plate in my head. I have no idea what the connection is, nor do I care to know. The answers to some questions are too flaky for deep contemplation.

After the army gave me a medical discharge, I went to the library and read up on the 1919 World Series. According to the history books, Arnold Rothstein did fix that Series. And a man named Sport Sullivan took part in the fix.

Look it up.

When I walked into my house, the phone was ringing. Captain Joe Patterson on the line. "We found Tara," he said without preamble. "In a gash joint on Mission Street, like you said. She was being held by a guy named Luther Gaston. He does odd jobs around the massage parlor. Passes out towels, warms the oil for the massages, that kind of shit."

"She's alive?"

"Yeah, she's alive. Better yet, Gaston had hidden her in an air vent, he intended to wait until nobody was in the building to have his fun and games with her. So she hasn't been harmed. My guess, this Gaston puke planned to rape her and then kill her, dump her body somewhere, probably tonight when fewer people would be likely to see him at work." Patterson cleared his throat. "You're expecting a thank you?"

"Not necessary." Would be nice though.

"Let me ask you something, Kevin."

All of a sudden we were on a first name basis.

"Do you know this Luther Gaston?"

"No, of course not." The question made me angry. "Don't go there, Captain."

"Do you know anybody connected with Luther Gaston? Any member of his family? Any of his friends? Any of the girls who work at the Starlight Dreamland massage parlor? Any of their boyfriends?"

"No!"

Patterson's teeth began their familiar grind. "If you don't know anyone connected with Gaston, how could you point me at him? I have to know that."

"I got a tip from what you sneeringly called *The Other Side*. Which, if I may say so, is a weird way for a cop to talk."

"I don't accept that." He sighed heavily. "I *can't* accept it."

"I understand how you feel. Yes, I got a tip from a source that's not really a part of this world. If I told you more, you'd try to have me committed."

"And you won't be going to the tv stations or the newspapers with this? Tell them how you solved the Hillyer case for the cops? Called in the spirits or goblins or whatever?"

The proverbial light bulb switched on over my head. Patterson was worried that someone outside the Police Department might get credit for tracking down Luther Gaston. "The media won't hear a word from me, Captain."

"This is crazy." I could hear him licking his lips, not a pleasant sound. "Some day I want you tell me how you knew where Tara could be found. I don't want to hear it today. But sometime, when I feel I can handle it, I want to know."

"Maybe."

"I want to *know*." Once again Captain Patterson hung up on me.

Later that night I watched the Channel 4 news and saw Luther Gaston, a pudgy and nondescript little man in shabby clothes, being hustled away in a police car with his hands secured behind his back by steel cuffs. Gaston looked slack-jawed and dazed.

I also saw a shot of Tara Hillyer being taken out of the Starlight Dreamland massage parlor wrapped in a blanket. A big uniformed cop carried her. Tara's parents were at her side, both in tears but smiling because their little girl was alive. The Channel 4 anchorman said Luther Gaston had no criminal record. However, a heavy wood dowel spotted with bloodstains, presumably the blood of Toby Hillyer, was found in a workroom at the parlor. Gaston's neighbors in the cheap Daly City apartment house where he lived came on camera to describe Gaston as "quiet but friendly." They were shocked to hear Gaston had committed such a terrible crime.

When I'd learned enough from the news reports to be sure Tara Hillyer would survive this horror in reasonably good shape, I switched off the tv and opened my last bottle of Carta Blanca. Before drinking, I raised the bottle and said, "Thank you, Sport."

Maybe he heard me, maybe he didn't.

CHAPTER 3

Summers are seldom good for me, I do better in other seasons. For example, my attention during June and July focused on a girl named Heather that I met during a stroll along the beach. Heather toiled as an account manager at a San Francisco advertising agency. She wore her blonde hair short and honed her figure to near perfection by thrice-weekly workouts. Add athletic legs and admirable buns and you have your basic California beach goddess.

"I come down to the beach every couple of weeks just to get away from the telephone," Heather explained when we first met. "I mean, the pressure of my job is intense. Don't you find your business is the same?"

"Right…intense." I didn't choose to reveal that on an average day my most intense decision is whether to wait until noon for my first Carta Blanca.

The fact that I was a portrait artist with a house on Half Moon Bay impressed Heather. Naturally I took pains to keep her from actually seeing the house. Instead I took her out several times, sometimes driving up to San Francisco and other times taking her to dinner at the Seaview Inn where she stayed when she came to Half Moon Bay. However, the time came when I couldn't avoid inviting her up to my digs. When she finally saw the place, her reaction was: "What happened here? A war?"

"Um, I leased out the place for six months to some people who trashed it." The lie rolled off my lips so glibly that I began to wonder about my basic honesty.

"What a shame!" Heather went through the house with the eye of a girl who knows real estate. "Your house has loads of potential, but right now it's just impossible."

"I have a contractor coming in tomorrow to give me an estimate on repairs." Another lie, but Heather had a wonderful body that I had not yet been able to fully explore. "And my architect's figuring out a way to jack up the right leg of the A-frame so the house doesn't look, you know, crooked." As long as I was inventing a contractor, I didn't see any harm in inventing an architect to keep him company.

Heather liked my paintings more than the state of my house, which was a relief. Until she began making suggestions about my work. Her ideas ran a spectrum that went something like this: "Why aren't any of these people *smiling*, Kevin? I mean, look at that pregnant woman. She should be happier about her baby, shouldn't she?" And "You should do portraits of corporate executives. I'll bet I could make a few phone calls and line up two or three commissions for you right off the bat." And "That man is so *ugly*. Nobody's going to buy a painting of an ugly man."

"You should see Cezanne's naked bathers," I countered, trying to get her off the subject.

"No, really," she insisted. "You should do pictures of good looking men and women, can't you see that? Your sales would soar! Kevin, I know marketing. People buy the sizzle, not the steak. You need to make these people *sizzle*!"

"Most of my subjects aren't the sizzling types." That's when I realized Heather and I were totally mismatched. I don't know why it took me so long to recognize that simple truth. I guess I was just looking at Heather's sizzle. When I finally told her I didn't think we should see each other any more, Heather took it pretty hard. For five or six seconds. Then she drove off in her red Mercedes convertible, throwing a jolly wave without actually bothering to look at me in her rearview mirror.

That pretty much sums up my summer.

In mid-July I wasn't too surprised to see a brief story in the San Francisco *Chronicle* that read:

Cop in Hillyer Case Retires From S.F. Police Department

Captain Joseph A. Patterson, who led the investigation that resulted in the arrest of Luther Gaston for the attempted murder of eight-year-old Toby Hillyer and the kidnapping of his five-year-old sister Tara, today announced his retirement from the San Francisco Police Department.

He will become director of security for the Race Software Development Corporation, headquartered in San Mateo. The Race Software Development Corporation is the eight billion dollar company founded only seven years ago by its chairman, twenty-eight-year-old Bobby Race. "We're lucky to have a man of Joe Patterson's proven talent as security director for our company," Mr. Race said. "His primary duty will be the protection of the company's intellectual property."

Captain Patterson, 43, joined the San Francisco Police Department more than 20 years ago as a patrolman. In his first year on duty, then patrolman Patterson won a citation for bravery when he single-handedly stopped a trio of armed men from robbing the Western and Home Bank on Montgomery Street. Patterson killed one of the armed robbers and subdued the other two.

During his long career, Captain Patterson was cited six times for bravery and twice won the department's Legion of Honor medal for outstanding detective work. His second Legion of Honor was presented only last month following the arrest of Luther Gaston. Captain Patterson led the task force that captured Gaston, who is currently awaiting trial.

The retired officer takes up his new position with the Race Software Development Corporation next Monday.

Didn't surprise me. The moment I met Patterson I knew he was on the make for something bigger and better than what he already had. His suit, his shoes, his haircut were too expensive for a cop. Together they cried out *I am an executive!* I didn't blame him for moving upward, everybody needs to shoot for something. Patterson hit the summit with the Race Corporation. Race had a reputation as the highest-paying outfit in Silicon Valley. Patterson should be feeling like Jimmy Cagney in *White Heat*, standing on top of a tower shouting, "Made it, Ma! Top of the world!" Of course, he wouldn't want to end up the way Cagney did in that movie—blown to pieces.

I can't say the summer was a total loss. Four of my portraits sold, including the one I call *The Long Day Of The Carpenter*. The prices were on the low side, but I was pleased to see *Carpenter* bought by a museum in Fort Worth for a show titled *America's Young Portrait Masters*. I was high for a week when I learned I'd be included in that show. Hey, I've got an ego, too.

If my ego was artificially high, it was driven back down to earth when I went into San Francisco the last week in August for a special show of impressionists at the De Young Museum. I went early, eager to see their work, and managed to be first in the door at nine a.m.

I spent about three hours at the show. Wonderful exhibition. Except that the work of genuine masters like Degas and Cezanne and Monet made me feel like a boy with a crude little coloring box. I'd studied their work, of course. Especially Cezanne. The brush work of the impressionists is always a joy, but I learned a few new things from this particular show.

Cezanne's *Boy With A Skull* got me to thinking about how important it is to surprise those who look at your work. In that painting, Cezanne showed a young man in a blue suit against a background that's essentially brown and ivory. The young man is seated at a desk that holds a stack of books, and also a human skull. What's the skull doing there? Does it symbolize the fleeting nature of youth and life? No way to tell, but the skull is definitely a surprise. Of course, Cezanne had a thing for skulls. It's said he kept a pile of human skulls in his bedroom. Go figure.

Another of the paintings in that show was Claude Monet's *Girl In A Garden With A Dog*. Guess what that one's about. Again, what the hell is the dog doing there? The dog is a major distraction from the main figure of the girl. Looking at that canvas, you spend as much time wondering about the dog as observing the girl. The dog's a surprise.

Monet gave us a different kind of surprise with *Monsieur Cogneret*. The subject was a friend of Monet's, a wealthy compass maker who bought several of his early works. Monsieur Cogneret was a rather ordinary looking man. Monet painted him in a brown suit, which made the dour little Frenchman appear even more ordinary. But that ordinary little man is wearing a violet-colored tie so vibrant that the entire painting takes your breath away.

I drove home from the exhibition feeling untalented, morose and totally defeated. Somehow I managed to reach my house without running into a tree or a roadside boulder. I plopped down on the couch with a six pack. It took three Carta Blancas to turn my thoughts from suicide.

I was feeling more sanguine when someone knocked on my front door. (They had to knock, my doorbell is broken too.) The knock was heavy, authoritative and insistent to the point of rudeness. Definitely a man's knock. Only very big knuckles, or possibly an earthquake, could make my front door shake that hard.

"Take it easy! I'm coming!"

I trudged to the door, opened it, found myself staring into the scowling face of Joe Patterson, former captain of San Francisco Police. "You!" (I'm not especially articulate after three Carta Blancas.)

"Yeah…me. You gonna invite us in?"

"Us?"

"You drunk or something?" His eyes zeroed in on the almost empty beer bottle in my hand. "At one o'clock in the afternoon? Jesus, the life of an artist. I'm glad none of my kids have any talent in that direction." He shoved past me. "Let us in, we don't have all day."

"We?"

A young woman sort of floated past me in Patterson's wake. I ran a hand over my eyes, trying to understand why these people were in my house. That didn't seem to help so I closed the door and followed Patterson and the young woman into my living room as if I were the visitor. Patterson made himself at home, taking my easy chair with a master-of-the-house expression and putting his feet up on my tattered old ottoman. He was even better dressed than the last time I'd seen him. His shoes were new and spit-shined, to use the army term. His tie had more vivid colors than most of my paintings. His suit was Italian and silk, it even smelled good.

"I read that you'd left the police force."

"That's right." Patterson fairly reeked of upward mobility. "I'm with Race Software now, director of security. This is Dorothy Lake, she's with Race too."

"Uh-huh." I was fighting a headache. And losing.

"Pierce, you've got a six pack of beer on the couch, three of them empties, your eyes are glassy and unfocused. You need some coffee before we can talk business."

"Business?"

"I don't think this is going to work," Dorothy Lake said. "Look at him. He's a mess. His house is even messier. He'll be of no help to us."

"Just make him some coffee."

"Why should I make the coffee?" she flared. "Because I'm a girl? Listen, Joe, I'm a director too, and don't you forget it."

"How could I? You wear your rank on your sleeve. Or maybe on your bra." Patterson heaved himself to his feet. "Fuck, I'll make the coffee."

"And don't use that kind of language in my presence."

"You're gonna bring a suit against me for using profanity?"

"I could do that. I will if you don't treat me as an equal."

"When I use profanity, I am treating you as an equal. Don't you understand that?"

They argued back and forth as if I weren't there. It occurred to me that perhaps I wasn't here. Perhaps this was a trick of some kind. Yes! Sport Sullivan was behind this! I closed my eyes, put my head back against the cushions of the couch and waited for these two new apparitions to fade away.

"Mr.Pierce, are you all right? Are you going to be ill?"

My eyes flickered open. The girl's face was about six inches from mine. She was staring at me with concern and maybe even compassion. "I'm okay. I just don't understand who you are or what you're doing in my house. Am I under some sort of arrest?"

"Not at all."

"I'm not drunk, I just had a bad morning. Cezanne's brushwork put me into a funk, I had a couple of beers."

"What?"

"At first you think he was just dashing it off, you know? It seems a lot has been left out. The faces are indistinct, the body lines vague. Then you realize it's real genius. By eliminating some specifics, he somehow managed to capture the depth of his people's characters and emotions. *Genius*, that's the only word for it."

The girl followed Patterson into the kitchen and I heard her say, in a voice not even low enough to avoid embarrassing me, "He's pretty far gone, he'll need a lot of coffee."

"I take mine black." I had hoped to embarrass them right back, but they were beyond that nicety.

"It'll be ready in a minute," the girl replied. "You should really clean your coffee maker more often, Mister Pierce. The coffee'll taste much better, I read a study on the subject."

"You can believe her," Patterson said. "She reads studies on everything. Try this on for size: Dorothy reads studies *for pleasure*."

"I don't drink much coffee, I just keep it for friends."

"You've been *so* busy with *beer*," Patterson sneered.

"You people just came here to insult me, is that it?"

"Not at all." Dorothy had somehow ended up making the coffee anyway. She thrust a cup into my hands and sat down across from me. "We're here to make you a generous business offer."

Without that fine layer of sludge inside the pot, the coffee didn't taste as good as usual. "There's no business we could do together. I'm a portrait artist."

"We want to commission you to paint a portrait of our company CEO."

"Bobby Race?"

"The one and only." Dorothy Lake smiled and all at once, coming out of my Carta Blanca fog, I realized she was not just a girl, but a beautiful girl. Much better looking than Heather. If Dorothy Lake were a flower, she'd be a perfect rose. If she were a bird, she'd be a morning dove. If she were an airplane, she'd be a sleek corporate jet. Dorothy was slender, very slender, not many curves. Some might call her skinny. Not me. To my eyes Dorothy had a delicate lightness of being that made me feel light too, just looking at her. Dorothy couldn't have weighed more than a hundred and five, yet her electric presence turned her into a very substantial person.

Dorothy's clothes were as expensive as Patterson's. Navy blue jacket and skirt, white silk blouse, black shoes with stiletto heels, the complete dress for success outfit. Her honey-blonde hair provided a dramatic frame for a face that was thin and quite pale, probably from spending years in front of computers. Her violet eyes seemed enormous in such a thin face. She had computer nerd written all over her, which made her beauty all the more surprising.

It hurt terribly to say no to Dorothy Lake. "I'm sorry. Really. I don't do portraits of corporate executives. Nothing against Mr. Race, it's just that I do portraits of ordinary people."

"And find something extraordinary in them, am I right?"

"That's what I look for. It isn't always there."

Dorothy nodded as if she were on my wave length. "It's the same for me with computers. I'm always looking for a breakthrough behind the numbers, some new pattern of zeroes and ones that unlocks a mystery."

"You're a programmer?"

"My title is director of advanced applications, but yes I'm basically a programmer."

Dorothy shook out her hair without any idea of how deeply that simple movement affected me. As far as I'm concerned, beautiful women are the great mystery of the universe. How do they turn a fairly bright man like myself into a hundred and eighty pounds of jello with one toss of their hair? "I really don't want to paint your boss. But I will paint you, if you'll let me. No charge, and you can have the painting."

Her smile was edgy and knowing. "Oldest line in the world. I expected more from someone with your interesting history."

"What do you mean by *history*?"

"Your military record," Patterson explained, slurping some of the coffee from a saucer. "Which ain't bad. Plus your credit rating, which is bad. The fact you were kicked out of high school for busting a teacher's chops. Very bad form there, Kevin, hitting a teacher because he didn't like the way you conjugated verbs or whatever."

"That particular teacher was trying to get in the pants of one of my classmates, a fifteen-year-old girl who didn't know how to handle him."

"You *handled* the guy all right. Put him in a hospital, according to the police file. Lucky you were only seventeen, your A and B conviction was purged. I understand the judge gave you a choice. Six months in Juvenile Hall or the army, you took the army."

"How did you get that information? Juvenile records are supposed to be sealed, you must have broken the law to get at them." I hate it when people know more about me than I want them to know. "I could have you arrested, Patterson. Wouldn't that be ironic?"

"Call me Joe, we're gonna be working together."

"No, we're not.

Dorothy studied me as if I were a butterfly mounted on a slide. "You'd be incredibly foolish to turn down this commission, considering your financial profile. Do you even know how much you owe on your Visa card? Never mind, consider this: the Race Software Development Corporation is willing to pay you fifty thousand dollars to paint Bobby Race's portrait. *Fifty thousand.* On top of that, Mister Race will prominently display the portrait in our corporate headquarters. That should bring in more commissions. Take the job, Mister Pierce. This is a once in a lifetime opportunity."

"Call him Kevin," Patterson suggested. "He's practically on board."

"I'm not interested." That wasn't quite true. "Actually, I'm very interested in the fifty thousand, but I'd make a hash of Bobby Race's portrait. I just can't paint execs. They don't slouch. Their clothes are too good. No stains on their lapels. They smile nonstop. And rarely do you find corporate execs with a harelip or a disfiguring scar to give their faces some character. How can you do portraits of people like that? Okay, some artists can. I can't."

"You're choosing to be a failure," Dorothy said. "That's pathetic."

"Let's have dinner tonight. We can discuss the matter more fully, maybe I'll change my mind."

Dorothy made a contemptuous sound and flounced away. I loved her flounce.

"Let's tell him the real deal," Patterson suggested.

She shot Patterson a warning look. "Bobby wants to tell him."

"Yeah, and Bobby's booked us onto his calendar for two o'clock. That means we have to get on the road..." Patterson consulted his watch "...like right now."

"What real deal?" I'd suspected all along they weren't here about a portrait. Patterson wouldn't cross the street to watch DaVinci paint the Mona Lisa. Nor did Dorothy Lake seem to think much of my talents, so why were they so eager to have me do Bobby Race's portrait? "Come on, let's hear it."

Patterson and Dorothy exchanged agitated looks that appeared to end with an unspoken agreement.

"All right," Dorothy said. "Go ahead and explain the project to Mr. Pierce."

Patterson put aside his coffee. "Kevin, we have a situation at corporate headquarters that you may be able to help us with. What we want is for you to spend a few days, maybe a week, at Race headquarters on the pretext that you're painting Bobby Race's portrait. Actually, you will paint the portrait. I mean, why not? If the painting comes out okay, Bobby looks like himself instead of an ink blot, we might even hang it up somewhere. But your real reason for being at our headquarters will be to look into this situation. Give us your advice. For this…and for the portrait…you'll be paid fifty grand. Not a bad payday, right?"

"What is this *situation* I'm supposed to look into?"

Dorothy broke in. "Our product is software, which is intellectual property, the product of the best software designers in the world. Mr. Pierce, some of our best people are threatening to quit and take their talent elsewhere. Why? Because they're frightened."

I could have listened to Dorothy talk for the rest of the day, but she stopped and waited for a response from me. After a confused moment I said, "Why are they frightened?"

"We've been having these, I hesitate to say it, this may sound crazy, but some of our people claim to have seen an *apparition* inside Race headquarters." She tittered like a child. "I'm sorry, I feel stupid offering you money to look into something like this."

But I wasn't paying attention to Dorothy. I was glaring at Joe Patterson, who at least had the grace to look uncomfortable. "What have you been saying about me?"

Patterson held up his hands. "I told Bobby Race you helped the police on a couple of major cases, that you've got some experience with the supernatural."

"Joe called you a cut-rate ghost buster."

He gave her an evil look. "That was a joke. Don't give Kevin the impression I was bad-mouthing him." Patterson smiled at me with what he perceived to be charm. "I told Bobby you're just the guy to help us out. And I really think you are."

Dorothy's eyebrows lifted. "Obviously there's a logical explanation for what our employees have been seeing. Frankly, we need someone familiar with the jargon of the supernatural world to come up with a convincing explanation. You appear to fit that bill."

"Why don't you go to Andersen Consulting, hire yourself three accountants and five Harvard MBAs. Those guys can explain anything."

"Bobby wants you," Patterson said with finality.

"No way."

Patterson groaned. "Kevin, I don't want to use my connections to make your life more miserable than it already is. I could have the Visa attorneys on your ass. Send the IRS after you, I'll bet your deductions are as phony as a Chicago election. And according to court records, you owe more than sixteen thousand dollars to a guy named Charlie Heavensent, an auto dealer in Dallas. He's been looking for you for three years. I could tell him where to find you."

"Heavensent sold me a used Corvette that fell apart two days after I bought it. I found out the odometer had been rigged, the transmission was held together with wire and spit, the tires had been regrooved, and Heavensent had loaded the engine with some sort of gook to disguise the fact that the valves and pistons were disintegrating. Guy's a crook! I drove the car back to the lot, told him to keep it. I'm sure he sold it to somebody else after that, so how can I owe him money on it?"

"That's between you and Charlie Heavensent and the Texas courts. I'd hate to be the one to send a crooked used car dealer after you, but you're not leaving me any choice."

"Do it! I don't care!" I jumped up and stormed out onto my deck, leaving Patterson and Dorothy looking at me in amusement. Despite my outburst, they both seemed to think they'd won the argument.

Dorothy was talking on her cellular phone. While I stared down at the slate blue ocean and fumed over this invasion of my privacy, Dorothy came out onto the deck and handed me her phone. "I have someone on the line who wants to speak with you." Her tone was almost apologetic.

I took the phone gingerly. The little cellular device only weighed a few ounces, but in my current state of mind it felt as heavy and lethal as a hand grenade. "Hello?"

"Kevin, this is great news!" I recognized the voice of my agent, Marie Spector. "A fifty thousand dollar commission! To paint the official corporate portrait of Bobby Race! How did you wangle that? Never mind, give me the full story later. The point is Bobby Race could hire any artist in the country to do his portrait, and he chose you! Kevin, this is the break we've been looking for. Do a good job on this portrait, and I know you will, and the rest of your work will be in great demand."

"Marie, I don't want to do Bobby Race's portrait."

"Are you insane? Race is the most charismatic figure in the information industry. He's a multi-billionaire. People hang on his every word. Fortunes are made or lost when he *farts*, for God's sake. Bobby Race has never had an official portrait done, though he's been approached many times. I approached him last year myself on behalf of another client who exclusively paints corporate execs. I can plant this story on every art page in every major newspaper in the country. And outside the U.S. as well. Kevin, this one portrait can make your career."

"I've never done a corporate executive, that's not my kind of art."

"Force yourself." Marie's voice had gone steely. "I've told you that art is also business. If you don't want to do business, you'll have to find someone else to represent you."

I couldn't afford to lose Marie Spector. I had no idea how to sell a painting on my own, I'd probably starve to death in a matter of weeks. She was right, of course, I was just being stubborn because every executive portrait I've ever seen looked colder than a New England winter.

Maybe I could make something out of Bobby Race, who from all reports didn't fit the typical corporate mold. "All right, I'll do it."

"Now you're making sense. Put Miss Lake back on the phone, I'll settle the contractual arrangements with her. Kevin, you won't regret this, I promise you."

"Sure, Marie." There was no way I could explain to Marie Spector I was being commissioned not as an artist, but as a *cut-rate ghostbuster* as Patterson had described me. I handed the cell phone back to Dorothy. "You've got a deal. Settle the arrangements with Marie."

While Dorothy and Marie were talking, I went inside and changed into less wrinkled clothes. I selected pencils and a pad of art paper, thought better of that and exchanged the pencils for charcoal. I felt mildly depressed at being pressured into this commission, but now that I was committed to the project I sort of looked forward to meeting Bobby Race. I'd seen his photograph hundreds of times, he seemed to have been on every magazine cover in America. He was in his late twenties, a certified software guru who was also a genius at business. His company developed and sold networking software, the kind of stuff that makes the Internet easy to use. He took the Race Software Development Corporation from nothing to eight billion dollars in revenue in the space of about seven years. The notion that Bobby Race's corporate headquarters might be haunted cheered me a bit, at least the guy couldn't control everything.

"That's it." Dorothy came in off the deck looking well satisfied. She folded up the cellular phone and slipped it into her purse. "I've made the deal with your agent. I wrote out the agreement while we were talking and signed it on behalf of the Race corporation. Where's your fax? I'll send it to Marie right now so she can countersign."

"I don't have a fax," I said. "Or, for that matter, a computer. Or a cellular phone. Or a pager. Or a personal digital assistant, whatever the hell that is."

Dorothy looked at me as if I were a prehistoric creature still learning to walk erect. "How can you operate a business without those things?"

"I keep all my business records on the backs of old envelopes. As long as I don't run out of old envelopes, I'm okay."

Patterson laughed and slapped me on the shoulder. "Kevin is an *artiste*. He doesn't have time for crass things like computers or faxes or cell phones. Or paying his bills."

"I always pay my bills," I shot back. "Eventually."

"Let's get on the road." Patterson consulted a gold Rolex. "Bobby doesn't like to be kept waiting."

CHAPTER 4

Everyone has heard Bobby Race's success story. He founded the Race Software Development Corporation seven years ago in a dingy 900-square-foot storefront on the tacky stretch of El Camino Real in San Mateo. At that time Bobby Race was a 21-year-old dropout from Stanford. Seems he was broke, couldn't come up with the tuition for his junior year, so he started his own company. He had a hunch that networking software for wireless computing would be the next big thing in the computer business. He was right. Today the Race Software headquarters consists of two starkly modern connected towers on the bay side of Route 101 in San Mateo. The towers are black, each resembling one of the strange black monoliths from Stanley Kubrick's *2001—A Space Odyssey*. Somewhere I read that Bobby Race is a big fan of Stanley Kubrick and that he personally designed the towers to look like the movie's monoliths. Race Software also owns scores of marketing centers around the world and sells its shrink-wrapped network applications through thousands of retail outlets. They'll also deliver new software to you right over the Internet. Not bad for a dropout.

As Joe Patterson guided his new BMW into a reserved parking space Dorothy said, "Welcome to the campus."

These days every high tech company in the Silicon Valley calls its headquarters complex *the campus*. As we walked toward the building, I decided Race Software didn't greatly resemble a college campus. Sure, the employees dressed casually, many in nothing more than jeans and t shirts and sneakers. There were picnic benches in the greenbelts between the towers. Six guys, three girls were playing a vicious game of volleyball. A few of the employees jogged or biked along a cinder path. But they all wore corporate badges and pagers clipped to their belts or hanging around their necks from plastic holders, they all had the same intense expressions, and the security in the buildings was as tight as a maximum security prison.

"In order for you to have the run of the building, you'll have to become a temporary Race Corporation employee," Patterson explained. At the front desk I signed an agreement to keep confidential any technical information I might come across at Race. In an alcove behind the desk, my photo was taken and electronically imprinted onto a magnetic employee's badge that also bore a five-digit serial number. Patterson clipped the badge to my shirt. "Now you're on the team."

"You are employee number twenty-five thousand five hundred and sixty." Dorothy flashed her badge at me. "I'm employee number seven. Know what that means? I was the seventh employee Bobby hired. The company was only three months old when I came on board."

"Is that like being one of the disciples at The Last Supper?"

Dorothy tossed her hair. "That's not funny."

"Do that again."

"Do what again?"

"Toss your hair."

"I will not!"

Patterson used his magnetic badge to open the door. "You have to watch yourself, Dorothy. Artists got nothing on their mind except booze and pussy, everybody knows that."

"Watch your mouth, Joe!"

"He's very crude." I gave her my winsome smile. "I don't use that kind of language myself."

Dorothy shook her head to indicate Patterson and I were both vulgarians and stepped ahead of us along the hallway. I followed willingly, caught up in the sway of her hips and the way her blonde hair shimmered. We took an elevator to the top floor. The interior of the building was done in varied tones of blue with some gray thrown in. Cool and restful. Executive suites occupied most of the top floor, each with a view of the lower part of San Francisco bay and the San Mateo bridge going across the bay toward Fremont. The suites also had a fine view of the jet liners making their approach up the bay to San Francisco International.

On the other end of the spectrum, the lower level employees worked in cubicles as starkly dull as those in the *Dilbert* cartoons.

The execs in the offices dressed as casually as the employees on the lower floors. In fact, Dorothy Lake and Joe Patterson were the only people I saw wearing business suits. I understood why Joe Patterson was suited up, he felt the need to advertise the fact that he was now an executive instead of a cop. Dorothy's reason for adopting an old-fashioned corporate look was harder to figure.

A secretary in a jogging suit greeted us. Patterson introduced her: "Kevin, this is Jenny Hartsong, Bobby's executive secretary. Jenny, meet Kevin Pierce. He's the artist who's going to do Bobby's portrait."

"How wonderful!" Jenny extended her hand. "Bobby's needed a portrait and I'm sure you'll do him justice."

"I'll try." Jenny looked to be in her early twenties, very young for an executive secretary. She had enthusiasm and energy jumping out of every pore. In her jogging suit, she looked more like the star of an exercise video than a high-level executive secretary.

"Come on in." Jenny ushered us into Bobby Race's private office. "There's juice, coffee, danish and nonfat milk on the sideboard. Bobby's in a meeting. Make yourself comfortable, he'll be right with you." Jenny gave us a brilliant smile and left us alone in Race's office, which was about the size of Candlestick Park and offered a magnificent view of the bay through two floor-to-ceiling glass walls. The other two walls were covered with posters from old movies and framed baseball cards. I saw a Mickey Mantle rookie card and an antique Grover Cleveland Alexander card. Among other treasures were a dozen Sandy Koufax cards, each one autographed. The largest display was a collection of at least thirty Pete Rose cards, also autographed.

"So, you like Sandy and Pete?"

Bobby Race, multi-billionaire, looking as relaxed and informal as he did on the cover of *Fortune* magazine and even younger than his twenty-eight years, came in from an adjoining conference room. He wore scuffed old black-and-white saddle shoes, a pink Ralph Lauren polo shirt with a slight tear in the underarm stitching and a pair of badly aged khakis you could pick up in a thrift shop for about three bucks.

"Yeah, Koufax was a great pitcher and Pete Rose the best hustler the game's ever seen. Remember the World Series game when Pete Rose backed up his catcher, caught a foul ball when it popped out of the catcher's mitt?"

"I sure do. They both pushed the envelope. Koufax was the first Major League player to make a hundred thousand dollars a year. At the time, back in the fifties, he got nothing but criticism for demanding a hundred k. Everyone said he'd ruin the game. No pitcher, no ballplayer, was worth that kind of money. Sandy was worth it, of course. Now the owners think nothing of paying five mill to some bozo who couldn't carry Sandy's glove, couldn't find the plate with a flashlight. Our values are screwed up." Race put his hand out and smiled broadly. "I'm Bobby Race, nice to meet you."

Forceful handshake.

"Kevin Pierce." My name sounded tinny and feeble next to his. "Good to meet you, Mr. Race."

"Call me Bobby. We're very informal around here, Kevin."

"Okay...Bobby."

I sat down with Dorothy and Patterson in flanking chairs. Race went swiftly back around the desk to his own chair, which resembled Captain Kirk's command chair on Star Trek. "Joe...Dorothy...thanks for bringing Kevin on board. We really need your services, Kevin. They tell me you're a unique individual and I expect you to prove your worth. Everyone on my team has to prove his or her worth every single day, that's part of our culture. Let me take a minute to brief myself on your background."

He swung around to his computer and hit a few keys. I could see the computer screen in a slantwise way. A color photo of my face popped up on the screen, my old army ID photo. Then one document after another flashed across the screen as Race clicked through my file. I saw my army record zoom past, documents that looked like credit reports, photos of some of my paintings, court records, a copy of my driver's license and high school transcript, my diploma from the Los Angeles Art Institute, reviews of my paintings from newspapers and magazines. In thirty seconds of speed reading Bobby Race knew as much about me as my mother did.

"Great military record. Silver Star for that action in Zaire. Purple Heart. Presidential unit citation. The reviews of your paintings have been positive. All of that's good, I'll be interested to see what your brush makes of me." Race flashed his boyish smile, leaned back in his Captain Kirk chair. "According to what I just read, you didn't take up painting until you got out of the army. Isn't that unusual? Don't most artists start early in life, when they're kids?"

"Most do. Growing up, I had no interest in art. No artistic talent either. I was twenty-one years old when I was wounded in Zaire. Head wound. The round that tore out part of my skull must have scrambled something in my brain, too. In the military hospital, when I was recovering, I picked up a pencil and pad of paper and began drawing a portrait of the guy in the next bed. Couldn't believe what I saw. My drawing was *good*. Not great, but a thousand times better than any-thing I'd ever drawn. I mean, in grade school and high school art was my least favorite subject. Now, all of a sudden, I had to draw. *Had to*. I didn't know why. Where'd I suddenly get the talent for it? Don't know that either. And what I wanted to draw was faces. All kinds of faces.

When I got out of the hospital, I went to the Los Angeles Art Institute. Since then I've been painting portraits."

"Interesting story." Race scratched his ear. "You really believe the head wound turned you into an artist?"

Thinking of Sport Sullivan. "That wound changed my life in a lot of ways."

Race swiveled to face Dorothy. "How about it, Dorothy? What's your take?"

"A few years ago I read a study titled *Psychological Effects of Life Threatening Trauma* that reported unusual changes in personalities following such events as car wrecks and gunshot wounds. There are documented instances of people who suddenly develop marvelous singing voices. Become champion bridge players. Great golfers. Develop other new talents. Scientifically, what happened to Mister Pierce is statistically rare but not unheard of."

Grinning, Race said, "Dorothy's a walking encyclopedia."

She glowed from Race's compliment.

"Wherever the gift comes from, I'm grateful for it."

"You should be, a bullet in the head doesn't usually give a guy a living. Get it? A living?" Patterson laughed, then switched back to his serious face. "Bobby, in order to get Kevin on board with us, I had to tell him a little about that other matter."

Bobby Race frowned. Not a pleasant sight. Because he was so young, I suppose, his disappointment gave his smooth features the countenance of a spoiled child. "I told you that I personally wanted to broach the other matter with him."

Patterson squirmed under his boss's glare. "I didn't tell him much, just gave him a taste. Isn't that right, Dorothy?"

She answered with an ambivalent shrug, unwilling to help Patterson wiggle off the hook of Bobby's displeasure.

"What did they tell you"" Bobby asked me.

Having been manipulated into taking this commission, I was in no mood to make life easier for Patterson. Or even for the lovely Dorothy. "They told me your headquarters is haunted, that the portrait I'll be doing of you is just a cover for some ghostbusting, as they put it."

"Haunted!" Race's closed fist slammed down on his desk. He raked Dorothy and Patterson with his eyes, which had gone crazy. "Are you two crazy? That's just the kind of talk I *don't* want! Can you imagine what our competitors would do if they learned I was concerned with supernatural events? That our headquarters might be *haunted*? They'd turn Race Software into the biggest joke in the industry!"

"Neither Joe nor I ever used the word haunted," Dorothy assured him. "Honestly, Bobby. We never did. Joe referred to our problem as a *situation*."

The poor kid looked so terrified that I regretted throwing the word haunted around. Even Joe Patterson, a tough cop who'd killed a bank robber in his first year on the force, was shaken. "She's right, Bobby." It felt strange calling a billionaire by his first name. "Neither of them used the word haunted. I inferred that from what little they did tell me. Which was vague stuff. Some sort of specter sighted in your buildings, that's the most they said."

"That was too damned much!" Race struggled regain control of himself. "Look here people, there's bound to be a logical explanation for all this. That's why we hired Kevin, to find the answer."

"And paint your portrait." If I had to be here, I wanted to do his damned face.

"That too. But let's watch how we talk about this problem. I don't want to hear the word *ghost* or *haunted* or *supernatural* from anyone. That kind of talk just fuels rumors, and we have enough of those already."

"What kind of rumors?" I asked.

Race rather grumpily deferred to Patterson. "Since you've already opened the subject, you might as well explain what's going on."

Patterson, much relieved to have his boss speaking to him in normal tones again, picked up a file lying in his lap. "Over the last four weeks, some of our employees have reported seeing strange things in the headquarters complex." He consulted the file. "On July 18 Julie Reed, a systems analyst here in Building One, reported a *red mist* hovering in the air in the hallway outside her cubicle on the eighth floor. She screamed. Two of her colleagues came running and claim to have seen the mist too. The sighting was accompanied by what two of those people called moaning, or groaning, or sobbing sounds.

"There was a similar sighting by eight employees on July 23. Just a couple of days later still another sighting of the same phenomenon, a reddish mist accompanied by strange sounds. Seventeen employees reported seeing and hearing that one. Another sighting two days after that. All told, we've had eleven sightings of the same kind of thing, a red mist usually accompanied by human type sounds. A total of fifty-seven employees have been involved. All good people. No weirdos. Except for one guy who believes we're regularly visited by alien beings and a gal who says she belongs to a coven, and you'd get a few of those in any cross-section of the population. I've interviewed each employee who reported seeing this thing, hearing the noises. They're sincere, they really believe they've seen something like a ghost." Patterson shot a glance at his boss. "Sorry, Bobby. I meant something out of the ordinary."

I felt obliged to ask some questions to earn my fifty thousand dollars. "Have any of these sightings occurred in a common place?"

"Yeah." Patterson consulted his notes. "Four out of the eleven sightings took place in the technical library."

"The library is now virtually deserted," Dorothy commented. "We may have to move the facility to another location."

"Fifteen employees have actually quit the company," Race put in. "Most of them we could afford to lose, but three were key players. We musn't lose any more key people over this…this…phenomenon."

"People are scared, productivity is down," Dorothy added. "We called in a psychologist, he diagnosed this is as a case of mass hysteria. Personally, I think he was on the right track." She cleared her throat. "Unfortunately, there was another sighting that moved through the library while the psychologist was interviewing people there. The psychologist took off, we haven't seen him since the incident and he won't return our calls."

"Doesn't that tell you something?" I suggested.

Patterson snorted. "Tells us the psychologist is a major wimp."

"I'm sure all these people saw *something*," Dorothy said. "I know many of them, they're a level-headed bunch. But what they've seen can't be supernatural. I've looked at studies that prove there are rational explanations for what are usually called supernatural events. For example, there could be some sort of electrical disturbance in our buildings. The buildings are so new that we're still working out the bugs. Elevators sometimes stop between floors. The air conditioning system occasionally puts out too much air or too little. That sort of thing. It's very possible we're experiencing powerful static electricity, static storms they're called. That sometimes happens in new buildings that have a lot of built-in electronic equipment, as we do, though they're seldom as powerful or frequent as what we've experienced."

"What do you think?" Bobby asked me.

"Possible." I thought of Sport Sullivan. Sometimes I wondered if he might be just a creature of my imagination. Or something like a static storm. "I'm sure there are simple explanations to a lot of things that seem supernatural. But I do believe there is a spirit world, too. These could be supernatural events."

"Prove it," Patterson said bluntly.

"I can't." They were paying me a lot of money and they knew everything about me anyway, so I decided to cross a line I seldom acknowledge. "All I know is that I'm what spiritualists call a medium. I'm sure that's in my file already, along with the name of my favorite breakfast food." Acknowledging nods and sarcastic smirks all around. "Go ahead, laugh. For reasons unknown to me I attract a spirit, one spirit only, who appears when I least expect him. I don't even like this guy, he doesn't like me. He comes, we argue, he goes away. I don't want him around, never did. Now and then he does something positive. He told me where you could find Tara Hillyer, you've got to admit that was clairvoyant. That's all I care to say about this spirit. Frankly, I look on him as a pain in the butt."

Patterson was shaking his head. "I still think somebody who knew Gaston tipped you off."

"As you're so fond of saying: prove it."

"What is this spirit of yours?" Bobby Race was reluctantly interested. "A poltergeist?"

I've read a few books on the supernatural, just out of self defense. I told him what I knew. "No, a poltergeist throws stuff around, makes a lot of noise. Poltergeists are heard, not seen. They make tapping sounds. Knock dishes off the table. Shake banisters. There are *studies...*" tossing the word back at Dorothy "...that validate the existence of poltergeists. That isn't what I've got in my life, and it's not what you've got here. Poltergeists appear in homes, not commercial buildings. Usually homes where there are children. Look it up, Dorothy. No, what you've got is either something as simple as static storms, or a genuine spirit who's pissed off about something."

"I'm betting on the static storm," Dorothy declared. "I've called in an electrical engineer from Stanford, he'll begin a survey tomorrow for any transient electrical disturbances."

"I've put Dorothy in charge of this problem," Race explained. "She has one of the best analytical minds in the company."

Again Dorothy looked like a flower in full bloom.

"Good idea," I agreed. "Attack the problem from several angles. Tell me, did any of your people report a sharp drop or rise in temperature when this red mist was seen?"

Race, Patterson and Dorothy exchanged uncomfortable glances.

"Yes," Dorothy said. "That was a consistent part of the phenomenon."

"Very common when a spirit is present. The temperature usually doesn't stabilize until it leaves. Is that the case here?"

Patterson grumbled that yes, everyone he interviewed said the temperature plunged when the mist came in and rose again when it departed.

"How long did these sightings last? The average is three to five minutes."

Again Patterson was forced to admit I was on target.

"Quite often spirits that make despondent sounds, sobbing or groaning, died in some violent way, murder or an accident. I don't suppose you've had any violent deaths at Race headquarters recently." I meant the comment as a joke. It was greeted with serious expressions. "You have? Someone died here? In a violent way?"

"We had an accident," Dorothy said. "In June."

"Is someone going to tell me about that?"

Patterson cleared his throat. "Happened about two weeks before I came on board here, but I'm familiar with the file. She was an associate purchasing agent named Cynthia Gooding. Twenty-four years old. Cal graduate. She negotiated prices with our vendors for disks and software packaging. Only worked here six months, but her three-month and six-month evaluations were excellent."

I prompted him. "What kind of accident could a purchasing agent have?"

"Cynthia Gooding died in a fall," Patterson went on. "Apparently she was using the technical library to compare our disk prices against those of our competitors. The library's three levels high, circular staircase, dramatic design. You can access information through workstations or you can use any of the hundreds of publications in the racks. Cynthia had gone to the third level. She'd taken down a copy of *Electronic News*. Apparently she stepped back from the rack from which she'd taken the magazine, tripped, went over the rail. She hit her head on the floor below. Massive brain trauma, that was the medical examiner's determination. Poor kid, only twenty-four, makes you sick."

"Cynthia Gooding died in the place where four out of eleven sightings of this red stuff took place," I pointed out. "If we're talking about a spirit, and it's possible we are, it's probably this girl Cynthia."

"Nonsense," Bobby snapped.

"Did anyone see this accident?"

"Cynthia was alone in the library at the time of the accident," Dorothy answered.

"There's no librarian?"

"Our people are professionals, they don't need to be led around a library by hand like a bunch of kids." Bobby was annoyed at having to explain this. "One of our technical specialists spends two days a week updating the magazines on the shelves. The publications accessed by computer are updated automatically."

I rather liked getting under Bobby's skin. "Your library sounds like a dangerous place. Anyone else have a fatal accident there?"

"You're out of line." Bobby tried to drive me into the wall with his eyes. I'm sure the eye thing works with his regular employees, certainly Dorothy and Patterson blanched at his anger, but I didn't have a future at Race Software to protect.

"You wanted my ideas, Bobby. That's what I'm giving you."

Dorothy jumped in. "The rail on the second and third levels of the library should have been higher. That was corrected. They were raised two feet after Cynthia...after the accident."

"Sounds like Cynthia's survivors have grounds for a lawsuit."

Bobby leveled a finger at me. "You'll have a lawsuit on your own hands if you repeat that statement outside this office. I have twenty-two lawyers on staff, Kevin. Plus the firm of Heidecker, Raymond and Willeston on retainer. They exist to suck the life's blood out people who annoy me."

I had already come to the conclusion that Race's casual clothes and movie posters and baseball cards and puppy dog enthusiasm were a disguise. The guy was about as laid back as a cobra.

"We did expect someone to come forth with a lawsuit on behalf of Cynthia," Patterson said. I think he was actually giving me support, trying to draw Bobby Race's flak away from me. "Turns out she didn't have any family. My first week on the job I tried to find a relative. There aren't any. Nobody even came forward to claim her body. The company had to give the girl a funeral. We're still holding her insurance money in escrow."

"I'd like to look at the places where this red mist was seen," I told them. "Especially the technical library. I'll bring my sketch pad along. If anyone asks what I'm doing, I'm making sketches of your headquarters to use as possible backgrounds for your portrait."

"That can be arranged." Race addressed Dorothy. "Take Kevin around the headquarters, use his cover story about the sketches. Also, have Jenny set up an easel over there..." gesturing toward the corner of the office "...along with any other equipment Kevin needs. He can go through the motions of doing my portrait while I'm working and having meetings. He'll have the run of the headquarters, but I don't want a single word to get out that he's investigating our little problem."

"I'm not *going through the motions*, Mr. Race. Bobby. I've been commissioned to do a portrait of you and I will. Otherwise, the deal is off."

Race shrugged in a surly way. "Whatever. Supply him with photos, Dorothy. He can do most of his portrait work from those." He turned back to his computer and became instantly oblivious to the three of us, so submerged in his work that I doubt he would have responded if we'd spoken to him.

None of us did speak, of course. Instead we rose quietly and left. No, that isn't quite right. We didn't leave. We escaped.

Dorothy spent the next hour showing me around the headquarters complex. I'd never seen so many computers. Every employee in the place had a laptop computer that he or she could pick up and take home. Bobby paid his employees top dollar, but he expected them to take their laptops home and go back to work after dinner.

On their desktops, the notebooks were attached to "docking stations" that included various devices, printers and such. The cubicles, though nicely designed, were still Dilbertland as far as I was concerned.

The places where the red mist had been sighted included coffee rooms, hallways, conference rooms, even a woman's room.

I was particularly interested in the technical library, where four out of the eleven sightings had occurred. A big facility, three circular levels connected by an elegant circular staircase, the same muted blue and gray tones found in the rest of the headquarters. Except for the floor, which was made of red Mexican saltillo tile. Which explained why Cynthia Gooding had cracked open her head. Standing in the center of the facility, I looked up at the clear plastic siderails along the upper levels at least five feet high.

"Those are new rails, I assume."

"Yes," Dorothy confirmed. "They were three and a half feet high before the accident. Obviously, not high enough."

The floor showed no evidence of the accident.

"There was blood." Dorothy guessing at my thoughts. "That's been cleaned up, of course. Bobby even had the stained tiles replaced."

"Very sensitive guy." My sarcasm wasn't very well concealed, she picked up on it immediately.

"That's unfair."

"He reminds me of my drill sergeant in basic training, a grinning charmer one minute and a rabid killer the next."

"Bobby's really very kind. You only have to look at our benefits, the best in the industry, to know he really cares about his people. This phenomenon has upset him terribly, that's all. He's accustomed to having total control over his own domain. The idea that something unpleasant is going on here that he can't stop is torture to a man like Bobby."

Dorothy was incapable of thinking badly of Bobby Race, so I switched the subject. "You've shown me every place where this thing was seen. Did you notice what they all had in common?"

Her eyes narrowed. "Nothing I could see."

"Your company colors are predominantly blue and gray. Yet every place where the red mist was seen has a very strong red motif, like this red saltillo tile floor. Think about it, the Coke and other vending machines in the coffee room are red. There was a print on the wall of that hallway, strong reds. The other places where this thing appeared, too. Otherwise your headquarters is cool blue with some grays."

Dorothy flapped her arms. "You're right. Nobody else noticed that, I wonder why?"

"I'm an artist, I notice colors."

"What does this mean?"

"I haven't the slightest idea. But your mysterious mist is red, too. Must mean something."

"Dorothy!" A black maintenance man in blue workclothes came running into the library. "There's been another sighting! Third floor coffee room, Joe Patterson wants ya right away!" Pointing at me. "He wants this guy too!"

We hurried out of the library to an elevator. The maintenance man used his elevator key to keep the door open and the elevator itself stationary on our floor. As soon as we were inside, he turned the key and punched the button for the third floor. The languid descent was nerve-wracking. I had time to take a better look at the maintenance man. He had a rough directness at odds with the oh-so-polite Race employees I'd met. The name Pepper stitched onto the pocket of his workshirt. His left hand missing. In its place he wore a wicked-looking hook.

"Pepper Johnson," he said, when he caught me studying him.

"Kevin Pierce."

As soon as the elevator stopped and the door opened, we charged into the hallway. Some panic in evidence. People pushing their way into the elevator we had just left and others huddled in frightened groups, the herd instinct at work. We eased past them, Pepper Johnson leading us toward a coffee room at the end of the hall. Bobby Race appeared and the employees made a path as if for royalty.

"It's in the break room," Pepper said.

Patterson stood in the doorway, arms gripping both door posts to keep others out. "Look at this." Awe in his voice. "Fucking thing's red all right."

We edged into a break room about fifteen by thirty feet in size. The room held a few chairs and tables, a lounge, a bank of vending machines including large red Coke dispensers, a microwave oven, a magazine rack. In one corner hovered the red mist. Deep red in color, it seemed to contract and expand almost as a beating heart would do. The thing wasn't solid, you could see through it. I suppose it was the size of a human being, except it had no human form. Just a pulsating blob. The walls vibrated with sound: "Aaahhhhh...nooo...oh oh oh oh...aieeeee...aaahhhhhh...." Sobbing sounds. Pitiful noises that wrenched at you like fingernails across a blackboard.

The temperature hadn't fallen by just a few degrees, it had dropped from perhaps 75 to less than 40 degrees.

"I don't believe this," Bobby said hoarsely.

"There has to be an explanation," Dorothy said, though she failed to offer one. "Kevin, what is it?"

"Beats me." The thing bore no relation to my experiences with Sport Sullivan, who walked and talked and looked like a former human being.

"Someone's playing head games with us." Patterson was the kind who, faced with something he couldn't explain, became angry. "I know what it is...one of them...whattayacallit...holograms! That's it. Somebody's fiddled with the air conditioning. Bounced some sound in here. Projected a goddam hologram. We're being conned!"

"I don't think so." Patterson's explanation was the kind of pat answer people fall back on when they're exposed to something beyond their ken. I watched the red thing move, heard the sobbing and other sounds emanating directly from the apparition, and believed it did have a supernatural basis.

"It is a hologram." Patterson sounded madder than ever. "I'll prove it to you!"

"Joe, don't go near it!"

"Stay back here," Bobby told him.

I grabbed for his arm, but Patterson dived into the apparition with his arms outstretched as if he could tackle the damned thing.

"No!" Patterson screamed and fell to the floor shaking like a drunk with the DTs. "Jesus, Mary and Joseph, I can't breathe!"

Dorothy's instinct was to jump in after Patterson and try to save him. Pepper and I held her back. I grabbed a chair and thrust it into the mist, careful to keep myself outside its borders. The metal legs of the chair were immediately covered with a sheen of ice. Pepper Johnson snared one of Patterson's legs with the hook at the end of his left arm and began to pull him out. The chair, which within seconds became completely covered with ice, slipped off. Pepper kept pulling until Patterson's leg emerged from the mist. I dropped the chair, seized Patterson's ankle and pulled him across the floor until he was free of that thing.

"Joe, are you all right?" Bobby grabbed an arm and the three of us dragged Patterson out of the break room and into the hallway.

Pepper pushed back the knot of onlookers. "Make room for him. Bobby, look at his skin, it's all burnt up!"

Patterson's skin had turned a terrible purplish red, with blisters on the face and at every joint of his hands. "Looks like severe frostbite," I said. "Call the EMS right away."

Pepper grabbed a communications unit off his belt and told the first floor security office to get an EMS unit headed this way pronto.

Dorothy touched Patterson's cheek. "I can't believe this, he's as cold as a block of ice."

"That's impossible, he was only inside that thing for fifteen seconds." Bobby timidly peered around the corner. "It's gone!"

The specter and its accompanying noises had indeed faded away and the temperature around us was rising. That didn't help Joe Patterson, who continued to shiver violently while his eyes fluttered and his mouth uttered unintelligible words.

The EMS unit arrived quickly and Patterson was swiftly moved out.

"Get him to the Stanford Medical Center," Bobby Race told the EMS crew as they entered the elevator. "Tell them I want Joe to have the best treatment!"

When the elevator door closed and the EMS crew was descending to the first floor, Bobby turned to the twenty or more employees still in the hallway. He cleared his throat nervously. "People, there's been an accident in the coffee room." He wrung his hands, smiled weakly. "Joe Patterson was injured, but he's going to be just fine. I suggest we all get back to work, meet the deadline on the beta tests for Redleaf."

My ears pricked up at the mention of something called Redleaf.

One of the employees stepped forward. He was older than the average Race employee, maybe thirty-five, a short balding guy with thick arms, trim waist, the stance of an aging athlete. His eyes, behind thick glasses, were fiery. "Bobby, that was no accident. There was some fucking *thing* in there, a red *thing*, I saw it myself, and it was crying, or moaning, it shook us all up. And Joe Patterson, the *thing* burned his skin to a crisp. I don't like what's going on here, Bobby. I'm going to Oracle or HP or Apple or even IBM if have to. I just can't work with all this shit going on."

"Greg..."

"Bobby, I'm sorry. This was just too much. You've got a problem here and I don't think it's going away." The complainer turned on his heel and pushed his way down the hallway.

"Greg, think this over. You can't do better someplace else." Bobby was talking to thin air. Most of the other employees, embarrassed but impressed by their colleague's declaration of independence, avoided meeting their boss's eyes. They melted away into the stairwells and elevators and nearby offices, leaving Bobby Race standing with only Dorothy and myself.

"That was Greg Tillotson." Race shot me a venomous look, as if I'd prompted the man's resignation. "He is...he *was*...director of the Redleaf program."

"What's Redleaf?"

"Our newest networking package," Dorothy told me. "It's in the beta test phase, the final tests before the product goes into general release."

"If Greg has really quit the team, the tests will be set back at least six weeks. Microsoft and Lotus and Oracle and all the others will be on us like a pack of dogs." Bobby continued to glare at me as if my presence alone had created the entire problem. "Every one of our competitors will spread rumors that we haven't worked out the bugs on Redleaf, we can't deliver the firewalls we promised in this package."

"We'll make all the deadlines," Dorothy promised. "With or without Greg."

Bobby, still full of restless anger, jabbed his finger into my chest. "Kevin, you were sold to me as an expert on the supernatural. You'd better figure out what's going on around here, and do it fast! If you don't deliver, you're off the team and you can kiss that fifty k goodbye. Dorothy, I'll be in my office until midnight. Keep me informed about Joe's condition."

Jenny Hartsong...Bobby's secretary...was the only other employee who hadn't fled the scene. Jenny came forward and put a hand on her boss's arm. "Let me talk to Greg," she suggested. "I'm sure I can change his mind. He doesn't really want to leave, I know that."

"Yeah...talk to him, Jenny...please."

Bobby stalked away with Jenny hurrying along at his side making calming noises.

"Well, fuck him," I growled. "I never claimed to be an *expert* on the supernatural. You people dragged me in here."

"Please…" Dorothy clutched my shirtsleeve. "Bobby needs you, he knows he does, he's just upset about what happened to Joe."

"Sure, that's why he's rushing over to the hospital to see how his chief of security is doing."

"You don't understand." Her eyes were moist. "The salaries of all these people, the expectations of thousands of our customers, not to mention what those backbiting analysts on Wall Street expect of Race Software, all ride on Bobby's shoulders. He works twenty-four hours a day to keep this company vital, to extend our success. The pressure is much greater than anything you can imagine."

"So that gives him the right to fuck over anybody he wants?"

"Don't talk like that around me."

Dorothy's mouth had become tight and prim. She still looked great to me, vulnerable as hell despite all the intelligence. I ached for her, and it had been a long time since I'd felt that strongly about a woman.

I waved my hand. "All right, the man's a prince. I should be burned at the stake for taking offense. Let's head over to the Stanford Medical Center. I want to see how Joe's doing."

While we waited for the elevator, I pointed into the coffee room. "More red Coke machines? Project Redleaf? The red misty thing that just attacked Joe Patterson? You have a study explaining all that?"

"No." Dorothy reached out and clutched my shirt. "We need you, Kevin. Please don't get mad and leave us."

Shit-oh-dear, I thought. She's got me.

We hung around Stanford Medical Center for the next few hours, waiting for news on Joe Patterson's condition. His wife Eileen was summoned. She came with their two sons, a pair of husky teenagers in letterman jackets who looked like they'd make good cops too, or formidable football players. Eileen Patterson was as petite as her sons were husky. She had a sharp face, trim figure, kind eyes. Dorothy, who knew Eileen, introduced me as a fellow employee at Race. Eileen Patterson had been a cop's wife for years so she didn't break down when told that Joe was in serious condition. Joe was conscious, she talked to him for a few minutes and came out of the hospital room looking pale but wearing a confident smile to buck up the spirits of her boys.

The doctor treating Joe was puzzled. "Your husband has deep frostbite, Mrs. Patterson. How did that happen? I mean, this is California, for God's sake!"

"I don't know." Eileen turned to us. "What was it?"

"An industrial accident," was all Dorothy could think of to say.

"The cause is being investigated," I said. "Bobby Race will be in touch with you, doctor. And you, Eileen. About the particulars."

"I was the one who urged Joe to leave the force, get a *safer* job," Eileen Patterson said bitterly. "More than twenty years a cop, never a scratch. Gunfights. Fist fights. Riots. He never got hurt. Six weeks as an executive and he's in the hospital. He's going to be all right?"

"Yes, he'll recover," the doctor said. "I'm afraid he's going to lose at least two fingers on his left hand. Maybe three. You saw how bad they were."

"Oh, no."

"Two fingers were frozen all the way into the bone. Very rare. They're almost gangrenous already, they have to be amputated. I really don't understand this. If I didn't know better, I'd say your husband was flash frozen. Anyway, as soon as you sign this authorization we'll get him into surgery." The doctor turned to me. "Are you Kevin Pierce?"

"Yes, I am."

"Joe would like to speak with you. I told him that'd be all right." He raised a warning finger. "You have only two minutes, we've already medicated him for surgery. You'll find him groggy."

I went into Joe Patterson's hospital room and found him swathed in bandages, his face deep red and blistered, his left arm propped up on a pillow with the hand exposed. Ready for surgery. The hand looked awful. Not just blisters. Blackened fingers, two of them already missing some flesh. His eyes were glassy but otherwise he seemed alert.

"You look lousy," I said.

He laughed hoarsely. "Everybody else tiptoeing around, telling me how good I'm doing. You have to be the honest one. Don't you know that isn't done in a hospital?"

"Do you remember what happened?"

"I remember the mist. The sobbing sounds. I thought it was a hologram? What a dumb idea that turned out to be." He swallowed hard. "I've got deep frostbite, the doc says. How long was I in there?"

"Just a few seconds."

"It was chilly outside the mist. Inside like the North Pole. You pulled me out?"

"Me and the maintenance guy, Pepper Johnson. The guy with a hook for a left hand."

"Thanks. Tell Pepper I appreciate what you guys did. I guess maybe there are ghosts." He laughed again, it turned into a cough. "Never thought I'd hear myself say that." He looked at his left hand. "I'm gonna lose those two fingers, the ones that look like burnt hot-dogs. And the doc says I'll be sensitive to light and cold for the rest of my life."

"You want some advice? Sue Bobby Race for ten million dollars, walk away from your new job and enjoy your family instead."

"You met Eileen?"

"Yes, she's great. And your sons look just like you."

"They're good kids, need a firm hand is all. Eileen's terrific with them, I wasn't around enough when I was on the job. That's one reason I went to work for Race, thought I'd have more time for the family. A soft berth. Another big mistake." He blinked several times in rapid succession. "I'm getting groggy here, Kevin. And I got something to tell you."

His words were becoming slurred from the medication.

"The girl who was killed…Cynthia Gooding…tried to get a line on her. She had no past…nothing there…just a degree from U.C. Berkeley and that turned out to be a fake. Credit history a fake, too. Also, Bobby was fucking Cynthia."

"Bobby Race and Cynthia Gooding? Are you sure about that?"

"Yeah…I'm…I'm positive. Bobby likes to dip into the employee pool…sex…two or three months. Then he drops the girl, picks up another. Endless supply. *Bobby's Harem* is what they call those girls behind their backs. Guy's an asshole. Brilliant, y'know…but an asshole. I like…she's another one."

I put my ear down just inches from his mouth. "Who's another one?"

"Dorothy. He's had her, too. He moved on afterwards…like he always does. That's the story. I like Dorothy…but…she still believes he loves her. Bobby's style…thinks he owns everything and everyone in the company." Patterson's eyes rolled back. "I'm fading."

I wondered why Dorothy remained so blindly loyal to a man who'd dumped her.

"When I was a cop…only three motives. Money. Sex. Rage. Ghosts or not, see who has the motive."

"You think Cynthia Gooding was murdered?"

"I'm real tired." His eyes closed and soon he was unconscious.

CHAPTER 5

The next morning I began to block out the elements of Bobby Race's portrait, working in the corner of his office that had been assigned to me. Bobby was there when I arrived but left soon afterwards at the head of a platoon of yes-men and of-course-Bobby-women. I think he went off to prepare the world for computer networks built into bathroom walls or something equally useless. Dorothy came in a few minutes later and looked over my shoulder.

"Is that going to be the background color for Bobby's portrait?"

"I think so, I haven't really decided." I was seated in front of the easel I'd set up with a good view of Bobby's desk. Usually it annoys me to have someone looking over my shoulder while I work. In this case, with Dorothy's hair swinging loose and fragrant against the nape of my neck, I decided she could stand there all day if she wanted, it would be churlish of me to complain.

"It's beige," she said.

"Mmmm," I replied, more a reaction to the wonderful aroma of her hair than her inaccurate description of the color I was using. "This is more of an ecru with shadings of cream. Makes a decent background, you can work with any kind of color in the foreground. But I'm still playing around, getting a sense of what I want to do. Nothing final about this."

"Race Software's company color is blue. The background for the portrait should be blue, too. Doesn't that make sense?"

The words *"No, that makes no goddam sense at all!"* made it as far as my tongue, but I bit them back. "Dorothy…" Very reasonable voice. "This is a portrait, not a company logo. There's a helluva difference."

"Bobby's portrait is bound to be reproduced in a lot of ways. We might use it in a company brochure, for example. Or in the annual report. We'd give color stats to magazines like *Fortune* and *Business Week*. Don't you see? Everything about Bobby becomes an extension of Race Software. Especially Bobby's personal image."

Her smile shattered my heart, but I retained enough resolve about my work to point out the fallacy at the center of her argument. "Dorothy," I said with utmost patience, "not everything is about business."

"Don't be silly," she countered. "Everything *is* about business. That's the first thing you learn when you leave school and get out into the real world." She'd slipped into the role of a teacher trying to impart an important lesson to a backward student. "All those college courses on history and philosophy, they were just window dressing. Economics. Science. Technology. That's what the world is truly about. You can't put art, not even your kind of art, into a box that separates it from the business world. I'll say it again with a different emphasis—*everything* is about business."

"You can't really buy that view of life."

"I do," she said.

"All right, everything is about business. Since portraits are my business, I'll do them my own way."

"Don't be so touchy, I'm just trying to help."

"Well…thank you. This is one area where I don't require help."

"Suit yourself." She left in a charming huff.

I hadn't been able to tell Dorothy in a more straightforward way to keep her artistic opinions to herself because I still had hopes of breaking through that brittle shell into her more intimate regions. I'm a weak person, okay?

A few minutes later Jenny came bustling in and looked approvingly at my easel and canvas plus the chair and a workbox full of paints, brushes, colored pencils, thinner, pads of art paper, rags. The usual flotsam of my life. "How're you doing, Kevin? Got everything you need?" This morning she dressed in a tank-top, runner's shorts, sneakers. She had the trim body and athletic legs of a dedicated runner. Her hair tied back in a runner's neat ponytail. Her face so clean-cut and wholesome it didn't need to be pretty. But of course, it was.

"I'm settled in just fine."

Jenny plopped a basket of goodies on an end table near my easel. "Here's some bottled water, juice, fruit, granola bars. If you need anything else, art supplies, whatever, just sing out."

"You're amazing." No exaggeration. Jenny Hartsong had more energy than a nuclear reactor. I had arrived at Race Software at 9:30 a.m., which seemed to me a civilized hour to begin a portrait, to find that Jenny had been calling my house. She informed me in a pleasant though cautionary way that most people arrive by seven-thirty in the morning and generally leave the office at seven p.m. or later, always taking their laptops home so they could squeeze in an hour or two of e-mail or "debugging."

Anyone who thinks California has a laid-back lifestyle has never have worked in Silicon Valley.

When I told Jenny her call missed me because I'd stopped at a Lyon's coffee shop for bacon and eggs, she suggested I get in by eight a.m. tomorrow and breakfast on the fat-free muffins or low calorie bagels in the company cafeteria.

Despite her iron determination to "help get you on track," as she put it, I genuinely liked Jenny. She'd do anything I asked short of eating a pound of rusty nails, and she might even do that to advance the fortunes of Race Software. She was, of course, ferociously dedicated to the personal needs of Bobby Race.

When the king returned to his office, he hardly took notice of this lowly serf. He was occupied giving Jenny two or three hundred tasks to do, each of which she scribbled onto a long list with cheery disregard for how late she'd have to stay that night to get them all done.

The part I heard went something like this: Bobby saying: "Circulate the results of the latest Redleaf beta tests to the A list, I want their reactions pronto. Call each of my direct reports and tell them I need their weekly financial summaries on my computer before noon. Tell Samuelson I won't speak at Comdex after all, he'll be pissed but I don't care. Set up my trip to Tokyo for November, I want an hour-by-hour itinerary on my desk six weeks ahead of time. I'm out of the granola bars I like, the ones with the raisins, get me a couple of twelve-packs and put them in my bottom left-hand drawer. I want to review the revised marketing plan for Redleaf with Hardesty, and tell him I don't want any of those goddam small-type ads this time around. See that some good charity for kids gets my private box for the Giants-Dodgers series, I won't be able to make any of the games, and tell the P.R. people to make sure my generosity gets into the newspapers. I did a bunch of charts last night, print and collate them for me (handing her a disk) but first change the greens and blues so they don't bleed into each other like a bad cartoon."

He went on like that for at least fifteen minutes. When her boss was through passing out work, all Jenny said was, "Consider it done, Bobby."

I was making good progress blocking out the portrait. If I had my way, I'd have painted Bobby Race crouched in a corner of the canvas counting out stacks of money, his mouth set in a cruel line, face flushed with greed, eyes fastened maniacally on his wealth, with various of his dead and defeated competitors impaled on sharpened stakes, their teeth yellowing as their life-giving juices faded into eternity.

Yes, I could easily paint Bobby Race as a cross between Scrooge and Vlad the Impaler. However, in the cause of getting my house fixed up I selected a more conventional attitude. I'd paint him at a quarter angle, leaning forward with characteristic aggressiveness but without the core of nastiness that lurked just below the surface. I'd give him his signature boyish grin, of course. He wouldn't be Bobby without the grin.

The hell of it was that Bobby Race really did have a face worth painting. Even the untutored eye could detect multiple layers of complexity behind Bobby's bland college boy exterior. Some of the layers were bright and shining, others hinted at the raw material for a dictator or mad scientist. You hear about people who have a "glint" in their eyes. Bobby really did have a glint. It was laserlike rather than twinkly and charming, a tool for cutting diamonds rather than the high-spirited signature of the leprechaun. But I could see how a ferocious glint would appeal to the ladies. With a glint like that, I'd get laid a lot more often myself. For now I'd have to settle for getting that glint just right in Bobby's portrait.

As usual, I slowly became obsessed with sketching the basic structure. His bones were light yet strong, more aluminum than steel. His cheekbones well defined without being sharp. His hair the texture of the aged brown straw you find underfoot in stables. The hair gave Bobby his plain guy look. At first I thought Bobby's look, the old shirts, faded jeans, scuffed tennies, must be totally cultivated. It wasn't. He just didn't give a damn about clothes and wouldn't waste time combing his hair. It took me a while to realized his hair wasn't the creation of some stylist. The unruly mop held even more appeal than the grin. It was a frame that defined his face.

"…with us, Kevin?"

"Huh?"

"I said: Are you with us, Kevin?"

I blinked a couple of times. Saw Bobby go around his desk and plop himself down in front of his computer screen. "Sorry. Guess I didn't hear you come in."

"Quite all right. I don't care much for people who can't lose themselves in their work. Nothing I enjoy more than watching an employee's eyes glaze over as he loses himself in his task. Speaking of which, it's time for you to get to work."

I waved my brush at the canvas.

"No, I'm talking about the *real* work I hired you to do." Bobby punched a button on his desk and Jenny appeared.

"Yes, Bobby?"

"You've got those appointments lined up for Kevin?"

"All set." She flipped back her note pad. "Eleven o'clock with Hugh Wilson…eleven-thirty with Pam Solter…noon with Greg Tillotson." She ripped the sheet out of her notebook and handed it to me. "Anything else, Bobby?"

"Not right now."

Jenny flitted out of the office like Tinkerbell in search of Peter Pan.

"What am I supposed to talk about with these people?"

"Pam's my director of human resources, she'll have some useful background on Cynthia. Hugh is corporate counsel, he holds everybody's employment contract. Maybe there's a factoid in Cynthia's contract that'll help you. And Greg dealt with Cynthia almost every day, she negotiated prices on the disks and CDs we'll put the Redleaf program on."

"So Cynthia's job was important? I got the impression from Dorothy that Cynthia held a fairly low level job."

Bobby tilted back in a twenty-thousand dollar leather chair. I knew the price because it had been mentioned in one of the magazine profiles of Bobby that I'd read. "Cynthia wasn't a key player, but she was working on an important program." He gave up a short laugh. "Some higher level employees were even jealous of her access to senior executives."

"What kind of access did Cynthia have to you?"

"What's that supposed to mean?"

"I understand you were sleeping with Cynthia Gooding."

"Who told you that?" Bobby jerked forward. "I want the name of the employee who's spreading rumors about me."

"What makes you think I heard that story from an employee?"

"That's just the kind of gossip corporate employees like to kick around." He shook his head. "I'll tell you something, Kevin. Corporate grunges are the ultimate rumor mongers."

"Then it's not true?"

"I work late almost every night, it's part of our corporate culture. A way of life you wouldn't understand. Now and then I'd run across Cynthia here on the campus at night, say hello, chat her up, maybe have coffee with her. That's all it amounted to. Enough to start a rumor, obviously."

"I've been told you sleep with all the best looking women here. That Cynthia Gooding was one of a group they call *Bobby's Harem*."

The famous grin slipped. "Do you enjoy your poverty, Kevin? You may be looking forward to a lifetime of it."

"Nobody enjoys poverty. And I'm not poor, Bobby. I'm broke. There's a distinction."

"You're doing some work for me on a sensitive matter. That's the sum of our relationship. My personal life is none of your business."

"What if this strange red glob floating around your headquarters is related to your personal life? What if Cynthia Gooding is haunting you." I held up a hand. "Hey, I know you don't want to hear that word. I'm just giving you some *what ifs* to think about. *What if* this weird red presence is the essence of Cynthia Gooding? *What if* Cynthia Gooding resented being treated like a member of your harem? *What if* she died with a grudge against you? *What if* she wants something from you?"

Bobby stared at me as if I had shit all over my face. "You've gone way over the line."

"What you want me to look into is bizarre. Any theories I come up with are liable to be equally bizarre."

Bobby pointed a finger at me. "When you speak to my executives, keep your crackpot theories to yourself. By now everyone around here knows you're doing my portrait. You can tell people you were also a personal friend of Cynthia Gooding and that I've given you permission to ask about her, try to find out why we can't locate any of her family or friends."

"Your well-known devotion to your employees manifesting itself yet again." Sometimes I just have to take the cheap shot. It's a weakness I'm working on, though not too hard.

"You've got more balls than brains, Kevin. Not a healthy trait." He turned back to his computer and began punching keys, an effective if insulting dismissal.

"Call me Pam, we're pretty casual around here. So you're the artist." Pam Solter, director of human resources, leaned back and munched on a Snickers bar. "You look like an artist."

"Thank you."

"That wasn't necessarily a compliment. You want a Snickers bar?" She reached into a desk drawer and offered me one. "I've got plenty."

"No granola?"

Pam Solter stuck a finger down her throat and mimed being nauseous. "I hate granola. I hate fat free muffins. Most of all I hate *raisins*. Everybody in this place carries those little red boxes of raisins. They're supposed to be healthy. Fuck raisins, give me a Snickers bar any day."

I liked Pam. For starters, she was quite a bit heavier than the fitness freaks around Race headquarters. She had a pleasant round face set off by kind brown eyes, a sprinkle of freckles under the eyes, a shrewd mouth, doughy cheeks. She wore a loose pair of jeans and a bulky sweater. She resembled a dumpling that could talk.

"So what am I doing here?" I asked. "Talking to you, I mean."

"I'm supposed to give you the usual Race Software orientation pitch. How leading edge we are. What a privilege it is for you to work for us, even as a grade one contractor. Ya-da-ya-da-ya-da. And I need your signature on the usual forms." She flipped open a file. "Sign these. First one's a non-disclosure agreement, says we'll sue if you disclose company secrets to a competitor. Believe me, we'd do that, keep you tied up in court for years, confiscate your bank accounts, your house, your dog, any small children you may have. Next is a form saying I've given you the orientation pitch, consider that done. Next is a bank form for a company credit card, usable for company expenses only. Then a California state income tax form. The green form's a next-of-kin statement so we know who to contact if you drop dead while you're doing Bobby's portrait. That's about it."

I'd been signing the forms without looking at them, barely interested in what they were about, until I heard Pam mention a credit card. "You said…what was it?…I'm signing for a credit card?"

She took a Visa card out of the folder and slid it across the desk. "Yes, you get a Visa card for company expenses. Let me emphasize that the card is to be used *for company expenses only*. I mention that because as a routine matter we ran a credit check and determined that the Visa people have a hit man looking for you."

"The people who run credit card companies have no souls," I explained. "They are the undead."

Her dumpling face came alight. "I know where you're coming from. When I was in college they were looking for me, too. The Visa Vampires, I called them. They only come out at night to eat corpses. Like, I was a few weeks late with a payment and they wanted my right arm for a meal."

"They want both my arms, which would make it awfully hard to paint portraits."

"Just be careful with that piece of plastic. I understand you're only going to be with us for a week or two. Even so, I don't want to have to terminate our business relationship on an ugly note."

"You have my word as a gentleman that I will be careful how I use my new credit card." Tucking it safely into my tattered old wallet.

Her eyes were knowing as well as kind. "Well, it's nice to have met you, Kevin. I'm looking forward to seeing your portrait of Bobby.

Everybody's talking about it, wondering how he's going to look. His physical image is important to the company, you know."

"That's what I'm finding out. Pam, I've also been asked by Bobby to try to find out more about Cynthia Gooding, the employee who died recently. Died right here in this building, I've been told. Cynthia must have signed one of these next of kin forms too. Given you an address. Yet nobody's been able to locate her family, her address, or any of her friends."

Wariness crept into her features. "Bobby asked you to look into this? Why would he ask you to do that? You're an artist who's here to do his portrait." Before I could answer, Pam went on almost angrily. "I looked for that girl's family, sent staff members to the address she gave us and hired a locator agency to find her family. They couldn't find any trace of Cynthia Gooding. It's as if she never existed."

"What do you make of that?"

Pam picked up her phone and punched in an internal number. "Hi Jenny, this is Pam Solter. Is Bobby there? I need thirty seconds." She drummed her fingers on the desk until Bobby came on the line. "Bobby, did you authorize this artist, Kevin Pierce, to ask me questions about Cynthia Gooding?" As she listened to his reply, her expression gradually lightened. "Okay…thanks…just checking." She put down the phone. "That's just like Bobby, still worrying over one of his people even after her death. You should have said you knew Cynthia, that explains why Bobby asked you to look into the matter."

I admired how smoothly Bobby Race could cover his tracks. "I didn't know her very well."

Pam called up a file on her computer screen and hit the print button. Instantly the personnel records for Cynthia Gooding began spewing out of the printer next to her desk. She collected the sheaf of papers and handed them across to me. "We scan all personnel documents into the computer. This is everything we have, including copies of all the forms Cynthia signed when she joined the company."

There was even a color photo of Cynthia Gooding. It showed her to be an attractive girl with reddish brown hair. "Pam, I've got a delicate question. Was Cynthia one of the girls in what they call *Bobby's Harem*?"

Pam's warmth went into cold storage. "I've heard that phrase and I don't like it. There was nothing between Cynthia and Bobby that I know of, and I know pretty much everything that happens around here. They saw each other fairly often because Cynthia was on the Redleaf team. She was a productive worker, put in long hours. Lots of people drift into Bobby's office in the evening just to gab and have a granola bar with him. When Bobby offers you a granola bar from his desk, it's like being anointed to an inner circle. You hear people say *She's one of the granola gang* a lot more often than *She's one of Bobby's Harem.*"

"But they do talk about a harem?"

She nodded curtly. "Don't believe every story you hear. Some of the girls want people to think they've been to bed with Bobby. Around here that's like sleeping with a movie star."

"You're sure Cynthia didn't connect in that way with Bobby?"

A groan. "Might have happened." Her eyes shifted around. "The truth? I've warned Bobby that at some point he might face a sexual harassment lawsuit from one of his *harem*. I'm telling you this because Bobby obviously has a special relationship with you that goes beyond having his portrait painted. It's stupid of him to sleep with an employee when so many other women would like to get him in the sack. He always seems to listen when I tell him that, even looks chastened sometimes, then I hear he's had another girl *working late* in his office." Her manner turned probing. "Does this have anything to do with our in-house ghost?"

"Don't use that word around Bobby, he denies the existence of supernatural beings."

Pam looked grim. "So do I, but I've talked to people who claim to have seen something unearthly in the break room yesterday. Whether Bobby wants it or not, there are weird rumors flying around the campus. I went to the hospital before breakfast to see Joe Patterson. He has no logical explanation for what happened to him yesterday and neither do his doctors. Do you?"

Bobby's instructions were to avoid mentioning the supernatural, so I did. "I have no idea what happened to Joe." That was almost the truth. The thing in the coffee room was as puzzling to me as the paintings of the Pre-Raphaelite Brotherhood.

"Are you a born liar, Mr. Pierce? Or did you take training in it?" She glanced past me at a secretary who stood in the doorway. "Can I help you, Esther?"

The pert young woman in the doorway was looking on me with disfavor. "If you're Kevin Pierce, you're forty minutes late for your meeting with Mister Wilson. You were supposed to be in his office at eleven. I had to track you down here."

"Sorry. I got confused and came to this meeting first." I got up and thanked Pam for her time.

Pam said, "Anything you find out about Cynthia comes directly to me as well as to Bobby."

"Fair enough." I had another thought. "I noticed a copy of Cynthia's driver's license in the documents you gave me. You wouldn't happen to have the original, would you?"

"I have Cynthia's purse in my private file because nobody else claimed it. Or her. We found the purse in her desk. I'm sure I saw her driver's license in there."

"Could I have the purse and its contents? I've got a particular use for the driver's license."

"I guess that will be all right." Pam unlocked a file and gave me a bulky package in an outsized gray envelope. I had to sign for it, of course. I was learning that you have to sign for everything at a corporation.

Esther, Hugh Wilson's secretary, tapped her foot with such a rich portrayal of impatience that I wanted to applaud. I settled for following her at a trot. She was small but shifty, maneuvering her way through the crowded hallways with the tenacity of an NFL halfback. Over her shoulder she continued to berate me. "Mr. Wilson practices calendar integrity and he expects others to do the same."

"I didn't know calendars had integrity. I thought they just had dates and times."

"Is that a joke?"

"Supposed to be."

"Well, you aren't a bit funny."

"That's what my mother used to say." I tried to placate her. "Really. She did say that a lot."

"You should have listened to her."

If pert little Esther was annoyed with me for missing the meeting, her boss looked fighting mad. I found Hugh Wilson running laps on a treadmill near his desk in nothing but sneakers and a pair of running shorts. According to the digital monitor, he'd run seven miles already and was panting for air. He sweated copiously and smelled awful. This probably explained Esther's lousy disposition. I hoped Hugh Wilson was high enough in the power structure to rate a private shower.

He expressed his displeasure with me in the following way:

"Kevin Pierce? You're forty minutes late." *Pant pant.* "That's unforgivable." *Pant pant.* "My time is worth roughly five hundred dollars an hour." *Pant pant pant.* "So your tardiness has cost this corporation approximately six hundred and fifty dollars." *Pant pant.*

"I apologize," I said, though I didn't really give a damn how much money Hugh Wilson made or how much I might have cost the Race Software Development Corporation and its far-flung empire.

Wilson dropped his belligerence but continued to run and sweat and pant and smell incredibly gross. I longed to tell him how terrible he smelled, but feared being sued for defamation.

"Hand me those papers on the desk." *Pant followed by a painful gasp.* "The ones in the..." *pant pant pant* "...blue folder." The guy looked like he was born to jog, meaning he was as lean as you could get. His bodyweight was probably only one percent fat, the rest would be brittle bones. Plus, of course, his enormous sweat glands. Wilson's face was as thin as an ax, his eyes gray and probing. I doubt that he was more than a year or two older than me. Which put him in his early thirties. But the eyes were as tired as a septuagenarian's. He had that humorless expression you see on the faces of runners who've long ago forgotten why they laced up their sneakers.

I picked the folder from a messy collection and handed it to him. A narrow desktop had been built into the frame of the treadmill so Wilson could work while he jogged. Piles of legal documents teetered on the desktop. He plopped the folder onto one of the piles and opened it without missing a pace. "This is your employment contract." *More panting.* "It's been vetted by your agent." *Panting followed by intense gulping.* "Put your initials on the line at the bottom right hand corner of each of the first eight pages. Then sign and date the last page."

"Excuse me, but you're sweating all over my contract."

He looked genuinely chagrined. "Shit, I'm sorry." Wilson punched a button that made the treadmill slowly grind to a halt. He stepped off, grabbed a towel and rubbed himself under the arms and around the chest, which only served to transfer some of the noxious fumes to a second surface.

As quickly as possible, I did the initialing and signing.

"You should always read a contract before you sign it," Wilson said in a severe voice.

"I became an artist partly so I wouldn't have to look over legal documents. Or read manuals. Or talk to people about things like bits and bytes."

He smiled and suddenly looked younger and more at ease with himself. "You want a laugh? I became a lawyer to right some of the injustices in our society." With a wave at the floor-to-ceiling bookcase filled with lawbooks bound in unattractive colors. "Instead I help corporations avoid their taxes."

"Sounds lucrative."

"Lucrative." He rolled the word around in his mouth. "I became the Race corporate counsel only three months ago. My predecessor died of a heart attack at this very desk. Died at midnight while rewriting an errant subjective clause in a contract. That's why I jog, so I won't end up like him. Fact is, I hate to run. No, the people who joined the team the first couple of years were the big winners. They had stock options at two dollars a share and today they're multi-millionaires. I draw a damned good salary, but my options are at *eighty dollars* a share. I'll never get rich off Race Software."

"Look on the bright side. Guys like me don't have a big salaries *or* stock options. On top of that, my roof leaks."

"You should sue your contractor."

"It's an old house."

"Sue somebody else then." Wilson settled more comfortably into his chair. "A neighbor. The realtor who sold you the house. Anyone. Don't you know it's the duty of the populace to keep lawyers employed?"

"Yeah, I remember now. It's written into the Constitution."

When Wilson laughed, the taut skin on his sharp face looked less leathery. He seemed the kind of guy who became more personable the longer you talked to him. A shy guy maybe. Needed to feel his way with someone new.

While he was in a good mood, I threw in a question. "Cynthia Gooding was an old friend of mine and Bobby's asked me to try to find her family. Could I look at her employment contract?"

His reluctance lasted less than a second. "Bobby's idea? Well, his whim is my command." Wilson sprang from his chair. "Esther! Bring in Cynthia Gooding's employment contract." In an aside to me: "Esther hates it when I jog. She never says anything, but I can tell that the aroma of physical exercise isn't her favorite perfume. Excuse me, I'll take a quick shower while you look over the young woman's contract. Don't think you'll find much of interest though. Standard contract."

Wilson pushed at something on the wall and a panel swung open. The bastard *did* have a private shower. He disappeared into it as Esther came in with the contract. The relief on Esther's face when she heard the shower running was a beautiful sight. I pinched my nose with two fingers and Esther actually giggled before scooting out of the office.

Cynthia Gooding's contract wasn't very enlightening. Too many legal terms. I did gag at the high salaries being paid even the lower level employees at places like Race Software. I also noticed that her signature was totally illegible. Bad handwriting? Or had she been trying to hide something?

Wilson came out of his private shower in more businesslike dress, khaki pants, blue linen shirt, brown loafers. "Find anything helpful?"

"Not much. I'm surprised at how much Cynthia was being paid."

"Let me see." Wilson took the contract and turned to the compensation clause. His surprise at the figure showed. "That's about forty percent higher than a person at her level would normally be worth."

"Who hired Cynthia?"

Wilson flipped to the last page of the contract. "Greg Tillotson, director of the Redleaf program. Cynthia reported directly to him."

I looked at my watch. "I'm supposed to be at Tillotson's office right now. Thanks for the help with the contract. Um, when do you think I'll get paid?"

"Within sixty days after you complete Bobby's painting."

So my termites had a sixty-day reprieve. The little devils could do a lot of damage over the next two months, them and their kamikaze mentality. I brooded over that while wandering the hallways looking for Greg Tillotson's office. Should have been easy to find, he was a high-level exec, but the hallways of Race Software were a maze and I didn't have my Boy Scout compass. After ten minutes of wandering around and asking hesitant directions, I entered a generous-sized corner office where Tillotson was working at a computer with fingers the shapes of sausages.

"Hi there, Mr. Tillotson."

He grunted without looking up from his work.

"We have an appointment."

Tillotson grunted again. Taking that as an invitation, I sat down.

After a few minutes he swiveled toward me, his eyes enormous and bloodshot behind thick glasses. "Oh, yeah. You're the artist I met yesterday. What the hell do you want? I don't have time for artists today. Matter of fact, I *never* have time for artists."

"Bobby sent me to…"

"Yeah, he sends dozens of people to see me every day. I'm under enormous pressure to bring Redleaf in on time, on budget, and Bobby expects me to talk with fools like…I repeat…what do you want?"

"Since you put it that way, I want to know why you hired Cynthia Gooding at a salary forty percent higher than her job usually pays."

The enormous eyes blinked rapidly behind the glasses. "What I pay the employees in my division is none of your business. Is that it? You had one question? Good. Get out, I'm busy."

He was swinging back to his computer when I asked him a second question out of pure spite. "Were you fucking Cynthia? Was that why she got the big bucks?"

At last I had his full attention.

He jumped up, raising himself to his full five foot two, quivering with anger. "Did Bobby send you to ask me that? No, I don't think he did. Bobby may have been sleeping with the girl himself, that's the rumor. I wouldn't know. I'm too *tired* and too *busy* to fuck anybody. Ask my wife, she'll give you a primer on the subject. I'm not fucking anyone because I have a *product program* to run. For your information, Race Software could go down in flames if Redleaf isn't everything the industry expects it to be. So I had no time for slinky sirens like Cynthia." His voice dropped. "God rest her soul." He crossed himself. "Why do you care what happened to Cynthia?"

"I knew her slightly," I lied. "I'm trying find her family, tell them what happened to Cynthia. Bobby asked me to do that. She worked for you. You paid her well. I thought you might know something personal about her. I was rude because you tried to blow me off. I'm sorry."

Tillotson slowly returned to his chair, put his elbows on his desk. "I didn't know Cynthia well. She was competent at her job, that's all I can say about her. When this company was smaller, I knew every employee by name. Most of them were friends as well. I'm ashamed to say these days I don't even know everyone on the Redleaf team. My own team. Six hundred people, more or less. I'm disgusted with myself. Bone tired from working seventeen hour days. Afraid I'll fail Bobby. Worried about that…*thing*…we saw yesterday in the coffee room." He looked me up and down. "Do you know what it was? Are you here to do something more than draw Bobby's picture?"

"I don't draw pictures. I paint portraits."

Small smile. "Every profession has its own jargon. And you haven't answered my question. I decided not to quit Bobby after all, but I'm very worried about yesterday's incident."

"I don't know what it was. I'm painting Bobby's official portrait and, as long as I'm here anyway, trying to find Cynthia Gooding's family."

The smile widened a few millimeters. "I don't envy you. I suspect it's even harder to paint Bobby's portrait than to run Redleaf. Have you run into the brain trust yet?"

"What brain trust?"

"You'll find out." He turned away from me. "Now I really do have to get back to work."

After talking with Tillotson, I put in another couple of hours on Bobby's portrait while he buzzed in and out of the office, yelled at people over the phone, worked at his computer. The idea that he might spend at least a few minutes posing for me, just so I could get his physical dimensions in proper scale, never occurred to him.

Okay by me. I didn't relish the idea of spending much time alone with him anyway.

Now and then one of his visitors would come over to glance at what I was doing. None of them said a word, yet I had the feeling they were judging me and that I was getting a low grade.

About two o'clock I began cleaning my brushes.

"Going somewhere?" Bobby and I were alone, his most recent gang of yes people having departed his office to do battle with Microsoft and Oracle.

"I'm going into the city. I have a friend there who may be able to give me a lead on Cynthia Gooding."

"You're still convinced she has a connection with our problem?"

"Yes, I am."

"What if our *problem* occurs again while you're gone?"

"Take two candlesticks. Make a cross. See what the thing does."

"What?"

"Just a joke."

The very notion of a joke made Bobby bristle. "That's not much advice for all the money you're being paid."

"The portrait will get done," I promised.

"You know I don't really care about the portrait."

"It'll get done anyway. This afternoon I'll try to find out who Cynthia Gooding really was and what she was doing here."

Bobby sighed and shifted around restlessly. "Yesterday's incident produced a dozen resignations from some damned good resources."

I hate it when corporate executives refer to flesh and blood people as "resources." Bobby began talking to me about business problems I didn't care about. While he talked, I cleaned my hands with thinner and thought about Hopper and the Ash Can School. I love the realism and drama of Hopper's scenes. His faces leave me cold.

"I'll see you tomorrow," I said, cutting him off.

He didn't much like to be cut off. "Where are you going? Who're you going to see?"

"Nobody you'd know." I was out the door before he could ask more questions. Not that I escaped Bobby's attention altogether. In the parking lot I found Dorothy Lake leaning against my car with her arms gracefully crossed.

"Bobby wants me to stay with you this afternoon."

"Doesn't he trust me?"

"He doesn't understand what you're up to."

I opened the passenger door of my old Karmann Ghia. When she hesitated, I said, "Don't worry, this just looks like an old car. It's really a superbly engineered classic automobile. Some day it'll be worth a lot of money."

"If it doesn't explode. Where are we going?"

"To talk with the best car thief in San Francisco."

CHAPTER 6

Big Sam Cody drove into my life more than ten years ago in a mint condition 1973 red Corvette, about forty thousand dollars worth of classic automobile at that year's prices. Sam had been transferred to Fort Riley, Kansas. He came onto the post with the Corvette's top down. Radio blaring out a rap song in which the word fuck was repeated at least three times in any ten-second sequence. New York plates. Bumper sticker that read *Honk Twice If You Want Kinky Sex.*

Before he got a hundred yards inside the post, Sam had a jeep full of Military Police on his tail. They pulled him over. Made him get out of the Corvette, put his hands on the hood, spread his legs. Searched him and the car for dope. Found none. Ordered Sam to scratch off the bumper sticker with his ignition key, which took about twenty minutes.

While Sam was getting rid of the bumper sticker, the MPs patched through on their radio to New York DMV headquarters for the Corvette's registration, which to their surprise checked out. They demanded to see his insurance papers, which also checked out. What they wanted to know, Sam Cody was a twenty-year-old army private, a black kid who never finished high school, where did he get a car like that?

"Won it hustling pool," was Sam's answer.

The MPs didn't believe him. Even after they got a nationwide report on stolen Corvettes and found no '73 models on the list, they thought the car must be stolen.

"Where's your uniform?" they asked him. "Don't you know better than to report to a new post wearing civilian clothes?"

"My uniforms are in the trunk, I was gonna suit up before reportin' into the replacement center. That's the drill, ain't it?" Sam opened the trunk, showed them his uniforms. They weren't the usual thing, either. He'd come to Fort Riley with a duffel bag filled with tailored uniforms. Not just his Class As, the fatigues were tailored too. One of the MPs guessed that Sam Cody had laid out four thousand dollars on uniforms.

"I like to look gooood," Sam explained.

The MPs made him get into the Corvette and change into his uniform right there behind the steering wheel. Sam smiled at each MP as if they were family and did as he was ordered despite the cramped quarters.

Luck of the draw, Sam Cody was assigned to the platoon I was in. Third platoon, Company E, Fourth Battalion, First Infantry Division. The barracks were laid out in two-man cubicles and Sam was assigned as my bunkmate. Luckiest thing that ever happened to me. Sam became the best friend I'd ever have. Over time we played chess against each other for money, got drunk while we speculated about our futures, covered each other's backs in fistfights, traded shirts and shorts when the laundry was late, went into Kansas City together on three-day passes. Like they say in the army, we lived in each other's pockets. I went to Arizona with Sam for his mother's funeral. He sat up all night with me sipping Bacardi 101 when the girl I was engaged to, June Pickard, sent me a Dear John letter. And it was Sam Cody who plucked me out of thin air when I got shot out of that chopper over the U.S. embassy complex in Kinsasha, Zaire.

But the first night we met, I doubted Sam and I would ever be friends. He looked me up and down as if I were his worst nightmare. "Stuck me with a whitebread bunkmate looks dumber than water, that's the final insult."

"I'm not as dumb as I look," was my brilliant riposte.

"No, Mister Whitebread, I guess you couldn't be. But you're not wired into company HQ if they stuck you with me, 'cause they don't like my style at all. I mean, they took one look and decided I don't belong in this outfit. What'cha think about that? "

Sam began hanging his tailored uniforms in his locker with great care. I sat on my bunk and watched him use a matchbook to separate with precision the space between each hangar. Each uniform faced in the same direction with the sleeves hanging straight down, one over the other, with equal precision. His shoes weren't standard issue, either. They were made in Italy and spit-shined to a high gloss.

"Good looking shoes. Never could get the hang of spit shining myself."

"Don't surprise me." Looking at the Class A shoes under my bunk. "Here, gimmee those trashy clodhoppers. I ain't gonna share a cubicle with a Mister Whitebread looks like some old Okie." He took out a pair of rags and a can of black shoe polish. Spit onto the toe of my shoe. Began polishing in a slow circular motion. "Good spit-shine takes patience. Care. And pride. You got pride, Mister Whitebread?"

"I like to think so. Where'd you hear that word?"

"What word? Pride?"

"Okie."

"Just read a book by a dude name of Steinbeck. *Grapes Of Wrath.* You heard of it? All about the Okies, had to move west back in the thirties. My old grandad, he came from Norman, Oklahoma, headed for California in 1935. Thanks to Mr. Steinbeck, I now got a feel for why he went west. Those were bad days for blacks, and for some whites, too. You might call them migrants white niggers, way they were treated by other whites." Sam put some more spit onto the toe of my shoe.

"You've got good taste in books."

"Got a bunch of books in the bottom of my foot locker." He nodded toward the steel locker. "You want to borrow some, go ahead. Might help smarten you up."

"Maybe I will." I squatted in front of the locker and looked over some of the titles of his books. *Spartacus. Thirty Days To A More Powerful Vocabulary. The Cat In The Hat. Best Known Works Of Oscar Wilde. All*

Creatures Great And Small. Tunes Of Glory. The Grapes Of Wrath. How To Win In The Stock Market.

"Can I borrow *Tunes Of Glory?*"

"I said help yourself. Don't say nothin' I don't mean." He held out a shoe at arm's length and appeared satisfied with the way the shine was coming up. "They stopped my old grandad at the California state line, wouldn't let any niggers or Okies cross over into California that year. That's how come I got born and grew up in Almost-A-Dog, Arizona."

"Is that a real place?"

"Almost-A-Dog?" Sam winked at me. He was a big young guy. Big hands, too. Extremely deep brown eyes with crinkles in the corners. A jaw that might have been broken once or twice. Skin so black it was almost blue. "Yeah, Almost-A-Dog's a real place. About as small as this shitpile of a barracks, but just as real."

"Where'd you get the Corvette, Sam?"

He dropped my shoe and reared back. "That's a dangerous question. And who said you could use my first name?"

"I'm not just your bunkmate. I'm your flank man in the platoon. I've only been in the army three months, but I learned one thing real fast. You have to cover me and I have to cover you. We've got no choice but to trust each other. That gives me the right to call you Sam."

He thought on that. After a minute he went back to work on my shoe. Making little circles with the polish. Slowly bringing a gleam to my cheap, government-issue army shoes. "For now you can call me Sam. Till I know for sure whether that trust talk is real or bullshit. I'll call you Mister Whitebread now and then 'cause that's what you are. What's your whole name?"

"Kevin Pierce." I put out my hand, which he ignored.

"Most whitebread name I ever heard. Guess you don't need to invite me to your family reunions." His first smile in my direction. "I wouldn't fit in."

"So tell me about the Corvette. Where'd you get it?"

"Won it hustling pool, like I told the MPs."

"Come on, where'd you *really* get it?"

"You ain't seen me shoot pool. I'm goooood."

At that point in my life I was a babe in the woods compared with Sam, but I wasn't green enough to buy that story. "If you were really a pool hustler, you wouldn't be sitting on your bunk talking to me about your old grandad and shining my shoes as a favor. You'd be down in the Day Room where the pool table is, playing eight ball for money. Hustlers, I'm talking about pool hustlers good enough to win a Corvette, spend every free minute with a cue in their hands and usually a shot of bourbon on the rail. That doesn't seem to be you."

"Maybe you ain't so dumb after all." Sam put down the first shoe, which now had a shine in which you could see not only your reflection, but shave from that reflection, and picked up its mate. "I lifted the 'Vette from a storage garage in Newark, New Jersey. Owner's in Europe for the summer, it won't be missed till after Labor Day. I forged a pink slip on my own press. State of the art printing technology, if I do say so myself. Re-registered the car in the state of New York under a phony engine number, they never double-check the engines in New York. Paid three months insurance up front. Gonna sell it before the end of August, make myself a real nice profit. Got a buyer lined up in Denver. I'll provide a different set of papers, they'll never trace it to him."

"You've done this before?"

Sam looked insulted. "You ain't talking to some *joyrider*. Fell in love with fine automobiles when I was ten years old, been stealin' 'em and movin' 'em ever since. This is a serious business for me. Combines my personal love for quality automobiles with an advanced form of what they call *laize faire* capitalism, you understand what I'm sayin'?"

"You're saying you're a car thief."

"Automobile broker." Sam winked. "A phrase you better commit to memory, you know what's good for you."

"Can I drive the Corvette some time?"

When Sam Cody laughed, his entire face came alive with the sweetest radiance I'd ever seen on a man's features. "Fuck yes, we'll take a run down to K.C next weekend, we don't have some shitass duty. Here you go, Mister Whitebread, wear 'em proud." My shoes were spit-shined to the highest gloss they'd ever seen. "Fifty years ago, only kind of work my old grandad could get was shinin' shoes in a four-chair barber shop. Suppose that's why I'm so good at it, runs in the family."

The next weekend Sam allowed me to slide behind the wheel of the Corvette and drive it a hundred and fifty miles from Fort Riley to Kansas City and back again. Sweetest ride I ever had.

I told Dorothy that story as we rode into the city. She was alternately outraged and fascinated. "That's shameful! This man is still stealing cars? He hasn't been arrested?"

"Arrested often, never tried or convicted."

"If the police know this Sam Cody person steals cars, why don't they just follow him around until they catch him at it?"

"From time to time the cops do keep an eye on Sam. But their work-load's too high to put somebody on him all day and night, every day of the year. They do send undercover people who offer him money to steal a particular luxury car, a Jag or an Infiniti, but he can tell a real buyer from a police informant. They also bug his office from time to time, so Sam does an electronic sweep every day. I doubt he personally steals many cars these days; he probably has people who do that for him."

"You sound proud of him."

"Sam's the Bobby Race of his chosen field. Maybe not a totally admirable person, but a guy who gets the job done."

"He should be in prison."

"A lot of people should be in prison. Have you ever loaded your computer with some software you didn't have a legal right to use? Bent the copyright laws? I understand that happens all the time in the software business."

Reluctantly, Dorothy allowed that she might have done something of the sort. "You can't compare that with stealing somebody's car."

"Why not? Intellectual property can be worth more than a car. Isn't that what Bobby's worried about? Somebody getting a jump on his company by stealing the codes for Redleaf? Isn't that Joe Patterson's job, keeping the software pirates at bay?"

Very grudgingly, "I suppose you're right. Still, I think car thieves do more damage to the fabric of society than someone who loads a software application on an unauthorized computer."

I was learning that Dorothy Lake hated to be wrong. A very human trait, I suppose. Dorothy's sense of self-worth was closely tied to being "the expert" at whatever subject came up. She reminded me of that old comedian, Professor Irwin Corey, who billed himself as "The World's Leading Authority." He never said what he was the leading authority of, he just blustered his way through whatever subjects arose with a minimum of fact and a maximum of humor. Dorothy had a lot of real knowledge. In fact, she was one of the smartest people I'd ever met. I just wished she'd let me win a conversational point now and then.

Sam's place of business was at the less fashionable end of Market Street. He owned a two-story brick building which housed a small auto showroom on the first floor, augmented by a lot next door on which a dozen or so cars were for sale. They were all luxury cars, Jags, a Lexus or two, a maroon Bentley with a right-hand drive, an antique BMW, a Mercedes that looked brand-new, a gray-green Infinity, other sets of wheels in the same price range. The sign over the showroom door read: *Cody Classic Cars*. The sales manager who greeted us was a tall black middle-aged woman dressed in an elegant pants suit, no jewelry except a plain gold wedding band and jade earrings. She was Jane Evanston, a widow raising three teenage boys on her own and doing a hell of a job at it. Her husband had been killed by a drunk driver. All three kids were on their high school honor lists and had good shots at making it into

Major League baseball. Sam Cody had sponsored their teams from T-Ball through Little League.

She extended her hand with a smile. "Good afternoon, Mr. Pierce. Good to see you again." Her voice revealed West Indian origins.

"Mrs. Evanston, this is Dorothy Lake."

"Very nice to meet you, Ms. Lake. Sam is expecting you, Mr. Pierce. You can go straight up." Jane Evanston carried in the pocket of her white jacket a battery-operated remote device which controlled access to the elevator. She reached into her pocket and pushed a button on the remote. The elevator door opened and we stepped inside.

"An elevator for a two-story building?"

"Sam's very concerned about security."

"In his business, he'd have to be. Are the cars in his showroom and lot all stolen?"

"Sam's classic car business is entirely legal. He does very well at it. You just saw a couple of million dollars worth of wheels down there."

"If he has a successful legitimate business, why does he still steal automobiles?"

"That's his recreation."

Dorothy was shaking her head when the elevator door opened. Sam had turned the entire second floor into a combination office and apartment. There were no walls. Gleaming wood floors ran the length of the building and the space was so artfully decorated you could hardly tell where the office left off and the living space began.

"Mister Whitebread, how you doin' today?" Sam came up and threw his arms around me in a hug that threatened to crush a couple of ribs. Over the past ten years he'd gotten bigger. Not much of it was fat, he worked on the weight machines at Boil's gym and did some boxing. Sometimes he took jobs as a sparring partner for the better local heavyweights, just to see if he could go four rounds with them. He was in demand. They paid him a hundred bucks a round for four rounds. Sam always donated the money to a homeless shelter in the Castro district.

"Doing good. Sam, this is Dorothy Lake."

He turned his attention on her with a gallantry that was only slightly exaggerated. Sam really did like women. They didn't have to be beautiful or sexy to rate his attention, he just seemed to have a special affinity for the feminine gender. "Ms. Lake, I'm proud to meet you. It ain't often Kevin brings a lady around. I mean, a real *lady* which I can tell you are."

"Kevin speaks highly of you." Dorothy shook hands with Sam the way the President of the United States greets the Premier of China, with a total absence of personal warmth. However, I could tell she was reluctantly impressed by Sam Cody. As usual, Sam was impeccably dressed in a silk suit by one of those Italian designers who wear sunglasses no matter how dark the surroundings. Sam was also wearing a Hermes tie and his customary Italian shoes. His shirts were made by a tailor on Montgomery Street and he'd invented a family crest which was hand-sewn onto the breast pocket of the shirt.

More impressive than Sam's tailoring was his bearing, which had become more imposing with each passing year. If anything, Sam was an inch taller, six foot two or three, at the age of thirty than he'd been at the age of twenty. How the hell did he do that? I wish I knew. Also, his shoulders were wider and his waist more narrow, a by-product of the tough years we'd spent together in the infantry and his work on the weight machines. Elegant but hard, a black man as much at home in a Nob Hill bistro as in a mean back street south of Market. That's how you'd have to describe Sam Cody.

"Please sit down, Ms. Lake. Would you like a glass of rasberry iced tea? I got regular iced tea, too. Or, you might prefer a lemonade or a glass of chardonay."

Dorothy looked surprised by the choices. "I've never had raspberry iced tea."

"You're gonna love it." Sam walked the length of the floor, past a living room setting of extremely abstract modern furniture in stark black and white and into a kitchen all stainless steel and gray tile. From an immense sub-zero refrigerator he took a container of raspberry iced tea and placed it on a tray with three glasses. He came back and poured out drinks for each of us.

"Can't help wonderin' why a beautiful and obviously brainy woman is hangin' out with our Mister Whitebread."

"You've heard of Bobby Race? I'm doing his official portrait. Dorothy's an executive at Race Software. We're working together on a little side project and we need your help."

"Kevin Pierce actually working? At a job? For a corporation?" Sam threw back his head and laughed. "Never thought I'd see Kevin do corporate work. Is the portrait any good, Dorothy? Has Kevin got the great Bobby Race down cold?"

"I don't know. Kevin just started on the portrait this morning."

"And he's already takin' the afternoon off? Now that's my Kevin. The man has never properly appreciated the good old American work ethic. Works a whole two or three hours a day when the mood strikes him. Which ain't often."

"On the way over I told Dorothy you were my best friend. I retract that statement."

"Don't get me wrong," Sam said to Dorothy. "For reasons I never really got a grip on, I like this whitebread fool. And he is a hell of an artist. Come over here, I'll show you somethin'."

Sam led us, glasses in hand, to the living room section of his habitat and waved at the painting on the wall behind his sofa. "That's what Kevin did with my ugly puss. What'cha think, Dorothy? Did he nail me?"

I'd painted Sam on one of his infrequent bad days. He had a hangover and was dressed in an old red turtleneck sweater instead of something Italian and expensive. We'd been up half the night playing poker with a couple of Sam's "business associates." Guys named Snake and Bullseye. Cigarette smoke had given Sam bloodshot eyes. On top of that, Sam had just received a telegram from Arizona reporting the death of a high school buddy, shot down during a robbery.

I painted Sam staring out the window with those bloodshot eyes. Face craggy with tiredness and with despair over his dead boyhood pal. The red turtleneck turned up almost to his chin. He never even noticed I was working because I'd just thrown a canvas on a table and went at my work like a demon, finishing the painting in less than an hour. Not a flattering portrait. I believe I punched through Sam's affable front and down into the devious, cynical, hard-bitten core of the guy.

A couple of days later, when Sam really focused on what I'd done while he was brooding, he surprised me by loving the portrait.

"You dig this kind of art?" Sam asked Dorothy. "See what the bastard did to me? I look *mean* and *belligerent* and...shit...I dunno...*poorly dressed*. Yet, I feel this is a guy other people would be interested in. Do you see that too?"

Dorothy didn't do anything lightly, including looking at a painting. She studied the canvas from several angles before answering. "I'd say Kevin used your face to reach right into you. I'm not sure I like everything I see, but I can tell from this picture that you're more than just a run-of-the-mill car thief."

Her turn of phrase made me wince. I hadn't meant for Dorothy to be so frank, which was my mistake. She had a directness that gave ground to no one. "I had to tell her what business you're in because of the kind of help we need."

Sam made a Japanese-like bow, hands at his sides. "Even though my good friend ratted me out, he's still my good friend." Giving me a slantwise glance ripe with irritation. "For now anyway." Then a graceful change of subject. "How you like the raspberry tea?"

"Delicious."

"Knew you'd enjoy it. Hey, I'm really glad you're in the computer business." Sam rubbed his hands together. "I'll help you with your project if you can solve a little computer problem for me."

"I suppose I can help you out." She followed him to the far corner of the floor where Sam had set up his office.

Sam slid into a chair in front of a computer already up and running. "My problem is, I just bought this new system. Had an old Presario, this new box is supposed to be top-of-the-line."

"It is," she confirmed. "You've got enough power to do anything except launch nuclear missiles."

"Too bad, 'cause there's a couple of dudes I'd really like to nuke. Kevin, you remember Bullseye Fratino? We played poker with him the night before you did my portrait? That bum's been in my face lately, I'd like to bust his chops. But right now, Dorothy, I'd settle for a few tips on how to toggle from one network to another. There must be a way to drag-and-drop stuff between networks, but I can't find it in the damn manual."

Dorothy couldn't pass up an opportunity to sing praises for her company. "Most software manuals are written by people who only talk to computer programmers. They've long ago forgotten how to communicate with real people. At Race, we make a point of writing manuals in simple, direct language anyone can understand."

She moved Sam out of the chair and seated herself at the computer. "Let's see what I can do. What are the two applications you want to work between?"

"One's called Autopilot and the other's a network that uses this logo." He employed the mouse pointer to single out an official looking icon. "I can get into both networks with no trouble; I just can't work between them."

Dorothy sent her fingers flying over the keyboard. "All you need is a macro that'll make it easy to toggle back and forth. Drag and drop. I can write a macro, put it on your hard drive, in ten minutes."

"A genius." Sam grinned at me. "That's what you've brought me Kevin, a certified genius."

"Any number of people could write you a macro. I'm surprised you didn't hire Compaq to do it for you. Or an independent software developer."

"That would have been my next move." Sam eased me away from the computer. "Come on, Kevin. Let the lady work."

We drifted over to the window that looked down on Market Street. When we were out of Dorothy's earshot, Sam said: "What the fuck's this all about? You and Race Software? Like they say down in Silicon Valley, it just don't compute."

"Doing a portrait of Bobby Race is kind of a cover. They've been having problems they think I can solve. They're probably wrong, but I have to give it a shot. They're paying me a bundle for the portrait, Sam. Best commission I ever had."

"What sort of problems?"

"People have been seeing strange stuff at Race headquarters."

"What brand of *strange stuff* we talkin' about? Kinky sex in the office? That's the usual thing down in the valley."

"Nothing that simple. People are seeing this…uh…specter, I guess that's what you could call it. I've seen the thing myself and so has Dorothy. It's unearthly, Sam. That's all I can tell about it."

"What?" Sam lowered his voice almost to a whisper. "You talkin' about your old friend Sport Sullivan? He's back?"

The second time Sport presented himself to me in the sick bay aboard the Carl Vinson, when I was recuperating from the wound I took when we lifted off from the embassy in that chopper, Sam was visiting me. He'd snuck a couple of beers into the sick bay to hasten my recovery. That was the only time Sam ever saw Sport, but over the years I'd given him reports on Sport's periodic visits.

"No, what I saw wasn't Sport. Though Sport did come around a few weeks ago."

"Scary dude." Sam shivered. "Never forget them orange eyes, the way he…I dunno…*glittered*. Thought he was gonna grab me, drag me down to hell."

"Sport's not in hell, he's in limbo. As he's always reminding me. No, this thing at Race is something else. I get the feeling it's a tortured spirit."

Sam snorted out a derisive laugh. "Tortured spirit? Don't go talkin' that way around anyone but me, okay?"

I told him how I'd been brought into Race Software by Joe Patterson and that I thought the incarnation at the company's headquarters might have something to do with a dead girl who used the false name of Cynthia Gooding. I asked Sam if he could use her driver's license to find out who Cynthia really was. Sam allowed he might be able to do that. Finally I described to him what the presence at Race Software looked like and how it had affected Joe Patterson.

"Shit, man, I knew Joe Patterson when he was on the force. Sounds like the guy's fucked up for life. What hospital's he at?"

"Stanford Medical Center."

Sam went to his phone and called downstairs to Jane Evanston. "Jane, there's a dude name of Joe Patterson recovering from surgery down at the Stanford Med Center. Have something nice sent to him, will ya? The usual flowers. Plus a bottle of real good champagne and a couple of glasses, boost his spirits with some spirits if you dig me. Throw in a silver ice bucket. Balloons, a whole roomful, lots of different colors. One of them circle cheeses from some foreign country, ten or fifteen pounds of cheese, goes good with champagne. Them little crackers from England? Two boxes. Maybe a Gameboy or some other electronic gadget, whatever's popular right now, give him something to play with. Plus half a dozen books. Best sellers, mystery novels, maybe a biography of some sports star. Nothin' real heavy. Light hospital readin', you understand? Thanks, Jane." He started to put down the phone, then quickly pulled it back. "Jane, don't include a card. Make it an anonymous gift, you dig?"

He came back to the window.

"I don't think Joe would take any gifts if he knew they came from me. He pulled me in two maybe three times when he was runnin' the auto theft squad. Tried hard to make a case against me. Sent guys to entrap me, that's part of the game. Paid snitches to look for my chop shop. Bugged this office, my home, my personal car. But he never got out of line, never called me a nigger or put a heavy elbow in my ribs like some of them do. Man shows me respect, I appreciate it."

"I sort of like him too, even though he doesn't seem to think much of me or what I do for a living."

"Old fashioned bull," Sam commented. "I'm surprised he quit the force, went corporate."

"Everybody's doing it."

"Yeah." Sam grinned. "Even you."

"I'm doing it just to get those termites out of my house, it'll fall down if I don't."

"You probably need a new set of wheels too. I'll bet you're still drivin' that old clunker." Sam peered down through the window at my Karmann Ghia parked in front of his establishment. With a groan, "Man, there ain't nothin' but rust holdin' that piece of trash together. Let me find you some better wheels. Nothin' fancy, just somethin' clean and reliable. Won't cost me a cent and you'll have a set of legit papers, you can sleep easy. How about it?"

"Thanks, but I'll stick with my Karmann Ghia. We're two of a kind."

"You're a stubborn piece of whitebread, don't know why I bother with you." He shifted his attention to Dorothy. "She's a funny one, ain't she. Flaunts her brains like they was boobs. Mighty cute, though."

"Not cute. Beautiful. I'll tell you something, Sam. When Dorothy's around, I have a hard time looking any place except in her direction."

"Feel the same way about my new best lady. Calls herself Neon. Real name's Eleanor Smith, she don't like her roots."

"Nobody seems to like their roots anymore." I continued to watch Dorothy work the keyboard with her right hand, the left hand behind her head twisting a strand of hair around the index finger. The graceful way she did so brought a serious lump to my throat. "I remember when roots were a big thing, everyone was supposed to love their humble beginnings."

"Humble sucks. That's the official word these days."

"What is this?" Sam and I both turned toward Dorothy, who was waving her arms like a symphony conductor. "I can't believe it. This is a Department of Motor Vehicles database!"

"You're into it?" Sam rushed to Dorothy's side. "Hot damn, Dorothy. You do know your stuff."

She swiveled toward Sam with eyes ablaze. "You've made me a felon!"

Sam hit the save key before Dorothy could wipe out what she'd done. "Take it easy, Dorothy. Just calm down. You did me a favor, I'll do one for you. That was the deal."

"It's against the law to hack into a state database. You've made me an accessory to your crimes. I could go to jail. Or be sued. My God, I'm a director of Race Software." The horror of that thought drained the color from Dorothy's face. "They could blame *Bobby* for this."

"Calm yourself, Dorothy. Drink your raspberry tea and think this through. You didn't tap into anybody's database, I did that myself. All you did was fix it so I could toggle back and forth between two databases, you didn't even know what they were."

"That's probably a crime too."

"Sam, you should have told Dorothy what you were up to here." I was as pissed as Dorothy. When Sam wanted something for his business, he let nothing stand in his way. Sam had a lot of charm, he was compulsively generous, truly warm, as good as his word, all that and more. But his business was his life. "You fucked us over, Sam. I'm disappointed in you."

There was a moment when I thought Sam Cody might deliver his big fist straight to my chin. Or worse yet to my nose, which I'd managed to keep handsomely straight for thirty-one years. Sam's eyes turned to flint. He shook his head as if regretting what he was going to have to do to me. I thought I'd lost a friend and gained a broken nose.

That moment passed.

"Yeah, I should've spoken up. I'm sorry, Dorothy. Mister Whitebread, I expect I owe you an apology too. Consider it said. But I gotta tell you, I was already into the DMV computer and Autopilot, the statewide auto registration system. That's where I get my papers, y'understand? The toggle macro makes it easier to work both systems at once, what you've done is gonna save me a lot of time. But I've been goin' in and out of those databases for about three years."

Dorothy was shaking her head. "Aren't you afraid the police will come in some day with a warrant to search your computer?"

"Let 'em search. Only thing they'll find is wires and chips. They don't have the right codes, this computer's just another box. No way to stop a good hack job just by confiscatin' a computer. Am I right, Dorothy?"

Grudging nod. "They could trace a computer break-in by backtracking to your phone lines."

"My lines go through phone numbers in other peoples' names. The cops backtrack the modem from this computer, all they'll find is an office down in South San Francisco that's empty except for a desk and six phone lines. I got bootleg lines all over town."

Dorothy was hot again, arms flailing and face gone crimson. "It's people like you who undermine the public's confidence in computers!"

"Just tryin' to make a livin'." Sam rubbed his hands together. "We shouldn't be tradin' harsh words, we should work on your little problem. Doin' somethin' positive for Race Software, isn't that what you're here for? Tell me how I can help."

I took out Cynthia Gooding's driver's license. "This license belonged to the girl I told you about. I don't believe her real name was Gooding. Can you use this to find out who she really was?"

Sam studied Cynthia Gooding's drivers license closely. Both sides. "There's guys around who'll sell you a fake license. This one's legit. Issued right here in San Francisco at the DMV office. Let's go into the computer and look at the backup behind the license."

He seated himself at the computer and began punching keys. I noticed that Sam kept his rather large body between the keyboard and Dorothy so she couldn't tell what codes he was using. That steamed Dorothy even more. She cut me up with her eyes, blaming me for tainting her with Sam's felonious conduct. Beneath her anger was heavy doubt that Cynthia Gooding had anything to do with the red thing that kept appearing at Race Software. She considered this visit a total waste of time, you could read that in the way she crossed her arms and in the incessant tapping of her foot.

"Here's the license itself." Sam had brought up a visual image of Cynthia Gooding's driver's license. "And here's the application, written test, the examiner's evaluation of her drivin' test. Looks okay." His shoulders stiffened. "Hello...this is good stuff."

"What is?" Hoping he'd found something to redeem me in Dorothy's eyes. "The license is phony after all?"

"Nah, it's a proper license. You see that signature at the bottom of the paperwork? That's the clerk who processed Cynthia's application. Guy named Maury Canselmo."

"You know him?"

"Shouldn't be telling tales out of school, but Maury's one of my contacts in the DMV. There's fifteen or twenty clerks between L.A. and Sacramento who'll issue you a license in any name you want. The price for a clean license ranges from one to three k, or whatever the traffic will bear. Mostly they sell licenses to illegal aliens. Ex-cons who want a second identity. Guys who've lost their licenses after a DWI conviction. I've bought a few off Maury myself, to accommodate clients."

Dorothy stamped her foot. "That's terrible! I can't believe corruption in a California state agency could be so rampant!"

Poor Dorothy. The afternoon was producing one disillusionment after another. "This is nothing new. Don't you remember the story in the papers last year? Half a dozen DMV employees arrested for selling licenses to ex-cons, foreigners with no entry papers, all kinds of illegals."

"That's my point, they were *caught*," Dorothy insisted. "Fired from their jobs. Sent to prison. I remember the attorney general saying the problem was localized in the San Jose and Santa Clara DMV offices."

Sam had a good laugh while I tried to suppress a smile.

"They catch one, three more take his place." Sam shrugged in mock apology." That's what keeps people like me in business." He looked at his watch. Turned off the computer. "Let's go have ourselves a nice lunch. I'll call Maury Canselmo. Ask him to join us. See what he knows about this Cynthia Gooding." Modest smile. "We'll take my Rolls."

CHAPTER 7

We had a fine lunch at the Fog City Diner on the Embarcadero while we waited for Maury Canselmo. I went for the jalapeno corn sticks as an appetizer, followed by mushu pork burritos and crabcakes with sherry-cayenne mayonnaise. Dorothy ordered the red curry mussel stew plus a small plate of heirloom tomatoes. A hearty eater like Sam needed the Mighty Meatloaf with tomato chutney gravy, garlic mashed potatoes, cheddar and Virginia ham grits, and a basket of dutch crunch rolls.

"I've never heard of mushu pork burritos." Dorothy wore her disapproving schoolmarm expression. "They can't be healthy."

"All I know is they taste wonderful." I hadn't eaten this well in weeks and was considering for dessert the warm banana chocolate bread pudding with rum caramel. For the healthful potassium in the bananas, of course. Dorothy was right, if you don't have your health, you don't have anything.

We were into the dessert—and the bread pudding really was delicious as well as healthful—when Maury Canselmo joined us. He was short, about forty years old, slightly built, a poster boy for male pattern baldness, with a sallow complexion and deep, permanent circles under his eyes. He wore brown slacks, a white short-sleeved shirt with yellowish sweat stains in the armpits, half a dozen ballpoints in a shirt pocket protector, necktie from K-Mart. While Sam did the introductions, Maury kept glancing around the restaurant and saying: "Uh-huh...yeah...gladameetcha...uh-huh...yeah...uh-huh." And finally, "What's going on here, Sam? You never brought me around to meet your clients before. This ain't businesslike."

"Relax, these aren't clients. They're friends of mine who need some information."

Maury suffered a full-body twitch. "Do I look like an encyclopedia? Is the word *Britannica* tattooed on my forehead?" Another violent twitch. "I shouldn't even be seen with you." Eyes swiveling all over the room. "The cops hear I've been talking with Big Sam Cody, they might start digging into my personal finances."

"This is no cop hangout, you know that."

It gradually came to me that Maury Canselmo's nervousness didn't have much to do with the presence of Dorothy and me; it was his permanent condition. The little guy finally deigned to look us in the eye. "Who are you people? What do you want?"

"Doesn't matter who we are," I said. "All we want is a small piece of information." I brought out the license I'd been carrying around. "About six months ago you arranged for this girl to get a driver's license in the name of Cynthia Gooding. That doesn't appear to be her real name. She's dead now. I want to know who she actually was…where she came from…whatever you know about her. You recognize the picture on this license?"

Maury gave the girl's photo a cursory glance. Did a double take. Dropped the license as if it were covered with maggots. "This chick's dead? Jesus…I mean…that's too bad. But I never seen her before." His voice was choked up. "She got no license from me."

"Your initials are on all the tests she took," Sam pointed out. "I should say the tests she never did take, somebody gave you a payoff to issue that license. Don't try to tell me different, Maury. I've looked at the paperwork, I know how your system works."

This time Maury's twitch went all the way into a seizure. "I don't know a goddam thing about that girl!" He lowered his voice when people in neighboring booths began staring at him. "And I won't sit here and listen to any more questions. You and me ain't doing no more business either, Sam. I been good to you, what do you do? Try to fuck me up with important people."

"What important people?" Sam demanded. "Who paid you for the license? Wasn't her, was it? Somebody *important* paid you? Who do you know that's important?"

"Nobody," Maury hissed.

"Tell us," I said. Maury shook his head, a definite no. As he started to slide out of the booth, I put my arm out and blocked him. "You aren't leaving until you give us a name."

"And not just any name," Dorothy put in. She seemed to have grown more willing to put some pressure on poor old nervous Maury. "The *right name* is what we want."

Sam grinned. "You don't want to mess with our Dorothy. She's a tough lady. See those bruises on her knuckles? She coldcocked a long-shoreman yesterday, handed him his own teeth."

"You people don't know what you're asking." Maury wheezed asthmatically. "Who you're fucking with, what can happen to me if I talk out of turn."

"I know what'll happen if you don't talk to us. I'll hang you out to dry, Maury. Not here in the Fog City Diner, of course. No sir, I don't intend to ruin my welcome in this fine establishment. But some dark night, cloudy sky, no moon, I'll pick you up, take you down to Pier 21, give you a swimmin' lesson."

Maury was near tears. "Don't talk like that. I'm just a clerk, I don't know much about anything."

Despite the civilizing effect of Italian tailoring, Sam could be quite menacing.

"Don't do this to me, Sam." One last plea. Then, in the face of Sam's hard determination, Maury folded. "Okay…shit…I'll tell you what I know. Which ain't much."

A waiter appeared at our booth. "Is everything all right?" Apparently he'd noticed Maury's crestfallen expression.

"Our friend's been put on a strict low-fat diet." Sam patted Maury's arm. "He wants the chocolate chile tart and we won't let him have it. For his own good, y'understand. You can bring us all some coffee, though. Who wants decaf besides me?"

When the waiter left, Dorothy impulsively reached across the booth and patted Maury's shoulder. "Mister Canselmo, you can ignore Sam's threat. It was just talk. I promise no harm will come to you, we know how to keep a confidence."

"No kidding, I don't know that much." He tapped the driver's license with a forefinger. "I don't even know this girl's real name. She was sent to me with an envelope full of hundred dollar bills. Two thousand bucks in all. Met her at a coffee shop around the corner from the DMV. There was a note in the envelope telling me to give this girl a driver's license under the name Cynthia Gooding. Plus her age, address, height, weight, other info I needed for the license."

"She didn't tell you her name?" I leaned forward aggressively, hoping to be a touch menacing myself. I don't think that worked because Maury showed no reaction. "What did she tell you about herself?"

"I don't think we exchanged ten words. All she said that was important to me was 'Izzy Valentine sent me.' That was all I had to hear. I told her to come to the back door after the office closed. She came a little after six, when I was alone there. I had the license all set except for the photo and signature. I'd already faked up the paperwork for the driving and written tests. I shot her picture. Had her sign the license. Transferred the photo to the license. She was out the door in jig time."

"Who in the world is Izzy Valentine?" Dorothy asked.

Sam knew the name. "Izzy sent the girl to you?"

"That's right." Maury was having second thoughts about telling us. "Jesus, Mary and Joseph. Please don't let Izzy know that I told you."

"You got my word." Sam appeared to be giving furious thought to this information. "You talked to Izzy personally?"

"No, 'course not. I got a phone call from one of his guys, I don't know which one. Guy said Izzy Valentine was sending a girl to the coffee shop at three o'clock, he wanted her to have a clean license. There was two grand in it. That's all I needed to know." Short laugh to relieve his own tension. "That's all I wanted to know."

"I repeat," Dorothy said in her most testy voice. "Who is this Izzy Valentine?"

"You might have seen his name in the papers," I said. "He was on trial for mail fraud, I think it was, a couple of years ago. And he was arrested along with a bunch of other people when a savings and loan went under. You see other stories about Izzy Valentine. You've probably seen his picture too. He goes to big parties. Does business with the city. Sponsors fund raising events for charity. You can't tell from the stories whether he's a crook or a celebrity. Not that there's much difference these days."

Dorothy had begun nodding along with me. "Yes…Izzy Valentine…I know who he is now. I think Bobby knows him."

"Was Cynthia Gooding the first person Izzy Valentine ever sent to you for a license?" I asked Maury.

"No, he's sent others from time to time. They always bring cash in an envelope."

"You can go, Maury." Sam had roused himself from deep thought. "And look here, you little prick, you need to keep your mouth shut. I don't want Izzy to know we're pokin' around in his business. You understand me?"

"Sure, Sam." Maury was sliding out of the booth, hungry for escape. "You can count on me."

"I'll snap your scrawny neck like a twig."

"Sam!" Dorothy the disapproving schoolmarm again. "Nothing like that's going to happen to you, Mister Canselmo." But the little man was already out the door and headed swiftly back to a rewarding life of public service. "That was dreadful of you," Dorothy declared, swinging her hair in exasperation.

A little moan may have escaped my lips, the sound I had come to make whenever Dorothy did charming things with her hair.

Sam gave me a slow smile. "Something you had for lunch gone bad, Kevin?"

"I'm fine, thanks. You seem to know Izzy Valentine pretty well."

"We came up together, you might say." The coffee arrived. We were silent until the waiter left, then Sam continued. "Izzy and me, we hit the San Francisco streets about the same time. That'd be eight years ago, give or take. Izzy comes from Buffalo where he got his start disposin' of stolen goods for the Lucca family. He's a deal maker, that's his big talent. Hated the cold weather in Buffalo, so he moved west. Started buyin' and sellin' stolen computer chips. When that became a federal crime, he bought two or three legitimate companies. An advertising agency. A vending machine outfit 'cause they deal in cash, great way to wash money. Isadore Valentine Star Enterprises is his holdin' company, big office on Montgomery Street. Izzy met a bunch of celebrities through his ad agency, started givin' parties. I been to some of them. Today he must own twenty companies. He's stubbed his toe a couple of times. Once when he and some other dudes cleaned out a savings and loan, he was tried but not convicted. The other time was the mail fraud thing, he beat that too without havin' to go to court."

"You know quite a lot about this man," Dorothy commented.

"Earlier this year Izzy offered to buy my auto agency, keep me on as general manager." Sam bristled. "Told him I don't have no ambition to be a hired hand in my own company. That didn't stop him, he offered deals structured this way or that. I kept sayin' no. Lately..." crooked smile "...I been having some business setbacks. Twice I had bricks tossed through the showroom window. And somebody breached my security one night, came onto the lot and slashed all the tires and did some other vandalism that juiced up my insurance rates. Then I got ratted out by some unknown party on one of my off-line deals. I moved a Lexus and two BMWs to a client in Alabama, he was nailed by the FBI before he could resell them. I was pulled in and almost indicted for interstate theft. Had to hire half the lawyers in town to wriggle outta that one, cost me some heavy bucks."

"You think Izzy Valentine is behind all that?" It surprised me that Sam Cody would have any problems. I'd always pictured him in complete control of his own little world.

"I told you back at the office I'd like to nuke Bullseye Fratino, dude we played poker with the night before you did my picture? See, I hear Bullseye and his pal Snake are now workin' for Izzy. I think Izzy hired Bullseye and Snake to harass me till I decide to sell my business to Izzy and take his paycheck. Bullseye's done a little work for me now and then, moved some of my special merchandise from one state to another. So he's in a position to know how to hurt me."

Dorothy couldn't help being the voice of reason. "If you concentrated on your legitimate business, you wouldn't have these problems." She saw that line of thought going nowhere with Sam and shifted to a different point. "Don't you think it's strange that all of us should be connected with Izzy Valentine through this girl who called herself Cynthia Gooding?"

"Not so strange," Sam said, "when you consider how many different pies Izzy's got his sticky fingers into. He's so big now he thinks he can take over any company he wants. Includin' mine."

"Do you think he has designs on Race Software?" All of a sudden Dorothy was taking the Cynthia Gooding connection more seriously. Anything that might affect the fortunes of Bobby Race was like catnip to her.

"Your company's way too big for Izzy to swallow whole," Sam said. "But he might try to take a bite out of it. The guy's got ambitions you wouldn't believe, plus access to venture capital. And lately he's begun to crave respectability."

Dorothy turned to me with more warmth than I'd ever felt from her. "I misjudged you, Kevin. You may have come up with something useful to the company after all."

My stomach did a flip, I was that startled by her smile. Just a slip of a girl, but she had an incredibly sensuous way about her that was all the more powerful because she didn't realize she had it.

"Let's say this Izzy Valentine person has some reason for wanting to cause trouble for Bobby." Her hand flipped back and forth. "I don't know his motive. Could be anything. He's causing vandalism at Sam's place of business. Perhaps he's doing something of the sort at our place of business too. The *red mist* thing. Could this Izzy fellow have devised it? A hologram as Joe Patterson suspected? A fog caused by dry ice and chemicals that give it a red halo effect? I don't know what it might be. I'll jump on the Internet tonight, see if I can trace anything similar to what we've been seeing."

My only answer was a shrug. "I suppose this guy might be behind the thing your people have been seeing. I sort of doubt that scenario. I'm no expert on the supernatural, nobody really is, I just know what I saw didn't have the look of something created by chemicals or any other kind of science."

"From what I've heard," she went on, "it seems likely that Mr. Valentine sent Cynthia to Race Software with a fake ID. Somehow Cynthia got herself hired and assigned to the Redleaf project. Is this a case of industrial espionage?" Dorothy drummed her fingers on the tabletop. "Is Izzy Valentine trying to steal Redleaf from us?"

"Don't get paranoid. Not everyone in the world is as fascinated with the fortunes of Race Software as you are."

"You think not? What about you, Sam? I'll bet you own some stock in Race Software, along with about a million others."

"Yeah, I got some Race in my portfolio. These days just about everybody does."

"I don't have any in my portfolio," I countered.

"You don't even have a portfolio," Sam laughed. "Nor a pot to piss in, for that matter. Excuse me, Dorothy."

"Point taken." My face felt hot. "What I'm saying is there's no evidence this Valentine character has any 'designs' on your company. Let's not focus too hard on that one idea, we might miss the real answer to Bobby's problem, okay?"

"Agreed," Dorothy nodded. "But we must give Izzy Valentine a close look."

"Of course." I had no idea how to give another person *a close look* except for the obvious moves of digging up old newspaper clippings about him and talking to his friends and neighbors. Dorothy and her boss were trying to turn me into some sort of private detective, a role for which I was spectacularly unqualified.

Our waiter presented the check. "I'll take it." I casually handed my new Visa card to the waiter, who trotted off to complete the transaction.

"You're buying lunch?" Sam shook his head as if exposed to an idea so bizarre as to cause dizziness.

Dorothy leaned forward with a quizzical frown. "That looked like a Race Software credit card. They're supposed to be used only for company business."

"That's what this lunch is all about," I replied blithely.

"Lemme understand this," Sam said to Dorothy. "You people gave Kevin Pierce a credit card? With what limit?"

"I think the limit is eight thousand," I said.

Sam cast his eyes to heaven. "What comes next, Lord? Forty days and nights of floods? Those Race shares I'm holdin'? I'm sellin' them tomorrow. Mighty sorry about that, Dorothy, but I see big deficits ahead for your outfit."

The waiter returned with the charge slip. I added a twenty percent tip, signed with a flourish, pocketed the receipt. "Excellent lunch. Great service. And the company was superb. I remind you, Dorothy, in case your gnarly little accountants question this expense, that we talked business for at least twenty minutes. By the way, where do you people keep your expense forms?"

Dorothy treated me to a rare soft smile. "Tomorrow morning ask Jenny to show you how to fill out an expense chit on the computer, she'll be glad to help. Jenny's taken quite an interest in you, Kevin. And not just because you're doing Bobby's portrait."

"Do I smell an office romance?" Sam pretended to admire my features. "Don't surprise me at all. Our boy's been a swordsman a lot longer than he's been an artist." He winced when I kicked him under the table. "What I should've said is our boy's real sincere…never treated a woman wrong in his life. Well…shit…except for that gal Angela we met in Junction City, Kansas. In a bar outside Fort Riley. One night Angela had a go at Kevin's throat with a steak knife. Didn't like Kevin turning his back on her to put his moves on another girl. And that made no sense. Angela was a pro after all. Only way you could insult Angela was to offer her less than fifty."

"We'd better head back to the office." Before Sam could completely destroy my chances with Dorothy, I slid out of the booth and helped her to her feet as any gentleman would do.

On the drive back down the peninsula, Dorothy took from her commodious shoulder bag what appeared to be the world's smallest computer. "Wireless mini PC," she explained. "Latest thing in mobile remote communications. I can reach all the way to Hong Kong on this. Sydney. Rio. Stuttgart. I can connect with anyone…anywhere…any time."

"I'm impressed." The truth is I wouldn't really give a fiddler's fart if every leading-edge computer in the world suddenly self-destructed. In fact, I'd probably cheer.

"The new wireless technology is terrific." Dorothy bent to her work over the mini-keyboard.

Over the years I've been shut out by girls for a variety of reasons: Competition from better looking guys. Parents suspicious of my intentions (they were always right). Political disagreements. Personality conflicts. The usual litany. A girl named Claire once dumped me because I liked the coyote and roadrunner cartoons better than Bugs Bunny. (She wasn't exactly the brightest star in the universe.) Dorothy was the first to shut me out in favor of a machine. That really hurt.

I let her work silently until we came to a halt in a traffic jam on the Bayshore freeway near San Francisco International. Then I lost it. Maybe I was pissed about all the time I was spending away from work that really matters to me. Maybe she'd pricked my ego. Maybe it was simple road rage, a popular pastime on the Bayshore. Whatever the reason, I found myself angrily punching the power button on her oh-so-marvelous-state-of-the-art-mini-PC and yelling "Turn that damn thing off and talk to me! Does every type of communication have to take place on one of those goddam black boxes? Don't you ever crave a genuine conversation with someone who actually cares about you?"

My outburst startled her. "Kevin, what's wrong?"

"Didn't you even pick up on those last few key words—*someone who cares about you*?"

"Why are you so angry?"

"I've done everything but handstands to draw you out, show you I care about you." The traffic started to move again in a vague stop-and-go fashion. I shifted into second and crawled along with it, all the while staring at Dorothy in feverish exasperation. "What is it with you? Don't people count?"

"That's insulting." Her hand drew back, I thought she was going to slap me. Instead she waved the hand in front of her face in an attempt to dispel the moment. "You don't know anything about me. Nothing. Less than nothing."

"That's my point. You won't let me in. Do you let anyone in besides the great Bobby Race?"

Then Dorothy did slap me.

A woman in a Toyota Camry, stuck next to us in the adjoining lane, watched as if we were a spicy episode of her favorite soap opera. Her mouth hung open in anticipation. The slap was good, but she wanted more. Would I slap Dorothy back? Would I pull a gun and shoot myself? Or Dorothy? Were we a married couple having a fight or two lovers caught up in a rancorous affair? She'd never know. I managed to creep a few feet ahead of the Camry, cutting off her line of sight.

"I apologize. That was rude as hell. I do care about you, Dorothy. Being close to you makes me giddy. That's why I'm acting weird. I want to spend more time with you, get to know you well. We're alone in a car, you're punching computer keys instead of talking to me, that makes me crazy."

While I was pouring my heart out, she had gotten her emotions together. Gone prim and straight-backed on me. "Kevin, you're a very attractive man. Every girl in the building is already interested in you. Hit on one of them."

"You don't like me? Is it that simple?"

"No, that isn't it. I have a life that suits me. Every day I accrue more intellectual satisfaction and financial stability than I ever thought I'd achieve. My parents were high school teachers in a poor district. Do you realize I'm a millionaire several times over, thanks to my stock options? I'm focused on my work because it has a big payoff, and because I love it. There's just no room for you in my life, Kevin." Dorothy moaned and rolled her beautiful head on her exquisite shoulders. "Or anyone else. Not even Bobby. Yes, the rumors are true. At one time I did have a thing with Bobby. It didn't work out. Would never have worked anyway, Bobby's a hit and run guy. But God help me, I can't handle relationships. Not at all. Every time I get involved with a man I become possessive, shrill, jealous, bitchy, hyper, grungy. All the bad comes out. It happened with Bobby, he dropped me fast and he was right to do it. I was engaged once, it was the same story."

"History doesn't always repeat itself."

A wan smile. "I think you've got your quote backwards. What George Bernard Shaw said was, *We learn from history that men never learn anything from history.* I think that applies to women, too. And it totally negates your point."

I had to laugh. "Do you know everything?"

"Bobby says I know everything worth knowing." She noted my creased brow. "Sorry, I do tend to wave Bobby's name like a flag."

I was seized with an irrational need to prove I was somewhat educated, too. "I think it was Pascal who said, *If Cleopatra's nose had been shorter, the whole face of the earth would have changed.* If Bobby ever took a really deep look at you, he wouldn't need all those other girls."

Dorothy gave me another of her soft looks. "That's a lovely thing to say."

My hands gripped the steering wheel much tighter than necessary. She reached over and patted them. The traffic began to move briskly and I gladly lost myself in the rote mechanics of driving.

CHAPTER 8

I remained morose when I dropped Dorothy at Race headquarters and my mood continued to be gloomy as I negotiated the switchback stretch of Route 92 down the mountain towards Half Moon Bay. All my own fault, of course. The move I'd put on Dorothy was about as subtle as Godzilla rising out of the sea. The next time I approached her, and there would be a next time, I'd plan a way to put my considerable charm to better use.

It didn't help my mood to have some hotshot in a Porsche hovering about six inches from my rear bumper all the way down the mountain, revving his powerful engine in a deliberately intimidating way at every hairpin turn. One of those dot.com millionaires you find all over Silicon Valley. His bullying finally got to me. On one of the critically tight turns I hit my brakes twice, as if I were about to slow to a crawl, then sped up when he tried to pass me. Mister Porsche almost went over the cliff. In my rearview mirror he revealed himself as the kind of guy who can't take a joke.

My spirits rose as I approached the intersection of Route 92 and Route 1, which runs along the ocean. There's a little place near that intersection called Manuel and Sadie's Not-So-Super-Market. Manuel and Sadie don't carry nearly as many items as the big Safeway a couple of blocks north, but they do have the largest stock of Carta Blanca in town, which makes it my favorite place to shop.

Sadie, the proprietoress, a large dark-complexioned Samoan, greeted me with her usual open smile. "Hey, Kevin. Couple six packs tonight?"

"Sadie, my love, I've come to make a major purchase. Four cases of Carta Blanca, if you please. No…wait." I made a hasty assessment of how much beer could be fitted into a Karmann Ghia. For the first time ever, I regretted owning such a small automobile. "Make that six cases. I'll need some help from your stock boy to fit them into my car."

"Six cases?" Sadie had often advanced me a six pack plus some milk and bananas on credit. I could see she was reluctant to advance me six full cases. "Don't know I can put that much on your tab. Manny might beat me."

"Not to worry." I flashed my new credit card from Race Software. "This week you'll find me well financed. I'd better lay in some food, too. Throw in the biggest bunch of bananas you've got, half a gallon of milk, and a king-sized box of Frosted Flakes."

"Half gallon?" Sadie's many chins bounced as she chuckled. "You really need all that milk? Your car so small, it take a lot of space you could use for beer."

"You're right, I have to do a better job of thinking ahead. Just between us, Sadie, my new patron could yank this piece of plastic tomorrow. So make that a quart of milk, a small bunch of bananas, medium-sized Frosted Flakes, and *eight* cases of Carta Blanca. We can tie a couple of cases to the rear hood, if necessary."

"You always a crazy man. I have the boy dolly them out to parking lot. You gonna need civil engineer fit them into Ghia."

"Necessity is the mother of invention." Not an original thought, but an apt one.

"You artists talk so smart." Sadie took the credit card and began totaling the sale. "So how come you all time gotta buy on tab?"

"That was just a temporary condition. My days of penury are coming to an end."

"What penury mean?"

"It means extreme poverty."

"Ah...okay...you no be broke no more. Good news for me and Manny. Good news for Carta Blanca company too."

Sadie gave me back the credit card. As I signed the charge slip, it hit me that you can put almost anything on a card these days. You could even use a credit card to pay a pest control man to get rid of termites.

The stock boy helped me load the beer into the car. He had a clever mind. Probably another future dot.com millionaire. He suggested that if we took all the beer out of the cases and carefully stuffed them into the back compartment and front seat bottle by bottle, we could probably fit a whole extra case into the Ghia. I ran inside and put another case on the card. Sadie guffawed and came out to watch us work, oohing in wonder when after great effort we managed to pack a total of *ten* cases of Carta Blanca into my car bottle by bottle.

Where are the people from the *Guinness Book Of Records* when you need them?

Weighed down as it was with bottles of beer, the Ghia's steering went sluggish and it took the hill to my house with great effort, the bottles clanking a jolly tune. Unloading my purchase took about half an hour. The beer completely filled my pantry, a beautiful sight.

The luncheon at the Fog City Diner was still with me so I had only a glass of milk and one banana for dinner. I was looking forward to a cold refreshment later on, but business always comes first with us corporate grunges. Somewhere in my messy desk was a written estimate from Rudgear Pest Control. A step-by-step search turned up the estimate, which was twenty-four hundred dollars. I called the home number on the business card I'd been given and was soon talking with Alvin Rudgear himself.

"This is Kevin Pierce. Do you remember me, Mister Rudgear? About six months ago you gave me a quote of twenty-four hundred dollars to get rid of my termites."

"Naw, I don't recall. Wait…okay…I remember you now. You're some kind of artist? You got that nice house above the highway. Redwood deck. Great ocean view. Needs a lot of work, as I recall."

I ignored his disrespectful tone. "That's why I'm calling. I'd like you to do the termite work tomorrow."

"Tomorrow? Not a chance. I got people ahead of you. Lady in Santa Cruz has so many silverfish in her house…"

"I'll double your fee. Forty-eight hundred if you do the job tomorrow. I want the whole job over and done with in a day. Can you handle that?"

"Double?" Rudgear chewed that over. "Well, let's see, it'd take me all day and into the night. I'd have to bring in a crew. You got extensive infestation, as I recall."

"Forty-eight hundred," I repeated. "If you won't do it, I'm sure I can force that amount of money on one of your competitors."

"You really got forty-eight hundred dollars?" A suspicious note had crept into Rudgear's voice. "No offense, but you looked like a hand-to-mouth guy to me."

"I have a credit card with a much higher limit than forty-eight hundred. Can you come over now? Run my card and take payment tonight if you want. I'll be out all day tomorrow, I'll give you my extra house key and trust you to do the job right."

"My reputation in this community is first class, Mr. Pierce. If I take your money, the job'll get done."

"I never meant to imply otherwise. How about it, can you come over right now?"

Alvin Rudgear, torn between irritation at my demands and greed for my money, hemmed and hawed and presently allowed as how he could come by in half an hour. I'd sign a contract and he'd run my card through his mobile credit system for payment.

His arrival was punctual. His surliness had vanished. He was dressed in the same workpants and shirt with *Rudgear Pest Control* on the back that he wore when he came to my house the first time.

Rudgear was a small man with a fierce expression, as if always expecting attacks from household pests. He wiped his feet carefully before coming into the house. Once inside, he stomped around examining the first floor baseboards, muttering to himself and shaking his head. Then he went outside to poke at the foundation. He crawled under deck and came up shaking his head more vigorously and declaring that I'd called him just in time. "Termites ain't like people, Mr. Pierce. They work all year round. Every damned day. That's why they do so much damage."

"So do I. I mean I don't do damage, I work every day."

"Uh-huh." Drenching the grunt with doubt. "Can I run your credit card now? Just want to make sure we're in this together, if you understand me."

Nice way of saying he wanted to make sure I wasn't the deadbeat he'd taken me to be. I gave him my Race credit card, which impressed him. Everyone in the Silicon Valley area knew the company to be wildly wealthy. While he ran the card, I held my breath. I don't trust corporations, they can turn on you in a second. For all I knew, my lovely credit card might already have been canceled. In which case Alvin Rudgear would at least make himself fifty bucks from the credit card company for confiscating that little piece of plastic.

"Okay." Rudgear sounded pleased and surprised when his mobile system kicked out an approval for the charge. "I guess we're in business. I'll be here with my crew at seven a.m., Mr. Pierce. (Very respectful tone this time.) There won't be much in the way of noxious odors to put up with. I do my job right, you won't even know I've been here. Except you won't see them nasty termites buzzing around the foundation."

"That'll be a pleasant change."

I ushered him out and was soon relaxing on my deck, enjoying a cold Carta Blanca and bidding a final farewell to the colony of pests living in the wood I was sitting on. Little did they know they were about to be zapped into oblivion by my good friend and admirer Alvin Rudgear.

The phone rang. A cultured female voice ringing with an English background said: "Is this the residence of Kevin Pierce?"

"Yes, this is the residence and this is Kevin Pierce himself."

"I'm Amelia Valentine. My husband, Isadore, asked me to invite you to a party we're giving this evening at our home in Hillsborough. I apologize for calling you on such extreme short notice. Isadore would be most grateful for your presence at his party. So would I, of course. There will be many other guests, but he pledges to make time to speak with you. May we expect to enjoy your company?"

It hadn't taken Maury Canselmo long to let Izzy Valentine know I'd been asking questions about him. We had lunch about two o'clock. My watch read seven-fifteen. "What time does the party start?"

"Eight o'clock. I'm absolutely *appalled* to be calling you so late. Isadore said to tell you there would be an ample supply of Carta Blanca on hand. He seemed to think that would be an inducement. Will you be with us tonight?"

The comment left me chilled. If Izzy Valentine wanted to demonstrate he could invade my private life with extraordinary ease, he'd succeeded. "Sure, I'll be there. What's the dress?"

"Jacket and tie would be appreciated."

"I can handle that."

"Good! I look forward to meeting you. I've seen your work, it's wonderful."

I was astounded. "You have? Where?"

"Why, in our own home. Isadore owns one of your paintings. I see it every day on the wall of his study. I thought you must know that."

"No, I didn't."

"How extraordinary." With a perky voice, "Well, that's reason enough to accept our invitation, isn't it?"

"You bet it is. If you'll give me directions to your house, I'll see you soon."

Izzy Valentine's house in Hillsborough sat on one of those fake country lanes created by a developer to resemble rural England. All the same, it was impressive. Large Tudor-style estates lined the road, each on a parcel of twenty acres or more. Each had a big iron gate. Some even had small gate houses where, I imagined, indentured servants struggled for a hard living in genteel poverty. Or maybe I've just seen too many episodes of *Masterpiece Theatre.*

The gates to Izzy's estate stood open. I went up a two-hundred-yard driveway to the front of the house where two red-jacketed attendants were parking cars. They greeted my old Karmann Ghia with morbid curiosity. After a quick coin toss, the loser took my keys and parked the Ghia in a line of luxury automobiles that would have made even Big Sam Cody suck air with envy.

Forty or more guests were circulating through the first floor of the house. Drinks in hand. Smiles in place. Those who didn't already know each other seemed to have quickly found common conversational ground. Which pissed me off. Whenever I walk into a party full of unfamiliar faces, I end up alone in a corner pretending to admire a picture or piece of sculpture.

While I was trying to guess which face belonged to Izzy Valentine, a waiter who looked like an old photo of Troy Donahue came up to me with a glass of beer on a tray. "Mr. Pierce? I was told to bring you a Carta Blanca as soon as you came in, and to make sure it was ice cold."

"Hey, thanks." I took the beer, swallowed, sighed in deep appreciation. "Who told you to do that?"

"Mrs. Valentine."

"I've never met Mrs. Valentine. Can you point her out?"

The waiter looked around. "Don't see her at the moment. Nice lady. Great voice too, sounds like Eliza Doolittle after the make-over."

"You're an actor, right?"

His chest puffed out. "You've seen me in something? The commercial for East Bay Chevrolet?"

"Uh…no…I don't think so. It's just that you look like Troy Donahue and you talked about Eliza Doolittle."

"Troy Donahue?" His friendliness vaporized. "You really know how to hurt a guy." A second later he disappeared, leaving me to wonder where my next Carta Blanca would come from.

I tried circulating, but it didn't work any better at this party than it had at most others. Nobody talked to me. After a few minutes, I did slip into a semicircle of people, two women and three guys, and tried to join a conversation that turned out to be about limited debentures. My contribution was to appear worried about the tax implications of new legislation. I did that for a while, frowning and nodding whenever the dreaded word tax was mentioned, then drifted off to look for Troy Donahue and a fresh beer.

I didn't see Troy. Near the refreshments table I did find a large wash-bucket filled with ice into which a dozen or so bottles of beer had been artfully inserted. I helped myself.

"Mr. Pierce? I'm Amelia Valentine. It was awfully good of you to come on such short notice."

I turned and tried, successfully I hope, to hide my surprise. Amelia Valentine was a lovely woman of about forty, fashionably slim, dark hair pulled back, eyebrows elegantly arched, a complexion that hinted at expensive weekly care by Elizabeth Arden. She wore a long black designer dress. And she was wheelchair bound. "Nice to meet you, Mrs. Valentine. Thanks for the invitation. I don't get out to big parties very often, so this is a treat."

"Manacled to your easel, I imagine," she said in that wonderful accent.

"Yes, I suppose."

"Well, I know what it's like to be manacled to something." She gave her wheelchair a friendly pat, as if it were a favored pet. "I don't get out much either, so we often invite friends and acquaintances to the house. It's easier for me that way."

"What part of England are you from?"

"Surrey. My father was a country vet. I came to the colonies about fifteen years ago to study veterinary medicine myself. I met Isadore and got married instead."

I suppose my eyes held questions because she went on to tell me more about herself. "Yes, I came from England to go to veterinary school in Buffalo, New York. I met Isadore, fell in love with him, partly because he was the smartest chap I'd ever gone out with and also because he was so wildly different from anyone I'd ever met. Once we were married, he let me continue my studies and indulged my love of animals." Her mouth tightened. "That turned out to be an unfortunate choice of passions. A horse threw me..." She cast her eyes down at the wheelchair. "That was twelve years ago. Come along, I'll show you where Isadore placed your painting. I think you'll be pleased."

Amelia Valentine's wheelchair was battery powered. She used a small control panel to expertly maneuver a path through her scattered guests, pausing now and again to say a few words to some of them, smiling at others, checking as she passed to make sure each had a refreshment. Amelia Valentine generated a quiet, well-bred warmth. Women bent to kiss her cheek. Men beamed at her. A path was magically opened for her.

We went through the living room and a library, down a wide hallway and through what appeared to be a second living room before entering a dark-paneled study. The paneling, heavy wood desk, solid chairs, golf clubs leaning in one corner, wall calendar from a Montgomery Street investment bank, Cross pen set and other decorations were masculine to a fault.

There were half a dozen paintings on the walls of Izzy Valentine's study. One was my portrait of Marty Sanchez, a scrappy bantamweight I'd seen fight at the Oakland Coliseum. I told Amelia Valentine that I went to watch Marty fight after I'd seen his photo on the sports page of *The Chronicle*. Just a one-column shot, but it was enough to make me want to see more. I bought a seat in the second row for his next bout and brought along my old 35 millimeter Rollei. The ticket was a good investment. Marty had a face that would cower a serial killer. All the sharp planes were long gone, beaten flat by thousands of blows. He had hypnotically aggressive eyes, a mouth twisted with hostility, permanent puckered scar under the left eye, split bottom lip, black hair with strands as thick as cables.

Marty won the bout. Afterwards you wouldn't have guessed it from looking at him. His opponent had cut a new scar up near the hairline and flattened his nose even further. I went back to Marty Sanchez's dressing room, told him I was an artist, asked if I could take some color photos of him as the basis for a portrait . Marty was not especially articulate. He listened, grunted his approval, demanded five hundred for the privilege of having photos taken and his portrait painted. I didn't have five hundred, or anything close to it. We negotiated a compromise: fifty dollars for five minutes.

I shot as many closeups as I could manage in the time. After four minutes he cut me off and hustled me out of his dressing room, he had a girl coming to "Gimmee some gash," as he put it.

"And that's how I happened to do Marty Sanchez's portrait," I told Amelia Valentine, deleting only the gash remark.

She'd been nodding along with me as I told the story. "Is he still fighting?"

"About a year ago I saw a story about Marty in the *Chronicle*. He was walking down Pico Boulevard in L.A. and fell over dead. Blood vessel burst in his brain, something like that. They say he took too many shots to the head."

"Everyone says boxing is too barbaric to be a real sport. You don't think much about it until someone you know, even if it's just someone you know from a portrait, dies. I'll never be able to look at this portrait in the same way." She rolled her wheelchair a few inches forward, a few inches back. "In Isadore's younger days, before I knew him, he was a boxer. Middleweight class? Do I have the terminology right? We had different classes of fighters in England."

"Middleweight would be the right term here. Was he any good?"

"I have no idea." She put a hand to her mouth. "Oh dear, do you think it's terrible that I don't know whether my husband was a good boxer?"

She had an easy way of making me smile. "Not at all."

"Isadore has a book of clippings from his days as a fighter. Every now and then, when he thinks I won't notice, he gets out the book and looks through it. Page by page. With such nostalgic eyes I want to cry for him." Her own eyes were glistening. "Isadore wants to be a boy again. Running around Buffalo, New York, with a gang of tough lads, plenty of birds to flirt with. And I'd like to be a young bird, preferably a bird with two strong legs. Growing older has quite a sad side to it, Kevin. But as you Yanks like to say, it's loads better than the alternative."

Amelia Valentine spoke so warmly of her husband that I found myself questioning Big Sam Cody's description of Izzy Valentine as a manipulative hoodlum, possibly even a killer.

"I like doing portraits of older people," I said. "Their faces tell stories."

"Are most of those stories comedies or tragedies?"

"Mostly tragedy, I'm afraid." I shrugged. "Or maybe I'm misreading what I see."

"No, I don't think you are." Her voice had become hoarse and her shoulders sagged. "There's tragedy aplenty in this world."

I felt I'd put my foot down on a landmine. "Looks like I've succeeded in depressing you with my story about Marty Sanchez. I'm awfully sorry."

Amelia Valentine resurrected her winning smile. "Don't be. Most of the conversations at our parties have so little substance, it's refreshing to have a serious interlude. Let's look for Isadore, shall we? He wants to meet you."

I followed in the wake of her motorized wheelchair. We went from room to room until we came to the library, where seven or eight people were looking at antique stereopticon slides through an equally antique hand-held viewer that was being passed around.

"Good Lord, this is a photo of the Paris Exposition of 1900," someone said. "If I remember my history, that exposition was a turning point in the industrial revolution."

"What you're looking at is nothing less than the very dynamo Henry Adams wrote about when he described the exposition in *The Education of Henry Adams.* Yes, that event was a turning point. For the first time, people from around the world came to realize that in the new century machines like the dynamo were going to surpass the efforts of human beings."

That extremely authoritarian statement came from a man of medium height and swarthy complexion who spoke in a gravelly voice with brisk, decisive gestures. I gathered from Amelia Valentine's glowing attentiveness that the speaker was her husband. Izzy Valentine went on for several minutes more about the significance of the Paris Exposition, bringing out additional stereopticon slides and passing them around to make his points. I knew of the Paris Exposition because some wonderful art came out of it. Izzy's knowledge of the event was impressive. He switched to the subject of stereopticon slides, calling them "the first serious attempt at three-dimensional art."

When the conversation wound down, Izzy Valentine excused himself and came over to us. He kissed Amelia's cheek and affectionately squeezed her shoulder. She responded by reaching up and patting the hand on her shoulder. "Isadore, this is Kevin Pierce. He was good enough to join us at short notice."

"Hello, Kevin." He spoke in a heavy Eastern seaboard voice. "I'm glad you could come, I see you found the Carta Blanca."

I hoisted my glass. "Found it...surrounded it."

He laughed and asked his wife if she'd shown me the portrait in the study.

"Indeed I have. Kevin even told me the story behind that painting. Quite a sad tale, I'm afraid."

"Let's go look at it again," Izzy said. "Excuse us, my dear."

"Very nice to have met you, Mrs. Valentine." I shook her hand. "Thank you for inviting me."

"Please come again."

Izzy steered me by the elbow into his study. He closed the door behind him and offered me a cigar from a humidor. "Cuban."

"No, thanks. I don't smoke."

"Too busy with beer, huh. Mind if I have one? Amelia's banished my cigars to this one room. Oh, she can be tough, don't underestimate her."

"Smoke up a storm. By the way, I like your wife a lot."

"You know where we met? Public reading room of the Buffalo library. She asked if I knew what a *cartouche* is. Happened I did know. We talked some more. Despite our different backgrounds, we really liked each other. Marrying Amelia was the best thing ever happened to me. Most people love Amelia as much as they dislike me."

That was said without any trace of self-pity. Izzy charred the tip of the cigar with a gold lighter to strengthen its draw before taking tentative puffs. He was dressed in a navy blue suit that didn't quite fit him despite its expensive and stylish cut. Izzy hadn't been a middleweight for some time. His paunch was substantial. His face bore faint marks of childhood acne as well some scar tissue around the eyes, probably a holdover from his days as a boxer. His eyes were a muddy brown under bushy, almost unkempt brows, his dark hair thin and combed straight back. He was ugly in a formidable way.

For a couple of minutes we just looked at my portrait of Marty Sanchez.

"Hell of a painting," Izzy said at last. "Amelia told you I started out as a fighter? Well, I bought this painting because it's what I would have looked like if I'd kept at it. This is Marty Sanchez, isn't it? Bantamweight from L.A.? I still subscribe to *Ring* magazine and I used to see his picture. Whatever happened to him? Did he retire?"

"As I told your wife, Marty collapsed on the street and died of a brain hemorrhage."

With a deep draw on his Cuban cigar, Izzy said, "Boxers have brain hemorrhages the way three-year-olds have earaches. I was pretty good, if I say so myself. Came out of high school with a solid right hand, started out in Golden Gloves, booked myself into some club fights, won fourteen out of sixteen bouts, got a rating. But I didn't have a put-away punch. Most of my fights were won on points." He seated himself on a couch and waved me into a chair opposite him. "You don't last long without a put-away punch. I was going nowhere in the fight game, so I took a job with Johnny Lucca's family because he was the smartest of the local wiseguys. I was never a real mob guy myself, despite what Big Sam Cody probably told you. I wholesaled merchandise that *fell off the back of a truck*, as they like to say. But Johnny Lucca did teach me how to make money. When I decided to move to California and go into business for myself, Johnny wished me well."

"I can understand why you'd want to get out of Buffalo. When I see the Bills play at home, the temperature's usually down around the twenties."

Izzy Valentine gave a hearty laugh. "The wind off that lake? Forget it!" He became more serious. "Actually, the winters didn't bother me that much, I grew up with them. The real reason for my move to California was Amelia's health. She's the one who couldn't take those winters. You want a fresh beer? I'll have one brought in."

"I'm fine." I sensed Izzy was about to approach the real reason for my invitation to his party.

"Guy called today, said you're asking questions about me. You want to know about my business? Talk to my accountants. I'll tell them to show you my books. I got nothing to hide, or very little anyhow. But you were asking personal questions about me, Kevin. Why's that?"

"I didn't ask any questions about you." His eyes narrowed dangerously when I contradicted him. In a flash I saw Izzy Valentine as he must have been as a kid in Buffalo, tougher than the harsh winters and meaner than the cold, desolate streets he grew up on. "That's the truth. Your name was brought up by someone else."

"By Maury Canselmo?"

"Yes." I didn't like Izzy's expression, it spelled trouble for Canselmo. "Don't get pissed at some clerk. He was pretty much forced into giving up your name. I believe Sam mentioned something about shoving the poor little guy off a pier at midnight."

Izzy chewed on his cigar. "Maury's not what you'd call a stand-up guy. What did you ask him?"

I took Cynthia Gooding's driver's license out of my wallet. "I'm trying to find out what this girl's real name is. All Maury knew about her was that you sent her to him for a driver's license in the name of Cynthia Gooding."

He gave the photo ID a quick look. "Yeah, I know her. Why do you want to find her? What kind of trouble is she in?"

"The worst kind. She's dead." I'd be willing to swear Izzy's surprise was genuine. But once upon a time I also believed that girls would flock to me if I was honest with them and had a great sense of humor.

"How'd she die?"

"Accidental fall, or so they say."

A derisive noise came boiling up all the way from his diaphragm. "Cindy wasn't the kind to die in an accidental fall."

"Cindy? What was her full name?"

"Cindy Pacini."

"Will you tell me what you know about her?"

"I shouldn't." Izzy looked at the door beyond which lay his guests and his wheelchair bound wife. "But it pisses me off to hear she's dead. I don't buy an *accidental fall* story any more than you apparently do. You think somebody snuffed her?"

"It's a real possibility. Who was Cindy Pacini? Why did you send her to a crooked DMV clerk for a fake driver's license?"

"I was doing her a favor, or so I thought." Izzy touched a button built into the end table next to him and within twenty seconds the waiter who looked like Troy Donahue came in. "Bring me a Wild Turkey, water on the side. My friend will have a Carta Blanca, make sure it's cold."

He pondered in silence what I'd told him until our fresh drinks were served and the waiter had closed the door behind him.

"Cindy was a prostitute, worked out of a nice apartment on Russian Hill. She had a small well-heeled clientele. I'm guessing she brought in eighty to a hundred large per year. I used her myself." He shrugged. "I love Amelia, but I've got some needs she wouldn't understand. I had three girls I was seeing at the time. They were prostitutes, but they all had their VD and AIDS checks every month, I insist on that. I won't do business with girls who don't take care of themselves. One day Cindy says she's quitting the trade, she's got something else going. Fine, I say. Good luck to you. I liked Cindy. She was smart and sexy. Honest too, in her way. There's plenty of call girls around, losing her services didn't mean anything to me. But she asks me for a favor. Says she's changing her identity so her new boyfriend won't find out where she came from."

"What'd she mean by *where she came from*?"

"You know, that she'd been a prostitute. Cindy claimed she was about to get married, settle down, maybe let herself gain a few pounds. All she needed was a new name and identity. I had one of my guys call Maury Canselmo and set up an appointment for Cindy to get a driver's license in whatever name she wanted. Until now, I didn't know that Cynthia Gooding was the new monicker she chose." He moved his head in approval. "Classier name than Cindy Pacini. Not that it brought her any luck."

"Did you give her the two thousand dollars she paid to Maury Canselmo for the driver's license?"

"No, Cindy put out her own money for that. Said she'd saved a sizable nest egg for her new start. I believe that. She was a first-class whore." He shot me a glance of curiosity. "Who'd she marry?"

"Nobody that I know of. When Cindy died she was single, according to her records, and working for Race Software."

Izzy Valentine let his glass of Wild Turkey sink toward his lap. "She was working for Bobby Race?"

"Not directly, though she did deal with him."

"I hear Bobby hits on all the good-looking women in his company. He must have gone after Cindy. She was hot, anybody'll tell you that."

"I've heard they got together." I felt a bit uncomfortable telling tales on my financial benefactor. "I don't know for certain that it's true."

"You're not saying Bobby Race had something to do with Cindy's 'accident'?"

"No."

"Then who arranged Cindy's accident? Why are you digging into her death? And why is my name being dragged into it?" Izzy got up and paced the length of his study with his head down. "This doesn't make any sense, unless somebody's out to smear me." He turned on me sharply. "You'd better not try to involve me in a murder, Kevin. I'll have your hands broken into so many pieces you'll have to hold your paint brush in your teeth."

"I'm not playing any games with your reputation. Not that it's a very good reputation anyway."

He sizzled at the remark. "You've been talking to Sam Cody." Izzy's jaw extended itself. "He's pissed because I want to buy him out. I don't mean Sam any harm, he doesn't understand he'd make more money if he came on my team."

"Sam's not a team player. He likes to work solo."

"You two were army buddies, I've been told."

"That's right."

"Decorated heroes, both of you."

"We did our jobs."

He pointed a long finger in my face. "You two had better not be trying to do a job on me."

"Sam sees it the other way around, you're trying to do a job on him. He's had some troubles at his place of business lately and thinks you're behind it."

With a wheeze of exasperation, Izzy Valentine soaked up some of his Wild Turkey. "All I'm trying to do is buy Sam Cody's expertise. Did you know he's developed a foolproof way of changing the engine number on an automobile? A system like that's worth a ton of money. I'm willing to pay, but Sam isn't willing to sell. That's not right. He should be willing to share his expertise with his friends, don't you think?"

"I don't try to tell Sam how to run his business, and I doubt he'll listen to you either."

"Stubborn bastard." He eyed me suspiciously. "You see where I'm going, I can't help wondering if you're trying to stir up trouble for me on behalf of your old army buddy."

"I'm only trying to find out about Cynthia Gooding as a favor to the people at Race Software. She was an employee. There are death benefits for her family. They can't find the family without knowing her true name."

"I doubt they'll find Cindy's family anyway. This is a whore we're talking about. She might have been on her fifth or sixth name by the time she started calling herself Cindy Pacini. From now on, stay out of my business. I've told you everything I know about Cindy."

"Except her address on Russian Hill."

Izzy gave me the address, which I dutifully wrote down. "I'll give you more than her address." He went to his desk and opened one of the small side drawers, from which he took a single key. "This is the key to the apartment where I used to meet Cindy once or twice a week. I have no idea whether she was still living there when she died. Like I said, I never saw her again after she told me she was quitting the business to get married."

"And she didn't say who this boyfriend was?"

"She knew I didn't really care who the guy might be."

Izzy didn't appear to be the jealous type, but a lot of men unexpectedly turned violent against women who try to leave them. Even against women who charged money for their sexual services. I couldn't discount the possibility that Izzy Valentine might be behind Cynthia Gooding's...or should I say Cindy Pacini's...death.

I couldn't call her by both names, so I decided to stick with Cynthia Gooding. Somehow I thought that's the name she would have wanted me to use.

"I'd better be on my way."

"I'll see you out." Before opening the door to the study, Izzy paused in front of my portrait of Marty Sanchez. "You know what I do when I buy a new painting? I hang it right here on the wall of my study for a year or two, just to get used to it. If, after a couple of years, the painting still pleases me, I promote it to the wall of my library or even to the living room. A lot of important people visit my house, Kevin. They admire my paintings. My pieces of sculpture. My other artwork. If an artist's name is new to them, they ask where they can see more of his or her work. That's how artistic reputations are built. I've been thinking of promoting Marty Sanchez's portrait to my living room, which over time would result in a significant rise in your stature and income. Don't fuck up your future. Not for a whore who probably had a dozen different names."

He took me to his front door, bid me good evening and patted my back as I started down the flagstone steps. I think he wished he was holding a knife in his hand.

CHAPTER 9

I should have gone home, eaten a couple of bananas and jumped straight into bed. Instead I drove back to the city to look for Cynthia Gooding's apartment. If I'd known how the night was going to turn out, I'd have driven to Canada instead and changed my name to Frederic Remington. Or maybe Henri de Toulouse-Lautrec. Those guys did all right in the art biz, didn't they?

Russian Hill has some narrow, complicated streets and you have to be a witch or, in my case, a warlock to find a parking place anywhere in the vicinity. I summoned up some witchcraft and found a slot for my Karmann Ghia on Taylor Street near Filbert. From there I walked up the hill until I found the address Izzy Valentine had given me, a four-story apartment building with bay windows and what realtors call "lots of old San Francisco charm." Translation: sky-high prices.

The name Cynthia Gooding was no longer on the mailbox for apartment 3-B. The name slot was blank. The lobby was small and elegant, thanks to a dandy city scene fresco on the largest wall. I lingered a moment to admire it, then walked up to the third floor. The stairwell and hallways were nicely painted in teals and grays and decorated with contemporary art I didn't care for, energetic stuff vaguely in the style of Jasper Johns and bold but depressing black-on-white monotypes. The apartments would be larger than most on Russian Hill, which meant the rents would be four thousand a month minimum. As condos, they'd be worth eight hundred thousand and up. Cynthia had been living awfully well for a company purchasing agent.

I put the key into the lock of 3-B but didn't immediately turn it. I didn't think I could be arrested for entering Cynthia's apartment so long as I had a key, but what I know about the law you could put into the glove compartment of my car. What if someone was legally inside the apartment, like a room mate of Cynthia or a person who had sublet the place from her? What if that person screamed and called out the window for the cops? What if I panicked and ran like a burglar? What if a police car happened to be passing? What if I panicked some more and tried to get away? What if one of the cops drew his gun and fired? What if…

Sometimes it doesn't pay to have an imagination.

I shivered away my misgivings, turned the key, opened the door. "Hello? Anyone home?"

The apartment was modern and empty of furniture. However, the living room ceiling light was on and clear plastic paint covers were spread around the floors. The aroma of fresh paint was quite strong. The walls had recently been done in arctic blue. At the rear of the apartment people could be heard moving around and from a radio or CD disk Elton John was singing *Candle In The Wind*.

"Hello?" I said again.

"Who's that?" The man who came into the living room was about forty years old. A tired forty. He wore one of those throwaway painter's hats, old jeans and a torn sweatshirt smeared with two shades of paint. The first was arctic blue and the second a deep cream that edged toward beige. I liked the cream better than the blue.

"Who are you? How'd you get in here?"

"I have a key." I showed it to him. "I'm sorry, I thought this apartment was unoccupied."

A woman about ten years younger than the guy appeared at his side. She'd been painting too. Her short brown hair was flecked here and there with arctic blue. She had a thin, aggressive face and very large breasts. "It certainly is occupied," she declared. "We're the Hoffmans. We just bought this condo, closed on it three days ago. Where did you get a key to our place?" She glared at the guy. "Bernie, I told you to have the locks changed." Her voice was shrill enough to shatter glass. "That's the first thing you do when you buy a place, change all the locks."

"I know, Penny. I know." Bernie apparently had heard this refrain before.

"I'm Kevin Pierce." I stepped inside and closed the door behind me. "The girl who lived here before you bought the place has died. Did you know that?"

"No!" Penny glared at Bernie. "Did you hear what he said? We bought a place from a dead girl! I told you we moved too fast."

"We bought from a real estate trust," Bernie explained patiently. "The girl was just leasing."

"If we bought from a dead girl, we overpaid!"

Bernie turned to me as a way of escaping his wife. "I still don't know what you're doing here." He put out his hand. "And I want that key."

"You should have had the locks changed," Penny snapped. "I told you that more than once."

"I know…I know." Bernie begged with his eyes until I handed over the key. "Thank you."

"Don't thank him, he's a trespasser." Penny Hoffman crossed her arms. "You'd better leave before we call the police."

"The young woman who died was named Cynthia Gooding. You must know that name, it would have been on the mailbox when you moved in."

"Yes," Bernie mumbled. "It was. We were told she was the previous tenant. Nobody said she'd died."

His wife nailed him with a venomous look. "I ordered this man to get out of our condo."

"Did Cynthia leave anything behind? She worked for Race Software and so do I." I showed him my shiny new employee ID card. "I've been sent to collect anything she may have left behind."

"The apartment was empty when we moved in," Penny Hoffman said. "Someone had collected all of her stuff when she gave up the lease. I mean, that's what we understood, the previous tenant had given up her lease."

"They didn't collect quite everything." Bernie winced as he realized he'd just contradicted his wife. He could feel her eyes on him and taste her displeasure. But having spoken, he was committed. "We were prepping the bedroom walls yesterday and found a panel that had been painted over to look like part of the wall. There was a little compartment behind the panel. We found a shopping bag there, bag full of papers. Computer printouts, looks like. You want the bag? I think it's still sitting in the corner."

Penny stepped in front of her husband, her considerable breasts standing at attention. "Just a minute, Bernie. We aren't giving those papers to this man. We don't know anything about him. Those papers may be valuable, we haven't really looked at them. They were in this condo when we bought it, so they belong to us." She looked at me defiantly. "That's our position. Do you agree, Bernie?"

With a tired sigh: "Yes, Penny."

I've met plenty of Penny Hoffmans. Sometimes they're women, sometimes they're men. Whatever their gender, they're just old-fashioned bullies.

"Mrs. Hoffman, you've seen my ID." I thought of Joe Patterson lying in his hospital bed. "My title is director of security for the Race Software Development Corporation. You're right, those papers are valuable. They represent important intellectual property of the Race Corporation. If you don't hand over those papers right now, I'll have an attorney on your doorstep at six a.m. We'll file suit against you in the Superior Court of San Francisco for withholding and possibly tampering with our corporation's intellectual property. If you don't cooperate, there'll also be a criminal charge of industrial espionage. Folks, I'm sorry to say your legal bills are going to be awfully high for the next year or two.

Certainly hope you don't lose this nice condo, what with the fresh paint and all."

Penny Hoffman had gone pale. Her right hand went to her throat and her eyes shifted back and forth between her husband and me. "Bernie?"

"For God's sake, Penny. We don't have any use for those papers." He gave me a curt nod. "I'll get them for you."

Bernie was gone less than a minute, an awkward minute between Penny Hoffman and myself. We avoided each others' eyes until Bernie returned carrying a yellow Nordstrom's shopping bag. "Here, take it and go."

"Thank you." The bag was heavy, filled with what Bernie had accurately described as computer printouts. A cursory look did me no good, the various symbols and icons I could see were gibberish to me. "I'm sorry to have intruded. Enjoy your new home."

Self-congratulation is a character flaw I dislike in others, but there are times when I can't resist patting myself on my own back. I left the Hoffmans to their inevitable bickering and hurried down to the street feeling pretty good about the way I'd handled the situation. I'd lied. Dissembled. Bluffed. Cajoled. Exaggerated. Threatened. And gotten what I wanted. Joe Patterson couldn't have done it better.

It remained to be seen whether the Nordstrom bag contained anything valuable. The fact that Cynthia Gooding had taken such pains to hide the material indicated it must be worth something.

If I hadn't been so full of myself, I might have been suspicious when a bulky character in khaki pants and a dirty denim jacket stopped me with the oldest line in the world. "Hey buddy, you got a light?"

"Sorry, I don't…"

That was as far as I got. I was hit across the back by something long and hard. All the breath went out of me. My knees buckled. I didn't collapse to the sidewalk only because two pairs of hands grabbed me from behind. I was yanked backward. The Nordstrom bag fell to the sidewalk and was scooped up by someone. I was dragged into an alley and pulled along for maybe twenty-five yards, far enough to be out of sight and earshot from anyone passing by.

As I began to be able to breathe, a fist clubbed the side of my head.

"Enough! What the hell do you…" I was hit again, another blow to the back, lower this time, a solid shot to the kidneys that robbed me of all my strength. These characters knew their business.

They stopped dragging me and I was thrown against a brick wall. I managed to stay on my feet, get my hands above my waist, brace myself. Three shadowy figures with large shoulders formed a menacing semicircle around me. "What do you want?"

"We got some e-mail for you," a rough voice said.

"E for easy to understand," said another vaguely familiar voice. "You got to leave this Cynthia Gooding thing alone. Go back to your paint box or you'll get hurt real bad."

I almost said *Are you threatening me?* Never in a moment of crisis have I said anything smart. Obviously I was being threatened. I just didn't know why. I did manage to say, "I never knew Cynthia Gooding."

"Then why are you asking questions about her? There are people who don't want those questions asked."

"I'm just helping a friend find out about Cynthia." My eyes were adjusting to the darkness. It was too dark in the alley to read faces, but I could see that my antagonists were three guys in their thirties to mid-forties, each dressed in work clothes, hard looking even in silhouette. They probably hadn't known Cynthia Gooding either. Somebody's hired thugs.

"What's this shit?" asked the one holding the Nordstrom bag.

"I don't know, just some stuff Cynthia left in her apartment."

"Bullshit. We was told to clean out the apartment, get rid of all her things, and we did."

That was interesting. "You missed this bag because it was hidden behind a panel in the bedroom wall."

"We didn't miss nothing."

The last voice was finally registering in my somewhat banged up memory box. Snake Ritchie. I'd played poker at Sam Cody's apartment with Snake and a similarly shady type who went by the name of Bullseye Fratino. Snake Ritchie was a large man with close-cropped dark hair, bloodshot eyes, bad breath. Bullseye Fratino was big too, with long hair tied in a pony tail, Y-shaped face. These guys fit that profile. "Yeah, you missed it, Snake. Your boss isn't going to be happy about that."

"I told you we should've bagged his head," one of the others said.

"Is that you, Bullseye?" These were definitely the two guys I'd played poker with, the ones Sam claimed were now employed by Izzy Valentine to harass his business. "You still drawing to inside straights, Bullseye?"

"He made you guys," said the third man. "This ain't good."

"Shut up, Louie," said Snake Ritchie. "Kevin, you're one dumb artist. You was smart, you would've pretended you didn't make me and Bullseye. This is gonna cost you."

I heard somewhere that the best defense is a good offense, so I kicked Snake Ritchie between the legs and threw a punch at the one called Louie. Snake howled and sank to his knees. My punch connected, but Louie's head was as solid as a bowling ball.

"Hold him, Louie!" Bullseye yelled.

Louie threw his arms around me and wrestled me against the wall, his beer gut holding me in place. Bullseye Fratino dropped the Nordstrom bag and jumped in to pound at my head with his fists. I caught one of the blows on my right cheek, jerked my head to avoid the second one. Bullseye yelped when his fist scraped the brick wall.

Snake was on his feet and Bullseye quickly recovered from his bruised knuckles. While Louie held me, they pounded on me from both sides until I began to sag. Then Louie stepped back and let me slide down the wall.

"We heard you was a tough ex-soldier, medals and war wounds, the whole deal." Snake was panting, but satisfied with himself. "That's why there's three of us. Guess we didn't need to bring Louie along, you ain't so tough."

"I've been drinking too much beer." I tried to sit up straight and failed. Until this moment I hadn't realized how out-of-shape I'd become. Ten years ago I'd have taken all three of them. Like the physical ed books say, Use it or lose it. "Who sent you, Snake?"

"None of your fucking business. Grab his arms."

Bullseye seized one of my arms, Louie the other.

"You're right handed," Snake said. "I remember you dealt the cards at Sam's place with your right. So you must paint with that hand, too."

For the first time, I felt afraid. "Don't do that, Snake."

"I was told to teach you a lesson, show you how to mind your own business. I thought a light workover would do it, I was wrong. What you need, Kevin, you need a broken hand. Sit on the beach for six months, can't do no painting, you'll know better next time than to ask a bunch of dumbshit questions."

The one called Louie forced my right hand down on the pavement. I squirmed and struggled, but these were guys who knew how to hold a man down.

Snake was all set to stomp on my hand. His foot was raised. A slant of light caught his face and I could see him smile, relishing the moment. My mouth was dry and my heart hammered. After six months on the beach I might never have the nerve to pick up another brush.

The slant of light on Snake's face grew brighter. His entire face was bathed in an eerie green glow. The light grew bigger. Brighter. Greener. It filled the alley. The glow was insidious. From inside the green light came a buzz like that of a big fly circling your head on a lazy summer day. Behind that came the crackle of lightning.

Snake's foot came down, though not on my hand. He backed away from me and the light. His mouth gaped, jaw hung, eyes bulged.

"Hey..." Louie's tough voice had become a raspy croak. "What is it?"

"It ain't nothing." Snake tried to assert himself by drawing a short-barreled revolver from under his jacket. "It's just...you know...a light." He pointed his pistol at the light. His hand began to shake so badly he had to lower the pistol.

"I'm outta here!" Bullseye turned and ran a dozen steps before he discovered the alley came to a dead end. He turned and ran back to us shouting, "You can't get out that way! It's a dead end, we're trapped here, Snake!"

Within a minute the hundreds of shards of light making up the green glow joined together to create a thing that was at first too blurred to be identifiable. A lightning storm occurred within the glow, which soon coalesced into the figure of a man. As I lay there, still feeling too pounded upon to be able to move very much, I could make out the features of my old nemesis Sport Sullivan. Bigger than usual. At least nine feet tall, he filled the alleyway with his jaunty presence.

"Kevin, you look like shit. These guys been beating on you?"

"Sport! I'm almost glad to see you."

"What is that thing?" Snake cried. "Is that a man? Or a...Or a..."

"Course I'm a man! What do I look like, a fucking zebra! I'm just in limbo, that's all." Sport towered over Snake Ritchie. "I'm as much a man as you ever was, sonny. Hadn't been for that bastard Arnold Rothstein, I wouldn't be in limbo. I'd be up in heaven where I belong. With what's-his-name...Saint Peter...all them other saints and angels."

Snake's gun dropped from his hand and he drew back from Sport with a whimper. "Let me outta here. Please."

With a cry of terror, Louie launched himself forward. He tried to run right through Sport Sullivan and down the alley. Instead, he bounced off Sport and fell in a sprawl on his backside.

"It's a goddam ghost!" Bullseye shouted.

"You fucking idiot, I told you already I'm just in limbo. L-I-M-B-O. That's a totally different thing." In his anger, Sport grew another foot higher and wider. His eyes were already redder than I'd ever seen them. Sport was working himself up to something truly terrible. His truculence unsettled me even though I'd seen him in some ugly moods before.

"Settle down, Sport," I said. "He didn't mean anything."

"These punks got big mouths."

Sport glared at Snake, Louie and Bullseye, who were now huddled together, too cowed to do anything except stare at the impossible sight of a ten-foot-high hunk of ectoplasm dressed in a gaudy suit circa 1920.

"You three wouldn't last ten minutes against Arnold Rothstein," Sport snarled. "He's the guy had me bumped off. Big time gambler, Arnold was. Arnold and me, we fixed the 1919 World Series. You guys heard about that, didn't you?"

"Let us go," Snake croaked.

"What, let you run off? After you beat up my good buddy Kevin? Naw, I don't think so. You saps seen this one?"

Sport put his thumb in his mouth and began blowing as if it were a balloon. Incredibly, his crackling green form began to expand. With every breath he blew into his thumb, he increased his height by about a foot and his width by several inches. Ten breaths later, Sport was ten feet taller. His head rose above the alley's roofline. Another several hearty blows into his thumb and he became a giant. Something out of Macy's Thanksgiving parade. My own mouth was agape. I was as rooted as the others.

When he finally stopped, Sport stood at least twenty-five feet in height. His face, long and especially cadaverous in moonlight, beamed with wicked pleasure. He leaned down and put that huge, grotesque countenance just a few inches from the faces of Snake, Louie, and Bullseye.

"Boo!"

Bullseye seized his chest with one hand, gasped for air, keeled over. His legs jerked spasmodically before he went limp. Snake bawled like a baby. Louie put his hands together and began to pray. Evidently Louie had received religious instruction as a boy because Latin phrases came pouring from his mouth.

Abruptly, Sport began to deflate. In a matter of seconds he managed to shrink down to about six feet in height. He remained scary, but without the imposing height no longer looked deadly. Snake and Louie seized the moment to leap to their feet and run past Sport, down the alley, out into the street.

Sport threw back his head and laughed. "We won't see those assholes again."

I crawled over to Bullseye Fratino and felt for a pulse. "This man's dead, Sport."

"No shit?"

"Looks like a heart attack. You scared the poor guy to death."

Sport's smile twisted with satisfaction. "Didn't know I could kill someone while I'm, y'know, floating around out here. That's something, ain't it? Frighten a guy to death?" When he laughed, his glow grew brighter. "I appreciate the call, Kevin. Gave me a chance to try something new. The way I blew into my thumb to get bigger, that was new for me too."

"I didn't call for you."

"Sure you did. Think it was just a coincidence, me popping up while those three bums was using you for a punching bag? You send out signals, Kevin. How long's it been since the last time we seen each other?"

"Couple of months."

"They find that kid? The one you asked me about last time?"

"Yes, they found her in the Mission District, just where you said she'd be. She wasn't hurt."

Sport preened himself. "Well ain't I the slick one? Last time I saved a little girl's life and tonight I kept your sorry ass in one piece. Don't I get a thank you?"

"Thank you."

"You piss me off, Kevin. No matter what I do, it ain't enough. You and Arnold, you're two peas in a fucking pod. Ungrateful bastards, the both of you." Sport began to shrink again. He went from six feet tall down to about the size of a bottle of Coke. "I got a feeling we're gonna see a lot of each other, whether you like it or not. You better work on your attitude or I might not be here the next time you need me."

"I didn't call for you this time, Sport. No matter what you think."

"Little gratitude, that's all I ask." There was a sound like a champagne cork popping and Sport Sullivan disappeared.

I lay there looking at the spot where Sport had been and thinking I might be, as they say in the army, as crazy as a shithouse rat. The entire incident might have been a wild hallucination if it weren't for the dead body of Bullseye Fratino lying faceup in the alley.

I couldn't afford to sit around in a dirty alley with a dead body for very long. I had get myself out of here. Wouldn't be easy to do. My left leg wasn't working, the kneecap felt like a pile of rusty hubcaps. My ribs were clanking around something awful. Bullseye and Snake were good at their work, such as it was.

I saw what looked like a cellular phone hanging out of Bullseye's jacket pocket. Did even head-busting thugs use cell phones to do their business these days? Another triumph for technology. I wondered if Bullseye received calls on the Muni bus that sent him off to beat up people like me. If so, what would the folks sitting near him on the bus think about those conversations? I worked the cell phone out of his pocket and held it up to what little light existed in the alley. Too many buttons, too little light. I punched the buttons with the precision of a drunk, which resulted in a brief conversation with a teenage girl in Pacific Heights baby sitting for a neighbor. She said I sounded cute and invited me over. I hit a button that ended the conversation and tried again. The second time I reached Sam Cody at his apartment.

"Sam…it's me."

"Mister Whitebread? You don't sound good, what's goin' on?"

"I'm lying in an alley next to a dead man and I can't seem to use my legs.".

"In an alley? Next to a dead man? Shit-the-bed, you must be on a cell phone."

"Yeah. And the dead man's eyes are open. He's your old pal…"

"Don't say the name! Don't say my name, either. You're a technological idiot, you know that? Somebody might listen in, cell phones got no security at all. Tell me where you are, I'll come get you. Keep it short."

I gave him Cynthia's address and described the nearby alley.

"I read you. Hang on, Mister Whitebread. I'm just a few blocks away."

I turned off the cell phone and started to shove it back into Bullseye's pocket, then realized my fingerprints would now be all over the thing. Bullseye's death was natural. Sort of. But I didn't care to explain what I'd been doing with him in a dark alley on the night of his death. I put the phone in my own pocket and tried to stand up, just in case my directions had been too shaky for Sam to find me.

Getting to my feet took a hell of a long time. I stood still for quite a while, using the brick wall for support. I was dizzy. The left leg still gave me a ton of pain. None of the blows that had rained down on my head and ribs seemed to have done any serious damage, but the leg was a disaster.

While I was still testing my leg, a car turned into the alley and its headlights picked me up. The car stopped twenty yards away and Sam came running toward me. "Kevin? Don't move, man. Just lean on the wall."

Sam was wearing a dark suit and black turtleneck sweater. He stopped to grab my arm, steady me, observe my injuries. "You don't look so bad. Tryin' to scare me, that's what you were up to."

He turned from me and knelt beside the still form a few feet away. "Whoa! This here is Bullseye Fratino. Remember Bullseye? We played poker together?"

"Indeed I do."

"What the hell's he doing here? How'd he get dead? You been up to your old army ways?"

"I'm not sure how he got here. Izzy Valentine sent me here with a key to an apartment around the corner. Can't be a coincidence that Bullseye and Snake Ritchie and another guy they called Louie showed up at the apartment house that Izzy pointed me at."

"You been busy since lunch. Come on, we'd better get out of here before anybody else shows up. I don't trust cell phones."

Sam put an arm around my waist and helped me to his car. Which was, of course, his Rolls Royce. "You drove a Rolls here when you knew I was in an alley with a dead man?"

"I can't afford to be seen in a Chevy or Ford, I got my reputation to think about."

I didn't remind him that his reputation consisted of multiple arrests for grand theft auto. That would have been churlish of me considering the circumstances.

"Sam, grab that Nordstrom bag."

He threw the bag into the back seat and we got out of there fast.

An hour later I was deeply immersed in hot water that bubbled and churned through Sam's black marble whirlpool tub. My leg was coming around and my other aches and pains were fading, too. There were bruises on my ribcage and back, a cut under my left eye, black and blue marks on my leg. Nothing broken. I couldn't completely credit the whirlpool for my quick recovery. My second cold Carta Blanca, sitting on the edge of the tub, had been therapeutic too. Though I've never heard beer referred to as a "miracle healer," that seems to me a rich field for medical research.

Depression nagged at me as I took frequent sips from the beer. Those three thugs had handled me much too easily. I can't say I was ever a badass in Sam Cody's league. But in my army days, which weren't that far in the past, I would have done a lot of damage to those three cut-rate thugs. I was drinking more of the golden brew than was probably good for me and that had to stop.

Soon.

But not tonight.

Sam's bathroom was done completely in black marble with stacks of bright yellow towels on a rack within arm's reach. From my comfortable position in the whirlpool bath, I could see through the open bathroom door and across Sam's loft all the way to the corner that housed his office. Sam sat hunched over his computer. On the desk next to him was Bullseye Fratino's cell phone. He was trying to tap into the phone company's computer to find out what numbers Bullseye had been calling and taking calls from.

Good luck to him. All I wanted was to get back to my easel. I'd made a mistake becoming involved in the business dealings of Race Software and people like Izzy Valentine.

Time to pull back and focus on my own work.

The doorbell at the street level rang, and Sam left the computer to go down and answer it. He returned with Dorothy Lake.

"Kevin!" Dorothy came rushing into the bathroom. "You look awful!"

"What are you doing here?"

"Sam called me at the office, I was working late. He said you'd been beaten up, you were in trouble, and that you'd found where Cynthia Gooding lived and reclaimed some of the company's documents."

Thanks to the whirlpool's churning water, Dorothy could see my injuries only from the chest up. I was about to object to her reckless invasion of my privacy when she began caressing my cheek and even running her hand tenderly over the welt on my rib cage where Bullseye had punched me once or twice. "What happened to you?"

"Three professional head-breakers dragged me into an alley and worked me over."

Dorothy sank to her knees next to the tub and began to gently probe and massage the worst of my bruises. "You poor guy, they really did hurt you."

Her hands were working miracles. "Can you do that a little lower? Down here under the waterline?"

She slapped the back of my head with a sudsy hand. "Now you're just being a pig."

"No…honestly…the pain down there is worse than anything you can imagine."

"Kevin, that's the dumbest line I've heard from you yet." She stood, dried her arms on one of the bright yellow towels and tossed it aside. "I'm going to look at the printouts you brought from Cynthia's apartment. Come out when you're ready."

I sulked in my tub, finished the Carta Blanca, started on another one. Sam called out to me: "Kevin! You're turnin' yourself into a prune. Dry off and get out here, I got some hot G-2 for you."

"I don't want any *hot G-2*. I'd rather have a fresh beer."

"You finished that last one already? Come on, soldier. Move your butt."

"I'm no longer a soldier. I'm an artist of considerable reputation who deserves greater respect from the auto theft community."

"You're an artist with interesting enemies, is what you are."

"I have no enemies. I'm beloved by everyone who knows me."

"You don't get no more beer when you start talkin' like Saint Francis."

"There is a resemblance. Animals flock to me. The birds alight on my shoulders. The small creatures of the forest gather at my feet."

"He always runs on that way after his third beer," Sam confided to Dorothy.

"I'm in complete control of myself." To prove the point I got out of the bath, dried myself, dressed in a pair of slacks and shirt Sam had loaned me, and went out into Sam's loft. "Where's the beer?"

"You shouldn't have any more," Dorothy said. "You've been beaten. You're obviously exhausted. Sam says he fed you a whole handful of aspirin before you started drinking. I read an article in the *Northeastern Medical Review* that showed an overdose of analgesic acid combined with just two ounces of alcohol can dangerously increase your heart rate. The data looked solid."

"Uh-huh. Well, I read an article in *The Alcoholic's Home Companion* that a fourth Carta Blanca taken internally could be instrumental in purging the human body of all pompous attitudes. That data looked solid, too."

When Sam chuckled, Dorothy said, "Don't encourage him."

"He don't need encouragement. Dorothy, I'm still tryin' to hack into the phone company data base to find out who Bullseye's been talkin' with on his cell phone. Can you help me out here?"

She put down the Race printout with a fidgety move. "We could all go to jail for hacking into the phone company's system." She riffled a thumb through the printout from the Nordstrom bag. "On the other hand, the material Kevin took out of Cynthia's old apartment is primary code for the Redleaf system. The code's gone through a lot of revision since the version you've got here. Still, it convinces me Cynthia came to work for us in order to steal the Redleaf code. She had no legitimate reason to have it hidden away in her apartment."

"We need to make the connections," Sam said. "I say Izzy Valentine's behind all of it. Guy's got his hand in all kinds of deals. He used this Cynthia to get hold of the code for your new product, just like he's been usin' Bullseye and Snake to pressure me into sellin' out to him."

"Hard to prove," Dorothy sighed.

"I'm not lookin' to put Izzy in jail." Sam stretched his legs and smiled in my direction. "Wouldn't mind sendin' him along to see his old pal Bullseye, though."

"We've got enough trouble, we don't need more." Having contributed something sensible to the discussion, I promptly fell asleep.

I was awakened some time later to hear Sam saying: "…son of a bitch hasn't made an honest dime since Lassie was a pup. Wanted my business and now he wants a piece of yours, too. He'll get what he wants, somebody don't stomp on him first."

"We haven't proved anything, Sam. All we have are suspicions and tenuous connections."

"What's going on?" I yawned. "Something's going on, I can tell."

Sam swung around to me. "Dorothy thinks she can scare Izzy with lawyers, the same Izzy Valentine who's rumored to have already planted one lawyer in a rubbish dump outside Buffalo. I got to hand it to Dorothy though." He gave her a respectful bow. "She sneaked into the phone company's data base, called up Bullseye Fratino's billing record. Sure enough, Bullseye received a call about eight-thirty tonight from a number that turned out to be Izzy Valentine's house."

"That call would have been placed very soon after I left Izzy's party." I came partially awake. "Izzy gave me the key to Cynthia Gooding's apartment, figured I'd go straight there. Which I did. And he had his goons waiting to work me over."

"After our lunch, I talked to Bobby about Izzy Valentine." Dorothy was sipping at another of Sam's special raspberry iced tea. "It seems Mr. Valentine had been borrowing money to buy up large blocks of stock in Race Software. Bobby says this man wants a seat on our board of directors. But we don't yet have much information. We have to turn this over to the lawyers. *Investigate. Litigate. Negotiate.* That's what Bobby always says."

"Kevin tried the investigating part," Sam pointed out. "Look what happened."

"What did happen?" Dorothy looked from me to Sam and back again.

"You haven't told me much."

"Not much to tell," I said.

"I don't believe you." When I wouldn't say more, she tossed her hair. Beautifully. "At least we know there's nothing supernatural about this. I mean, Race Software isn't really *haunted*. What we're dealing with is simple industrial espionage and, possibly, extortion."

"Don't be so quick to write off things you don't understand," I said. "You people who are *scientifically grounded*, as you like to call yourselves, don't know much. This little planet is just a speck and each of us is a sub-speck. Sub-specks are ignorant by nature, and you're being stupid when you don't realize that. There are things that go bump in the night, Dorothy. Some of them come from a place none of us ever sees."

"Thank you very much for that insight," Dorothy replied coolly.

I hadn't meant to bite her head off. I was weary and cranky and sick of being taunted for knowing from experience that there is indeed a spirit world. So I went ahead and told Dorothy everything, including my history of arguments and infighting with the boastful spirit of Sport Sullivan. I described Sport in detail, from his snappy 1920 suit to the spats that covered his button shoes to his claim to having helped Arnold Rothstein fix the 1919 World Series.

Of course, Dorothy didn't believe a word of it. She stared at me first with amusement. Then with worry. Followed by astonishment. Finally with sympathy.

"Kevin," she said when I was done. "Please don't take offense, but you were hit several times on the head tonight, you told us so and I can see that much is true, and you may have a concussion. I shouldn't have let you doze off, that's one of the signs of a head injury. Let's go to the nearest emergency room. They'll give you a Catscan and we'll know for sure whether your injuries are serious."

"Dorothy, try to believe him," Sam said. "I saw this Sport Sullivan for myself in the sickbay on board the Carl Vinson. Sport is a fuckin' ghost. I didn't want to believe it either, not at the time. Kevin's description is accurate right down to Sport's mother-of-pearl cufflinks. Sport *materialized* right in front of me. He talked. Bragged. Bitched. Walked around. Told tall tales. Then he *dematerialized*. I'm not bullshittin' you. There are ghosts. One ghost anyway."

She delicately arched an eyebrow. "Has anybody seen this Sport Sullivan besides, pardon my descriptions of you two, an emotionally unstable artist and a career car thief?"

"Yes," I answered. "Snake Ritchie and his pal Louie saw Sport Sullivan tonight. So did Bullseye Fratino. That's why Bullseye's dead. Sport frightened him to death."

Dorothy rolled her eyes. "Three more of society's outcasts heard from. Hardly a persuasive case. I don't know what drunken party Sport Sullivan first emerged from, but it must have been magnificent. I'm almost sorry I missed it. I must admit to being mistaken about one thing. Nobody here needs the emergency room. What you both need is long-term psychiatric care." She looked at her watch. "I'm going home."

Chapter 10

I came awake a few minutes after nine a.m. still in Big Sam's comfortable leather chair. He had kindly thrown a black terrycloth robe over me. I felt pretty good.

"Hot shower'll fix you right up. Razor, shaving cream, toothbrush set out for you in the bathroom." Sam came from his bedroom slipping on a gray gabardine jacket over a darker gray silk shirt. He also wore charcoal slacks and Bally loafers. "Coffee on the stove. Juice in the fridge. I have to go out." He winked. "Pick up a couple of fine automobiles I've had my eye on. Oh yeah, I found that comical old junker of yours where you parked it last night, bottom of Russian Hill. Put it in my lot next door, key's in the ignition. Please get it outta there soon's you can, okay? No offense, but it lowers the tone of my business. I mean, your ugly old Ghia's parked right between a Rolls and a Mercedes. What'll people think?"

"When did Dorothy leave?"

"Two a.m. or thereabouts. Don't you remember? You told her all about Sport Sullivan? She laughed in your face? Mine too, when I backed up your story?"

It came back to me. "Yeah, I remember."

"Don't ever again ask me to say I've seen your personal ghost. When I told Dorothy, I sounded crazy even to myself."

"But you have seen him!"

Sam raised both hands. "That time on the Carl Vinson must have been combat fatigue. Or temporary insanity. Give it whatever name you want, I'm all right now. Don't look at me that way, Mister

Whitebread. We could get ourselves committed, we talk to the wrong person about seeing a ghost named Sport Sullivan. And Dorothy might be the wrong person."

"Dorothy's okay."

"Thinks we're crazy .Might tell other people."

"She'll come around. Dorothy loves the truth."

"Truth? Uh-uh. That girl loves facts, which is a whole different territory from the truth. I never met anyone who's read so many articles, monographs, white papers, shit like that. Dorothy's got a hard head, Kevin. Beautiful head. Smart head. But goddam hard. Facts facts facts, that's her mantra. Like my mantra is cars cars cars. You'll never convince her Sport exists. I'm not convinced myself, and I've seen Sport's big green face up close. Except I deny that really happened, like I said it was just combat fatigue."

"The essence of Cynthia Gooding is still on this earth and she's putting in appearances at Bobby Race's corporate headquarters. Dorothy's in denial, still looking for *logical answers*. Sooner or later she'll have to accept what's going on there. When she does, the idea of Sport Sullivan won't sound so crazy to her."

"Find another girl," Sam advised. "Plenty around."

"No others quite as lovely as Dorothy."

"Like Dorothy's gonna let you take her away from her big job and six-figure salary, move into a termite-infested beach house. She's too smart to hook up with a down-at-the-heels artist can barely pay for his beers."

"Things have changed for me. By now my termites have been sent to termite hell and at the moment I have ten cases of Carta Blanca in my pantry." I paused to let that impressive number sink in. "Ten cases."

"You know you've got yourself a real problem with beer?" Sam picked up a pair of leather driving gloves and rang for his private elevator.

"I'm working on that."

"Glad to hear it. My liquor bill's been up in the stratosphere since you started your love affair with Carta Blanca."

The elevator came and Sam went off to steal a luxury car.

Limping my way along the corridor to Bobby Race's office, I was stopped by several people who said I looked pretty well despite my "car accident." Said they hoped my injuries would heal fast. I muttered thanks for their concern and limped on, wondering where they'd gotten the idea I'd been a four-car pileup on Route 280 the night before.

Dorothy caught me in the hallway and pulled me into her office where she told me she'd spread the accident tale. "I didn't want you putting out the real story about where you got those bruises. You look better than I expected. I thought you wouldn't sleep well in that chair, but neither Sam nor I could get you out of it." She half giggled. "I should have known you'd be okay, you were snoring up a storm when I left."

"I never snore, I'm too refined."

This was my first visit to Dorothy's office and I took the opportunity to look it over for clues to her personality, and whatever else I could learn about her. The office was big enough so anyone could tell Dorothy was a senior executive. But that's all the office said about her. There were no family photos on any of the shelves. No cartoons taped to the wall. No university diploma up there either. No personal memorabilia of any kind in sight. Stacks of computer printouts, of course. Lots of disks. Heavy technical volumes on the bookshelves, the kind that would put me to sleep in about three minutes. Everything from pencils to books were squared up perfectly. One piece of art on the wall, a poster of a computer called an LYZ-something-or-other made by one of those acronym companies. Art's the wrong word, of course. My opinion, only reason to put up a picture of a computer is to cover a hole in the wall.

"Nice office," I lied.

Dorothy looked around proudly. "I put in lots of hours and plenty of hard work to get it." She appeared embarrassed by that simple admission. "If you knew what this office has cost me…" She closed down the subject with an echo of bitterness that probably had been under careful control for many years. "So the leg's okay?"

"It only hurts when I pole vault."

A great sigh arose from that slight body. "Why do you have to joke about everything?"

"I never joke about my work. I take my profession as seriously as you take yours."

"I hope your sense of humor makes it through the day."

"What does that mean?"

"Nothing in particular."

"You're trying to tell me something."

"Kevin, whatever you hear today, I want you to know it wasn't my idea, my decision. Try to remember you're working within a corporation. Lots of people are involved, not just you and Bobby. Big money on the line. Don't lose your temper, okay? Just stay calm and listen. You might even learn something."

"I don't have a clue to what you're talking about, Dorothy. If, during the course of the day, I do get a clue, I'll take your advice. Try to stay calm and learn something."

"Good." Pity in her eyes. "That's all I ask." She glanced at her watch and stood up. "I'm late for a meeting with Bobby. See you later."

She scooted out and I followed slowly, more upset by her veiled warning than I cared to admit.

I've noticed that working in a corporation tends to make people paranoid. Everyone I know who works in what they call *the corporate environment,* or sometimes *the private sector,* sooner or later develops a wide streak of paranoia. They think their bosses are spying on their private lives. Or a competitor has their phones bugged. Or the HR manager is keeping a desk file on their little faults and failures. Or somebody in the mail room is reading their private memos. Quite often they think someone's after their jobs. To give those people their due, they're often right about that one. Someone said even paranoids have real enemies. So when I left Dorothy's office, I tried to avoid letting her weirdly circumspect warning inflame my occasional tendency to see trouble around every corner.

On the way to Bobby's office I ran into Pepper Johnson, the one-handed black maintenance man who'd helped me drag Joe Patterson out of the red mist. He was having difficulty holding the new thermostat against the wall with the hook while he screwed it in place with the screwdriver in his good hand.

"Can I help?" I took hold of the thermostat and held it to the wall for him.

"Thank ya."

Though the man had only the one good arm, it was a hell of an arm. Long, heavily corded with muscle, black as anthracite, biceps that bulged like melons and scarred in three places besides. One I judged to be a knife scar. The other two were bullet wounds, I'd seen plenty of those. I watched in fascination as he used the powerful arm to screw the stat to the wall. He hit a stud but that didn't stop him, his thick wrist had plenty of torque.

"That does it." Pepper stepped back and slid the screwdriver into a slot on his workbelt. "How's the artist today?"

"Artist-in-residence," I said.

Pepper laughed at my joke, not riotously. "Thanks for the help. Can I buy ya coffee, Kevin? Break room's straight down the hall."

"Sure."

We went into the break room and took a table by the window. Pepper Johnson was about a head shorter than me, but when we sat across from each other at one of the tables he gave the impression of being bigger. Pepper was probably in his late fifties, maybe even his sixties, so I took a wild guess based on the bullet wounds and the familiar watchfulness in his eyes.

"I've got a feeling you were in Vietnam."

"Ya got that right. I hear on the grapevine you done some soldiering yourself."

"People here know I was in the army?"

"You're a good looking young guy, all the girls are talking about ya. They know ya was a decorated soldier. That you're single. Not gay. Live down by the beach. Girls even know your brand of beer. You're a Carta Blanca man, right?"

"Si, senor."

"And ya wear boxer shorts. Blue boxer shorts."

"How'd they find that out?" Paranoia began to feel almost natural in this place. "I don't think I've had my pants off in this building, I'm sure I'd remember if I did."

"I'll share a secret, and ya better keep it to yourself. In the sixth floor mens room, the secretaries from the word processing center got a hole in the wall right near the urinals. It goes through from the womens room. They like to peek at all the guys' dicks, do their comparison shopping. Yesterday morning, when ya used the men's room on the sixth floor, a couple of the girls gave ya a pecker check. They saw your blue boxers and a lot more besides."

I admit to gaping like a shocked teenager.

Pepper added enough sugar to his coffee to revive the Cuban economy. "The girls liked the looks of your dick, I can tell ya that. Play your cards right, ya could make out real good around here."

"And all these years I thought corporations were dull. How do you know I won't rat out those girls?"

"I can't see an artist, a guy who rumor say lives on Carta Blanca, ratting out some girls cause they're having a little harmless fun." He added a guy-to-guy wink. "Specially when those same girls gave your goods a four-star review."

"I suppose I should be flattered." A couple of seconds floated by. "Now that I think about it, I am flattered. How'd you find out about the spyhole?"

"The girls took up a collection, paid me a hundred bucks to drill the hole."

"Does it work both ways? Would someone be able to see into the womens room?"

"On their side they got the hole stuffed with toilet paper. They only take the toilet paper out when they want to do their dick shopping."

"Clever girls. You're a valuable guy, Pepper. And I still owe you a thanks for helping me pull Joe Patterson out that red thing yesterday."

"Joe hasn't been at Race very long, but from day one he treated me like I was a rich white guy with two good hands."

"Can I ask why you chose a hook for a left hand instead of one of those prosthetic devices."

"Only prosthetic hand I was offered was white, so I opted for the hook."

"That had to be two or three decades ago, they must be making them in basic black by now."

Pepper looked at the hook as if it were an old and valued friend. "Yeah, they do. But now I'm used to the hook. It's got some advantages, ya know. Like, I don't have to stand in many lines. People look at the hook, my size, by ugly black face, I get ushered right to the front."

"I wonder if Joe Patterson will need a new hand." I remembered my first meeting with Joe, his sarcastic and dismissive attitude toward me. "I like Joe, too. Though I didn't feel that way the first time I met him. He gave me such a hard time I wanted to punch him out. He was still a police lieutenant then, so I didn't."

"Guy can be a pisser when you get on his wrong side," Pepper agreed.

"I'm going over to the hospital later to see Joe. Want to come along?"

"Sure."

"Two o'clock?"

"Meet you in the lobby."

As we left the coffee room, Greg Tillotson, the director of the Redleaf program, came out of his office with a sweaty, red-faced scowl. "Pepper? Where the hell have you been? You were supposed to fix the air-conditioning in my office this morning. I can't work in all this heat!" He noticed me and said, "Oh…hello, Pierce…you feeling okay after that car wreck?" Without waiting for an answer, he switched his focus back to Pepper Johnson. "Look here, Pepper. If you can't fix a simple air-conditioning problem, I suggest you find a different line of work."

"Thermostat here in the hallway controls your office, Greg. It went dead, so I just put in a new one. The temp in your space oughtta be just right in ten, maybe fifteen minutes."

"Took you long enough to find the problem," Tillotson grumbled. "A little advice, you could spend less time in the coffee room. Beats the hell out of me why Bobby likes you so much. If I were running this place, you'd be out of here."

Pepper replied with an equanimity I could never have matched, "Then I guess I'm lucky ya ain't running this place."

Tillotson's face went a deeply unflattering shade of red. "Don't give me any of your famous backtalk. You're just a goddamn janitor, Pepper. Don't forget that or you will definitely be looking for a new job."

"I'm not a janitor, Greg. I'm a building maintenance technician."

Pepper's calm dignity seemed to inflame Tillotson. "Just do your job!"

"I pledge to do my best…Greg…sir."

Tillotson, at a loss for a snappy reply, turned on his heel and went back into his office. The door slammed behind him.

Jerking his thumb towards Tillotson's office, Pepper said, "The girls checked out his equipment, too. They weren't impressed. Usually Greg's okay, he's just stressed out these days 'cause of all the problems with Redleaf."

"Do you make a habit of butting heads with high level execs? And calling them by their first names?"

"When the mood comes on me."

"Then you must be independently wealthy."

"I was the first maintenance man Bobby hired when his whole operation was in a dumpy old building on El Camino Real. I held that place together with spit and bailing wire till the company started making real money and Bobby could buy a good piece of property and build a real headquarters. Me and Bobby, we get along. Sometimes, end of the day, Bobby calls me on my pager, asks me to come up and talk baseball with him. Guys like Greg think a maintenance man got no business hobnobbing with the CEO."

"Tillotson doesn't appreciate artists, either."

Pepper cocked an eyebrow. "Ya know what a nanosecond is? Or a gigabyte?"

"Gigabyte? Sounds like something you put in your toilet tank to keep the water clean."

"How it works around here, the executives think folks who don't talk nanoseconds and gigabytes are morons."

"I had a nanosecond once, but I lost it at the movies."

"Gotta take your nanoseconds seriously. Real important around here, how many nanoseconds it takes to do this, how many nanoseconds to do that. Means money to Race Software."

"I'll try to keep that in mind." I snapped my fingers. "Oops, there it went. Lost the thought in just over a nanosecond."

"I gotta hunch," Pepper said, "you're gonna be outta here before the paint dries on that portrait you're doing."

"I sincerely hope so." I clapped Pepper on the shoulder. "Two o'clock in the lobby."

At the threshold to Bobby's office I encountered Jenny, who today was dressed in the tightest tee-shirt yet and pink shorts that almost gave up her deepest secrets.

"Kevin! Look at you!" She began stroking the bruised areas of my face. "You need aloe!" Jenny took me to her desk and began dabbing my face with a sweet-smelling cream. Her hands were soft and she smelled like a spring day. Not that she used perfume. Jenny was too environmentally conscious to spray herself with a chemical concoction. She just naturally smelled like a spring day. Her hair shimmered and her clean-cut face glowed.

"I'll bet you have other bruises too." Jenny peeked down my shirt. "My, you have great pecs."

"Pecs?"

"Pectorals…chest muscles. You must work out every day."

"I never work out." Seeing her disappointment, I hastily added, "For religious reasons."

"Oh, I hope I didn't offend you."

"Jenny Hartsong, there is nothing you could do that would offend me. Especially when you're wearing that t-shirt and those shorts."

"Are you flirting with me, Kevin?"

"I certainly am."

"Hmm, that's promising. I thought you only had eyes for that stuck up Dorothy Lake."

"I do like Dorothy."

"All the guys do," Jenny groused. "Those slim hips, I suppose."

"Nothing wrong with your hips."

"Except they're not attached to a girl who brings home four hundred thousand a year."

"Dorothy makes that much? I may ask her to marry me."

"You didn't hear it from me." Jenny leaned close to my ear. "And that doesn't include her stock options. The girl is rolling in money." She straightened up. "Why am I building up my competition?"

"You have no competition. You're the most beautiful girl at Race Software. There are a lot of them, my head's been spinning ever since I

got here. You're head and shoulders above all of them. I was just thinking that you always smell like a spring day. How do you do that?"

"Dove soap." Jenny's eyes glinted. "You're wonderful at flattery. I like
that in a man." She sighed. "To be continued later. Bobby's been asking
for you all morning, so you'd best get in there."

They took other things besides nanoseconds seriously at Race
Software. Bobby was huddled in his lavish office with Dorothy and
Hugh Wilson, the thin and edgy corporate counsel who'd huffed and
puffed on his office treadmill yesterday while explaining my employment contract to me.

Bobby floored me by coming around his desk, grabbing my right
hand and shaking it heartily. "Kevin, that was great work last night. I'm
sorry you got beat up. I'll make it up to you, that's a promise."

"I'm impressed," Hugh Wilson conceded. "You unearthed a major
leak in the Redleaf program."

"The material you found last night came off the hard drive of my
own computer." Bobby's face flushed with the admission. "Just between
the four of us, I did have a close personal relationship with Cynthia. She
took advantage of her access to my office to copy Redleaf code off my
drive. I let her come and go here late at night, my mistake. Fortunately,
the code you found last night has been rewritten several times over."

"Cynthia had to be working with someone," Dorothy said. "She didn't
have the expertise to make use of such complicated code herself. The
question is, who is that person? And is that person still around? Still
stealing Redleaf code? Maybe with the help of some other employee?"

"Those are four questions," Hugh Wilson, ever the lawyer, pointed out.

"What we need is someone with Joe Patterson's expertise," Bobby
declared. "Unfortunately, Joe's going to be out of the loop for quite a
while. I went by the med center about six a.m. The doctors thought
they'd have to amputate two fingers on his left hand, they ended up taking three."

We all winced.

After a few bleak moments, Hugh unpursed his thin lips and said, "There's a private investigation firm in Palo Alto that specializes in tracking down hackers who steal intellectual assets. I could hire them to see what else they can find out about Cynthia and to audit our current security procedures."

"Good." Bobby made a tent with his fingers. "I expect each of you to keep my involvement with Cynthia confidential."

Hugh nodded vigorously. "Of course, Bobby."

"Yes, Bobby," Dorothy added.

"You're a little late in closing that barn door," I said. "Everybody around here knows you were having it on with Cynthia."

You could flash freeze vegetables with the chill that descended on the office.

"I'm sorry…it's just…the first day I was here several people told me about you and Cynthia. Seems useless to…" I searched for words that might warm up the atmosphere when I caught Dorothy's low-key signal to shut up. I tried to wiggle out with a promise. "You can count on me to be discreet."

"I doubt you know the meaning of the word."

Bobby's icy comment closed the meeting. Hugh and Dorothy flew from the office like a brace of pheasants. That left me exactly where I didn't want to be, alone with Bobby Race.

"If you hadn't gotten yourself beaten up last night protecting the interests of this company, I'd be tempted to make you pay very dearly for embarrassing me the way you just did."

Bobby's voice had gone deceptively mild. I was getting to know him. When he lowered his voice into that particular tone, he was really pissed.

"I apologize."

"Don't apologize. Just don't embarrass me like that again."

"Deal."

Bobby picked up a copy of the San Francisco *Chronicle* from his credenza. "The Dodgers are playing the Giants tonight. Who do you like?"

"With that new kid Connelly pitching for the Giants? I like San Francisco, of course."

"Connelly's ERA is pretty good." Bobby gave me his trademark grin. "I'm a Giants fan too, but I'll bet you five k the Dodgers take the Giants tonight."

"Five k? Like in five thousand dollars? Where am I doing to get that kind of money?"

"If you lose, I'll deduct it from your fee. If you win, I'll pay you cash. I generally carry about ten k in cash. In hundred dollar bills. You know why? I don't want anyone finding out from credit cards companies how I spend my money."

It wasn't hard to see what this was all about. I'd embarrassed the great Bobby Race and he was determined to embarrass me right back. If I lost, I wouldn't have the resources to pay him in cash. If I won, he could belittle me by peeling off hundred dollar bills from a monstrous wad.

Only one thing to say: "Bobby, you've got yourself a bet."

CHAPTER 11

The great thing about doing work you like is that it totally absorbs you. That's the one thing Bobby Race and I had in common, we both loved our work. I think that's why Bobby's hero was Pete Rose, who may never make the Baseball Hall of Fame even though he slammed more hits than any other player in the history of the game. When Pete Rose stepped on the field, he never for one second took his mind off the game. A thousand percent is what he gave. Every minute of every game. I can't say I'm at the top of my profession, the way Pete Rose reached the pinnacle of his. My achievements aren't in Bobby's league, either. But like those two guys, every errant thought does flee my mind when I'm at my work.

I worked at my easel for maybe three hours without pause. Now and then I was vaguely aware of Bobby talking on his phone or snapping orders at some poor soul. People came and went from meetings with him. He pounded away at the keyboard of his computer. None of that touched my mind. I was absorbed with the image I was trying to build of Bobby Race.

If you want a straightforward image of a person, take a photograph. A portrait is a unique opportunity to peel away the outer layers and get at the core. The more complicated the person is, the tougher it becomes to reach the core.

Bobby was like a typhoid carrier, except that what he carried was intelligence. A great many people who came in close contact with him seemed to become infected with his own need to excel.

That's what I was trying to capture. The image of a brilliant, petulant little boy who suddenly finds himself crowned as a king and somehow has the smarts to really be a king.

I felt I was getting into that when Jenny came bustling in with Pepper Johnson and another maintenance guy.

"Sorry to bother you, Kevin. It's time to move your easel into the conference room for the meeting."

"What meeting?"

"The one o'clock executive conference." Jenny was puzzled. "You must have read the memo, I taped it to the front of your canvas where you'd be sure to see it."

"That was a memo?" I had vaguely noticed a piece of paper taped to the canvas. "I think I used it to clean some lint off my brush."

"Oh Kevin, I do love you. You're so out of place." She pinched my cheek, then turned to the workmen. "Move the easel and canvas to the east end of the conference room. Please take care. This portrait of Bobby is very important to the company."

"I don't understand." I looked around for Bobby, but he'd left the office. "What's the meeting got to do with me? Why do you need the painting?"

"Kevin, the meeting is *about* your painting. Bobby wants his executive committee to look over what you've done so far." Jenny used her considerable kinetic energy to hector Pepper and the other maintenance guy into moving faster.

"Sorry about this," Pepper muttered.

"A meeting? About the painting? It isn't even close to being finished, so what's there to discuss?"

"Poor Kevin." Jenny seemed wistful about my inability to understand the purpose of the meeting. "All will be revealed in about..." she consulted her watch. "...two minutes. Let's go, guys. Chop chop. Meeting's about to begin."

I trailed along with a growing sense of dread as my easel was moved into the adjoining conference room. Pepper and his pal relocated the easel and canvas to a position near the head of the table. Jenny quickly put out yellow legal pads and freshly sharpened pencils at each place around the table. The doors at each end of the room opened and men and women began coming in and filling up the chairs. Most didn't bother to look at the painting, they were busy discussing weightier business subjects. A few had brought battery-powered laptops and were tapping away at the keyboards.

"Sit here, Kevin." Jenny patted the backrest of a chair near the head of the table. "I reserved this seat for you."

Most of the faces were new. I did recognize a few people. Greg Tillotson, the Redleaf program director, owl-like in his oversized glasses, looking as impatient and out of sorts as usual. Pam Solter up from the personnel section; she winked at me good naturedly. Hugh Wilson again, ever the lean-mean lawyer, reviewing a thick stack of contracts while waiting for the meeting to start. A moment later Dorothy slipped in and took a seat at the other end of the table.

A guy wearing a shirt with a polo player on the pocket plopped down next to me and offered his hand. "Ray Waters, director of communications. Nice to meet you, Kevin. Heard great things about your work."

"Thanks." Ray Waters' unlined face was decorated with a salesman's smile. His excessively jovial manner made me pat my hip pocket to make sure my wallet was still there.

"Yessir, this portrait of Bobby is going to be a valuable component of our branding program."

"Branding program? What's that?"

"Our company's brand. Bobby Race is the brand. The brand is Bobby. What you're really doing, Kevin, whether you realize it or not, is helping to build our brand equity. See what I mean?"

I felt like Dorothy and Toto in Munchkinland. "No, I don't."

Ray Waters considered expanding on his thoughts. Instead he stood and cleared his throat. "I guess I'm chairing today's executive meeting. Thanks for coming, we'll try to keep this net." He gestured at me. "Some of you have met Kevin Pierce. He's doing Bobby's portrait. A very respected portrait artist, we're lucky to have him on board. This is what he's got so far." Indicating my canvas on the easel. "Bobby's asked us to look it over, provide the usual feedback and direction. Who'd like to open the discussion?"

I considered grabbing my canvas and making a run for the nearest exit. Before I could follow through, a hand was raised.

"I don't like the pink shirt." A short, bespectacled man with frown lines etched into his forehead was speaking from halfway down the table. "Let's face it, a segment of our customers, especially men, probably think of pink as an effeminate color. We all know that's ridiculous, but we have to consider the brand implications. Kevin, I suggest you change the color of Bobby's shirt."

"I couldn't agree more." Ray Waters was utterly serious. "Good suggestion, George. Kevin, make a note of that. Anyone else?"

A black woman with long, sensuous arms raised her hand and waggled a pencil to get our attention. "Bobby's smile could be bigger. Another hundred watts should do it."

Some laughter, lots of nods.

A man with half a dozen pens in his shirt pocket said, "I understand Kevin is using oils for his painting of Bobby. I suppose oils are okay for the ordinary painting. But I did a quick dip into our materials database and discovered that acrylic is a much stronger material. Water soluble pigments held together by a plastic binder. Ideal. If we plan to make Bobby's portrait a key element of our marketing plan, the painting's going to get a lot of use. I assume we might move it from city to city. Put it under hot lights for photography. So why not go with acrylic? I know, Kevin, you've already started with oils, but you've only been on it a couple of days, they tell me. You can start over, can't you? We backtrack all the time in engineering."

It took every bit of self-control I possessed to stop myself from charging down the table and tearing out the engineer's throat. "Oils seemed to work pretty well for Rembrandt," I said calmly. "For Picasso. For Van Gough. For Dali. For scores of other fine artists. So I guess oil is good enough for me, too. Oils are subtle, they convey emotion, they lend warmth to a portrait. That's why I use them."

"Picasso used all kinds of materials," Dorothy put in. "He wasn't afraid to experiment."

"Bless him." I attempted to hide the fact that I was pissed at Dorothy for joining the enemy camp. "I've experimented with lots of materials and I still like oils. Also, I'm the artist. It's my prerogative to choose the colors, the materials, the point of view, everything else about this portrait."

Hugh Wilson, who hadn't appeared to be listening, looked up from his stack of legal documents. His hawklike face held a frown. "That's not quite accurate. Look at the contract you signed, you'll see that what you're doing is termed *work for hire*. Which means this corporation retains all rights to your completed work. That also means we have a lot to say about the way the portrait is done. You aren't freelancing on this one, my friend."

I thought about walking out and never coming back inside this zoo. Thought about it hard. What stopped me, that was my painting on the easel. Leaving it would be like abandoning my own child.

"And we need more blue. Blue is the Race Corporation's corporate color," Ray Waters was saying. "We won't have much use for a portrait of Bobby that doesn't incorporate the color blue as a major element."

"Everyone will expect to see a lot of blue." Never before had I found myself explaining the way I work. I promised myself it would never happen again. But now, at this particular moment, I wanted to puncture their self-satisfied thinking. "Throwing a ton of blue into Bobby's portrait won't surprise anybody. Everyone will expect that because, like you said, blue's the magical *corporate color*. On the other hand, the essence of a great portrait is the amount of surprise it arouses in the viewer. That's what gives a portrait its impact. Surprise. A daring viewpoint. Maybe you can order me to do the portrait the way you want it, I don't know, reading contracts is something I'm not good at. What I know is you're asking me to do a conventional portrait of a truly unconventional man. And I also know Bobby Race would hate to look conventional."

Worried glances around the table. Except for Pam Solter, who smiled. "Kevin's right. When we hire a senior programmer, somebody with superb credentials, we don't second-guess every damned line of code that person writes. We let the programmer do his or her job. Kevin's an artist, let him do his job, too. Let him paint Bobby the way he seems him."

"But blue's the corporate color," Ray Waters insisted.

"Fuck blue," I said. "I don't see Bobby with a blue background. It's that simple."

Disapproving murmurs from most quarters.

"I told Kevin myself that the portrait needs a blue background and he wouldn't listen." Dorothy's arms were folded, she had a testy tilt to her chin. "Kevin's a fine artist. I've looked at some of his work. I guess I've come to agree with Pam, let him do Bobby's portrait his own way. Otherwise it'll be nothing but a mess."

Surprise. Surprise. From her body language, Dorothy had seemed certain to throw in her cards with the naysayers. Our eyes met briefly and she allowed herself an enigmatic smile. I couldn't tell whether she was supporting me or just giving me enough rope to hang myself. Didn't matter why she'd come to my defense. I needed her support. Dorothy was even more brainy than she was beautiful and everyone at the table knew it. They'd follow her lead. She commanded enormous respect at Race Software, you only had to watch the effect of her words to realize that.

Besides, everyone knew she had Bobby's ear.

People were nodding in reluctant acquiescence. So much tension had bled out of the room that even when Ray Waters cried out in a plaintive voice, "Folks, the corporate color is a big issue here, we're talking brand impact!" nobody paid him much attention. He asked for other comments but none were offered. A man with longish hair tied in an unnecessary ponytail got up, muttered a quiet apology and slipped out of the room. A young woman folded up her laptop and followed him.

"I'm running a benchmark," Greg Tillotson announced. When he stomped out, others followed by twos and threes and then by general stampede. The meeting had imploded in Ray Waters' face. I looked for Dorothy. She'd been among the early escapees.

I was left standing at the head of the long and empty conference table with Ray Waters, who flashed an insincere smile. "I suppose congratulations are in order. It appears, Kevin, that your approach to Bobby's image just received a ringing endorsement from the executive team."

"I wouldn't say that. Looked to me like everybody was too busy with their own responsibilities to give my little picture much serious thought."

"Whatever." Waters shrugged as if failing to gain control of my painting was not a personal defeat for him. "We'll see what happens when your *little picture* is finished." That parting shot was fired over his shoulder as he strode out of the conference room.

Jenny appeared wearing a big smile. "You won, Kevin!"

"I took round one on points. Ray Waters seems to think I can't go the distance. All he's seen so far is my footwork. It's my counterpunch he has to worry about."

"I love it when you talk in metaphors." Jenny's eyes sparkled. "Guys around here don't do that. It's all techno-speak with them."

"I'm a throwback to a more romantic time," I said with what I thought was self-mockery.

"Yes, you are." As Jenny went past me, she let her forefinger run down my arm. "Pepper will put your painting back where it belongs." Before she went out the door, Jenny turned and said, "Are you going to be home tonight, Kevin?"

"I expect to be."

"Bobby said he'd dictate some notes later today about your painting. Since you don't have a fax machine, I'll deliver the notes to you personally later tonight."

"You don't have to do that. I live way over in Half Moon Bay."

"I'm here in San Mateo, it's only fifteen minutes over the hill to the ocean. Besides, some of the girls were saying you have a fabulous house overlooking the water. I'd like to check it out."

"You may be disappointed."

"I don't think so. See you about eight o'clock."

Pepper and his fellow workman were moving the painting and easel back to Bobby's office and once again I floated along in their wake.

"Ya must know it ain't your house Jenny wants to look at," Pepper said when his companion had gone on to another task. "They tell me Jenny elbowed some of the other girls aside for a peak at your goods through that hole I mentioned."

"Didn't think I was Jenny's type. I don't eat granola or jog in the park or drink guava juice."

"Then it's your goods that must be Jenny's type. 'Cause she ain't coming to your place tonight to deliver no set of business notes."

"You know everything that goes on around here, don't you, Pepper."

"I been with this company almost since Bobby went into business. Got the profit sharing. Got the good benefits. Got friends here. So I pay attention to what's going on around this place, protect my living."

"Always a good idea." I looked at my watch. "See you in the lobby at two."

As Pepper and I entered the Stanford Medical Center, we ran into Eileen Patterson heading home for a few hours of rest. She was so preoccupied that I had to reintroduce myself and Pepper to her before we asked about her husband.

"They ended up having to take three fingers off his left hand instead of two." She twisted a tear-stained handkerchief between her fingers.

"He's going to be all right otherwise?"

Her eyes were baleful but brave. "Yes, he will. It'll be another couple of weeks before he can come home, though."

"Think it's all right for us to go up and say hello?"

"Sure, he'll be glad to see you."

When he went up to his room, Joe did give us a warm welcome. "Come in, guys. Kevin, thanks for coming by. Pepper, good to see you."

Both of us tried to hide our shock. Joe looked even worse than he had immediately after the incident. The blisters on his face were red/black. Puckered. Oozing pus. Half his hair was gone, obliterated by the blisters along the most frostbitten areas of his scalp. Even his eyelids were black and swollen. Joe looked like he'd spent a week on Mount Everest without any sunscreen. His left arm was fitted into a special device that kept it elevated and stationary. The hand was swathed in bandages.

"*The Beast From The Black Lagoon.* Remember that one?" Joe's gravelly laugh had a lot of pain in it. "The beast looked better than I do."

"Yeah, but he didn't have any dialogue." I patted Joe's arm lightly. "We met your wife downstairs, she said it was all right for us to come up."

"I finally got Eileen to go home for some shuteye. She's a trooper. I've been feeling kind of sorry for myself, she's been trying to buck up my spirits."

"Fact is, Joe, you're one lucky guy." Pepper looked wistful. "Three fingers gone? That could be worse." He held up the stump of his left arm so that the hook glinted under the fluorescent lights. "I'd be glad to have my arm back, even it only had two fingers. Plus you've still got Eileen. I lost my wife and son ten years ago to a doped-up truck driver. Damn near wiped me out."

"I didn't know," Joe said quietly.

Pepper's strength and vitality faded when he spoke of losing his family. "Yeah, well, I don't talk about it. Just don't think ya should wallow around in that bed feeling sorry for yourself. Not with a wife like your Eileen." Pepper used the point of his hook to lift the lid on the cover of

Joe Patterson's untouched lunch. "Or maybe you've got a right to feel sorry for yourself, they feed you this shit. What's that gray stuff, Joe?"

"Mashed potatoes, I think."

Pepper dipped the tip of his hook into the food, licked a bit of it off, made a face. "They served better chow in the army. And more of it."

Joe asked what was going on at Race. I told him what I'd learned about Cynthia Gooding and her ties to Izzy Valentine. He saw the marks on my face so I explained that Izzy had sent a couple of goons to try to take away the printouts I'd found at Cynthia's apartment. It didn't seem wise to bring up Sport Sullivan or the fact that my private ghost had literally frightened Bullseye Fratino to death.

Pepper seemed more outraged about Izzy's unscrupulous behavior than Joe Patterson did. Of course, Joe was an ex-cop who'd seen it all.

"We can't let this Valentine guy worm his way into the company!" Pepper said.

"Izzy Valentine has built himself a mostly legitimate business since he moved to San Francisco." Joe shifted to a more comfortable position. "The guy's mobbed up, no doubt about that. But over the last few years Izzy's been polishing his image. I'm surprised he resorted to his old tricks. Could backfire on him."

"He wants a seat on Race Software's board of directors," I said. "That would give him a shot at controlling a hot company and cranking up his respectability at the same time."

"Bobby'll never let him in," Pepper said.

"Bobby may not have a choice." Talking about this was helping me understand Izzy's purposes. "Let's say Izzy hired Cynthia Gooding to get hold of the Redleaf code. I'll bet he could hurt Bobby pretty badly by selling the code to some other company. Hell, he could even buy some small company and go into competition with Race Software. But I don't think that's Izzy's game. He'll use the Redleaf code to force Bobby to bring him on the board of directors."

"Bobby'll sue his ass off," Joe said. "He'll put Hugh Wilson and his staff of lawyers on Izzy's case. Those guys are cannibals, they'll eat Izzy's liver."

"Legal actions take time," I pointed out. "Meanwhile, Izzy could do plenty of damage to the company. Bobby might think it would save a lot of money and hassle to put Izzy on the board. At least temporarily."

A nurse came in to give Joe his "meds" and gingerly daub a thick yellowish cream on his burns. She also changed his bedpan. Pepper and I looked out the window until she was finished and gone.

"They don't leave you much dignity in a hospital," Joe complained. "That's the worst thing about the place."

The new application of cream was obviously causing Joe some discomfort. I thought perhaps Pepper and I should leave. On the other hand, the conversation might take his mind off his aches and pains.

"I'm still trying to figure out what did this to me," Joe said. "I'm a nuts-and-bolts, bacon-and-eggs, yes-or-no kind of guy. There's not much room in my mind for ghosts."

"You probably go to church, though," I suggested.

"Sure I do."

"The Holy Ghost sound familiar? The human soul? Archangels? Satan? Those are all accepted, conventional religious entities. Doesn't take much of a leap to get from there to other forms of spirits." I decided to be as honest with Joe Patterson as I could; he'd certainly earned it. "Don't look at me like I'm crazy. I've told you that now and then I'm visited by a spirit myself."

"I don't buy it. I'm not calling you a liar, I just think you've got an overactive imagination. You're an artist, it comes with your paint kit."

"How else do you explain the way I delivered Tara Hillyer's kidnapper to you?"

"There's a lot I can't explain. Doesn't mean I believe in the supernatural."

"I do." Pepper had been listening intently to our conversation. "I've seen that kind of thing myself. This was over in 'Nam. One of my buddies,

Pug Scott, took a sniper's round through the chest. I dragged Pug back to where a medic could work on him. Pug died while the medic was trying to save him. When the medic crawled off to help some of the other wounded, I sat there looking at Pug and trying to stop myself from shaking, trying to get up the nerve to go back to my squad."

Pepper licked his lips and rubbed a hand through his salt-and-pepper hair. His coal black skin had become as dry as dust.

"That's when I saw Pug's spirit rise up out of him. Wasn't red, like the thing that got ya, Joe. Wasn't ice cold, either. What come up out of Pug was like a warm white vapor. It had a form. Not a human-shaped form, just a shimmering center. Drifted up and away. When that happened, Pug's body sort of deflated."

"Gasses," Joe said. "Lots of dead bodies lose their gasses, I've seen that happen."

"Not ten seconds after they die," Pepper persisted. "Believe me, I've seen more decomposing corpses than I like to remember. It takes a while for the gasses to build up."

"But you only saw one that had a spirit rise up from it," Joe pointed out. "How come that never happened to any of the other corpses you saw over there?"

"How should I know?" Pepper looked to me. "You're the expert, Kevin. You explain it to him."

"I'm not an expert. I'm just a reluctant believer."

Pepper scratched his head with the tip of his hook. "So what was that red, misty thing that put Joe in the hospital?"

"For lack of a better word, I'd call it a chimera."

"Say what?"

"A chimera is any kind of impossible or wild incarnation that can't be explained."

"Well fuck," Joe said. "That's just a fancy word for a ghost."

"The difference is," I explained, "when you call it a chimera, you don't sound as crazy."

Joe just stared at me, Pepper laughed.

"And I still believe this particular chimera is whatever remains in our world of Cynthia Gooding. Whose real name, by the way, was Cindy Pacini. We know Cynthia was stealing Redleaf code, probably for Izzy Valentine. I think someone, maybe on Izzy's orders, deliberately pushed Cynthia over the rail of the highest level in the library. She hit the floor and died. For some reason, her spirit has stayed around. The chimera is trying to tell us something, though I'm damned if I know what it is. Trying to get its revenge, maybe."

"You're nuts," Joe said.

"Listen, there have been hundreds of documented cases where the spirits of people appear in the places where those people died. Remember the ghost of flight 901?"

"What are you talking about?"

"It was all over the newspapers when I was a kid. An Eastern Airlines flight crashed in the Florida everglades. For several years afterwards the spirit of the navigator was seen by passengers and crew members on other Eastern flights. Turned out that each of the flights on which the navigator's spirit was seen carried salvaged parts from the plane that went down. Look it up, there's documentation."

"Was Elvis on any of those flights?"

Joe laughed uproariously at his own joke. I let him have his laugh because it was probably good therapy.

"That's just one example." I suppose my story sounded lame even though it was true. In self defense, I almost told him all about Sport Sullivan. What stopped me was that anything I might say about Sport probably would have made Joe laugh harder.

"I'm glad to see ya laughing so soon after what happened to you," Pepper said. "But something weird robbed you of three fingers. I saw it myself and don't know what it was. I'd like to find out."

Joe sobered up real fast. "So would I, guys. So would I."

CHAPTER 12

Jenny Hartsong appeared on my doorstep about seven-thirty that evening. She'd changed from the gym shorts and t-shirt into a skirt, a blouse that you could almost (but not quite) see through, and Gucci sandals. Her hair wasn't in a pony tail; it fell to her shoulders as softly as an Irish rain.

"You seem to have the *Dress For Success* thing totally backwards. At the office you wear shorts, sneakers and the world's tightest T-shirt. At night you slip into what passes in California for formal wear. Explain this to me."

Jenny took a walking tour of the first floor and I followed along.

"Working for Bobby is like running in a marathon, it takes every bit of energy I've got so I wear light clothes. Marathon clothes. Fine with Bobby, he doesn't care how I dress or what I look like." She noted my cynical reaction. "No, it's true. Bobby didn't hire me because I've got a good figure and a cute face. I could be the world's ugliest secretary, he would have hired me anyway because I'm a damned good executive secretary. Bobby doesn't pay attention to how any of his people look, or how they dress. He's only interested in the quality of our work."

"Admirable."

"So when I finally get off work after a twelve or fourteen hour day, I like to dress up." She glanced up the steps that led to the second floor. "How many bedrooms?"

"Just the one big loft up there."

"Cool." Jenny scampered up the steps for a look at the loft. "You need a housekeeper," she said when she came down.

"I value my privacy. Besides, I can't afford a housekeeper."

"You'll be able to afford one after Bobby's portrait is done. You'll be fighting off all the new clients, Kevin. I guarantee it."

"Maybe."

"No maybe about it. Being selected to do Bobby's official portrait is an incredible coup. Haven't you figured that out yet?"

"People keep telling me how lucky I am. Meanwhile, the bill collectors are still circling my house like vultures."

"You don't seem too worried."

"I'm way past the worrying stage."

Jenny was sniffing the air. "What's that aroma? Smells sort of like a hospital."

"I had a pest control guy out here spraying for termites. He must have done a good job. I haven't heard the little bastards chomping on the foundation even once since I got home."

That caused Jenny to shudder. "Chemicals! I hope for your sake he used biodegradable materials."

"I think he used some sort of gas. Serin he called it."

Jenny jumped almost out of her see-through blouse. "Serin! My God, that's a deadly...oh...you're yanking my chain, aren't you."

"Just a friendly tug."

"I take myself too seriously sometimes, especially when it comes to things like health and the environment. My degree is in physical therapy, with a minor in nutritional science."

"You have a degree in physical therapy? And nutritional science? What are you doing...I mean...you're working out of your field."

"You mean why am I working as a secretary? For money, of course. Bobby pays an awfully good salary. Plus bonuses. Plus stock options. Do you have any wine?"

I stirred myself into action. "Sorry, I'm not a very good host. Too few visitors. Sure, I have wine. I'll bring it out on the deck. It's a fine night and even though it's dark you can hear the surf."

"I prefer white wine, if you have it," Jenny said on her way out to the deck.

"Coming right up."

Somewhere in the back of my pantry there might be, if I was lucky, a bottle of wine I'd bought when I was seeing Heather, the upwardly mobile advertising exec who'd wanted to market me like a box of cereal. I couldn't remember whether that wine was red, white or blue. Or whether it was still there. I shoved things around in the pantry until I did uncover a dusty bottle of wine.

White wine!

As Hemingway said when he survived a plane crash in Africa, *My luck, she is running good.*

I was glad Jenny had gone out to the deck. Better she shouldn't see that the wine I was about to offer came out of a bottle with a screw cap instead of a cork. I cleaned a decent looking glass, poured the wine, opened a beer for myself, and went out to her. Jenny had turned on the deck lights. Far below, a series of whitecaps could be seen against the moonlight. Jenny looked even better in moonlight. I could feel my physical desires shifting from Dorothy to Jenny, like a compass needle searching for true north.

"White wine. As promised. And it's definitely bio-degradable."

She took the wine and tasted it. I half expected her to make a sour face. But she smiled and said, "Nice."

Abruptly, I remembered the reason Jenny had given for this visit. "Did you bring Bobby's notes about the portrait?"

"He didn't have time to dictate any notes. I decided to come anyway because I was curious."

"About what?"

"Your house. Your work. You." Jenny moved closer to me. "I've never known an artist before. Oh, I've met guys who dabbled in what they called *the arts.* But you're the only man I've met who's committed his entire life to something so risky. So adventurous."

"Everything in life is risky. From the little I've seen, the computer business makes portrait painting look steady and reliable."

Jenny was shaking her head. "Even the also-rans in the computer business manage to bring home a lot of money. We're talking a trillion dollar industry, Kevin."

"I don't even know how many zeroes there are in a trillion."

"Enough so that there's money for everybody."

"Somehow I don't see you as a girl who's interested exclusively in money."

She moved maybe an inch closer. "My long-term goal is to start a health institute, sort of a cross between a spa and a nutrition center. I'm especially interested in geriatric nutrition. My grandmother raised me. She lived most of her life in bad health and died at fifty-five, when I was just seventeen." Jenny's eyes glistened. "Grammy could have lived in good health well into her seventies if she'd eaten better food and gotten some moderate daily exercise. I think I can help older people live longer and be more active and satisfied with their lives. Some day, when I've proved out my ideas, I'll turn them into a book that can help millions of people."

"An ambitious goal. Sounds expensive, too."

"That's why I'm with Bobby. Soon I'll have enough to go into business for myself. Not a big business like Race Software, but I'll be doing my own thing."

"You'll make it. You've got brains and energy to spare."

"Brains and energy." She looked chagrined. "Is that all you see in me?"

"I didn't think I had to add the part about beauty. You're a gorgeous person, Jenny. You're electric. You make sparks fly."

She moved smoothly into my arms. "Do I have enough electricity to jump-start your motor?"

"I have a feeling you could jump-start a whole fleet of cars."

"I'll settle for bumping up your voltage a few watts."

Her wine glass and my beer were put onto the deck's railing and we kissed for so long that I became literally breathless. After a while Jenny said, "How about giving me a guided tour of your loft?"

"Nothing up there but the...uh..."

"The bed," Jenny prompted.

"Exactly."

We finished our drinks and left the empty glasses on the rail. Upstairs, Jenny undressed swiftly and I did the same. I flicked off the light and slipped under the sheets next to her.

Good foreplay is one my best qualities, so I've been told. This time it didn't last long because Jenny was eager for the main event.

Making love to Jenny was like performing in an exercise video. In her usual energetic fashion, she took me through a complete and exhausting workout. I'm not implying Jenny lacked passion. Quite the contrary. Jenny let me know at all times how vividly she was enjoying herself. The walls of my A-frame veritably shook with howls of joy. What was I feeling? Great sexual satisfaction, no doubt about that. But I also felt traces of disloyalty to Dorothy even though she'd rejected me. I was reminded of the old musical refrain: *When I'm not near the girl I love, I love the girl I'm near.*

Was I that the kind of guy?

Evidently.

When our exercise video ended, Jenny fell back onto her pillow with a glowing smile. "You were wonderful, Kevin. How about you, did you enjoy yourself?"

"Absolutely. It was like making love to the Flying Walendas."

Jenny laughed and ran a hand along my leg. "Someday you'll be serious about something and I'll wonder if the man I'm talking to is really you."

"I had a seriously great time," I said.

"Me, too."

The phone next to the bed rang and I reluctantly removed my hand from Jenny's firm breast to answer it. "Yes?"

"Hello, Mister Whitebread. How you doin'?"

"Just fine at the moment."

"Wish I could say the same." Sam Cody's voice sounded uncharacteristically strained. "I'm callin' from the San Francisco county lockup. Got busted this afternoon for…well…you can guess why they tagged me."

"Auto theft? After all this time you were *caught*?"

"Somebody set me up. You can guess who that is, too."

"Izzy Valentine?"

"Bingo."

"What makes you think it was him?"

"The bastard left his fingerprints all over this one. I'll explain later."

"You need some help, Sam?"

"Yeah, I do." He lowered his voice. "My lawyers'll get me outta here, but not until after the arraignment tomorrow mornin'. Meanwhile…" Sam's voice dropped another notch "…there's a green Lexus, this year's model, in the parking garage at the Hillsdale mall. Right near Crate and Barrel, y'know the area I'm talkin about?"

"Sure."

"Can you go pick it up for me right now? Move it someplace else, anyplace else, three or four blocks away is fine. In fact, put it in the train station parking lot the other side of Camino Real. Leave the key in the ignition. Maybe I'll get lucky, somebody else'll steal it."

"Hold on one second." I told Jenny I'd have to take this call downstairs, slipped on my shorts, and hurried down the steps. "Okay, I'm back. Where's the ignition key?"

"Little magnetized box under the left front fender."

"Sam, how do I know the police don't have the Lexus staked out, too?"

"No, Izzy set me up with a hot Jag. I can hardly believe it, I'm always so careful. But the Lexus leaves me exposed, some people saw me drop it in that mall lot. Ordinarily, that's no big deal, I'd have moved it myself by now. But somebody on the auto theft squad might notice the theft of a new Lexus, then the mall's security people might check the hot sheet and call the cops, and one of the folks at the Crate and Barrel folks might have seen me drop the Lexus there. So I need the Lexus moved before any of that shit happens. Dig?"

"Yeah…sure. Listen, are you certain the police aren't listening in on this call? I mean, you are in a jail."

"This phone's used by prisoners talkin' to their lawyers. Anybody tapped it and they were found out, the D.A.'d have a whole bunch of his convictions reversed on breach of attorney-client privilege. Your problem, Kevin, you don't know nothin' about the wonderful world of law enforcement."

"I'm learning, thanks to you."

"Just move the Lexus, okay?"

"Consider it moved."

"Thanks."

I hung up, took the steps to the loft two at a time and literally dived back into bed with Jenny.

"Whoops! Nice landing!" She laughed and hugged me. "What was that all about, Kevin? You said something about auto theft? Izzy Valentine? He's the man who wants a seat on our Board of Directors. Bobby doesn't like him, I know that much. I heard Bobby tell Hugh Wilson that Valentine might have been behind Cynthia's theft of our Redleaf code. Are you still working on that?"

"Sort of. That call was from a friend who's having his own problems with Izzy Valentine."

"Doesn't sound like a very nice man."

"No, he isn't a nice man. Funny thing, his wife is lovely. She's in a wheelchair, but he seems to dote on her."

Jenny reached across me for her purse. She pulled out two granola bars and handed one to me. "I know…I know…most people have a cigarette after sex…Jenny has a granola bar…ha ha ha. Sorry, but I don't smoke and I'm usually hungry after sex."

"Hey, I'm starting to like granola bars." A lie. I unwrapped mine and took a nibble. The difference in taste between granola and cardboard is, in my opinion, negligible. If anything, I'd give cardboard the nod on points. Still, I wasn't about to turn down Jenny's granola bar. I'm not exactly a gentleman, but I'm not an ungrateful cur either. So I chewed and smiled and made vague noises of satisfaction. After awhile I said, "Is there some strawberry in this one?"

"Yes, good isn't it."

"Delicious." Lie number two. "Jenny, I'm afraid I have to go out. That friend who called needs me to do an errand."

"Is it dangerous?" Jenny sat up straight in bed, revealing her well formed breasts in all their glory. "Can I come along?"

"No, my errand isn't dangerous. And no, you can't come along."

"Why not?"

"Well, what I've been asked to do may not be altogether proper."

"Proper. As in illegal?"

"Some narrow-minded people might put that interpretation on what I have to do." I got up and began to dress with the granola bar sitting in my stomach like a rock. I needed a stream of cold beer to break the granola down into its basic molecular structure. Unfortunately, there was no time for that. Sam had made my errand sound pretty urgent. I suppose I should have dressed without first jumping into bed with Jenny, but that would have been even more insensitive than turning down the granola bar.

"Really, you can't come along." Jenny was dressing faster than a girl would ordinarily do, quite obviously determined to leave the house with me. "Why don't you wait for me, I'll be back inside an hour."

"If there's skullduggery to do, I want to be in on it."

"Where did you hear the word skullduggery?"

"My Grammy used to say that."

When we were both dressed and walking downstairs from the loft, I said, "No kidding, you can't come along."

"No kidding, I am coming with you," she countered.

"Jenny…"

"You wouldn't want me to sort of let it slip out at the office that we've had sex. I mean, Dorothy would be sure to hear about it."

"Jenny, that's blackmail."

"It's only blackmail if you care what Dorothy thinks about you. And if you cared about her, you wouldn't have slept with me. Would you?"

Trapped. "Okay," I said. "You can come along."

Jenny squealed with delight and squeezed my arm.

"You'll have to stay in the car, though."

"No way I'm going to *stay in the car* like a child."

"You're impossible."

"Thank you," she said.

Jenny took one look at my old Karmann Ghia and insisted we go to Hillsdale in her car, a snappy red Miata as fast and whippy as herself. She drove with the top down and we got over the mountain on Route 92 in no time with Jenny downshifting like an Indianapolis 500 driver.

"Relax," Jenny laughed. "We're almost there."

"Thank you, Jenny. You've taught me what the phrase *white-knuckled* really means."

We came down onto Camino Real and went a mile south to the Hillsdale mall. "Pull into the parking garage near Crate and Barrel," I told her. "Just cruise through the garage. At a much slower speed, if you don't mind."

"You've got it. What are we looking for?"

"First, a green Lexus. Then, any security cars."

"There's a Lexus."

Jenny began to turn toward the car. "Don't go near it yet," I said. "I want to look around the parking garage first."

There were few cars in the lot. It was nearly 9:30 and the last shoppers of the day were leaving as the stores began to close. The parking garage was a two-story structure and I asked Jenny to take the ramp to the upper deck. There were only eight or ten cars up there. I had feared the police might be up there, looking down through one of the stairwells at the Lexus. Nobody suspicious in sight on either the upper or street-level decks.

"What we're going to do," I told Jenny, "is park your car about five spaces from that Lexus. Then we'll walk over to the Lexus, I'll get a key from a magnetic box under the left front fender, we'll get in and drive away."

"What about my car?"

"We're only going a few blocks. We'll drop the Lexus at the train station and walk back to your car."

"Why are we doing this?"

"I told you. Favor for a friend."

"A friend who steals cars?"

"He's an automotive consultant."

The only car parked near the Lexus was a blue Dodge van with bumper stickers plastered all over its rear and sides, the old Peace sign from the 60's painted on one door, a broken aerial, and a left rear tire that was very low. Looked like something one of the mobile homeless might live in.

"Park right over there." I couldn't take my eyes off the old van. "When I was in high school in Texas, I bought a beat-up old van something like that one. I used it mainly to make tequila runs down to the border where liquor was really cheap and they never asked to see an ID."

"This okay?" Jenny parked exactly five spaces from the Lexus.

"Just fine." I looked around the parking garage. A few people were still reclaiming their cars as the last of the stores in the mall closed up. I didn't detect anyone watching the Lexus. "Change of plans. I'm going to get out by myself, take the key from under the left fender and drive the Lexus to the station. Follow and pick me up there, okay?"

"No! You said I could go with you! Driving in a stolen car, that'd be a kick!"

"I won't put you in a position that..." All of a sudden I felt a rush of fear. "Kiss me, Jenny."

"Why, Kevin. I'm glad to kiss you. Anytime...anywhere."

We went into an extended embrace that continued long enough so that I almost forgot why it had begun. Jenny finally drew back, her big eyes blinking. "Wow! Looks to me like we're going back to your house for an encore!"

"Right...encore."

"What's the matter?"

"Nothing...kiss me again."

Suddenly the back doors of the nearby van popped open and two uniformed officers jumped out. They hustled up to us and the one with lieutenant's bars on his shoulders said, "What are you people doing here?"

"What does it look like we're doing?"

"Lemmee see some ID," the lieutenant said. "Identification," he added, as if I were too dim to understand the acronym.

I dragged out my wallet and handed him the driver's license. Jenny, who had lost her perkiness at the sight of the two officers exploding from the back of the van, nervously produced her license.

"You guys are wearing San Francisco Police Department badges," I remarked. "What are you doing this far down the peninsula?"

"None of your business. We got authority to be here, that's all you need to know." He wrote down our names in a notebook. "I'm gonna ask you just once more. What are you two doing here? Right here at this particular spot?"

"We pulled in to switch drivers," I said. "My girlfriend doesn't like to drive at night."

"You cruised around the lot like you were looking it over for something."

"We thought there might be a place open where we could get coffee. Looks like everything in the mall's closing up, though."

The lieutenant didn't especially like my story because he had the inbred suspicion of all policemen. But he didn't really believe I was there to pick up the stolen Lexus either. He was probably with the San Francisco auto theft squad and I was sure he'd been tipped off to expect a well-known and well-dressed black man named Sam Cody. Evidently he didn't know Sam had already been picked up moving a different stolen car. The cop's main concern would be to get Jenny and me out of the area so we wouldn't scare off his real suspect.

"You two get outta here right now," the lieutenant said. "You're inhibiting a police investigation and that could get you in real trouble." His manner softened as he ogled Jenny's nubile flesh. "There's plenty of better places to have sex than a little Miata."

"I couldn't agree more."

The lieutenant returned our driver's licenses and Jenny hastily started up the Miata. She threw it into gear too fast and it stalled. With a nervous smile at the two officers, she went through the startup procedure more carefully and we drove slowly out of the Hillsdale mall garage.

"Oh, my God!" Jenny started hyperventilating when we were out onto the boulevard. "We could have been arrested! The police were watching that car!"

"Take slower breaths. That's better. Does picking up a stolen car still seem like fun?"

"No! Why were the police watching that car?"

"Somebody set it up, just in case the first trap didn't work."

"Trap?"

"It's complicated. Two different traps were set for my friend. The first one worked, you and I almost fell into the second one. It was a backup trap, you see what I mean?"

Jenny was driving erratically, drifting from lane to lane, pressing a hand to her chest. "I may be having a heart attack."

"You aren't having a heart attack, you're just shook up. Pull over and let me drive."

She pulled into the lot of the movie complex down the street from the mall and parked at the far end. "Whew! Kevin, is that why you kissed me? You realized the police were watching us?"

"The van was sagging from all the people and surveillance equipment inside. I wasn't certain there were cops in there, but the whole deal all of a sudden felt bad to me."

"Instinct." Jenny looked at me with admiration. "I read your personnel file. You were a soldier, won medals, got shot, survived. I guess that's where you learned to depend on your instincts."

I had to laugh. "You should've seen me last night, my instincts were nonexistent. I let three guys beat the crap out of me, I never even saw them coming."

"That's how you got those bruises? It wasn't a car accident?"

"My car can't go fast enough to get in an accident."

Jenny still had her hands on the steering wheel. Though she was breathing normally again, her face remained pale. "Kevin, I don't know if I can handle your lifestyle. The way you live isn't healthy."

"I drink a little beer, that's all."

"I'm talking about the things that happen to you, the people you know. I've come to the conclusion you have some real bad karma."

"Jenny, I have no karma at all. I lost it at the movies."

"If I'd been arrested tonight, convicted of a felony, the state of California would never give me a license to open the kind geriatric facility I hope to have some day." Jenny turned sad eyes on me. "I guess I made a mistake trying to insinuate myself into your life."

"Not to worry. From my side, it was a very pleasant mistake."

We talked for a few minutes. Jenny told me more about her grandmother and her plans for the future. We held hands. With the top down and a cool breeze, it was a lovely time. I hardly paid attention to the Mercedes limo that slid into a nearby parking space until the driver got out an approached us.

He was a large man with a bald, elongated head reminiscent of those stone statues that stare out to sea from Easter Island. He wore a perfectly pressed black chauffeur's uniform. "Mr. Pierce, my employer would like to speak with you for a few minutes. He apologizes for this interruption. This is important, he says."

"Would your employer be Izzy Valentine?"

"He would, sir."

"And how did you happen to find me? I mean, parked here in a movie lot? Never mind, I know how you found me. And I'm not interested in talking with your employer."

"Just for a few minutes."

The chauffeur was more than a professional driver, he had too many muscles and his eyes were much too cold. Actually, the driver with the Eric von Stroheim head didn't scare me. Neither did the presence of Izzy Valentine. If Izzy had planned any rough stuff for tonight, he'd be thirty miles away in the company of a bank president, a Nobel Prize winner, and a priest.

The chauffeur leaned closer. "I can't go back there without you. You know what I mean?"

"You'd be in a lot of trouble," I said.

"Mr. Valentine doesn't understand the word no. Come on, nothing unpleasant will happen. He had no idea Mr. Cody would send you to move the car. You should've heard him explode when you showed up, my ears are still ringing."

"He doesn't know Sam's already in jail?"

The chauffeur's eyebrows, the only hair on his head, lifted. "No kidding, Sam was picked up with the other car? We hadn't heard. So how about it, will you give him a couple of minutes?"

"I suppose."

Jenny had been following our conversation with glazed eyes. I knew she understood what was going on because she stiffened when Izzy Valentine's name was mentioned. "Jenny," I said, "can you drive yourself home?"

"I'm fine now. How will you get home?"

"Tell you what I'll do, miss," the chauffeur said. "I'll see Mr. Pierce gets home safe and sound. You have my word."

Jenny had doubts about Eric von Stroheim's word, as did I.

"When I say something, miss, I mean it," the chauffeur said.

"I'll be all right," I assured her. "I'll see you in the morning. I'll even have a fat-free muffin when I get to the office. Okay?"

"This is the weirdest date I ever had," Jenny said as I got out of her car. "Bobby's not going to believe it."

"You can tell Bobby. Don't tell anyone else," I warned her.

That's when I realized Bobby had sent Jenny to sleep with me.

CHAPTER 13

When we were driving up Camino Real towards the Route 92 turnoff, Izzy Valentine said, "I'm glad to have this chance to talk with you again, Kevin. You comfortable? Need anything?"

Izzy wasn't as well dressed as when I'd met him last night at his home. Tonight he wore old khaki pants, a pair of weathered boots gone white around the soles from salt water and an old, greasy fishing vest splattered with fish blood. At least I hoped it was fish blood. "I'm fine," I said. "You've been fishing?"

"Went out this afternoon for salmon. Caught some nice ones. I'll put one in your refrigerator, once we get you home. Nothing like fresh salmon. Right now you look like you need a beer." With the touch of a button, Izzy lowered the glass between the driver and passenger sections. "John, do we have any cold beer in the little fridge?"

"Afraid not, sir. I can stop at a liquor store if you'd like."

"Not necessary," I said.

"No trouble at all. I see a liquor store on the next corner." The chauffeur pulled over into a small parking lot next to the store. "What's your brand, Mr. Pierce?"

"He drinks Carta Blanca," Izzy said.

"Anything'll do," I said. "Or nothing."

"Sir, if you prefer Carta Blanca, that's what you'll get." The chauffeur went into the store.

"John'll find some C.B. for you. He's a very determined kind of guy. If I'd known we were going to see each other tonight, I'd have put a couple of bottles on ice."

Through the window, the chauffeur called John could be seen talking with the liquor store clerk. At first the conversation appeared amiable. Then, after an exchange of words, the chauffeur gestured in an angry way. The clerk responded in a similar manner. The chauffeur then reached across the counter and viciously slapped the clerk. More heated words followed. The clerk made a placating gesture and went into a rear room, followed by the chauffeur.

Izzy laughed. "I guess John had to convince the clerk to go look for your brand. Like I said, he's a determined guy."

"I don't like seeing some poor clerk pushed around over a lousy bottle of beer."

"I'm sure John asked politely for your brand. The clerk evidently said he might have some Carta Blanca in the back, but he wasn't going to look for it at this time of night. John simply reminded him that good service is crucial to a successful business and went into the back to help the guy find your brand."

"I'm touched by John's solicitude."

"He's known in certain circles as Pure John. You want to know why?"

Izzy was intent on telling the story, so I sat back and listened.

"About fifteen years ago John was a loan shark in Philadelphia. He had a lot of hair in those days, I'm told. Back then they called him Johnny Flash because he drove a red Ferrari, wore flashy clothes, had his hair styled. He worked for the Mendicinis. One day old man Mendicini got it in his head Johnny Flash was skimming money off his end. No proof of that. In fact, it wasn't true. In his own way, Johnny Flash was scrupulously honest. But old man Mendicini was almost eighty, a touch senile, probably thought Johnny Flash was somebody else, someone who skimmed money off him fifty years ago. So he ordered some dumb beefcake to hit Johnny Flash. Kill him, you understand?"

I stretched my legs, there was plenty of room in the back seat of Izzy's limo .

"But Johnny Flash wasn't so easy to hit. The beefcake got behind John in line at the deli, moved to put a knife between his ribs. Johnny Flash sensed it coming, grabbed the deli owner's knife, which was being used to slice a nice brisket for his sandwich, and killed the hit man. Put the knife in through the guy's jugular. Case closed.

"Of course, Johnny Flash had to get out of Philadelphia right away, so he headed for the state line in his red Ferrari, his flashy clothes, his styled hair. Naturally, the police spotted John right off and picked him up before he reached the New Jersey turnpike. John went away for six years for manslaughter. When he got out, what do you suppose Johnny Flash did?"

"I couldn't guess."

"Changed his style completely. Shaved his head. Got himself fitted for three black suits and two pairs of black Florsheim wingtips. Bought a nondescript Chevy for his personal car. On the rear he puts bumper stickers that say things like *Jesus Is Our Savior* and *Heaven Is Just Around The Corner*. He looks so pure, acts so pure, talks so politely, no cop will ever again stop him. John also gave up loan sharking and became my personal driver. That's why he's called Pure John these days instead of Johnny Flash."

"Fascinating."

"You want to paint Pure John's portrait, be my guest. He's an employee, he'll do what I say."

"No, thanks."

Pure John opened the door and put a bucket of ice in the back seat. Nesting in the ice was a six-pack of Carta Blanca. "Here you go, Mr. Pierce. They'll be cold before we cross over Route 280."

"Thanks…John."

"My pleasure, sir."

When we were back on the road, Izzy pushed the button that raised the glass barrier between the driver and passengers. Then he opened a compartment that held crystal glassware and a dozen or so bottles of whiskies and exotic liqueurs. "Last night I overdid my drinking. Amelia was upset with me so I'm only having a small brandy tonight. By the way, Amelia was quite impressed with you. She's talking about having a portrait done of the two of us. Are you interested in the job? Amelia would really appreciate it."

"Sorry, I don't do portraits of rich people posing in front of their estates."

"We wouldn't be *posing in front our estate,* for Crissake. Putting it that way makes us sound like a couple of no-class bozos. Besides, you're doing Bobby Race's portrait and he's a *rich guy* too."

"That's a special case. I'm sorry, I really do hate to disappoint Amelia because I like her quite a lot."

One of Izzy's curly black eyebrows rose. "Implying you don't like me?"

"Why should I? Thanks to your stupid little power games, I was almost arrested tonight."

"I didn't expect you to show up at the Lexus. I set up that little sting to entrap your good friend Sam Cody." Izzy raised a hand. "Not that I want to see Sam in prison. Hell, no. I'm just putting pressure on the guy. He got caught with the other car? The stolen Jag? No problem, the charges'll be dropped as soon as he agrees to sell me his company and work for my organization. Tell him that for me."

"Oh, I don't think I'll have to do that. I'm sure you'll be hearing from Sam personally."

"You really want your pal Sam to come up against me and Pure John? I know Sam Cody's got a reputation as a tough guy, but he ain't no Pure John."

We drank our respective refreshments in silence as the limo crossed over Route 280 and began snaking down the narrow, twisting road to Half Moon Bay. Pure John was a fine driver, I had to say that for him. He took each hairpin turn with confident grace. Our drinks remained steady on the narrow sideboards where we occasionally set them down. I wanted to ask Izzy Valentine a dozen questions. I settled for just a few.

"Do you know a couple of guys named Snake Ritchie and Bullseye Fratino?"

Izzy's gaze went from me to Pure John before settling back on me. "I've heard their names. They may even have done some work for my companies from time to time. Why do you ask?"

"After I left your party last night, I took the key you gave me to Cynthia Gooding's apartment on Russian Hill and drove up there."

"What'd you find out? Anything useful?"

"Her apartment had been cleaned out and sold to some other people. The new owners gave me a bagful of papers she left behind, some confidential information stolen from Race Software. When I left the apartment, three guys dragged me into an alley and worked me over. Two of them were Bullseye Fratino and Snake Ritchie."

He pursed his lips until they looked like two sausages on a breakfast plate. "You think I sent them? Get that idea out of your mind." A pause. "I read in the *Chronicle* this morning that the body of a man identified as Frank Fratino was found this morning in an alley on Russian Hill. Am I right that Frank was Bullseye's real first name?"

"I wouldn't know his real first name. But yes, Bullseye was dead when I left that alley."

Rubics of respect came into Izzy's eyes. "I'm impressed."

"No need to be. Bullseye had a heart attack, I guess he tired himself out beating on me. Snake and the third man took off."

"Sure he did." Izzy did an imitation of a wise old owl. "That's a good story, I hope for your sake the cops buy it. No shit, I didn't send those guys to lean on you. Your Cindy Pacini business...or Cynthia Gooding...whatever you call her...has nothing to do with me."

"I understand you're angling for a place on Race Software's board of directors."

Izzy looked surprised. "Who told you?"

"Deep Throat."

"Who?"

"Doesn't matter. The point is Cindy…Cynthia Gooding…was systematically stealing the programmers' code for a new networking product. Bobby thinks you planted her in his organization, that you were going to use the stolen code to force him to put you on his board. If that's the case, you wouldn't want me poking around in your business. I thought that's why you sent those guys. I still think that."

Izzy sniffed his brandy as a stall before addressing my accusation. He chuckled and drank off some of the brandy. "Goddamit, I wish I had come up with that idea. Using Cindy to steal some code? Then using the code to shoehorn myself onto Bobby's board? Great fucking idea. Unfortunately, I didn't make that move. Didn't send any tough guys after you, either. I mean, how the hell could I know you'd go straight to Russian Hill from my house? Sure I want a place on Bobby's board. I'll get it, too. You watch me."

"You could have had those guys follow me from your house."

"You're on the wrong track."

As we turned onto the lane where I live, Izzy said, "I'm gonna do you a favor, Kevin, by not telling Pure John you were involved in Bullseye's death. He and Bullseye were buddies. They used to go shooting together."

"Birds or people?"

Izzy laughed and slapped my leg. "Skeet shooting, but I gotta remember that one."

When we arrived at my house, Izzy insisted on personally carrying in one of the salmons he'd caught. "John'll filet it for you, only take a few minutes."

"Where do you keep your knives?" Pure John asked.

I didn't really want to point Pure John toward my knives, but my options seemed limited. "Top drawer next to the stove."

Like everyone who visits my house, Izzy Valentine took a strolling tour. "Interesting," is what most people say after they've looked over my place. Some say "Charming." Or "Different." Or "Eclectic."

"What a dump," is the way Izzy Valentine put it.

"My decorator had a nervous breakdown."

"I hope they've still got him in the hospital, he's a very sick person."

Pure John had removed his black suitcoat and rolled up the sleeves of his crisp white shirt. His bald head gleamed under the fluorescent lights in my kitchen. His expertise with a knife was a bit chilling. His big hands moved as lightly as feathers. With only a few cuts he was turning a salmon that weighed at least fifteen pounds into an assortment of beautiful filets.

"You'll get three or four dinners out of this, Mr. Pierce," Pure John said.

"Well, thanks for fileting it for me. You really didn't have to do that."

He smiled. "I enjoy working with knives. Your knives need sharpening, if I may say so."

"I don't use them very often."

"Never let a knife get dull. That's a mortal sin."

Pure John's smile made my skin crawl.

"There we go." He picked up my unopened copy of that morning's *Chronicle* and used pages from it to wrap up five different packages of filets. "An unopened newspaper is the most sterile thing you'll find in most homes. You can use it to wrap fish, meat, whatever. You ever have to deliver a baby at home, you should immediately lay the baby on a clean newspaper."

"I'll try to remember that."

"I had to do that very thing," Pure John said. "I was just a kid, fourteen years old, my older sister Rose had her baby at home. Her husband was drunk, they had no money for a hospital or doctor, no insurance. So I delivered the baby. Put it on a fresh newspaper. Cut the umbilical cord. Then I called 911, they sent a doctor to check out my sister's condition. I did everything just right, the doctor said."

It was difficult, though not impossible, to imagine a fourteen-year-old Pure John, plenty of hair, maybe still carrying some baby fat, delivering his sister's child. I could certainly picture him cutting the umbilical cord.

Pure John washed his hands in the sink clear up to his elbows, like a surgeon scrubbing up. "Try a nice Pinot Blanc with the salmon," he suggested.

"That would be a good choice," I agreed.

"I'll wait in the car," Pure John said to Izzy. "Good night, Mr. Pierce."

When he'd left the house, Izzy said, "I know. He gives me the creeps too, but he's a great chauffeur. Do me a favor, will you? When Sam Cody's bailed out tomorrow, tell him I'd like to meet with him. Straighten out our differences to his satisfaction and mine. He can choose the meeting place. Something public is fine with me."

"I'm sure you'll be hearing from Sam real soon."

"Tell him the reason I'm leaning on him is simple. One of my business associates down in Mexico has a need for thirty late model luxury cars every month. With the great papers and other backup Sam can supply. We need him and we can make him rich."

"Sam is already rich."

"Richer." As he went out the door, Izzy said, "Enjoy the salmon."

CHAPTER 14

Life style changes don't come easily for me. I tend to put them off until tomorrow. And then the next day. And the next. Until they're forgotten altogether. So I surprised myself by rising at six a.m., throwing some running clothes into a bag, and driving over the mountain into San Mateo where my little Karmann Ghia chugged onto Highway 101 with about four million other Silicon Valley commuters.

At the back of my mind was the fear that in the very near future I'd need to be in better shape. I couldn't say why, except there's always the prospect of physical activity when you associate with guys named Izzy Valentine and Snake Ritchie and Pure John.

I already felt virtuous just because I hadn't helped myself to a beer for breakfast. I felt positively saintly when I pulled into Race Software before seven a.m. and found a parking place right up near the entrance. At the hour I usually arrived, I always had to park way at the rear of the lot.

The jogging trails were already getting some use. I went to the locker room, changed into a t-shirt, shorts and running shoes and began jogging slowly along the paths. In the army our platoon usually began each day with a ten-mile run. Sam and I liked to take the lead and see who might be able to stay up with us. Generally, we were still in the lead when we completed the circuit back to the barracks ten miles later.

I wasn't taking any leads this morning. I set a very leisurely pace for myself and checked my pulse about every quarter of a mile. I was heartened to find my wind was still good and even when I stepped up the pace, my pulse rate never climbed above sixty. Evidently I wasn't in such terrible shape after all.

I did sweat like a racehorse, though.

I'd done three miles when Jenny Hartsong fell into stride beside me. "Kevin, you're here early. And you're jogging! What's the story?"

"I'm training for the Olympics."

"No…really."

"The Olympic Drinking Team."

"Oh, those Olympics."

When Jenny laughed, her ponytail swung free in a wonderfully sexy manner. She wore spandex and her shapely legs glistened with perspiration. I had a brief, compelling memory of the way Jenny had clamped those long legs around my waist in bed last night.

"What happened last night?" she asked. "With that Valentine person."

"His chauffeur drove me home and Izzy put a salmon in my refrigerator."

"That's all?"

"Izzy claimed he didn't ask or hire Cynthia Gooding to steal Redleaf code in order to force his way onto your board of directors."

"You believed him?"

"He was convincing. On the other hand, he's bound to be a superb liar." A marker went by while we were talking. "What'd that marker say?"

"That was the mile one marker again. We've passed it twice now."

"I've seen it four times, so I must have started running before you did."

"You've done four miles?" Jenny looked slantwise at me. "You aren't even breathing hard."

She was right, I was running pretty well. Early in the run I'd developed a slight stitch in my side, but it faded as the miles rolled by. Even with the stitch, I felt I could do ten miles without hurting myself. Not that I intended to go that far on the first hard run I've taken in three or four years.

Jenny was a bit surprised, maybe even annoyed, that I could match her pace. She showed her annoyance by picking up speed and trying to pull away from me. I came up even with her and then, just for the hell of it, went a couple of steps ahead. She matched me and then some. I matched her and went three paces ahead. By then we were in a genuine race. Jenny leaped to lead, grinning over her shoulder at me.

"Let's see what you've got!"

From the rear, I could see very well what Jenny had. Tantalizing buns, among other things. I forfeited that privileged view by stretching the length of my stride by about eight inches. Though the stitch reasserted itself, I didn't slow down. Jenny's arms and legs were pumping like mad and my own instinct to compete took over. We passed a couple of slow, startled joggers. Ran another jogger almost off the track.

"First one to the next mile marker wins!" Jenny yelled.

"You got it!"

Jenny heard the rasp in my reply and poured it on. My lungs turned into twin containers of pain and the stitch felt like somebody was cutting into my side with a letter opener. I caught up with her and held my own for another hundred yards, then she slowly began to draw ahead. I lengthened my stride again and paid for it with a cramp in my left calf. Fifty yards later I was limping and Jenny was showing me her marvelous buns from long distance.

I slowed down so much that soon even the slowest joggers on the course were passing me by. A few minutes later I limped up to the mile marker where Jenny was doing stretching exercises off on the grass. She was sweating hard and breathing harder. At least I'd given her some competition.

I collapsed on the grass next to her. "Do you give up?"

She laughed and ran her tongue sexily around her lips to wipe away some the sweat. "Yes, Kevin. I give up. Does that satisfy the old male ago?"

"Yes...definitely...God, I think my left lung has collapsed."

"You shouldn't run so hard after laying off for a long time. And drinking a lot of beer probably for a longer time. And eating yucky food like bacon."

"Okay…okay…this morning I'll have one of those fat-free muffins you've been leaving by my easel."

Jenny went into a stretching exercise that was particularly revealing. "What's behind this change in lifestyle, Kevin? I'd like to think I helped you see the light. I doubt that's the case."

"Did you tell Bobby we ran into Izzy Valentine last night?"

"When I got home I sent him a long e-mail."

"Did he reply?"

"No, I'll see him in the office pretty soon. I'm sure he'll want to talk to you."

"Fine, I plan to spend all morning working on Bobby's portrait."

"I have to shower. It's almost seven-thirty, Bobby will be yelling for me." Jenny stood and did one more stretching exercise. "Thanks again for a great evening, Kevin. I'm sorry we can't do it again. You seem to be the kind of guy who attracts trouble and I'm not comfortable with that."

"I understand."

Jenny smiled sympathetically and jogged off toward the showers.

Truthfully, I didn't really understand because I'd never thought of myself as a man who attracts trouble. How much trouble can a portrait artist get into? I mean, usually?

I worked pretty well that morning because for once I was left alone. Bobby spoke to me only in grunts and people came and went as rapidly as they do in airports. One of them was director of communications Ray Waters, splendid in a mauve Ralph Lauren shirt and cream slacks. He shot me a contemptuous smile that showed off a lot of expensive orthodontia. Some of the others gave me a wave or a smile. Pam Solter came over to look at my progress on the painting and said, "I like it."

Jenny was like a traffic cop, running people in and out of Bobby's office and making sure they didn't stay so long that his next appointments were kept waiting.

I took a break about ten o'clock. Drank a Snapple and then used a phone in an empty office to call Sam. It was a relief to hear him say, "Mornin' there, Mr. Whitebread."

"You're out!."

"I'm out *for now*. On bail. Arraignment comin' up next week. Just took my third shower, I smelled so evil after a night in the tank. I tell you, Kevin, my old granddad back in Almost-A-Dog would've been disgusted with me, letting myself get suckered into movin' a Jag the cops were sittin' on. Gonna cost me an arm and a leg to keep myself out of jail. Did you get the Lexus moved?"

"Afraid not." I told Sam what had happened, the cops sitting on that car too and Izzy Valentine's sudden appearance after I drove away from the Lexus. I also repeated Izzy's promise to make Sam's legal problems disappear if he'd enter into a business arrangement with him.

"Bastard! Hey, I'm sorry, Kevin. I didn't figure Izzy had set *two* traps for me. You could've ended up in the next cell, the one that held a pair of three hundred pound transvestite muggers wearin' hairnets and not much else."

"Might've been a better evening than the one I had. That chauffeur of Izzy's, calls himself Pure John, gave me the creeps."

"Pure John Braggia? Looks like an undertaker with muscles? Yeah, I know that dude."

I told him about Izzy driving me home in his limo and then coming into the house so Pure John could filet a couple of salmon Izzy had caught.

"You let Pure John into your house? Led him to your knife drawer? Oh man, lotta guys never survive a mistake that big. Pure John is one mean mother-fucker, that's why Izzy keeps him close."

"Does a hell of a filet, though."

"You still got stones, Mr. Whitebread."

"So what are you doing about this situation, Sam?"

"Umm, I'm lookin' at my first prison time, that's kind of a pain in the ass. Best I can do is hire primo legal talent, hope they can keep my black ass outta San Quentin. Gonna cost me big. Quarter of a million, maybe more. I handed a fifty k retainer to Jefferson Tyler this morning, that's just the start."

I'd heard of Jefferson Tyler, a high-profile criminal defense attorney with a long string of victories. "I thought only murder trials cost that much."

"Not these days. Not when you're caught flat-out, way I was. And not when you hire an attorney like Jefferson Tyler, eats money for breakfast instead of bagels."

"Izzy really wants you under his thumb. Are you sure you can't come to some sort of accommodation with him?"

Sam snorted. "Izzy! He don't appreciate who he's dealin' with! No, I can ruin Izzy any time. A few months ago, when I realized Izzy was gonna be all over me, I took certain steps. Believe me, I can fuck up Izzy's life whenever I damn well feel like it. Put him in so much shit he won't have time to worry about Sam Cody's little old business. Ruin his fuckin' reputation, that's what I plan to do. I'll let him think he's got me on the run, then I'll pull the fuckin' rug out from under the prick."

Sounded like one of Sam's grandiose statements. "I wish you well, pal."

"Thanks. And I'm sorry again, Mister Whitebread. About last night I mean. You could've stepped in shit up to your armpits doin' that little favor for me."

"Don't sweat it. I got some beautiful salmon filets out of the deal."

He let out a rolling laugh. "You artists are crazy folk. Talk to you soon, man."

I went back to my easel and worked straight through lunch. Bobby came and went and came back again. I did look up from my work when I heard Bobby talking to Hugh Wilson about something other than arcane legal matters. Bobby was angry, which wasn't unusual, his temper erupted like Old Faithful. This time Izzy Valentine's name was mentioned.

"That goddam Izzy Valentine is definitely buying up stock," Bobby was saying. "On borrowed money."

"That's his legal right," Hugh pointed out.

"He doesn't have a *legal right* to a seat on my board of directors, but that's what he wants. I heard from his attorney this morning. That *gangster* is officially petitioning for a seat on the board. Izzy Valentine, or Isadore M. Valentine as he signs his name, has also sent a copy of his petitioning letter to every board member, and to our major stockholders including the institutions. Even the California pension board. He's asking for their proxies!"

Hugh fidgeted with his papers. "Calpers is our biggest institutional stockholder." He seemed to recover. "So he sent a letter. So what? The board will never accept a man with Valentine's background."

"The man's never been convicted of a felony, Hugh. Charged, yes. Never convicted. And over the last few years he's been polishing his image by doing *good works* all over the peninsula." Bobby looked over at me. "Kevin, join us here, will you?"

When I took a seat across from him and next to Hugh Wilson, Bobby smiled and slid a granola bar across the great length of his desk. "Jenny tells me you're on a health kick. Good for you! Try one of these, I think you'll like it. So...Kevin...I hear you stonewalled the brain trust yesterday. Sold them your vision of my portrait. When Ray Waters was in here earlier, I sensed he was really pissed at you. Nice work, that bunch can be a tough sell."

"Thanks." That was just Bobby being charming. I knew he'd switch to the subject of Izzy Valentine in a nanosecond. My God, he had me thinking in terms of nanoseconds! What was happening to me?

"Jenny also told me you had a run-in with Izzy Valentine last night over a stolen car. Is there any way we can use that against Izzy?"

"I don't think so. Izzy took pains to avoid any personal connection with the stolen Lexus. He was trying to entrap a friend of mine into getting caught with the car. Didn't work. Jenny and I showed up instead."

Bobby wheeled on Hugh Wilson. "You hear what Kevin said, Hugh? That's the kind of man who wants a place on my board." He slammed his fist down on his desk. His face had gone fire engine red. "I won't allow it! I don't care how much of my stock Valentine controls. I won't let it happen!"

Hugh made a placating gesture. "I agree, Bobby. We can't let that happen. And we won't." He turned to me. "What did Valentine say about Race Software?"

"I asked him if he'd placed Cynthia Gooding in the company to steal your programming code. He denied having anything to do with Cynthia getting a job here."

"Of course he denied it," Bobby grumbled. "Hugh, I want you to get together with Jenny. Set up a schedule for me to talk by phone with every member of the board, every large stockholder, every institutional investor. I especially want to talk with Thurmond Wales, he's been buy- ing up a lot of our stock, too. Maybe he's in league with Izzy Valentine."

"I can't see those two working together."

"And I must talk with Clarence Wells. The man owns almost a billion dollars of Race stock and I've never even spoken with him!"

"Clarence Wells lives in Baltimore, Bobby. At least that's where his dividend checks go. He's never responded to any of our letters or calls. His telephone is unlisted. His attorney won't help us contact him. The only time we hear from Clarence Wells is when he sends in his proxies for the annual meetings."

Bobby leaned forward. "Hugh, pay attention here. If Izzy Valentine buys or otherwise gets control of both Thurmond Wales' and Clarence Wells' stock, he may be able to grab himself a place on my board. Get to Wales and Wells right away. I want assurances they won't sell out to Valentine. If necessary, I'll buy out their shares at a premium price to keep it out of Valentine's hands. Do you understand me?"

"Yes, Bobby." Hugh's lean face creased with worry. "I just don't how this Clarence Wells might be found."

"Hire a detective. Contact the FBI. Buy a pack of bloodhounds. Just do it!"

"Yes, Bobby." Hugh gathered up about a half pound of legal papers and scuttled out of the office.

"Lawyers." Bobby offered me a twinkly grin. "You know what a thousand lawyers at the bottom of the sea is?"

"A good start," I answered.

"Shit, everybody's heard that one." He pressed a button on his desk. "Jenny, tell Ray Waters to contact that gag writer in Hollywood. I need a fresh set of jokes."

"Will do, Bobby," came Jenny's reply.

He took out a granola bar, unwrapped it, and began munching away like a schoolboy rushing to finish his recess snack.

"You read the sports section this morning, Kevin?"

"I was too busy with *The Wall Street Journal.*"

Bobby shook his head. "Always the smart mouth. You should've read the sports page of the *Chronicle*. You would've found out you won our bet."

The bet! I'd completely forgotten the damned bet! I'd bet Bobby five thousand dollars I didn't have that the Giants would beat the Dodgers. "I won?"

"Giants six, Dodgers zip."

I watched Bobby Race calmly count out five thousand dollars from a stack of hundred dollar bills and my mouth began to water. Good thing I hadn't won ten thousand, I'd probably have been drooling down my shirtfront. To make myself look even worse, I snatched the five thousand out of Bobby's hand with a greedy, snarling laugh that would have done justice to Ebenezer Scrooge.

"Hey, leave me the hand!" Bobby's accompanying laugh had a high component of satisfaction. He'd lost what to him was just a few dollars. In exchange, he had the pleasure of watching The Great Artist grovel for those dollars. I tried to recoup some dignity by slipping the bills nonchalantly into my pocket and asking, "Who do you like for tonight's game?"

Bobby didn't deign to answer. He rose and said, "Let's take a look at what you've done with my face."

I always dread letting a subject look at what I've done with his or her face while I'm still working on the portrait. Not that I can't take criticism. Okay, I can't take criticism. Big deal, show me someone who can. The real problem is that I paint what I find in a person's face, which is often at odds with what they see in themselves.

"It's only about half finished," I warned. "You really can't tell much yet."

"I understand." Reassuring nod. "I just want to see what direction you're headed."

For a full minute, Bobby studied the portrait without expression. When his eyebrows arched, I braced myself for the worst. He surprised me by following up the arched eyebrows with a smile. "This isn't what I expected. I thought you'd do something passable, commonplace, suitable for commercial uses." He waggled his hand. "You know, the conventional view of Bobby Race, a workaholic grunge with a college boy look, touch of sinister around the mouth, the obligatory scarecrow hair. Instead you're making me look like an interesting person, an original personality, somebody who's still evolving."

"Yep, that's the way I see you, Bobby. Somewhere in the middle of the evolutionary scale."

Instead of laughing, he gave me a supportive nod. "I'm pleased. Keep it up."

Praise from Bobby Race? I could only suppose his opportunity to humiliate me over the baseball bet had put him in an unusually good mood. "I'll get back to work then." I half expected Bobby to suddenly wheel around and tell me what he *really* thought of my efforts. But he just went back to his work, which quickly absorbed him. As did mine.

CHAPTER 15

"All the girls here giggle among themselves about what a *hunk* you are. They even seem to know the size of your *thing*." Dorothy's chin was trembling and tears had formed in the corners of her eyes. "Do you have any idea how terribly humiliated I feel?"

"No, I don't. In fact, I haven't the vaguest idea what you're upset about." Dorothy had snagged my arm in the hallway as I was returning from a trip to the men's room and pulled me into her Spartan office. She was frantic with rage. "Tell me why you're sore."

"You know very well." She twisted a handkerchief as if she wished it were my neck. "First you made a big play for me, flattered me, gave everyone at Race the impression I meant something to you. Then, at the first opportunity, you jumped into bed with the lusty Jenny Hartsong. That's absolutely despicable."

"Wait a minute, back up a day. Remember when I told you that I cared for you? That I wanted to see you outside this high-tech lunatic asylum? Do you also remember blowing me off, telling me you're too focused on your career to have time for me?"

Tight, angry nod.

"So when you threw me over the side, I didn't have the right to reach for a life jacket?"

"That's what Jenny is to you? A life jacket? I'm sure she'll be pleased to hear it."

"Bad metaphor." I was too pissed to think straight. "Did Jenny tell you we slept together last night?"

"No, she told two or three dozen of her closest friends, knowing the news would get back to me within thirty minutes."

"She shouldn't have done that. But why are you upset? You don't care about me anyway, you said as much just yesterday."

"I didn't say I don't care for you." Her eyes dropped. "I said my life was too busy for you."

"Same thing."

"No, it isn't." She began to cry in earnest. "You might have worked harder to change my mind. Maybe I want to be pursued. I might've come around, if you'd taken just one or two more steps in my direction. Now everyone's laughing at me behind my back."

"That's what you're really upset about, your precious reputation at Race Software."

"Of course I'm concerned. This place is my life, these people are the only friends I have."

"That's the problem."

"I know, you're going to throw that old line at me. *Get a life.* This from a down-and-out artist who can't pay his bills, doesn't have much of a professional reputation, won't take responsibility for anything in his own life, sleeps around like some...some.... whoremaster!"

"Wow, I haven't heard that word since the last time I read William Makepiece Thackery. Dorothy, I'm a straightforward kind of guy. I told you I was attracted to you. You advised me to get lost. I took you at your word. And I didn't go looking for Jenny as a consolation prize. She showed up at my house last night on her own, revved up her considerable charms, I succumbed. Shoot me, I'm human."

"I'd like to shoot you," she bawled.

"Please don't cry." I said that even though she looked adorable with tears streaming in passionate rivulets down her cheeks. For some reason her hair was becoming frizzy as she sobbed, which only contributed to her waifish beauty. Could the tears be creating her own personal zone of humidity? "Come on." I gathered her into my arms. "Nobody's laughing at you behind your back. You've got the big salary, the big office, the title. Dilbert you're not."

"They're laughing at me as a woman."

"Got to be jealousy. You're one of the best looking girls in this crazy place."

"You've studied them all, I'm sure."

"Down to the color of their undies." I threw up my hands. "That was a joke! Dorothy, you have to loosen up."

"I don't know how."

She made those few words sound like a confession to a priest.

I took her hands just to stop them from flailing around. "Come over to my place tonight. Do you like pasta? That's the one thing I cook really well. Rigatoni…angel hair…penne…you name it. I do my own sauce, by the way." A total lie, my culinary skills are nonexistent. "We'll have wine, I'll put a candle on the table. What do you say?"

"What did you serve to Jenny last night?"

"She didn't have dinner at my house."

"Just a fast fuck and out the door?"

Profanity doesn't work for Dorothy, it makes her sound like a kindergarten teacher on amphetamines. "Wasn't like that." My reserves of patience were shrinking, but I persisted. "Come over tonight. I'll show you my etchings. Very few seducers who use that old line can actually produce etchings at the crucial moment. I can."

The beginnings of a smile crept through the tears. "You're incorrigible. I suppose that's why all the girls like you. The Bad Boy Syndrome, it's called. I read a monograph about people like you."

"Nonsense. My larger-than-life personality could never be captured in a mere monograph."

Dorothy's sobs flattened out into a series of wheezes which tailed off into deep breathing as she used her handkerchief to wipe her cheeks dry. I loved the way she did that. Even when she became semi-hysterical, her movements had grace and beauty. Dorothy was a swan, Jenny was a hummingbird. I guess I prefer swans.

Eventually she said, "What time should I be at your house?"

"Eight o'clock okay?"

"I usually don't leave the office until eight, or even later."

"Tonight you'll play hooky."

"All the years I was in school, I never cut a class." Wistfully. "I always wanted to, I could never take the plunge."

"This is your big opportunity." Taking a chance, I leaned forward and kissed Dorothy's cheek. She didn't object. Nor did she give me a gush-and-blush. She simply lowered her face demurely. "Eight o'clock," I repeated.

"I'll be there." Her face slowly came up towards mine. "Don't expect me to be Jenny. I'm not ready for that."

"Just be Dorothy, that's enough for me."

I spent a lot of the afternoon trying to infuse Bobby's portrait with the right *chiaroscuro*, those delicate gradations of light and shadow that provide a painting with its atmosphere. Visions of Dorothy intruded. I pictured her smiling at me over the dinner table, the candlelight playing artfully on our faces as we sipped wine and rubbed each other's insteps under the table.

On the way home I'd stop at Scarlatti's to pick up two ready-to-go dinners. Angel Hair, I think. In their great marinara sauce. Sourdough bread, too. That way I wouldn't have to do anything except slip the food in the oven, keep it warm until dinner, pretend I know how to do more in the kitchen than open a bottle of beer. With five thousand unexpected dollars in my pocket, I could afford wine with a real cork.

While I worked, I occasionally eavesdropped on Bobby's various conversations. He was whipping his execs to finish Redleaf, get it out on schedule, make it the best network software on the market, ya-da-ya-da-ya-da as Seinfeld would say. Sometimes he cajoled. Sometimes he threatened. In one case, he fired a guy who apparently fucked up something called a "benchmark." Tough business.

One rather tense meeting between Bobby and Greg Tillotson seemed to be going badly for Greg. The Redleaf project director shifted his thick body around uncomfortably while his fingers drummed the arm of his chair.

"I'll tell you, Bobby," Tillotson was saying, "the people at Zebulon-Perry are talking up their new networking protocol and it sounds very much like Redleaf. They could beat us to the same niche your marketing people have targeted."

"Zebulon-Perry's an also-ran." Bobby's tone was contemptuous. "They can't even beat IBM to market."

"I hear they've finished their Beta tests, got their channels signed up, independent software vendors are slavering to write applications for their new product," Tillotson said. "I think ZP's a real threat. Could they have gotten hold of any of our Redleaf code?"

"Absolutely not." Bobby leaned forward. "I think you're just looking for a reason to push back the Redleaf announcement again. We've got to get that package out before Microsoft and the others take control of our niche."

Pepper Johnson picked that moment to drift into Bobby's office, no appointment, the hook that took the place of his left hand spiking a copy of the *Chronicle's* sport section.

"Hey, Bobby, we got the Giants versus the Dodgers again tonight. Ya want to spot me ten bucks on the Giants? I got a feeling the Dodgers are gonna have a big game."

Greg Tillotson swung around at Pepper. "Can't you see we're in a meeting? Get out of here!"

"Hey now, Greg, chill out, this'll just take a minute. Me and Bobby like to have our daily ten-spot bet."

Tillotson's face went into a shade of crimson seldom seen outside the velvet walls of an old-fashioned whorehouse.

"It's okay, Greg." The tension had drained from Bobby's face. "You know Pepper and I like to get a bet down about this time of day. You got it, Pepper. I'll take the Giants for ten."

"Gonna cost ya." Pepper peeked at my painting, nodded approvingly. "Looking good there, Kevin." Then he drifted back out of Bobby's office.

As soon as he was gone, Tillotson began his complaints. "Bobby, it's not right that a broken-down janitor has more access to you than most of your senior executives. Lots of your execs resent it, and I'm one of them. Pepper wanders in and out as if this was his office."

"Pepper's more than a janitor. He's been with me almost from the beginning." Bobby pinched the bridge of his nose with two fingers. "Now and then I need some relief from the business. Don't you? This time of year, Pepper and I talk baseball. The playoffs are coming up, can the Giants make it? I hope so. Pepper doesn't think they have a shot. In the winter we try to figure out why the Raiders can't put it together anymore. In May we hold prayer meetings for the Lakers."

"I don't like him," Tillotson growled. "He's insolent."

"That's not insolence, it's confidence. You must have heard Pepper didn't lose his left hand in an auto accident. It was shot off in Vietnam. The way I heard it, and not from Pepper himself, is that a Vietcong machine gun shot off his hand, left it hanging from just a few strips of skin. He kept advancing anyway, used his good hand to empty a full clip from an M-16 into a machine-gun crew that had already killed three of his squad. Ten minutes later a medic amputated what was left of his hand. Things like corporate titles just don't impress a guy like Pepper Johnson."

Tillotson, weary of the argument, waved away any further discussion. "Forget Pepper. I'm still worried about Zebulon-Perry beating us to market."

"And I'm saying forget ZP. They're not a threat and I want Redleaf totally debugged by the end of the month. Get your team on the stick, Greg."

"They're already bleeding from every pore. Fifteen hour days and seven day weeks. What else can I do?"

"Whatever it takes."

As soon as Tillotson left, Bobby called Hugh Wilson into his office. The corporate counsel evidently had been working at the tiny desk set up on his treadmill because he arrived in t-shirt and shorts, out of breath, smelling like a dead skunk in the middle of a road.

Bobby recoiled. "Hugh, take a shower before you come into my office, will you?"

"Jenny said you wanted me right away." Hugh managed to look aggrieved and ready for action at the same time. "What's up?"

"Greg heard a rumor that Zebulon-Perry is test marketing a network package very much like Redleaf. I told Greg to ignore the rumor, it couldn't happen. He's under enough pressure already, I don't want him worried about ZP. But suppose Izzy Valentine made a deal with ZP's management. We don't know how much of our code Cynthia managed to grab or where it went."

Hugh Wilson shook his head. "ZP's not that aggressive, they've never led the pack. I can't see them having the guts to steal our intellectual property and their pockets aren't deep enough to fight us in a court battle over software piracy."

"That was my first reaction. Just to be safe, I want you to put that firm of private investigators on ZP, dig up some background on this hot new product of theirs."

"Will do, Bobby."

From my corner, I wondered how many times a day the phrase "*Will do, Bobby*" was uttered in this office.

Jenny came trotting in. She looked at me, then Bobby, then Hugh as if unsure which of us to address. Bobby being the undisputed master of all he surveyed, she spoke to him. "Mrs. Isadore Valentine is on line two. She wants to talk with Kevin."

"*Mrs.* Valentine." Bobby's shoulders hunched into a question mark. "Are you sure it isn't *Mr.* Isadore Valentine? Wanting to talk with *Kevin*?"

"Yes, it's a woman. Mrs. Isadore Valentine is how she introduced herself. Wants *a few minutes of Mr. Pierce's valuable time*, she said."

Never before had anyone said my time was valuable. It felt good. "I told you yesterday I met Amelia Valentine at Izzy's house, I'm sorry, at his mansion, he'd be insulted if I called it a house."

"What does she want?" Hugh asked me.

"Gee whiz, I left my Batman predictor ring at home. I'll probably have to actually talk to her to find out what she wants."

Bobby motioned to a bank of telephones on his desk that resembled the command center of Captain Nemo's submarine in *Twenty Thousand Leagues Under The Sea*. "Take the call right here. I'll put Mrs. Valentine on the speaker phone so Hugh and I can listen in on your conversation."

"Amelia's husband may be a crook, but she's still entitled to privacy in her personal conversations. I'll be happy to tell you what she said after I've talked to her."

"There's no legal reason we can't listen in," Hugh said. "The California statues on privacy explicitly state…"

"Hugh, stop being a lawyer for a minute. This is a nice woman in a wheelchair, not The Godfather. I'll take the call at Jenny's desk and come right back." Before they could object, I went out to Jenny's spacious cubicle and punched the button for line two. "Hello, this is Kevin Pierce."

"Kevin! Thank you so much for taking my call. I hope I didn't interrupt your work. I really needed to speak with you and just called on the spur of the moment, as you Yanks say."

Amelia's warmth triggered an automatic smile. "No problem. It's always a pleasure to hear from you. What's up? You need a single guy for dinner? I'm expecting a guest tonight, but I'll be free tomorrow evening."

Her laugh was quick and genuine. "You'd be welcome at my table any night, dear boy. However, that's not why I'm calling. I have an artistic commission that may interest you."

I hate it when people offer me an *artistic commission*. That usually means they want a portrait painted of their grandfather or a cherished nephew or maybe the family dog. "I'm sorry, Amelia. I don't do commissions. Usually I just stumble onto a face that absorbs me and then I go ahead and paint it. Not a particularly profitable way to work, I admit. The portrait I'm doing of Bobby Race is a rare exception to the way I work."

"I understand." Amelia chuckled vigorously. "That's exactly what I want you to do, look at some absorbing faces. I'm sure you aren't aware that I'm president of the Bayside Childrens Shelter. No reason you should know. The shelter is a volunteer organization, we take temporary custody of physically abused children in the eight to twelve-year-old range. San Mateo County sponsors us, though most of our funds come from private donations. We intend to print a poster to put in supermarkets around the South Bay. We need a child's face for that poster. There are some beautiful children here, boys and girls with incredible sadness in their eyes, terrible desperation, and a longing for gentle love. You could do that face, Kevin."

Amelia's offer was the last thing I expected. "Well, hell, that really is an interesting project."

"And it's not *pro bono*, as the solicitors say. We've put four thousand dollars into the budget for the poster's artwork."

"That's generous." I toyed with a lovely piece of quartz on Jenny's desk while I thought about the offer.

"I don't expect you to say yes over the phone. Can you come by the shelter on your way home this afternoon? Just for fifteen minutes? I'd like you to see the facility and the children. Especially the children. Then you'll know whether you'd be interested in this commission."

Even Saddam Hussein couldn't have said no to that one. "I'll be delighted to stop by."

"Splendid!" Amelia gave me the shelter's address and we agreed to meet at six o'clock. "I'm very enthused, Kevin. You have a wonderful eye and I believe you'll decide to take this commission. I will personally be extremely grateful if you do. Ta-ta."

Nobody had ever said ta-ta to me, either. That felt good, too. I went back into Bobby's office and explained what Amelia Valentine's call was about. Bobby looked skeptical. Hugh thought it might violate my employment contract with Race Software to negotiate a new agreement before completing my current assignment.

"You'll have to speak with my attorney about that," I replied in a haughty manner. "Actually, I don't have an attorney. When I feel the need to have my pockets picked, I go North Beach in San Francisco."

"Okay," Bobby said, "let's forget about the childrens shelter. Except, Kevin, if it looks like a worthwhile effort you can tell Amelia Valentine to put me down for a contribution of ten k. That's the kind of community project I like to support."

"You mean..." I still didn't quite get the k business "...ten thousand dollars?"

Bobby was amused. "Yes, Kevin. Ten thousand American dollars."

"Okay, I'll tell her." Sometimes I think Bobby Race is an asshole, other times I think he's a great man. I wish he wouldn't confuse me.

Jenny came trotting in with a strange wobble, minus her customary verve, slack-jawed, panic plastered across her face like a bumper sticker. "It's back!" she squealed. "That thing is back!"

"Jenny, get hold of yourself," Bobby said. "Are you saying that red mist is here again?"

"Yes!!!"

Bobby stood up with a jerky motion, then sat down again. Heavily. He looked at Hugh Wilson, ace attorney, a skinny guy in smelly shorts and t-shirt, and voted no with his eyes. Then at tearful, hyperactive

Jenny cringing at Hugh's side, her arms thrown around him. Another no vote. Finally at me. "Kevin, take care of this problem. Get that thing, whatever-the-hell-it-is, OUT…OF…MY…HEADQUARTERS!"

I thought I knew what the spirit of Cynthia Gooding was going to do. "I don't have to go get it. It's coming right up here to your office."

"That's ridiculous," Bobby snapped.

Pepper Johnson came running in, as sweaty as Hugh, apparently from running up several flights of stairs in order to beat the elevators. His hook was waving around as he gulped for air, trying to speak, till finally he wheezed out, "Hey guys, we got the red monster in the building again. It didn't even stop at the front desk to pick up a visitor's badge."

"It was in the lobby?" Bobby's eyes rolled. "How many people saw it?"

"Lots." Pepper gasping, trying to catch his breath, put his head down between his legs.

I went to the window overlooking the entrance to Race headquarters. Twenty or thirty employees were running for their cars as if the hounds of hell had fangs up their butts. They escaped into the parking lot, headed pell mell for their individual cars. One of the drivers sideswiped a brand-new Ford van in his haste to get away. A woman tripped and fell, nobody stopped to help her up. Somebody else ran to the bay's edge with his laptop computer in his hand, jumped in, began swimming clumsily in the general direction of Oakland.

"Full-scale panic going on down there." Though I tried to speak calmly, my voice broke on the last word. I cleared my throat. "Is it moving, Pepper? Coming this way?"

"Yeah." His head still between his legs. "I think so. It went from the lobby to the second floor, that's when I ran up the stairs. Getting too old to run up six flights."

Pam Solter and Greg Tillotson appeared in the doorway.

"You heard?" Pam's eyes darted around the room. "Yes, you've heard. Bobby, it's coming up floor by floor. People are running…"

"Running for their lives!" Tillotson barked, making it clear he wished he knew which way to run himself.

Dorothy rushed in, a hand thrown to her throat, her face compacted with alarm. "Is it back?" She quickly absorbed the fear in Bobby's office and hurried to her CEO's side for safety.

Bobby's management team didn't look like much of a team at the moment. Except for Pepper, they huddled as close to Bobby as possible, all their highly developed management skills profoundly useless in the face of a mysterious red mist. Custer's Last Stand, that's what I was reminded of. All eyes went to me.

"Hey, I don't know what to do."

"You're all we've got." Pam Solter made it a complaint. "Do *something*."

"She's right." Pepper had recovered his breath, his head was up, his eyes were on me, too. "Everybody here is into computer science, zeroes and ones, digits, bytes, bits, that's what they dig. You're the only one's got juice with the spirit world."

"That's not true!"

"Yes, ya do," Pepper fired back at me. "You're wired into this shit, Kevin. So stand up for us!"

I wanted to crawl under Bobby's desk and hide. Except there was no room for me, the desk was too congested.

Somebody in the hallway screamed. Feet pounded. Crashing noises, too, as employees madly dashed for safety. From all the panic, I cleverly deduced this incarnation was even more chilling than the earlier sightings. Or, what if I was totally wrong? What if this thing had nothing to do with Cynthia? What if it was simply some horribly evil and ugly wraith for which there was no explanation at all? You can't fight something like that. You can't outsmart it, reason with it, or send it back to wherever it came from. I felt stupid for ever giving these people any reason to believe I could deal with unearthly matters. Mostly I felt useless and as frightened as everyone else.

"Just don't move, any of you." A needless order, Bobby and his team were frozen in place. "Whatever happens, don't panic and run." Among other worries, I didn't care to be trampled in a stampede.

The temperature began to slide lower, just as it had the last time this thing appeared. My own body temperature seemed to drop as I imagined my blood going thick and icy and moving through my body like so much industrial sludge. This was nothing like one of Sport Sullivan's occasional visits, which were more irritating than scary. All Sport wanted was to brag that he helped fix the 1919 World Series and complain about the way Arnold Rothstein double-crossed him. This thing, whatever it was, had a serious agenda.

Suddenly the temperature went below freezing and everyone began to shiver.

"It's here!" somebody croaked.

"Well, fuck it," Pepper Johnson said. "When it comes in, everybody give it the finger, just so we don't look like a bunch of weasels."

Somebody behind me whimpered. I tried to stiffen my backbone and come up with a course of action. Nothing intelligent occurred to me. Then it came through the doorway. I should say it floated through the doorway.

"Oh no..." somebody said. "It's a woman!"

Right. This was no red, misty blob. It now had the shape of a woman. The vaguely formed face bore a resemblance to the photos I'd seen of Cynthia. It drifted around Bobby's office as if looking for something or someone.

"That's Cynthia!" Jenny squealed.

"Shut up," Hugh looked past the apparition. "Just keep quiet for once. Kevin, you do the talking."

Talking? What do you say to the ghost of a murdered woman? Okay, a question did come to me. "Are you Cynthia Gooding?"

Nothing. The thing just continued moving throughout the room in a swaying motion that suggested the presence of a breeze, though all I could feel was the dreadful chill.

"Cindy Pacini?" She might react to her real name. In fact, she did stop moving about. When she settled into one place, her features became better defined. Her face was much longer than it would have been in life. Eyes sunken. Cheeks hollow. Still the face of the woman known as Cynthia Gooding. The body was less distinctly drawn, though the shape was clearly that of a woman rather than a man. The whole apparition floated about a foot above the floor. I also became aware of a sound emanating from her, the kind of high-pitched hum you get when you hit a tuning fork.

"What do you want?"

The humming sound became shrill, then retreated.

"How did this happen, Cynthia? Cindy? Were you murdered? Was it an accident? How can we help you?"

The hum escalated into a wildly high pitch a hundred times more aggravating than fingernails across a blackboard. I resisted putting my hands over my ears. I had no idea what her reaction meant, or which of my questions, if any, might have drawn that reaction. Behind me, somebody bolted and ran out of Bobby's office. I glanced over to see Jenny running through the door. Hugh Wilson yelled "Jenny!" and ran after her.

Cynthia moved through the room again, finally coming to a standstill in front of the wall that displayed Bobby's collection of baseball cards. She continued to sway and hum in that position. Meanwhile, the misty quality of her form came and went with a pulsating beat. For a second or two the form would be quite solidly red, then become more ephemeral, then pulse back to a more solid red. I had the impression she had no control over her vibrations, no way of communicating, no way of righting whatever wrong might have been done to her. And that she was miserable about it.

"Make it go away!" Bobby barked.

Bobby leaned forward aggressively, his face chalky. Pam Solter had backed herself into the big glass window behind Bobby's desk. Dorothy simply stared, trying to get her logical mind wrapped around the concept of a ghostly being. Tillotson's customary bluster had vanished. Pepper scowled at the spirit and looked ready to make some kind of move on it. They all shivered from the cold. Their breaths came in white puffs.

"Stay put, Pepper," I said. "Remember what happened to Joe Patterson."

"We gotta get that thing outta here!"

Remarkably, an idea did come to me. "Pepper, you're closer to the door. There's a piece of ornamental crystal on Jenny's desk. Can you slip out the door and get it for me? Take care not to let our visitor touch you."

Much as Pepper wanted to take action, he had a hard time making himself move.

"Now," I prompted.

Pepper went sideways through the door, keeping his eyes on Cynthia's image every second. When he didn't immediately return, I wondered if he'd just kept on going. I wouldn't have faulted him. I wanted to run myself. Pepper leaned back in the door, juggling in his one good hand the crystal I'd toyed with during my phone conversation with Amelia. "Is this what ya want?"

"Yeah, that's the one. Toss it to me."

I caught the heavy piece of quartz and squeezed its rough surface while trying to figure out how to use it.

"What the hell are you doing?" Bobby said.

Dorothy found her voice. "The molecules in quartz crystals are arranged in a pattern repeated regularly in three dimensions. Some people believe that arrangement of molecules gives crystals the kinetic energy to generate supernatural powers. A ridiculous idea."

Trust Dorothy to have read about crystals.

"Psychics also claim that spirits fear crystals," I said. "Because of the energy."

"Waste of time!" Bobby thundered. "Do something that makes sense!"

"This is the best I can come up with. If you don't like it, call 1-800-GHOST." I went down on one knee and rolled the crystal across the floor, trying to make it come to rest just under Cynthia's pulsating red form. Though I missed by about six inches, the presence of the crystal did trigger a reaction. Cynthia's form suddenly telescoped down to half its size. With an accompanying shriek that sounded all too much like a frenzied scream, it began zooming around the room like a balloon with the air let out, bouncing crazily off the walls, windows and ceiling

Then, with a dreadful parting shriek that made all of us insane, Cynthia's ghost was out the door and gone.

CHAPTER 16

You ever been to a bar where there's a flea-bitten dog sleeping on the floor? Two guys in tank tops arm-wrestling at a back table? Credence Clearwater on an ancient juke box? Sawdust on the floor? Somebody's throw-up in the corner? Hardly enough light to read the label on your beer? Permanent smell of stale whiskey and lots of dirty laundry? Most of the customers looking like they once had numbers on their chests?

Then you might have been to Billy Jack's Bar & Texas Barbecue on the bad side of Redwood City, only a few miles from Race Software but light years away in lifestyle. After our "ghostly visitation" nobody wanted to stay in the headquarters building. Bobby shut the place down early, a first in the company's history, and I suggested we huddle at Billy Jack's for a *post mortem* on the afternoon's events. On reflection, *post mortem* might have been a poor choice of words.

Most of the management team came along. Bobby and Dorothy looking shaky. Pam Solter smoking foul-smelling black *cigarillos* one after another as if they were some form of tonic. Greg Tillotson once again argumentative. Pepper Johnson, too, pensive and tired. Hugh had taken Jenny home, her in tears and him still in his jogging togs.

We grabbed a large table at the rear of the place, near the sleeping dog. Everyone felt uncomfortable except me. I felt right at home.

"Why are we here?" Tillotson demanded. "I don't like this place, it smells putrid."

Bobby stirred. "We're here because it's the last place on the peninsula the media would think of looking for me. Isn't that why you brought us to this...uh...colorful establishment, Kevin?"

"That's right," I said.

There had been a dozen phone calls from the media before we left. Somebody had called the police. They showed up, stomped around, shrugged and left when told there had been a power failure that scared a lot of employees and forced the shutdown of the headquarters buildings. Pepper already had gone down to the engineering room and closed off most of the electrical systems to give the story credence. Bobby had delegated Ray Waters to put out the power failure story, even though he knew the media would get a totally different angle from any employees they could reach.

As we were leaving, vans with reporters and tv cameramen from Channel 4 and Fox News pulled up to the company gates.

"You picked a good place to hide out." Bobby grinned, which couldn't have been easy for him after the day he'd had. "What's the cuisine like?"

"Grease with various aromas. But they get all the Giants games on tv."

"Recommendation enough."

Pam said, "I don't like the looks of that bartender. Oh my God, did he hear me? He's coming over here."

The bartender's booming laugh preceded him. He was big enough to qualify for his own zip code, a shambling wreck of man with a scraggly beard, a bulbous veined nose, red face, a smile that would still be boyish when he reached eighty if he managed to live that long. "Hey there, Kevin, good to see yew! Yew don't come around here often enough, boy."

I stood up and we shook hands. "Folks, this is Billy Jack Henderson, the proprietor. We're from the same town in Texas, he was two years ahead of me in high school."

"I almost graduated, too," Billy Jack told our little group. "Would've graduated with a C minus average…C minus!!…if I hadn't robbed the Seven Eleven. Tell 'em, Kevin. C minus!"

"Billy Jack was one of our star students. He could've had a scholarship to the Bible college down the road, he hadn't gone into that Seven Eleven with a .38."

"Didn't set out to rob it," Billy Jack explained. "Clerk treated me like a field hand." He smiled all around. "I know what Kevin wants. Carta Blanca, same as he drank in fifth grade. What'll yew folks have? By the way, first drink for every new customer is on the house. So order up the best."

"Draft beer," Greg Tillotson said. "In a clean glass."

Bobby ordered champagne, just for amusement. When Billy Jack said, "No problem, I'll send the boy over to Safeway," Bobby changed his order to Anchor steam beer.

I knew some of Pam's cynical humor had returned when she said, "I'm on a health kick, so I'll just have the juice from a pint of vodka." Dorothy quietly ordered a club soda and Pepper asked for a boilermaker.

"Lemmee bring yew a double shot of Wild Turkey for the boilermaker," Billy Jack offered. "Makes your fingernails grow in spirals." He noticed the hook at the end of Pepper's left arm. "Sorry there, pardner. Didn't notice the meathook right off."

"No offense, Billy Jack. Ya got a good idea about the Wild Turkey. Let's go with it." When Billy Jack hustled off for the drinks, Pepper said, "This is a good joint, I'll be coming back to it."

"Let's move on to business," Bobby said. "Give me your opinions on what you saw today."

"I don't know what the hell we saw." Tillotson was, as usual, the first to speak. "At the time, it scared the hell out of me, I'll admit that." His customary glower deepened. "But I'm a man of science, I don't believe in supernatural beings. What we saw must have some basis in the real world."

Dorothy immediately agreed. "That was not the 'spirit' of Cynthia Gooding, or of anyone else. Someone rigged a very clever show. Clever enough to scare all of us. Thinking back, I'd compare it with the Wizard of Oz. Like that other Dorothy, the one from Kansas with the little dog, I was too frightened to look behind the curtain. I don't know how it was done, or why, but I'll find out. Bobby, you've seen many equally elaborate computer-produced special effects. We've written programs for special effects ourselves, on contract to movie studios. Some of our own people, sellouts to Izzy Valentine, could have organized the show. Do you really think it's a coincidence that today's special effects took place on the day Valentine began his campaign for a seat on your board?"

"No, I don't." Bobby's keen eyes focused somewhere above everyone's heads. "Izzy's the source of our current troubles, there's no doubt in my mind." His eyes turned to Pam Solter. "What about you, Pam? What was your take?"

"Bobby, I'm a rationalist." Pam's throat was raspy from all the *cigarillos* she'd smoked over the last hour. "I don't believe in the tooth fairy, the Easter bunny, or that the coyote will ever catch the roadrunner. But I believe what we saw today was not of this world."

"If it looks like a ghost, acts like a ghost, feels like a ghost, then it's a fucking ghost," was Pepper's contribution.

"I'll second that," Pam said.

An argument broke out between the pro-ghost and anti-ghost contingents, with Bobby and me sitting quietly on the sidelines. Billy Jack delivered our drinks, along with a complimentary stack of barbecued ribs almost too greasy to pick up. The drinks were eagerly snatched up and consumed. I drank my Carta Blanca and nibbled on a rib while the argument raged, well stoked by the alcohol.

"You know we're gonna lose some key people, which is bound to set back Greenleaf," Tillotson said. "No way around it."

Bobby's reply had the rasp of a dentist's drill. "It's your job to keep the program on track, Greg. You can't do the job, you're out."

Tillotson dropped his eyes and shifted his attention to his beer.

"We're almost over the hump on Redleaf," Dorothy said to fill the silence that followed. "We can deliver the product on time if we to contract out some of the work."

"No! We'll contract out nothing," Bobby retorted. "That's how you lose primary code to your competitors, and we've had enough of that already. All the development work stays in-house."

"A mistake," Dorothy said. When Bobby looked irritated, she added, "After today, we'll need a lot of new programmers."

Pam Solter agreed. "I've been pulling employment applications this week, looking to see who's out there, how many experienced programmers we might hire on short notice. There aren't many who can do the quality of work you expect, Bobby. I say contract out the least important work, keep the critical code in-house."

Bobby thought over their comments. "I'll consider it," he said finally. "Meanwhile, no code leaves the house."

"I don't know nothing about programming," Pepper declared, "but you people can do anything, ya set your minds to it." He glared around, challenging his drinking partners to live up to their reputations. "I've seen ya hack your way through worse shit than this."

"The competitive landscape is a lot different than it was two years ago, even one year ago, our competitors are more aggressive than ever," Tillotson complained. "This nonsense about a ghost is going to aggravate all of our problems."

"Greg, I learned the hard way there's only one thing to do when the enemy's got ya surrounded." Pepper used the sharpened hook at the end of his left arm to gouge a long deep scar into the wooden table top. The gouge was aimed at Greg Tillotson's heart. "Ya go straight at the fuckers."

Before Tillotson could reply, Bobby lifted his hands and applauded lightly. Tillotson's face flushed, he didn't appreciate a lesson in strategy from a "maintenance technician."

"Pepper's got the right idea," Bobby said. "Okay, everybody's been heard from except Kevin, and we know where he stands. He believes in the supernatural. Frankly, I was terrified. I'm as much a man of science as Greg, but at the time I thought we were looking at Cynthia's ghost. Now, a couple of hours later, I'm not so sure. Dorothy's right, these days you can create any effect you want with a computer. I suppose even the building's climate controls could have been tampered with to create that frigid atmosphere." He turned on me. "Kevin has a relationship of sorts with Valentine and his wife. He uncovered the connection between Izzy and Cynthia. And he did appear to stop the thing in its tracks, send it shooting out of the building. I'm grateful for all that, Kevin."

With rib meat in my mouth and grease all over my chin, I could only nod and grunt my thanks for the boss's approval.

"I want you to meet with Amelia Valentine today, just as you were scheduled to do..." Bobby consulted his watch, which had so many built-in high-tech gadgets he could hardly tell the time "...in about half an hour. Probe her about Izzy's letter to my board of directors and major stockholders. Report to Dorothy this evening on her reaction."

"Ummm...umhuh...umffah," I answered around my rib.

"I'll assume that's a yes." Bobby focused on Tillotson. "Greg, I'm well aware we're going to lose some of the Redleaf team over today's events. Your job is to keep the program on track no matter the cost. I repeat: *no matter the cost*. We're shooting the moon with this product."

"I understand." Tillotson didn't look happy, but he obviously understood his job was on the line, ghost or no ghost.

"We'll watch tonight's tv news," Bobby continued, "see what their angle is on the story, and check the morning papers. I expect the worst—a *ghost story*." He twisted the phrase so it sounded obscene. "Ray Waters will continue to handle the media inquiries. Any senior manager who gives an interview to the media about this afternoon's events is fired. I'm sure some of our employees will talk about what they saw—*think* they saw—to their friends. I don't want any employees let go for that. Fire only the ones who talk directly to the newspapers and tv people."

The management team looked as glum as a convention of Chicago Cubs fans, but they had their marching orders from Bobby. I had to admire the bastard. He didn't flinch at making tough decisions, listened to the thoughts of plain working guys like Pepper, knew how to bounce back.

Billy Jack reappeared. "How about another round, folks? This one's on your tab, of course."

"Hit us again," Bobby said. "And thanks for the ribs. They're delicious, best I ever tasted."

Billy Jack beamed. "I'll bring yew another side, no charge."

Bobby hadn't actually touched the ribs, he was just shmoozing the help because he knew I'd appreciate anything he did to make Billy Jack feel like an ace restaurateur. The guy was always polishing his image. Right away I didn't like him again. "I'd better get going, Amelia will be waiting." I looked pointedly at Dorothy. "How should I get in touch with you after I talk to her?"

Dorothy pretended to think that over. "Why don't I come by your house later, about eight o'clock."

Very smooth, Dorothy. "See you then."

The Bayside Childrens Shelter was located on some very expensive real estate in Palo Alto, one of the toniest communities in Silicon Valley. You can't throw a laptop in that town without hitting a high-level computer executive. The shelter sat in the middle of about ten leafy acres off Route 280 close to Stanford University's linear accelerator. When you go through Palo Alto on Route 280, you actually drive over the linear accelerator, which burrows along the ground for at least a couple of miles through otherwise unspoiled countryside. I always worry that my testicles might be fried if I happened to drive over the accelerator just when billions of atomic particles are sent racing down that long tube. So far I haven't noticed any singe marks on my balls, but I usually check them after a trip along 280.

I parked in the visitors lot below the complex and walked up a set of redwood steps to the shelter's main building, which resembled a well-financed suburban grammar school. There was a smaller staff parking lot at the top of the hill, right next to the main building. One of the cars in that lot was Izzy Valentine's limo. I didn't recognize the car itself. Limo identification isn't one of my strengths. I did recognize the chauffeur leaning against the limo, his big arms crossed, the black suit crisply pressed, bald head shining in the late afternoon sun.

Pure John Braggia greeted me politely. "Good to see you again, Mr. Pierce. How was the salmon?"

"Haven't had a chance to try it. I have a guest for dinner, maybe I'll serve the salmon to her. I'm not much of a cook, though."

"Salmon's easy, just broil it with a little lemon butter, it'll melt in your mouth."

"Are you driving Mrs. Valentine today?"

"Yes, sir. She doesn't get out much. When she does, Mr. Valentine likes me to watch over her. You'll find Mrs. Valentine in the dining room. It's dinner time for the brats. Dining room's straight down the hall through the main entrance."

"Thanks, I'll go find her." I took a couple of steps, then turned back to tell Pure John something that had been on my mind since I first met him. "I've been wanting to say you're the only person I know who can be insolent without being insolent, you know what I mean?"

"That's one of my many talents, Mr. Pierce."

"You see? Again you're being insolent without being insolent. How do you do that?"

"It's mostly in the voice. Subtle inflections here and there."

"Like when you pronounce *Mr. Pierce* and *sir* as if you were saying *dogshit.*"

"Exactly…Mr. Pierce…sir."

"You're good." I went into the main building and followed the aroma of food to the dining room, which was laid about pretty much like a small grammar school cafeteria. What immediately struck me was that the thirty or so eight to twelve-year-olds having dinner there weren't nearly as boisterous as most kids their age. If anything, their voices were muffled. Heads down. Plates being scraped clean, not a bite left by anyone. They moved more like residents in a senior center than a bunch of kids.

"Kevin, over here!" Amelia Valentine waved from a table at the far end of the dining room. She backed her motorized wheelchair away from the table, turned it smartly and came rolling down the center aisle to greet me.

"Hello, Amelia. Good to see you again." I bent to kiss her lightly on the cheek, her warmth inviting that small familiarity.

"Thank you for coming, Kevin. I'm most grateful."

She made me feel like a long-lost relative returned to the family hearth. I followed the wheelchair, which Amelia operated with the panache of a Formula One driver, back to her table. Amelia introduced me in glowing terms to a short, heavy-breasted woman of about fifty with plump, damp fingers that loosely shook my hand. Susan Wells, director of the shelter.

"Would you like me to get you something from the buffet?" Miss Wells asked.

"No, thanks. I'm having dinner with someone a bit later."

"I'm very excited about this project." Miss Wells' face glowed with enthusiasm, "Once you've observed our children for a while, I'm sure you'll take this commission. We'll be putting our posters in supermarkets and other businesses throughout the Bay area. The point is to let the public know there's a safe place they can bring an abused child while legal actions are being taken."

"They're unusual kids," I said. "Awfully quiet."

"There's a reason." Amelia pushed aside the empty plate in front of her in order to lean closer to me and speak in sotto voice. "Take a look at that girl." Pointing with her chin. "She's eight years old, her name is Mary Crystawski. What do you see in her?"

Mary Crystawski could have been a pretty girl, except that her hair was stringy, complexion sallow, eyes downcast and constantly shifting, shoulders slumped. She used her fork to play with the food on her plate. "From her posture and blank stare, I'd say she's in some sort of shock. But I don't know much about kids."

"In shock?" Amelia smiled sadly. "Yes, that's the essence of her problem. You'll notice, for instance, that Mary Crystawski is wearing a long-sleeved dress. Susan found the dress for Mary because both the girl's arms are covered with cigarette burns. Whenever Mary incurred the wrath of her parents, which was often, she was punished with a cigarette burn."

"Both parents ganged up on her?"

"Both of them," Susan Wells confirmed. "From time to time Mary was also locked in a closet for two or three days with just a pot to do her business in, a jug of water, and a bit of food. That usually happened when the parents took one of their gambling jaunts to Reno. God help Mary when the Crystawskis lost in Reno. If they came home from the gambling resorts broke, they'd tie Mary to a chair and beat her with the buckle ends of their belts."

"And that's not even the worst case here," Amelia added.

"Where are Mary's parents?"

"In jail." Amelia sighed. "For the moment, anyway. When they get out, they intend to petition the court to return Mary to their custody. They claim to be *outraged* that their darling girl has been taken from them. Believe it or not, some judge may decide to send Mary home with them." Amelia's aristocratic chin quivered. "That happens more often than you'd believe. It's appalling how often."

"Let me know if it happens this time." I looked at Mary Crystawski. "I'd be willing to pay a call on Mary's parents and I have a friend who'd enjoy making that call with me. Between us, we might be able to persuade them to leave Mary alone."

"Violence is the problem, not the solution," Susan Wells said softly. "Abused children often grow up to be abusers themselves. We seldom have children in our care for long, only until the courts decide whether to send them back home or assign them to foster parents. While we do have these youngsters, we try to show by example that violence is a crude and unnecessary reaction to life's problems. Your way of 'persuading' the Crystawskis would only help to legitimize violence in Mary's mind."

"I see your point." I'd pegged Miss Wells as a lightweight innocent, like the house mother in a really gross fraternity. She forced me to revise my opinion. I suppose the real Florence Nightingales never look as smart and determined as they are. Three cheers for Susan Wells.

"Which of these children might be good for our poster?" Amelia asked.

I peered around, hoping to find a face with enough zest to make an interesting portrait. These kids had been so abused that a lot of their juices had curdled. I did spot a boy of about ten whose round face had all sorts of qualities. He looked impish, frightened, curious, loving, bold and cautious all at once. His eyes were enormous and wide-set. "Who's that kid? I like his face."

"That's Aron," Miss Wells said. "But he's being returned to his home tomorrow."

"Why's he here?"

"You'll notice his left hand."

"Can't see it," I said. "His left hand's in his lap, he seems to be doing his eating with his right hand."

"His left hand is bandaged. Aron's father does woodworking as a hobby, has an extensive collection of tools. Aron broke one of the tools, I think he was doing something at his dad's garage workbench." Susan Wells leaned forward. "Yes, I remember now, it was the blade from a sabresaw that got broken. Anyway, the boy's father lost his temper. To teach Aron a lesson, he put the youngster's hand in a vice. Closed the vice until most of the bones in Aron's left hand were broken."

I was amazed the kid's face still showed so much spunk. "A blade for a sabresaw only costs a couple of bucks. And they're sending Aron home to that guy?"

"His father has gone through a program of psychological counseling. Some sort of rage workshop." Amelia raised a hand with her fingers crossed. "Let's hope it works. You know, there are legal problems associated with using any of these childrens' faces for a poster. For example, Aron's father would never give permission. An obstacle of that sort might be dealt with by our lawyers, but that would take time and money. I'm wondering, Kevin, if you could do a poster based not on one of our actual clients, but a boy or girl who is representative of those we care for."

"A composite?"

"Yes." Amelia's face folded into itself as she considered the concept. "You've now seen some of our young charges. Perhaps after additional observation you could use the emotions, reactions, whatever else you find in these children, to invent a face that would appropriate for our uses."

"That's possible. I've painted a lot of faces that just came out of my imagination."

"I think that's the most practical approach," Miss Wells agreed.

We discussed that possibility for a while. In the end, I agreed to do a poster for the shelter. Not just the face, but the total design, for a total of four thousand dollars. I made appointments to spend time with Susan Wells here at the shelter. I wanted to watch the kids doing a variety of things, playing and doing their schoolwork and just interacting. What concerned me most was finding the right tone for the poster. I gave Amelia the name and phone number of my agent so a proper contract could be drawn up.

"Let me show you out," Amelia said when our business was done. I shook hands with Susan Wells and thanked her for the chance to do this job. I really was excited.

Amelia efficiently maneuvered her wheelchair through the aisles and out into the hallway leading to the front of the building. "A very productive meeting," Amelia said. "I'm sorry to have interrupted your work at Race, but I want to get this project underway as soon as possible."

"Quite all right. By the way, Bobby Race wants to make a ten thousand dollar contribution to the shelter."

"How nice of him! I'll send Mister Race a thank you note tomorrow."

I had my opening. "Did you know that your husband caused some chaos at Race Software today?"

Amelia's eyebrows arched. "Isadore at Race Software? I thought he spent the day at his office in San Francisco."

"No, he wasn't physically at Race. He sent a letter to the Race board of directors and some key stockholders today demanding a seat on the board. That generated a lot of activity. As a result, Bobby Race didn't have much time to sit for me."

"Really? Isadore did that?"

We left the building and Amelia brought her wheelchair to a halt at the top of the steps leading down to the parking lot. Twenty yards away, Pure John managed to lean insolently against the limo without looking insolent to anyone except me.

"I don't know much about Isadore's business," Amelia went on. "He still suffers from the rather rough-and-tumble way he began his career. People hold his beginnings against him. As a result, Isadore is often very aggressive in his business tactics." When she spoke of her husband, her tone was wholly affectionate. She apparently had no idea that murder and physical intimidation might be some of Izzy's favorite 'business tactics.' "I can say that every company Isadore has bought into has done well through his participation. You might mention that to Bobby Race.

I understand he's as driven as Isadore. I suppose that's one reason Race Software looks attractive to my husband."

"Could be." Lame comment, but I was out of my element discussing things like corporate maneuvering. Beer I can talk about. Art I can talk about. Women I can talk about. "Thanks again for the chance to do the poster. I'll do your kids justice, I promise."

"I know you will. Ta-ta."

Amelia's wonderful face fairly sparkled. I bent for a kiss on the cheek and was enveloped by the classiest perfume I'd ever encountered.

Pure John gave me an insolent smile as I went down the steps. It wouldn't have looked insolent to anyone else, of course. I still couldn't figure out how he did that.

CHAPTER 17

"The sauce is wonderful." Dorothy's face, illuminated by the single candle in the middle of the table, glowed with her particular brand of beauty. "I wouldn't have believed you could cook a meal this grand, Kevin." She cut some of her angel hair pasta into smaller lengths. "Your kitchen doesn't show much evidence of being used for, well, actual cooking."

"I do my best." My modesty was well deserved since the pasta came from Scarlatti's restaurant in Burlingame and the crunchy sourdough bread from Shlotzky's. "More wine?" I added some Field Stone merlot to her glass. I'm not accustomed to uncorking wine. I'd botched the job with this bottle, resulting in a few stray bits of cork floating harmlessly at the top of Dorothy's glass. Wisely, I'd kept the light too low for her to take notice.

I told her about my meeting with Amelia Valentine, then asked, "How's Bobby holding up?" I was curious to learn whether he'd had any delayed reaction to the visit from Cynthia's ghost. Over the years I've run into people who've had, or claimed to have had, supernatural encounters. In each of the cases I considered legitimate, there was a three-stage reaction. Fear. Followed by denial. Ending with soul-searching. I wondered if Bobby had a soul he could search, or if at some point he'd bartered it away for his great big piece of Silicon Valley.

"We talked for a while after you left, everyone except Greg who went home to work on Redleaf from his laptop." Dorothy sipped at her wine. "Bobby kept probing for a logical answer to what we saw. We didn't come up with one tonight."

"The no-ghost theory continues to hold?"

"Uh-huh." The grunt came out as a rebuke to my own theories. "Bobby pointed out that his office doesn't have any predominantly red colors, like the other places the thing was seen."

That hadn't occurred to me. "You're right. Sort of blows my observation all to hell, doesn't it."

"All to hell," she repeated apologetically.

"This time it did resemble the pictures I've seen of Cynthia."

"That's what convinces me, and Bobby too, what we saw was some kind of elaborate theatrical production."

"What else did Bobby say?"

"Not much. We would've kicked the subject around some more except a fight started and we decided to leave."

"Billy Jack would've broken up the fight."

"Billy Jack started the fight. Those fellows in tank tops, the arm wrestlers, made a nasty crack about the bar and Billy Jack hit one of them. The other arm wrestler jumped into the fight and so did somebody else who was sore at Billy Jack. Bottles were flying. Then Pepper grabbed one of the arm wrestlers by the shirt with his hook, you should've heard the guy scream. Somebody got a piece of ear bitten off, too. When Pam and Bobby and I left, maybe I should say when we escaped, Pepper and Billy Jack were toasting each other with those things Pepper was drinking—boilermakers."

"Stop it, you're making me homesick for Texas."

"Is that what you'd be doing if you'd stayed in Texas? Getting into bar fights? Biting off ears?"

"With luck."

"I can't imagine you in such a tawdry life."

"At seventeen I was a hell-raiser, like my dad. He worked on oil rigs, died when I was fifteen. A well he was drilling shot its string of tools back to the surface, decapitated my dad. Or so they said. They wouldn't let me look at his body. I had a lot of rage from that. As a result, my behavior in high school made Billy Jack look like the Kiwanis Club Student of the Year. That's how I ended up in the army. A judge gave me a choice between a road gang and military service."

Her sigh was light as a feather. "I've never understood how people could waste so much time drinking and fighting. Or, for that matter, going to ball games, taking long lunches, reading paperback novels…"

"Enjoying life," I suggested.

Dorothy's face colored as it did whenever someone challenged her. "That's your interpretation." She was wearing jeans with a silk blouse in almost the same shade of pink that now appeared on her cheeks. These were different clothes than she'd worn to the office and to Billy Jack's. Dorothy had gone home to change before coming to my place, an encouraging sign.

"I never had much time for the things you probably enjoyed as a teenager," she explained. "My parents were awfully smart, but not well-off. I think I told you they were high school teachers in Bridgeport, Connecticut. They weren't touchy-feely people, I was hardly ever hugged or kissed, but they had great respect for me. You've probably never been to Bridgeport, it's an old Eastern seaboard working class city, a tough town. I have three brothers. They were the ones who had fun. Drank, ran around town in old cars, knocked up girls, ended up in unemployment lines. I went to school and did well."

Dorothy looked past me, thousands of miles to the east. "I was expected to win scholarships and carry the family banner into a more prosperous world." Her chin came up. "I've done that. My parents are extremely proud of me, and I make sure they share in my financial success. They don't live in Bridgeport now, I bought them a condo in Greenwich. I'm the Mickey Mantle of my family. I was born and bred to use my brain to make money, just as Mantle was born and bred to use his physical reflexes to make money." She leaned forward in a forlorn way. "It's not my fault the software business isn't as exciting as baseball."

That said, she swiftly downed the last of her merlot.

"Dorothy, your parents have every right to be proud of you, and not just because you bought them a condo in Greenwich. There's nothing wrong with making sacrifices to achieve financial security." I shrugged lightly. "That's not my style, but most people would admire everything you've done. You're pointing out, in a nice way, how different we are."

"Exactly."

"That however much we might be attracted to each other, we don't belong together."

She looked sad, but did not disagree.

"Then why are you here tonight?" The question was a simple one, and we both knew the answer.

"I guess..." A cocktail of wary, uncertain emotions came flurrying to the surface. "I don't know, I suppose I want some forbidden fruit. Maybe I envy my brothers' lifestyles. Maybe I secretly crave having sex without worrying about how it'll affect my responsibilities and without factoring in how the sex might advance my career." Her coloring deepened. "As I did with Bobby, I admit that."

"If that's the worst thing you ever did, you'll probably go to heaven anyway."

"Do you think Billy Jack will go to heaven?"

"He's got as good a chance as any U.S senator I can think of."

"Ah-ha, I've caught you out, Kevin. You don't know anything more about after-life than I do. I think it was probably a big mistake to hire you as a ghost-buster."

"I'm not a ghost-buster, never claimed to be." I was achingly aware of Dorothy's fragile beauty, even though I once again felt cut off from her. She had an emotional shield she could raise and lower at will. "It was you people who insisted I look into your problem. Once in, I've done my best to find out what is. I can't help it if Bobby, or you, or Greg Tillotson, disagree with me."

"I know."

"We may never solve your mystery, Dorothy. Not every terrible thing in this world can be explained. Look at rap music."

"That would be a tragedy for the company." Her aloofness lifted as swiftly as a San Francisco fog. "Hey, you're the one who says I spend too much time on business. Can I change the subject?"

"Sure."

"I was just thinking about the first time I had Italian food in a restaurant. Guess I was about eight years old. I ordered angel hair because the phrase is so wonderful." Her manner turned mischievous. "The taste, the presentation, everything was very much like tonight's dinner."

I reared back. "Are you accusing me of feeding you restaurant food?"

"Kevin, everyone on peninsula's eaten at Scarlatti's. I'd recognize their angel hair anywhere, it's wonderful."

There are times when confession really is good for the soul. "You've got me, Detective Lake. I'll go quietly, just let me wipe the sauce off my mouth before you cuff me."

"You are such a humbug."

"Humbug? Isn't it against company policy to use that kind of raunchy language?" Actually, I was thrilled at the fond tenor of her conversation. These were the warmest words I'd ever gotten out of her. Dorothy was such a slight thing I could've reached across the table, picked her up and held her in my arms. Which was exactly what I intended to do.

Of course the phone rang at that exact moment. I groaned and tried to ignore the stupid instrument while I directed nasty thoughts at the memory of Alexander Graham Bell.

"Better answer it," Dorothy said. "Might be Bobby."

Bobby replaced Alexander Graham Bell as the object of my anger even as I got up and went to the phone. "Hello?"

"Mister Whitebread, how you doin' tonight?"

"Fine until you called." I lowered my voice. "Dorothy is here and you just interrupted a tender moment. So go away."

"Kevin, listen to me. Somethin' you should know…"

"Tell me in the morning." I put down the phone and followed the wire to the place where it plugged into the wall. When I pulled the cord from the wall, the phone in the upstairs bedroom was also killed. Satisfied we wouldn't be interrupted again, I went back to the table.

Dorothy was laughing. "You have a rotary telephone with a cord? In the age of cordless phones, pagers, cellular phones, satellite transmissions, cable tv, wireless communications of all kinds, you still have a phone that needs a *cord*?"

"I don't have cable tv, either. And my toothbrush doesn't have a battery. It gets worse. Where I grew up in Texas, everybody brushed their teeth with baking soda. That's what I still use."

"You're making that up."

I crooked my finger at her. "Come on, I'll show you."

With just a touch of reluctance, Dorothy followed me up the stairs, through the bedroom, into the bathroom. I presented her with a can of Arm & Hammer baking soda as if it were a key piece of evidence in a murder case. "Exhibit A: baking soda. Exhibit B." Gesturing toward the baseboards around my bedroom. "No cable outlets. Exhibit C: another telephone with an actual cord."

"Why do you revel in rejecting technology? Does it make you feel superior?"

"Maybe I'm just content with things as they are. I don't need the newest phone, seven thousand tv channels, a computer, a fax machine, a satellite dish on my roof, a personal digital assistant or more than one brand of beer to be content. Is that so wrong?"

"You're looking into the past instead of accepting the present." Dorothy's arms flapped as if she were trying to take flight. "We're completely incompatible."

"Not completely." I bent and kissed her. At first she went rigid. Then, slowly but with rising involvement, her arms encircled me and she let her body press into mine. Her mouth was hungry for me. Our kisses were as wet and hot and hard as they could possibly be. Dorothy's ingrained cautions seemed to fall away like old clothes and for the first time since I'd know her she was wildly uninhibited. The change was startling. Her eyes were almost crazed, her skin searing to the touch.

"Over there…" She pulled me towards the bed where we fell onto the mattress as if it were an especially springy trampoline. In moments we were undressing each other with horizontal vigor, pulling and tugging and maybe even tearing when the need arose. I'd never come upon such small, perfect breasts. Courbet's *Woman With White Stockings* slid through my mind, an exquisite girl lying on her back to undress while she tempted her lover with flashes of smooth flesh.

The foreplay was frantic. When we finally made love, Dorothy's eyes closed so tightly they might have been welded together. Her hands gripped my shoulders with incredible strength. I managed to bring down her level of passion a few clicks so that presently we were enjoying each other's bodies in synch instead of just shooting off random fireworks. We reached the plateau together and Dorothy screamed, almost for mercy, until finally we stopped writhing and slipped quietly into each other's arms.

"That was the best," Dorothy whispered a bit later.

"The best," I agreed.

We lay together and talked for a while about nothing more than movies, families, traffic on the Bayshore, and when El Nino would be back. Neither of us wanted to move, we were content with the moment and each other.

Then the air started to shift. I hardly felt it at first, just a rustle among the curtains, maybe a breeze from the beach. The rustle became louder, a sustained tremble. The temperature dipped. Dorothy sat up. "Earthquake!"

"That's no earthquake."

"Yes." She grabbed a bedpost. "Can't you feel it?"

Dorothy started to get out of bed and I stopped her. "Stay right here."

"We should get under a table, or into a doorway!"

"This isn't an earthquake." A hard sell, when the room seemed to be rocking up and down. "Just hold on, Dorothy. The bastard! What the hell's he want now?"

"Who? What's happening?" Dorothy's fingers dug into my arm. "Kevin, I'm afraid."

"We'll be fine."

Presently my bedroom stopped its rockin' and rollin' and the inevitable tornado of light pinballed around the room. Dorothy shrieked. The shade flew off a table lamp and a few other items fell to the floor. Out of it all came my old nemesis Sport Sullivan.

"Hiya, Kevin. Look who's back." Sport was dressed, as always, in his ludicrous out-of-date gambler's clothes, derby perched at a jaunty angle, the bullet holes in his suit redder than usual against the green glow that permeated his shimmering form. "Hey, you got someone with you? A woman, for shit's sake?" Sport's eyebrows wagged up and down. "Caught you kids having a quick fuck, didn't I. Well, more power to you. I ain't been laid in, I can't even tell how many years. Centuries for all I know."

"Kevin?" Dorothy drew the sheet up to her neck and pulled herself close to me. "What's going on here?"

"Sport Sullivan at your service." Sport swept off his derby and bowed. His technique with women had probably been formed somewhere around the turn of the century. When he leered at Dorothy, his teeth and gums showed a horrible unworldly black that caused her to squeal.

"What is that thing, Kevin?"

"Dorothy, this is what I can only call the true spirit of Sport Sullivan, who died back in 1920 from the gunshot wounds you see right there on his chest."

"No, that's impossible! I *refuse* to believe such a thing!"

"Oh, it's true, Dorothy." Sport sat down on a chair next to the bed, driving Dorothy even deeper into my arms. "I'm in what they call limbo. What happened was that Arnold Rothstein, you must've heard of him, hired me to help him fix the 1919 World Series. I went to Chicago..." Sport was off and running on his favorite subject: himself and the big double-cross Arnold Rothstein had pulled on him. As Sport talked, his color continually changed in strobe-light fashion, bright flashes of reds...blues...greens...yellows...a whole palette of colors, one shade brighter and more bizarre than the next.

Dorothy watched and listened and cringed, fascinated despite herself. "I don't believe this," she muttered at one point. "I *can't* believe this, it's too absurd!"

"Your second ghost today." I patted her shoulder. "That can't be easy to deal with." Sport was so wrapped up in his own life story he couldn't even be bothered to notice our whispering. "And this ghost is an asshole. I mean, listen to Sport, he's got no interest in anything except himself."

"You've seen him...it...before?"

"I told you about Sport. Big Sam even confirmed my story, and still you wouldn't believe me. Sport comes around every so often to piss and moan about being in limbo, insult me and my art, bitch about Arnold Rothstein, tell me his life story over and over. Guy's a total pain in the ass."

"This isn't a light show? Computer-generated animation? Anything like that?"

"I wish to hell he was a light show. I'd switch him off. Listen to him, he *talks* and *talks* and *talks*."

"Maybe we're both having psychological breakdowns."

"Both of us at the same time? Come on, Dorothy. The guy is a ghost. G-H-O-S-T. I imagine a parapsychologist would have a bigger, better word for it, but what you're essentially looking at is the remains of a guy who died back in 1920."

Eventually Sport's monologue wound down. He got up and walked around my bedroom like a home buyer inspecting a property. "Sleep in the raw, Kevin? I always did. No nightshirts for me, except maybe on those frigid January nights in New York." He winked grotesquely at Dorothy. "And you, little lady, should spend all your time in the nude. The closer the bone, the sweeter the meat is what I always said, and you're proof of that."

Dorothy cleared her throat. "Uhh…you…Mr. Sullivan? You're in what state?"

"Limbo, sweetheart. I ain't quite dead and I ain't quite alive. I dunno why. Somebody up there's pissed at me, I suppose."

Slowly Dorothy disengaged from me. With the sheet still pulled up to her chin, she inched forward for a better look at Sport.

"Can you feel anything?"

"Sometimes yes, sometimes no. Comes and goes."

"How do you make these appearances?"

"Dunno that, either. Sometimes, wherever I am, I get the sense Kevin's calling for me. When that happens, here I come! Just like now."

"I didn't *call for you*," I said. "Do you think I'm an idiot? I'd *call for you* while I'm in bed with a beautiful woman?"

"No, you ain't an idiot. I'm the idiot for coming whenever you call."

I was obscurely annoyed when Dorothy snickered.

"You sure you ain't in any trouble, Kevin?"

"Sport, I'm just fine, so you can go away right now."

"Hey, I ain't leaving yet. I go for decades without talking with a woman gorgeous enough to be a Gibson Girl."

Dorothy frowned. "Gibson Girl?"

"They were famous showgirls back when Sport was fixing the World Series," I explained.

"And you could've been one of them, Dorothy." Sport's electric eyes didn't seem to bother Dorothy any more. If anything, she appeared fascinated by him.

"How about buying me a beer, Kevin? I been thinking about that Mexican beer you were drinking that time. Got any in the house?"

"Yeah, there's some in the fridge."

"What's a fridge?"

"In the icebox. But how are you going to drink it?"

"We'll figure something out. Just go get it for me, okay? I can't bear to tear myself away from this lovely Gibson Girl."

Sport was nauseating when he tried to be gallant. Nonetheless I slipped into my boxer shorts and padded down to the kitchen. When I brought the beer upstairs, I found Dorothy and Sport chatting like old college chums. Dorothy had slipped into a t-shirt of mine that came down way past her butt. She was on her knees on the bed, about five feet from Sport, gaping at him in utter fascination. I couldn't help noticing that her eyes were brighter than they'd ever been when she looked at me.

Dorothy and Sport? Sport and Dorothy? I couldn't get my mind around that one. It would be like pairing Adolph Hitler with Minnie Mouse.

She was blurting out questions at the rate of about six a minute and eating up Sport's answers. Mostly she wanted to know more about Sport's life, a subject with which he was equally fascinated, and about his untimely death at the hands of Arnold Rothstein's gunman.

"Here's your beer. I repeat, how are you going to drink it?"

Sport pondered the problem. "Dorothy, why don't you pour that golden juice into my mouth."

"That would just spill beer all over my carpet," I said.

"With your carpet, that don't hardly matter," Sport countered.

Again Dorothy laughed. I'm not easily insulted, but listening to Dorothy and Sport joke about my threadbare carpet made me burn.

"Let's try it." Dorothy eagerly took the bottle of Carta Blanca from me and twisted off the cap. "We'll think of this as a scientific experiment." Her eyes slid toward me. "If I don't think of it that way, I'd have to conclude I was insane." She capped that remark with a manic giggle.

I gave her the beer. Dorothy lifted the bottle to Sport's open mouth and tipped it until beer began to run out. I was right, most of the beer splattered into the carpeting. But not all. Some of the liquid, maybe a tenth of it, dissolved into gas somewhere in the general area where Sport's stomach would have been if he were alive.

"That's good stuff! I had the Mexicans all wrong."

"You could taste it?" Dorothy was hanging on Sport's words. "What was it like?"

"Heavy taste of wheat," Sport said immediately. "Hops, I oughtta say. The best hops you can buy, I know my beer. Knew my beer, anyway. Damn! I feel funny, I better sit down." He plopped back into a chair.

"Sport, are you drunk?" This was really too much.

"Just a little dizzy. I ain't had any beer in…what?…seventy…eighty years?"

"Sport, you're fascinating! I'm going to write a paper on you for *The Scientific American*." Dorothy was speaking in racehorse fashion. "This is an unexplored field! There must be ways to apply computer technology to research on the supernatural. A government grant? Surely I can get a grant. The government is sponsoring research into the possibility of communications with extraterrestrial life. Is this so different?"

"I'm feeling better." As Sport stood, he went through about six different shades of green in as many seconds. "But I'm fading, folks. Got the jangles. See you some time…"

"Don't go!" Dorothy begged.

There was the usual champagne cork pop and Sport Sullivan dematerialized.

"He's gone," Dorothy wailed.

"Thank God. I'm sorry, this was worse than usual. The son of a bitch just won't leave me alone."

Dorothy whirled on me. "Call him back, Kevin. Please. I need to know more about him."

"No."

"Then let me call him." There was a touch of hysteria in the way her hand flew to her throat. "How do you reach him?"

I always knew Dorothy was too tightly wrapped. She had a lot of obsessions: with her professional status, with Bobby Race, with money, with her grooming, with the expensive clothes that made her stand out from all the other women at Race Software. She was a zealot. A beautiful, mixed-up zealot. "I don't know how to reach him. He shows up, I can't explain how or why. He seems to make his obnoxious appearances during periods of crisis. Now that he can hit me up for beers, I'll probably see even more of him."

"I've got to reach him." She stripped off the oversized t-shirt and began throwing on her clothes. "We've made some important scientific breakthroughs today. First Cynthia Gooding. Now Sport Sullivan. There's a whole other world out there waiting to be explored."

"So now you do believe that was Cynthia's spirit swishing around Race headquarters?"

"Yes, I do." She cast down her eyes in apology. "We've all been fools. You were right, Kevin. I was wrong. Does that give you satisfaction?"

"It should." Dorothy wasn't just dressing, she was getting herself ready to leave. "Look, don't get involved with the supernatural beyond figuring out what's going on at the company. People have been studying the occult for centuries, going all the way back to the Gnostics and even before that to Zarathustra in the seventh century and a lot of others besides. You'll never get to the bottom of it just because you're good with computers."

"I have so much research to do." Talking more to herself than to me. "What's incredible is I never even suspected the existence of creatures like Sport Sullivan."

"Calm down, don't make yourself crazy."

"I have to go. I'll be on the Internet the rest of the night." She grinned with what I can only describe as a fierce joy. Then she was out the door.

CHAPTER 18

I should have seen it coming. Anyone who suddenly converts usually goes all the way. When smokers give up their cigarettes, they want to shoot everyone who's still smoking. Born-again Christians are ten times more pious than those brought up in the faith. Friends who start jogging after years as couch potatoes always want to run a marathon. Same thing with Dorothy. After scoffing her whole life at anything not rooted in science, she had now embraced the occult with hysterical fervor.

All my fault.

After cleaning off the dinner table, half-heartedly washing the dishes and downing a couple of cold Carta Blancas, I retreated to my easel. Work is the best antidote for depression, at least that's what all the self-help books say. So I began playing with some ideas for the poster Amelia had hired me to design. It would take a few trips to the shelter, observing the kids, before I could nail down an approach. It wouldn't hurt to noodle around a few concepts.

I wondered if the clear, pure colors produced by tempera might work well for the job. This wasn't a portrait that would hang on a wall for years to come. It would become a printed poster. Tempera would give whatever face I put on the poster a vivid sense of life. I decided to mix the egg yolk and water for tempera myself, you get the best colors that way.

Boy or girl? I couldn't make up my mind which would be most effective.

Someone knocked on my front door. The interruption annoyedme because I felt on the verge of a decent idea. "Who is it?"

263

"Uh...yeah...this is Tom Rudgear. Alvin Rudgear's son. We did your termite work."

"Oh, sure." I opened the door to Tom Rudgear, stocky, hairy, deep-voiced, dressed in the same brand of workclothes as his father, picking his nose expertly with one hand, holding a clipboard with some sort of form in the other. "What's up, Tom?"

"I need to get this work order completion report signed by you, says we did a satisfactory job of eliminating your pests."

"I assume you did, the termites haven't complained. But then, if you did a good job, they couldn't complain, could they?"

"Huh?"

"Yes, I'll sign off on the job."

I unlatched the screen door. Tom came through the door fast, his shoulder slamming into me as hard as one of the bumper cars at Pier 39. Next thing I knew I was lying flat on my back in my own entryway. Three guys poured through the door. I kicked the first in the kneecap, the one who'd claimed to be Alvin Rudgear's son. He swore and staggered sideways.

"Grab him, pin his arms!"

As they grappled for me, I rolled backwards and brought my legs clear back over my head, coming to my feet pretty quickly for an ex-soldier halfway out of shape. I pivoted on my left foot and slammed the ball of my right foot into somebody's chest. One of them crashed into a wall. Another lost his balance.

I don't own guns. But there were plenty of knives in the kitchen, so I jumped through the door and grabbed the first one that came to hand. Ten-inch blade, maybe longer. As I spun back toward the door, the phony pest controller came charging at me, his face as red as the stripes on an American flag.

The good news? Only one of them could come through the door at a time.

The bad news? That's what they did.

I slashed the pest controller's arm and he screamed like a banshee. Just like a banshee. Okay, Sport, you were right, you bastard, I was in trouble and didn't even know it, you just arrived a little early. Where are you when I do need you? The pest controller staggered against a cabinet, breaking the glass front and cutting himself some more.

The second man through the door was bigger, heavier, wider and smarter, probably because he was older. He had a barrel chest and thick, tatooed arms. His hard, flat-nosed face held no emotion. Rather than rush me, he picked up a kitchen chair and swung it. I feinted to one side and stepped back. He still managed to catch me with a piece of the chair. The knife flew out of my hand. I never punch anyone with my fist. Not because I'm afraid of injuring my delicate artist's hands, but because fist-fighting is inefficient. Instead I jabbed a thumb into the neck of the older thug, just below the Adam's apple. He gagged and grabbed his windpipe with both hands. I sent him to the floor with an elbow smash.

"Enough!" Pure John stood in the kitchen doorway, a 9 millimeter Browning Hi-Power pointed at my chest. Pure John's black suit was immaculate and still perfectly pressed, he hadn't waded into the fights. "Sit yourself down, Mr. Pierce. I don't want to shoot you, but I will if that's what it takes. This thing is loaded with Black Talons, they'll take your head right off."

I picked up a kitchen chair and sat down. The other two were coming slowly to their feet, gasping, cursing, shaking their heads, dabbing at cuts and probing at sore spots. As he was getting up, the older one gave me a backhanded slap that rattled my molars.

"Lay off," Pure John said. "We don't want Mr. Pierce looking all beaten up and disheveled." He noticed the dishes drying on the kitchen sink. "How was the salmon?"

"We had pasta tonight."

"You should've broiled the salmon while it was fresh."

"Don't know what I was thinking. By the way, what's this all about?"

"You know you've been putting your nose where it doesn't belong. That stops as of this evening."

"Amelia will be disappointed, she really wants me to do the poster for her shelter."

"I'm afraid Mrs. Valentine will have to find another artist." He prodded his two companions into action. The ersatz pest controller grabbed some of my napkins to doctor his cuts while flat-nose produced a short length of rope that he used to loosely tie my hands behind my back. The loose tie gave me a chill; I could think of only one reason they didn't want to leave marks on my wrists.

"Why the rope?"

Pure John ignored my question. He was busy straightening up my house. Putting chairs right. Dumping the broken glass in the trash. Cleaning the knife I'd used and then slipping it back into its woodblock sleeve. "You're a good housekeeper."

"Have to be, I'm a lifelong bachelor," he explained.

When the house had been put right, they hustled me outside to a large maroon sedan that was not Izzy's limousine. I was dumped into the trunk with my hands still tied behind me. The trunk lid was slammed shut. I heard the three of them get into the car and we began to drive.

We went downhill toward the beach. He came to a highway that could only be Route 1, turned left, drove another few minutes, turned right. The ocean sounds were now clear even inside the trunk. When the car began bouncing along rough, unpaved ground I knew where we headed, the flat bluff that led to cliffs overlooking the ocean.

I began chafing my wrists against the rope. If they were going to do what I feared, I wanted the medical examiner to at least find abrasion marks on my wrists.

We stopped. Car doors slammed. The trunk lid opened and I was dragged out by flat-nose and the pest controller.

"Treat him gently," Pure John said.

"He didn't treat us so gentle," flat-nose complained. "Guy's an artist, we didn't expect him to cut us up, loosen our kneecaps."

Pure John was about as sympathetic as a slave overseer. "I told you in advance the man was a decorated combat soldier before he became an artist. You should've taken him seriously."

"Gonna be a treat watching the great artist learn how to fly," the pest controller said.

"Shut up." Pure John took my arm and walked me toward the cliffs, the muzzle of the Browning was pressed into my side. His two pals walked close behind me and the cliff could be seen no more than twenty yards ahead. I'd walked this rocky part of the bluff often for the exercise and the sheer beauty of the view. The drop from the cliff would take me about ninety yards down to a cluster of jagged, half-submerged rocks. If I somehow survived the drop, the tide would carry me out to the proverbial watery grave. My options were narrowing fast.

Five yards from the cliff, I let myself trip on a loose rock and fall flat on my face.

"Get up, cheap fakery won't help you," Pure John said.

"Can I at least have a cigarette?" I don't smoke, but just this once I needed a cigarette.

"You want a blindfold too?" He laughed. "Okay, why not. Rudy, give the man a cigarette. He wants to go out like a gentleman, I can appreciate that. Untie his hands first, it's time to do that anyway."

My hands were untied. Rudy, I had a name for one of the executioners, I didn't have to call him flat-nose anymore, fumbled for a pack of smokes and a match. I closed my eyes and listened carefully. Sometimes my army training still comes in handy. I learned early on that any soldier foolish enough to light a match in darkness is going to be blind for three to six seconds. A cigarette was put into my hand. Then Rudy did something more stupid than striking a match; he flipped on a lighter, which has an even brighter flame.

I quickly rolled to my left because the ground sloped in that direction. My feet hit Pure John's ankles and knocked him down. He swore. Rudy yelled "Where'd he go? I can't see!"

I continued rolling because if I stood and ran they'd see me sooner rather than later. For maybe fifteen seconds I set an Olympic record for rolling along a downgrade. Behind me I heard a flurry of cursing and stamping of feet. By the time they got their act together, I was about twenty-five yards down the slope and well back from the cliff itself.

"He went down the slope," Pure John called. "Go after him."

They put about five yards between themselves and came cautiously in my direction. Did all of them have guns? I didn't think so. Pure John was armed, but he wasn't anxious to use his pistol. If he shot me, his plan for making my death look like a fall from a cliff would be spoiled. Also, a gunshot might attract attention. The California Highway Patrol cruised Route 1 all the time and there were only two roads out of Half Moon Bay, Route 1 or Route 92.

I couldn't understand why Izzy Valentine wanted me dead, but this wasn't the time to ponder the question.

A cloud moved across the moon and in an instant I was on my feet and running south parallel to the cliffs. Somewhere up ahead, maybe a mile or so, were houses and people and automobiles.

"He's running!" one of them yelled. "That way!"

"Go get him!" Pure John called back. "Put him over the cliff!"

I'd been heading away from the cliffs. To confuse them, I cut back toward the cliffs. Still moving south but running much closer to the sheer drop. The ground became rough. This wide strip of land was an old railroad right-of-way San Mateo County had taken over and wisely left in its natural state. I knew the ground a lot better than they did and as a consequence I could move more quickly and surely. They were falling farther behind. I could hear them stumbling and warning each other about the rockiness of the ground.

The Bible warns that pride goes before a fall. Just when I was congratulating myself on making my escape, I stepped into a hole and fell noisily onto my face.

"He's down," Pure John called. "Keep your eyes open. Find him."

My ankle was twisted. I could probably stand. Probably hobble. I couldn't run. Somebody was approaching and the cloud that had given me cover was about to move past the moon and spread more light around.

I hugged the ground and kept my head down. I was wearing khakis and a dark green shirt, so at least I didn't stand out against the sand and scrub grass along the cliff. Footsteps came directly toward me. I held my breath. Just then a foot came down on my left hand. I grabbed an ankle with my right hand and pulled. Rudy, the bigger and heavier of Pure John's two helpers, gave a yelp as he fell.

"Where are you?" Pure John called.

My right hand closed on Rudy's thick neck. I managed to keep him from answering though he was struggling hard, thrashing, trying to hit me with his fists. One of his fists connected with my brow. I was on my knees by then, my grip on Rudy's throat holding as I pushed and pulled the big man toward the cliff's edge.

His body sagged. Then his weight evaporated. I let go as he vanished over the cliff. He screamed as he went. The sound of the waves made it impossible to hear his body hit the rocks below. When the scream was cut off, I knew Rudy hadn't been able to grab a bush or a rock to save himself. He'd gone all the way down.

"Rudy got him!" the pest controller called.

"No." Pure John's reply was sober. "That was Rudy who fell."

"Let's get outta here, John."

"You're here to do a job, Tom. Find him. He's down, he's hurt, we can handle him."

Tom sounded frightened, which was encouraging. Bastards thought they could toss me off a cliff, give the wimpy artist the old heave-ho, they were learning better.

My ankle felt stronger. I was about to rise when a gray shadow fell over me. I looked up to see Tom grinning down. "Got'cha." Then he looked pained and surprised. His head wobbled. Blood trickled from the corner of his mouth. His legs failed him. He was grabbed from behind by someone else, not Pure John, and lowered silently to the ground.

Sam Cody knelt next to me. "Can you walk?" he whispered.

"Where did you come from? Pure John's over there somewhere. He's alone now but he's got a Browning Hi-Power."

Sam folded up the blade of the razor-sharp Gerber he always carried, slipped it into his pocket and put a supporting arm around my waist. "Stay low and we'll scoot outta here." He went the opposite direction I would have gone, north toward the place where Pure John had pulled me from the trunk of his car. By the time we'd gone a couple of hundred yards I was able to limp along without Sam's help.

Sam's car, the Rolls of course, was parked in the same vicinity as Pure John's though well back from it. He helped me into the passenger seat. The Rolls engine turned over so quietly that Pure John didn't hear us leave any more than he'd heard Sam arrive. Sam kept the lights off as we drove silently away. Even on rough ground the ride was as smooth as fine crystal. There are some practical advantages to luxury cars after all.

A couple of hours later, it must have been midnight by then, I had my feet propped up on a leather ottoman in Sam's loft, a beer at my elbow, a bowl of Maui chips to munch on. My nerves had settled. The security system for Sam's building had been double-checked in case Pure John was still on the prowl.

"You pulled the cord on your damned phone before I could talk business with you, so I decided to drive on down to Half Moon Bay. I got to your place when Pure John Braggia was stuffin' you into the trunk of his car," Sam explained. "Didn't take much brains to figure you weren't checkin' out the trunk in case you might want to buy John's car. Figured you were safe enough while you were in the trunk, so I followed you to the beach."

"You make a habit of saving my life," I said. "It's starting to be embarrassing."

"So next time should I let Pure John do what he wants with you?"

"No, I'd rather deal with the embarrassment. The thing I'm wondering, should we tell the police?"

Sam snorted. "I ain't tellin' the cops nothin' about tonight."

"It was self-defense. They were hired thugs, I'll bet they both had police records."

"I put my knife through a man's kidney from behind. If I try tellin' a cop that was self-defense, he'll laugh in my face. And you threw the other dude off a cliff, does that sound like self-defense?"

"I didn't exactly throw him, it was just a little shove. I don't suppose Pure John will go to the police, either."

"No, he'll go to Izzy Valentine with some song and dance about why you aren't dead so he can save his job. On top of that, Pure John will have an alibi for tonight."

"I still can't figure out why they made that kind of move on me." I saw myself as an inconsequential artist, a gentle man if not a gentleman, no enemies, admired by many for my talent and good works, a friend to all mankind. The idea that someone disliked me enough to make an attempt on my life sort of hurt my feelings.

"You must be makin' headway on this ghost thing." Sam poured himself a second tequila and dropped a slice of lime into the glass. "If Izzy thinks you might spoil his chance to get onto Race's board of directors, that'd be enough for him to make a run at you."

I'd told Sam about my eventful day. The visit from Cynthia's spirit. The discussion at Billy Jack's bar. Dinner with Dorothy. Sport's untimely appearance. Dorothy's sudden conversion to true believer. Pure John and his pals bursting into my house. The full catastrophe.

"How's the great Bobby Race takin' all this?"

"Freaking out in a quiet way."

Sam scratched his chin. "His business is hurt already. I saw a segment on the seven o'clock news, pretty girl with a microphone sayin' the Race headquarters complex might be haunted. Employees evacuated, company shut down early. scary shit goin' on. She made it sound funny. Worst thing can happen to a company is to have the media makin' fun of you. Stock price goes down. Sharks like Izzy move in."

"That's exactly what worries Bobby." Sam had the gleam in his eye that usually appears when he spots a cream puff luxury car, a Jag or better, that he just had to have. "What's on your devious mind, Sam?"

"Huddled most of the day with my lawyers." He took a handful of Maui chips, crunched a few in his mouth. Chewing around them, Sam said, "It's gonna cost me a bundle to beat the auto theft charge Izzy set up. Then there's lost business. The whole tab's gonna run half a million dollars 'cause I'll have to lay low for a year, not steal even a bike, live off legitimate income."

"What a shame."

"Hey, this is an emotional time for me, Kevin. Don't make fun."

"Sorry."

Sam sipped tequila, licked the rim of his glass. "I saw this comin', so about six months ago, I set up a sting of my own against Izzy. But I fucked up bad, let Izzy get in the first shot."

"What kind of game are you running?"

He smiled hugely. "Izzy's been playin' the solid citizen. Money to charities, political contributions, buyin' up quality companies, the full-court press. The move on Race is the big enchilada for him. He wins that board spot, he's part of the Silicon Valley establishment. What Izzy don't know is that I got a way to totally fuck up his shiny new reputation."

"So do it."

"I intend to." Sam put his feet up on the ottoman next to mine. "Why should I do it for nothin'? I figure Bobby Race might buy into my sting, help offset my legal expenses."

"Let me understand this." I began to see the outlines of Sam's deal. "You want Bobby to pay you to smear Izzy?"

"I'm thinkin' of askin' Bobby for two hundred and fifty thousand to fuck up Izzy. Spread Izzy's name all over the newspapers and tv news, worst kind of story you can imagine. I do that, Izzy's run at Race Software is dead in the water." Sam peered at me over the rim of his glass. "When you hung up your phone on me, I drove down to Half Moon Bay to ask if you think Bobby would go for a deal like that."

"Depends on what your game is all about. You tell me what you're going to spring on Izzy, I'll tell you what I think Bobby's reaction would be."

Sam took ten minutes to share all the details of his master plan with me. You'd have thought his sting was a new baby boy, he was so proud of it. He did have something to take pride in. The longer he talked, the wider my smile grew. By the time he finished, I was laughing so hard I choked on my beer and chips. "Brilliant!" I coughed, tried to clear my throat. "Sam, you're a genius! If you were an artist, you'd be Picasso!" I let the coughing wind down. Waited until my thoughts settled. Finally I said, "Not only will Bobby buy it, he'll want to make the phone call himself."

CHAPTER 19

The next morning the media was still camped outside the gates of Race Software: Channel Seven…Channel Four…CNN…Channel Five…MSNBC…Fox News. Plus some channels I'd never heard of. Also reporters from The San Francisco *Chronicle*, San Jose *Mercury-News*, *Wall Street Journal*, other newspapers. On the fringe, writers from the computer trades.

The morning papers had used some juicy quotes from Race employees to the effect that a ghost or spirit or poltergeist had made several appearances at the company headquarters. *Red Phantom Terrifies Race Software* was the lead story in the business section of the *Chronicle*. The *Wall Street Journal* went with *Silicon Valley Battles Ghostly Presence*. Somehow the *Chronicle* found out I was doing Bobby's portrait and updated its *Psychic Of Half Moon Bay* piece about me. Lots of speculation about my connection with Race Software, very few facts.

Sam inched his Rolls through the crowd toward the front entrance. None of the reporters could see us through the smoked windows. The most aggressive pressed their faces against the glass on the theory that anyone in a Rolls Royce must be worth an interview. Twenty or so new guards from one of the big security agencies on the peninsula were keeping reporters and curiosity-seekers off the property. They elbowed the press away from Sam's car. One of the guards checked my name against the employee list, gave Sam a suspicious once-over even though he was immaculately dressed, finally let us both drive through when I refused to go inside without Sam.

"Happens every time," Sam said in disgust. "White guy sees a black man in a luxury automobile, automatically thinks it's a stolen car."

"You are a professional car thief," I pointed out.

"Don't change the principle."

The atmosphere inside Race headquarters reminded me of those tv reports on the fall of Saigon. People were rushing back and forth, piles of papers in their hands. The usual building maintenance had not been done. Waste paper baskets overflowed. The floors were scuffed and marked. Some of the office furniture stood askew. Lots of new security guards stood around looking unsure of their duties. Moving men were carrying things out of the building and loading them into trucks and painters were carrying rollers and brushes and paint into one of the elevators.

"Sinkin' ship, no rats in sight," was Sam's evaluation.

The first face I recognized was Pam Solter's. She escorted a young man in a corduroy jacket to the front entrance, shook his hand, asked one of the guards to escort the visitor safely off the property.

"Pam, what's going on?"

Though distracted, Pam managed to focus on me. Then on Sam.

"This is Sam Cody, a friend who I think can help clear up the problem you've got here."

"If you can do that, I'll have a sandwich named after you at Max's Opera Cafe. Plus you can have my body, such as it is, to do with as you will." Pam threw her hands around. "About twenty percent of our people didn't come in today. Some called to say they'll be working at home for the rest of the week. I hope they do. A lot of them are out looking for new positions. I'm interviewing programmers, making offers, trying to keep us staffed up."

"Bobby in his office?"

Pam shook her head tightly. "The executive floor has been closed until further notice. I've cleared some space in the basement for the execs, brought in computers, hooked up phone lines. That's where

Bobby and Greg and the others are working from." Her eyes shifted to Sam, back to me. "Nobody wants to set foot on the sixth floor until our crisis is...what should I say...resolved?"

"What are all the moving men doing? And the painters?"

"Bobby is having all the red furniture and fixtures taken out of the building. All the red walls or posts or whatever are being repainted in blues and grays. The bright red Coke machines were the first to go, everybody has to drink tea or coffee from brown urns."

"That's crazy."

"I know." Pam rolled her eyes. "Bobby's developed a siege mentality."

"Have you seen Dorothy?"

"She's down in the basement, too, and as hyper as a kid on Hershey bars." When I started to move toward the elevators, Pam took my arm. "A word of advice. Don't make any comparisons between our basement and Hitler's bunker. Bobby overheard that kind of remark from one employee this morning, fired him on the spot."

"Thanks, Pam."

"Nice lady," Sam said as we went down one floor in the elevator. "You really think she could get a sandwich named after me at Max's? I've always wanted that."

"I'll talk to her about it. That's on top of the two hundred and fifty thousand, right?"

"Right."

"Is the sandwich a deal-breaker?"

Sam thought it over. "Guess not. Sure be nice, though."

The basement normally housed all the building controls, maintenance equipment, cleaning materials, toilet paper for the restrooms, all the stuff necessary to run a building. The whole mishmash had been pushed haphazardly out of the storage rooms into the one long basement aisle to make room for desks and computers.

We picked our way through the littered hallway looking for Bobby's office. I finally located Jenny near the north end of the aisle. She was holding a whispered conference with Hugh Wilson who today looked very lawyerly in a blue suit and sober tie. When they saw me coming, their faces shifted into embarrassed smiles.

"Kevin!" Jenny grabbed my hand. "Bobby's been asking for you. I'll show you where he's camped out. First I want to apologize for running out on you and everybody else yesterday. God, I was terrified! I cried all the way home, didn't I, Hugh?"

"Jenny was really frightened. I wouldn't have bugged out on you guys if she didn't need someone to drive her home."

"I don't blame you, I wanted to get out of there, too. This is Sam Cody. He's going to get Izzy Valentine out of Bobby's hair. We both need to see Bobby right away. You should be in this meeting, Hugh, there are legal implications."

Sam burst out with a laugh nasty enough to make Jenny and Hugh nervous.

"Legal implications, that's a good one." Though Sam was at least as well dressed as Hugh in a dark suit, charcoal gray shirt, red tie decorated with white Corvettes, there was no way a two-thousand dollar suit could offset his predatory bearing.

"I'll show you where Bobby's working." Jenny led the three of us to the room at the end of the hall, a cave-like space. The door held a plastic plate stamped with Pepper Johnson's name. Bobby using Pepper's office? There weren't even any windows down here and the smell of cleaning fluid dominated.

"About time you got here." Bobby looked up from a laptop resting on Pepper's tiny, scarred desk. The floor was grubby tile, the walls an indifferent gray, same as Bobby's complexion. "Look at this."

I grabbed the sheet of paper he tossed to me. A letter from Dorothy. She was resigning from Race Software "…as of the day Redleaf is announced in order to pursue a promising new field of study."

"What do you know about this?" Bobby demanded.

"Nothing."

"You were with Dorothy last night. She came in early, told me all about this…this other…whatever it was…she saw at your house." His gaze shifted around Pepper's small kingdom. I'd never seen Bobby nervous and defensive. "Now, because of *you* and *it*, Dorothy wants to go off and do *research* on the *occult*. She wants to create a worldwide database of supernatural events, find a common denominator that can be used to *make contact* with the spirit world. Dumbest idea I ever heard. Kevin, you've got to talk her out of it. I can't afford to lose Dorothy."

"I'll do what I can."

"Who's this? I don't have time for him, I've got a hundred problems to solve by the end of the business day."

"This is Sam Cody. He's here to solve the Izzy Valentine problem."

Bobby pointed a bony finger at Sam. "I've heard all about you from Dorothy. You're the car thief."

"I own a classic car agency." Sam politely placed his business card on the desk. "Izzy's movin' in on me, just like he is on you. I can put a halt to his shit for a price. You interested?"

"Sit down." Bobby waved Sam into a chair. "Sorry for the cramped quarters, I'm sure Kevin has explained our situation to you."

"Yeah, he did. You got a haunted house."

Bobby's mouth tightened. Jenny, reading the signs, disappeared. Hugh and Sam and I found three chairs, which were about all Bobby's temporary office could accommodate.

Sam provided a quick summary of his own problem. "Izzy wants me to sell him my business, go to work for him. He's not after my stock of classic cars. What he wants is access to my contacts in the DMV and with specialists who know how to acquire cars, print legitimate titles, manufacture fake plates, change engine numbers. Izzy's doin' this to accommodate some of his business associates. Latino drug dealers, in the main. Those dudes use up luxury cars real fast."

Hugh Wilson squirmed. "Am I really needed in this meeting?"

"Yes," I said. "Go on, Sam."

"This week Izzy fingered me on a grand theft auto charge. For the first time in my life, I'm gonna be indicted. I can beat the charge, my lawyers say. Gonna cost me a bundle in legal fees and lost business. Five hundred thousand dollars over the next year is the outside figure. For half that, two fifty k in cash, off the books of course, I can ruin Izzy's reputation. Get him charged with a crime that makes grand theft auto look like a parkin' ticket." Sam's mouth twisted in a way that made it resemble a wolf's snarl. "That'll get him off your back as well as mine. Nobody'll vote to put Izzy on your board when I'm done with him."

"What exactly is your plan?" Bobby wanted to know.

"And is it legal?" Hugh leaned forward. "We can't afford to be involved in an illegal or unethical attack on Izzy Valentine. Not with the media watching us so closely. He has a top-flight legal team, he could sue us."

"He ain't gonna sue nobody," Sam promised.

"Paying money off the books is in itself illegal," Hugh pointed out.

"We've done it before on confidential projects." Bobby tried to find a more comfortable position in the steel-backed chair he was using. He missed his specially built, twenty-thousand dollar executive chair, which never would have fit into Pepper's cubbyhole. "Mr. Cody, if you have a way to make Izzy go away, we have a deal."

Sam put his hand across the desk. After a moment's hesitation, Bobby shook it. I hoped Bobby understood that a deal with Sam Cody had to be honored. Otherwise he might get run over crossing the street.

"Six months ago Izzy gave me his first hint that he wanted to 'buy into' my operation. I declined his generous offer. I knew he'd be back, so I took precautions."

Hugh tensed up. "What kind of precautions?"

From a large manila envelope, Sam took an eight-by-ten color photograph. "This is an aerial photo of Izzy's twenty-acre estate in Hillsborough. The house is toward the front of the property. Big rose gardens over here, see them? Six car garage, very roomy. Italianate fountain in the center of the turnaround. Impressive layout, but Izzy left most of the property alone. Fifteen acres with no plantings, mostly oak trees and scrub grass and this nice stand of eucalyptus. Izzy don't pay much attention to the grounds. There's one gardener. He takes care of the grass and rose gardens, never goes to the back of the property.

"Back here…see this acre? See the plants growin' right there? Four months ago I hired a marijuana grower from Humboldt County to scale the fence at the rear of Izzy's estate. Gave him a near-new BMW to sneak onto Izzy's estate and plant about an acre with cannabis seeds. Took six hours, nobody saw him. What this picture shows is a real nice one-acre crop of marijuana on Izzy Valentine's estate. Izzy don't have a clue it's there. Plants are about three feet high now, ripe to be harvested."

Bobby smiled, probably for the first time since coming into the office. "Or ripe for a call to the Drug Enforcement Agency?"

"Hey, you read my script. Yeah, that's the plan. We rat out Izzy. The DEA swoops down, raids Izzy's estate. We tip off the media, watch the eleven o'clock news."

"An acre of marijuana growing in the middle of Silicon Valley's most exclusive community." The image made Bobby smile. "Even if he escapes prosecution, Izzy will never live that down." Bobby noticed Hugh Wilson's unease. "What's the matter?"

"This company can't be involved with a vendetta against Izzy Valentine," Hugh said. "We shouldn't even be aware of what he's doing. And there's certainly no way Race Software can pay a quarter of a million dollars off the books to Mr. Cody. That would make us co-conspirators in a drug case."

"It's a done deal," Sam reminded the attorney. "Handshakes count with me. Try to back out, there's gonna be consequences. I don't mean legal consequences, I'm talkin' about trauma to your personal body."

Hugh moved a few more inches away from Sam. "Part of my duty as corporate counsel is to steer Bobby and the Race Corporation away from any criminal charges or civil litigation."

"There are only four of us in this room," I pointed out. "Nobody here can afford to talk about this."

"Money can be traced," Hugh said.

"Move funds from one of the offshore accounts." Bobby swiveled around and punched some keys on his laptop. "Look, there's plenty of yen in the Japanese product development fund. I'm sure Sam has an offshore account of his own. Transfer the funds from Mitsubishi bank in Japan to that private bank we use in London, the Chichester Bank. From there into Mister Cody's account, wherever it may be. Sam, you don't mind being paid in Japanese yen, do you?"

"Fine with me," Sam agreed. "So long as there's enough of them. Don't want none of those Eurodollars, though. I'm a fiscal conservative."

"Hugh, you handle the payment. Do it today."

Sam wrote down the name of his Swiss bank and the account number, which he gave to an unhappy Hugh Wilson.

"I want to be the one to call the DEA," Bobby said. "We'll do that today, too."

I gave Sam an I-told-you-so wink.

"Afraid not," Sam said. "This has to be handled just right. One example, the DEA tape records all its phone tips. You don't want your voice on a DEA recording, those people got equipment to do voice analysis. Plus, the DEA moves faster on physical evidence than on phone tips. So I'll get a fresh copy of this photo, nobody's fingerprints on it, into DEA hands right away. They know exactly what an acre of marijuana looks like from the air. I'll put a typewritten note with the photo, give them the location of the crop. Make it sound like Izzy stiffed some people, they decided to rat him out on the marijuana."

"You're sure the DEA will move quickly on this?" Bobby asked. "And that the tip to the DEA won't be traced to you or to Race Software?"

"That's what you're payin' me for. Don't worry, I already laid the groundwork with my contact inside the DEA," Sam assured him. "This guy and some others'll get part of your dough to push the case against Izzy. Don't ask me no details. Just transfer the money. And like they say on Eyewitness News, stay tuned for further developments."

CHAPTER 20

The truly bizarre parts of the day were yet to come.

After the meeting, Sam happily went off to destroy Izzy Valentine's reputation. He gave me his cell phone number and told me to keep in touch.

I tried to go up to the sixth floor to retrieve my portrait of Bobby so I could do some of the work I'd actually been hired for. Couldn't do it, the elevators had been programmed not to stop at the sixth floor. I didn't realize that until I'd been pushing buttons for a frustrating five minutes, going from the first floor to the fifth floor and back again half a dozen times.

I tried sneaking up a stairwell, guards stopped me at the sixth floor landing. I argued with them for access to the sixth floor. I pleaded with their shift lieutenant. I appealed to Jenny and metaphorically got down on my hands and knees to beg Pam Solter for special access. No use. The executive floor was off limits until further notice, Bobby's orders.

Which left me effectively unemployed.

After that I strolled around looking for Dorothy. She wasn't in the small basement office assigned to her. In my wanderings I saw only a few people working at their terminals. Most employees huddled in small groups to speculate about when the next ghostly sighting might take place. I heard Cynthia Gooding's name mentioned. A few people claimed to have recognized her face on the spirit that had wandered the halls yesterday.

They're right, I thought. That was Cynthia. But what the hell did she want? How did she really die? Was she murdered? How could we communicate with her?

Plenty of questions, no answers.

More red furniture was being carried out to waiting vans by the moving men. Anything, it seemed, with a hint of the color red was being junked. I doubted that would put a halt to the sightings of Cynthia. Worse, the media vultures were bound to see red furniture and fixtures going out the door and use it to embellish their stories. They'd also hear that anything red and stationary, like walls or posts, was being repainted.

Not my problem, I decided. I'd done what I could for Bobby. From now on I'd stick to my palette and canvas, let the world go as crazy as it wanted. I'm not a detective or a ghost-buster or a PR consultant.

Ray Waters, who was a PR consultant, ran up and grabbed my arm. "Are they here? Have you seen them? You'll help me find places to put them, won't you, Kevin?"

"What are you talking about?" I disengaged Ray's hand from my arm. He hadn't changed clothes since I'd seen him yesterday. He was unshaven and bleary-eyed from having worked here throughout the night.

"The crystals! Bobby ordered fifty crystals from one of those New Age stores in San Francisco. They were supposed to be delivered by nine a.m. and distributed around the complex. We're going to use them to ward off…" his voice dropped to a hush "…the visitor."

"You can't spread crystals around like fire extinguishers. Or, in this case, ghost extinguishers."

"Don't use that word!"

"Ray…" I put a calming hand on his shoulder, which was trembling. "You're exhausted. Go lie down, get some rest. You'll collapse if you don't."

"I'll rest when we've turned this crisis around." He shrugged off my hand. "Bobby's depending on me."

"Ray, we don't know whether that crystal had any actual effect yesterday or whether our ghost…excuse me…our visitor…just went away on her own."

"Bobby's convinced the crystal did the trick."

"Whoever's delivering the crystals probably can't get past all those guards at the entrance anyway."

"You're right!" Ray rushed off towards the building entrance.

The loyalty Bobby Race instilled in his people was both impressive and depressing. The only other person I've known who had that kind of leadership was First Sergeant Tenney, a tough old infantryman who led the platoon Sam and I served with for so long. Sergeant Tenney's style was somewhat different from Bobby's. He spoke rarely but with quiet authority, so when he gave an order you felt obliged to leap to whatever task he assigned you. Like Bobby, Sergeant Tenney treated everyone the same regardless of rank, I'd seen him chew out majors and light colonels when they fucked up. He often took on the toughest, dirtiest jobs himself just to set a standard for how those jobs should be done.

Maybe that's the essence of leadership. Possessing only a modest taste for leadership myself, I wouldn't know. I'm not a leader. I'm not a follower. I like to go my own way. This had been a bad week for going my own way.

I came upon Dorothy lingering over coffee in the cafeteria, the last place I would have looked for a workaholic like her. She wasn't alone. Across the table from Dorothy sat a man in his forties with long grayish hair streaked fashionably with yellow, a scarecrow's stick-thin body, hawkish nose, remarkably deep-set eyes. He wore a herringbone jacket with leather patches on the elbows.

I'd seen him somewhere, not here at Race Software. Dorothy's left hand lay on the table. He held it with both of his hands and spoke to her intensely, as if they were on a higher plane than everyone around them. For once Dorothy had come to the office in casual clothes and with her hairy sort of frizzy instead of carefully groomed. She looked not just relaxed, but blissful.

"Hello, Dorothy." Clever opening, I could go anywhere from there.

"Kevin!" Though I startled Dorothy, at least she looked happy to see me. "I'm so glad you found me. Sit down, please." Her hawk-nosed companion looked at Dorothy's hand as if it were a piece of property he might buy, then released it. "This David Maximilian, I'm sure you've heard of him."

"Yes, I have." Saying to myself: Oh no, anything but this.

"Then you know David is director of the Institute for Psychic and Paranormal Research in Napa Valley. I was on the Internet most of the night looking for someone who's done a serious analysis of supernatural phenomena. Fortunately, I stumbled on the institute's web site. I called David at six a.m. and he agreed to come down here for a consultation. David, this is Kevin Pierce."

Maximilian extended his hand. "I've heard a lot about you."

I shook his hand without enthusiasm.

"Your name was familiar to me before this week. From time to time I considered inviting you to visit the institute, but I'd been told you had no real interest in the paranormal."

"You were told right."

He didn't react to my cold reply, just went on smiling and talking. I had the feeling he'd be impossible to insult. Some people use that technique to get their way. Hell, I use it myself when I'm trying to talk someone into posing for me.

"Dorothy's told me all about the visitations they've had here at Race, and about the appearance of this Sport Sullivan at your home last night." His deep-set eyes sparkled. "Fascinating! Every bit of it! Placing a crystal within the spirit's aura was a brilliant move. You must come up to the institute, Kevin. You obviously have a channel into the afterlife. I've developed an extensive set of psychological and physiological tests that can determine an individual's ability to connect with the spirit world. When we measure your APC, that's what we call it, we'll have a new baseline for comparison with our other subjects"

"There's no way I'm going to take one of your phony tests. I paint portraits, that's all I care about."

Maximilian went rosy with equanimity. "I think you'll change your mind at some point."

I was right, the bastard couldn't be insulted. I'd read about Maximilian. Usually he used just the one name, like Madonna or Cher. His two books on the occult hadn't sold very well even though he often appeared on talk shows. California has thousands of gurus. Maximilian was in the second or third tier of that peculiar breed. He hoped to use Race Software's problems and my connection with Sport Sullivan to raise his visibility in the media. Anything I told him would end up in one of his bullshit books and television tapes.

"No, I won't change my mind."

Maximilian persisted. "You should take some responsibility for your gift. This character from the 1920s, Sport Sullivan, sounds like an example of what I call The Lost Soul Syndrome. The institute could help you find a way to make more frequent contact with him."

"That's the last thing I want. Sport is a pain in the ass, he gives me nothing but grief."

"That's the wrong attitude," Dorothy said. "Sport has so much to say about…"

"He's got too much to say. About everything. I've heard the story of Sport's rise and fall over and over. What I really need is a way to get rid of him."

Maximilian's bony fingers tapped the table. "An interesting thought. Perhaps we could find a way to transfer Sport's appearances from you to Dorothy."

"Great idea!" Dorothy could hardly contain her new ambitions. "I'd love to be Sport's familiar."

"His what?"

"That's what we call a person who has a special relationship with a spirit," Maximilian explained.

"Listen, if you want Sport, you can have him."

"You'd have to come to the institute, take the tests, help us find a way to disengage you from your spirit partner."

"He's not my *spirit partner* and I won't have anything to do with your tests. I know what you're looking for, Max."

"Maximilian," he corrected.

"Grist for your next book, anecdotes for a talk show. That's all you care about."

Maximilian stiffened theatrically, putting on a nice show of being tragically misunderstood. "We take our work seriously at the institute. It isn't fair to criticize us without even coming up to Napa Valley to see what we do. Dorothy's joining my staff, you know. Does that give you any incentive?"

"She's what?"

"As soon as Redleaf is released, I'm out of here," Dorothy confirmed. "I've already given Bobby my resignation. I've got plenty of money, enough stock and other types of savings to see me through. This a chance to apply computers to something really exciting. Don't you see, Kevin? Meeting Sport Sullivan turned my life around. I was blind to the possibilities of communication with The Other Side. You're the one who opened my eyes to this incredible phantom world. You should be proud of that."

"I knew about your resignation, Bobby asked me talk you into withdrawing your letter. He seems to think he can't operate this place without you."

"He'll have to."

I jerked my thumb at Maximilian. "This goof doesn't know anything about The Other Side. You can't 'study' the ghosts of Sport Sullivan or Cynthia Gooding any more than you can 'study' how not to die."

Maximilian sighed deeply, making a production of his disappointment.

"I think you're wrong," Dorothy countered. "The large body of empirical evidence on paranormal experiences has never been properly analyzed. That became obvious to me from just one night on the Internet. Analysis is my skill. I'm going to build a worldwide database that will help David and others find new paths to the afterlife."

"Good luck." Dorothy couldn't be dissuaded, at least right now. "As somebody once said: Include me out."

CHAPTER 21

"Pepper Johnson is missing," Bobby said.

"Have you called his home?"

"Of course."

"When did you last see him? At Billy Jack's last night?"

"That's right."

"Did Pepper have a lot to drink?"

"He probably drank three boilermakers. Enough to put me flat on my back, but Pepper didn't seem much affected."

"He could be at home sleeping off a hangover."

"I sent someone to his house this morning. Pepper wasn't there."

Again Bobby surprised me. His concern for Pepper didn't appear to have anything to do with business. "Why are you bothered by this?"

It took a while for Bobby to answer. "Pepper's my only friend. I'm uncomfortable when he's not around."

"Come on, everybody wants to be your friend. You know a thousand people and you've probably got more women than Roddy Mellow. Don't ask me to feel sorry for you."

"Who's Roddy Mellow?"

"A legendary San Francisco pimp."

Bobby didn't find that amusing. He set his face in a look of disgust which also managed to convey a sense of being flattered by the comparison. "It's true. Pepper's the only person around here who doesn't want something from me. The old rascal actually likes me."

Bobby suddenly seemed even younger than his twenty-eight years. "My father's about the same age as Pepper, but he doesn't like me very much. Never did. I'm sure you're thinking Pepper's a surrogate father to me. Not quite right. Eight years ago, when I was only twenty and just getting this company started, Pepper came on board to sweep the floors and generally keep the old building I was renting from falling down around our ears. There were only about twenty people in the whole damned company then, so we all spent a lot of time together. Every single employee was important. I listened to what Pepper had to say as much as I listened to anyone else. I still do.

"From day one Pepper showed confidence in me. So what if he was just a maintenance man, a one-handed black janitor, not even a high school education. At the time I was just a twenty-year-old college dropout myself. No reputation. Hardly any money. Just the conviction that networking software, especially for wireless communication, was going to be the information industry's next gold mine. Pepper was convinced, and he convinced me, that Race Software would be a success, which is more than I thought when what little money I did have ran out."

"How'd you survive then?"

"I got lucky, a wealthy gentleman in Maryland put a million dollars into our stock, saved the company. Clarence Wells, that's the investor I've been trying to reach. Seven years later and I've still never met him. Apparently Wells travels constantly, he has business deals going all over the world. I suppose all he cares about is that his million dollar investment is now worth about a billion. Izzy Valentine's trying to reach Clarence Wells, too. He wants the proxies for Wells' stock. You know what? I'd rather lose Clarence Wells than Pepper Johnson."

Was that moisture in the corners of Bobby Race's eyes?

"I get it now. You won't let me onto the sixth floor to work on your portrait because you want me to find Pepper for you. Okay, you win. I'll do it."

"You will? Good." Bobby leaned forward crisply and handed me a slip of paper. "Here's Pepper's home address, maybe you'll find something there to tell you where he went. Maybe he'll even be home by the time you get there, I hope so. If not, Pepper might go back to Billy Jack's, he liked the place. And I've also written down the names of a couple of other bars where Pepper likes to hang out. Working class places."

Wait a minute. Had I just been masterfully manipulated? Those tears in the corners of Bobby's eyes seemed to have dried out awfully fast.

"Pepper usually has dinner out, says he doesn't like to cook," Bobby went on, still crisp and cool. "I know he eats most of his breakfasts and dinners at a *taqueria* near his house. Pepper's a widower. If the Giants were playing, he'd be at Pac Bell park. Sometimes he plays chess at the San Jose Senior's Club. That's about all I can tell you that might help find him."

You bastard, I thought. You can turn it on and off like a faucet. I was about to tell Bobby to go find Pepper himself when Jenny came rushing in with some urgent matter that immediately captured all of his attention.

I was concerned about Pepper too, so I decided to go find him before Bobby could manufacture any more tears.

CHAPTER 22

I took the Bayshore Freeway to Milpitas and found the street where Pepper Johnson lived. He was near The Great Mall, a former Ford assembly plant cut up into retail stores. The neighborhood consisted of smallish houses built in the 1950s for workers at the old Ford plant. Some were well maintained, others not. Older cars were haphazardly parked, torn newspapers and advertising flyers blew around in the gutters. Pepper had a beige stucco bungalow with a well-tended front yard planted in low-maintenance ivy. The trim was freshly painted. The windows gleamed. No cracks in the cement driveway. My house should look so good.

I went up the steps and rang the bell. No big surprise when Pepper didn't come to the door. By looking in all the windows, I learned exactly nothing except that Pepper owned a three-foot-high white plaster cat identical to the one my grandmother kept in the corner of her living room for many decades. Only difference, Pepper kept his in the corner of the dining room.

So much for detective work.

I had Bobby's list of places where Pepper might be found. I could spend the day checking out each place and only by the grace of God would I stumble into Pepper. However, the *taqueria* where Pepper took most of his meals sounded promising. Not because I might find him there, but because *taquerias* serve Mexican beer.

A five-minute drive through the neighborhood was all it took to locate Ernesto's Cafe and Taqueria about two blocks from Pepper's house. The place was painted an electric shade of pink. Next to the front door stood a full-sized statue of a pink flamingo. You couldn't drive past Ernesto's without noticing it, which I suppose was the point.

The pink motif extended to the inside of the establishment. However, the interior of Ernesto's was spotless and the aromas mouthwatering. I even liked the background music, Gloria Estefan singing soulfully in Spanish.

"Welcome...*Buenos tardes*." Behind the counter, a wide-chested Mexican with jet-black hair touched with gray was filling sugar containers. He was in his fifties, heavyset and had the proud air of a proprietor. "What can I get you, *amigo*?"

I slid onto a stool and picked up a menu which turned out to be printed in Spanish.

"Ain't to worry. Got the menu in English, too."

"Don't really need a menu." I pretended to give my order some thought. "Think I'll just have a Carta Blanca."

"Sorry, we only carry Dos Equis."

"I'm crushed, but I'll take it."

"I like a man who'll drink a brand that ain't his own." The proprietor reached into a cooler and pulled out an ice-cold bottle of Dos Equis, which he poured into a frosted glass.

"And I like a man who serves a really cold beer." I lifted my glass. "Your health."

"*Salud*." The proprietor lifted the cup of coffee near his elbow. "Sure you don't want some *huevos rancheros* to go with your beer?"

My stomach growled as if it had overheard the offer. "My gastric juices vote a resounding yes."

"*Bueno*." He called the order into the kitchen and came back with his cup of coffee. "My son Guillermo is the cook and *huevos rancheros* are his specialty. You ain't gonna regret your decision."

"You're Ernesto?"

"In the flesh." He patted his ample belly. "Too much damned flesh, runs in the family."

"I'm lucky, my family runs to thin people. Except for my Uncle Bubba back in Texas, who lives mostly on Hershey bars and blueberry pie. Bubba's up to about four hundred pounds."

"Makes me feel skinny. What's your Uncle Bubba do for a living?"

"He's a cardiologist."

Ernesto laughed and went off to freshen someone's coffee. It was about eleven o'clock, not many customers, so he soon returned. "You're a pretty good liar. What's your name?"

"Kevin Pierce."

"Hey, you're the horny artist! Pepper Johnson told me about you, he likes the way you paint and admires your way with the ladies. You looking for Pepper?"

"I'm told he eats here."

"I been feeding Pepper for twenty years. He don't like to cook. Since Rosie died, his wife, he's been eating breakfast and dinner here four, five times a week. Such a good customer, I give him a twenty percent discount." Ernesto hitched up his pants and looked wistfully at the ceiling. "Pepper ain't only a good customer. He's a true friend. Ten years ago he did me a really big favor, loaned me money to build the second story on this place so I could live above my business. Also helped paint the building pink and found the flamingo for me. You like it?"

"Love it." Ernesto was right, I'm a pretty good liar.

"You ain't gotta make nice, I know my place looks like a Disneyland wannabe."

"A little pink does go a long way with me," I admitted. "So Pepper loaned you money to expand? That is a friend."

"That was after he finally got the insurance settlement for the death of his wife and Joey, when he was still looking for things to do with his money."

"Who was Joey? Pepper's son?"

Ernesto frowned. "You didn't know? Twenty years ago, more or less, Pepper's wife Rosie and his son Joey were both killed. Rosie was taking

Joey to the beach, driving over the Santa Cruz mountains on Route 17. You know what a killer that road is. Truck went over the center line, wiped them out. Came out later the driver was high on cocaine. The trucking company settled with Pepper, after ten years of legal bullshit, for three million bucks. After the lawyers took their share, Pepper had a couple million dollars. That's how come he could help me out."

"How old was Pepper's son?"

"Fourteen. First Pepper lost a hand in Vietnam, then his family in an accident. Guy ain't had much luck."

"I'm surprised Pepper stayed in the house when he had money to move someplace else." I pictured Pepper wandering from room to room, touching things that belonged to his wife and son. I understood why the interior of his home had a dated look, he probably hadn't changed anything in all the years since Rosie died.

"Pepper says the years in that house, with his wife and son, were the best of his life. He likes to remember it all, have their stuff nearby."

Guillermo Suarez, a somewhat slimmer version of his father, brought out a platter of *huevos rancheros* about the size of a manhole cover. The enormous platter was heaped with eggs, refried beans, onions, chili peppers, potatoes, *sopapillas*, little pot of honey on the side.

"You could feed half of Mexico City with this."

"Dig in," Ernesto said. "I get you another Dos Equis."

I was beginning to see Pepper in a whole different light. Ernesto returned with another beer and a freshly frosted glass. "If Pepper settled for two million dollars, what's he doing working as a maintenance man?

"Oh, Pepper ain't got the money any more. He used it up. Gave Stanford University a million bucks for a scholarship in Joey's name. Then he loaned out a lot of *dinero* to friends, some of them didn't pay him back. In case you're wondering, I did pay back the twenty thousand he loaned me."

Between bites I said, "I wasn't wondering. Pepper wouldn't still be eating here if you'd stiffed him. He may be a saint, he isn't a sucker."

Ernesto nodded as if to say *damned straight*. "And then he invested a lotta bucks in one of them Silicon Valley startups. Guess he lost it all, he ain't never talked about it again."

"You're right, Pepper's had a load of bad luck." I dipped a *sopapilla* in the honey and ate it in two bites.

"You don't know the half. When he got the money, maybe a thousand con men came outta the woodwork at him. Guys pushing phony stock, cemetery plots, ostrich farms, beachfront property in Arizona, rare stamps, Swiss franc time deposits, Bolivian tin mines, beekeeping farms, offshore oil rigs, paper mills in Louisiana, you name it. Got so bad, Pepper began using his mother's name."

"You mean Pepper Johnson isn't his real name?"

"You need more tabasco sauce on them *huevos*." Without asking permission, Ernesto poured enough tabasco over my eggs to incinerate the city of Cleveland. "That's better, huh? Yeah, Pepper dropped the name Wells and started using his mom's maiden name. Johnson. After a couple of years, he stopped getting calls from every con man in California. He ain't never gone back to his other name, still calls himself Johnson."

I took another bite and the tabasco sauce not only cleared my sinuses, it reamed out every brain cell I owned and turned my eyeballs into fiery bowls of soup. "Ernesto, I can't breathe!" The words *strangled cry* would be appropriate here.

"You be okay in a minute." Nonchalantly. "I thrash my own tabasco sauce. Good for you to clean out your system. Everybody oughtta have a few ounces tabasco every single day. Ask your Uncle Bubba, the cardiologist."

Presently I was able to breathe again. The tabasco had dulled my antenna or I might have reacted sooner to Ernesto's offhand comments about Pepper's name. Or maybe I shouldn't blame the tabasco sauce. My antenna is more like one of those coat hangers you see sticking out of the fender of a rusted old Nissan.

"You said Pepper's real name is Wells? W-E-L-L-S?"

"That's it."

"Then Pepper must be a nickname. Do you know his real first name?"

"I did." Ernesto shrugged. "Ain't heard it in years, though."

"Could it be Clarence?"

"That's right, Clarence Wells. He never liked the name Clarence, always went by Pepper. Except, I suppose, on legal papers and such."

Legal papers. Like stock certificates. Whoa! I began to see what happened. Pepper collected a big settlement after his wife and son were killed, took a building maintenance job at Bobby·Race's little startup company under the name he was using to duck all those salesmen. Found he liked Bobby Race, thought his company had a future, put most of the money from the settlement into Race Software under his real name: Clarence Wells.

Which meant Pepper Johnson, or Clarence Wells, was an incredibly wealthy man. How much had Bobby said Clarence Wells' stock was now worth? A billion dollars? Yes, dammit, that's what Bobby said. A billion fucking dollars!

"Holy shit!"

"Tabasco still bothering you?"

"No, I'm fine." Bobby apparently had no idea his building maintenance man was his biggest individual stockholder. "Does Pepper come from Maryland?"

"Yeah, he does. Still got family there, too. Goes back to Baltimore every chance he gets. Owns a little vacation place on the Maryland shore, I think."

A little vacation place. Probably next door to the Duponts.

Okay, I also understood why Pepper felt so proprietary about the Race Software Corporation. Why he felt free to mouth off to high level execs and drop into Bobby's office whenever he felt like it. Why he made a point of knowing everything that went on at Race. Pepper owned the company, or at least a nice piece of it. He was just looking after his investment.

A major shit-eating grin spread slowly across my face. I wanted to be the one to tell Bobby that Pepper Johnson and Clarence Wells were the same person. And tell Greg Tillotson and Ray Waters and Dorothy and some of the other execs, too.

What a hoot!

"You never said whether Pepper came in for breakfast this morning."

"Oh, he was here. Had his usual. Pancakes, eggs, refried beans, wheat toast. Then his friends picked him up right when he came out of my place."

"What friends?"

"I ain't never seen them before." He reached for the bottle of tabasco.

"No more tabasco…please…who were these friends?"

"I dunno. Two of them in a big car. I figured they were from Race Software, came to take Pepper to work. I ain't telling you no secret when I say Pepper had a hangover this morning, probably didn't want to drive."

"What did these people look like?"

"I only saw the one guy real good. Maybe fifty years old, bald, dark suit."

Had to be Pure John again. Did the guy never rest? How was he able to leave his coffin during the daylight hours?

Bobby had said Izzy Valentine was also looking for Clarence Wells in order to get his proxies. With control of the proxies, Izzy would be a cinch to win a seat on the Race Software board of directors. Had Izzy discovered that Pepper Johnson and Clarence Wells were one in the same?

I hoped to hell he hadn't.

But how else could you explain Pure John picking up Pepper this morning? Unless, and I didn't even want to think about it, Pepper and Izzy had formed some sort of alliance. "Did Pepper go willingly with those two guys?"

Ernesto stepped back a pace. "Sure, I didn't see nothing unusual. What's wrong? Pepper in some kind'a trouble? Is that why you're looking for him?"

"No, I just need to talk with Pepper. Look, I'll take some more tabasco, my stomach's starting to adapt to it." I quickly finished my *huevos* and left Ernesto's with a burning sensation that may have come from the spicy meal or, more likely, from my fear that Pepper was in the worst kind of trouble.

CHAPTER 23

According to an article I read, a professional burglar can break into any home within thirty seconds. Took me almost half an hour to figure out how to enter Pepper's house. Of course, I wanted to get in without breaking a window or otherwise damaging any part of his property. Maybe I shouldn't have been so finicky, considering the urgency of the situation. But I couldn't prove Pepper had been abducted, or even that he was in any sort of danger. So if the police had shown up after I'd jimmied a door or broken a window, I'd have been hauled off to jail.

First I tried the old trick, everyone's seen it in the movies, of sliding a credit card between the door jam and the lock. Works in the movies every time. All I managed to do was snap my brand new Visa card from Race Software in half.

I almost cried.

Then I went from window to window looking for one that might be unlocked. No luck there, either. Sometimes people leave extra house keys in a flower pot or under a mat or some other place near a door. The Bible says *"Seek and ye shall find."* I sought, I didn't find.

Though neighborhood watch signs were posted along the street, none of the neighbors called the police on me or came over to ask what I was doing. I could have jacked the house up, put it on a flatbed truck, driven away with it. Some neighborhood watch.

When I was almost to the thirty-minute mark, it occurred to me that Pepper might hide a spare key in a place easily reached with his hook. I noticed a bird feeder hanging from a nail driven into a tree right next to the back door. No feed in it, though. Maybe Pepper used it for something else.

I reached up and felt around the feeder on the side that was out of view from the porch. Yes indeed, a spare house key hung from one of the out-of-sight perches.

"Thank you, Pepper."

I let myself into the house and did a quick walk-through. You could tell Rosie had picked out the furniture. It was solid maple from some established maker of early American pieces. Ethan Allen. Pennsylvania House. One of those. Good stuff, but in a style a man would never buy on his own. Pepper kept it polished. Treated right, furniture like this would last for generations. I imagine that's what Rosie had expected, generations of children, grandchildren, great grandchildren gathered at this dinner table or watching a ballgame from these chairs and couches. A dream as traditional as the furniture. A dream that never came true for Rosie Wells or her son Joey.

There were family photos in every room. Rosie Wells had been almost as tall as Pepper. Her face was round and, in every photo, extremely serious. Not that she frowned. Rosie had just been one of those big, serious girls determined to make a success of life. In three photos she held a Bible. In every photo that included Pepper, she held his hand tightly. Nothing was going to interfere with Rosie Wells' vision of an ideal family life.

Except a truck operated by a coked-up driver.

Their son Joey was well represented in Pepper's photo collection, too. Walking from room to room, I watched Joey grow from a fat little baby with laughing eyes to a five-year-old with a devilish grin to a twelve-year-old proudly dressed in an Oakland A's shirt and hat. Where Rosie was serious, Joey had a light-hearted smile for every occasion. He also had Pepper's muscular shoulders and arms. Joey would have been in his mid-thirties now, if he'd lived.

The room I wanted was a study off the main hallway that looked out to the street. I sat down at Pepper's desk and began opening drawers.

Pure John had taken Pepper right off the street from in front of Ernesto's *taqueria.* If Izzy wanted Pepper's proxies, he'd need more than Pepper himself. I had a vague understanding that Race Software, like every other corporation, sends out a proxy form every year to each of its stockholders. Most stockholders either ignore the proxy form, if they own only a few shares, or sign their proxies over to the company's board of directors. Sometimes a major player, or another corporation, will make a move on a company by rounding up a bunch of proxies.

How had I learned all this impressive stuff? Not through my extensive stock holdings, which are nonexistent. No, most of my expertise on corporate financing comes from reruns of old tv shows like *L.A. Law.* What I hoped was that Izzy didn't have Pepper's stock proxies. Without the proxies, it wouldn't help him much to have Pepper.

The paperwork I found proved that Pepper Johnson was, legally, Clarence E. Wells. The deed to the house, home insurance policy, auto policy, other legal documents were all in the name of Wells. I even came across a birth certificate and marriage license for Clarence E. Wells. Also Pepper's army discharge in that name.

I was about halfway through the files when a car pulled up to the curb outside the house. Pure John, as dapper and dark and insolent as ever, left the car and came up the walkway. He held a large ring of keys, maybe fifty in all. Big industrial key ring I'd last seen swinging from Pepper's belt.

My hands moved as fast as a magician's, though a hell of a lot more nervously, as I wildly stuffed papers back into the file drawer. Pure John was sure to be carrying the Browning Hi-Power with the Black Talon loads. "Shit-oh-dear!" I dropped half a dozen manila folders, sending papers skittering all over the floor. I went down on my knees, and not to pray. Well, I did some of that, too. Mainly I was scooping up pieces of paper and stuffing them helter skelter into any manila folder that came to hand.

Thank God Pepper carried so many keys. Pure John didn't know which one fit the front door to Pepper's house, so he had to try each of the most likely one by one. In the background, I could hear the keys being tried in the lock. *Scratch scratch. Scratch scratch. Scratch scratch. Scratch scratch. Scratch scratch.*

Then…*click*…as one of the keys fit and the door was unlocked.

I tiptoed out of the study, looking ridiculous I'm sure, and into a nearby closet just as Pure John began his own walk-through of Pepper's house. He pretty much followed my route and ended up in the same place. The study. I left the closet door cracked a couple of inches and could see Pure John's back as he took a seat at Pepper's desk.

He found the file drawer and began going through each of the manila folders. No doubt Izzy wanted the proxies. Another few minutes and I would have had those babies in my own hands.

With Pure John's back to me, I might have been able to come up behind him and bash in his ugly bald head…strangle him…knock him cold…pin him to the floor…whatever. The operative word was "might." All I could do safely was watch and wait.

After a time, he uttered a satisfied grunt and separated one of the manila folders from the others. After reading through the file a couple of times, he picked up the phone on Pepper's desk and made a call.

"Hello, this is John. I'm in his home and I have the proxies." Long pause. "Thank you. They were easy to find. Yes, I'm sure these are the current year's proxy forms. Shall I bring them straight to you? All right." He started to put down the phone, then quickly brought it up to his ear. "Oh, I'll stop at the Kinko's in Palo Alto to pick up copies of a standard last will and testament. Yes, okay. If they have more than one kind of will, I'll get both. You can decide which to use. If it comes to that. Yes, I'll see you soon."

Pure John put down the phone. He spent a few minutes straightening up Pepper's desk, putting away files. I saw him flip through Pepper's address book. He wrote down a few phone numbers from the book on a slip of paper and put it in his wallet. You would have thought he was sitting in his own study, Pure John was that relaxed.

After a while he rose, looked around the study and left the house. Locking the door behind him.

Before Pure John reached his car, I already had picked up Pepper's phone to call Big Sam Cody's cellular number. I tapped my foot while the call went through. All of a sudden Sam's booming voice came on the line. "County morgue, things are dead around here."

"You're in a good mood."

"Kevin? Yeah, my sting is startin' to play out. I'm sittin' in my car, top of Route 92. I can see a DEA helicopter makin' passes over our friend's property. They're takin' pictures, confirmin' the tip I gave them. Two or three hours and they'll have a team on the ground."

"Meanwhile Pure John has picked up one of Bobby's employees. I think they're holding him somewhere. Even Bobby doesn't know that the guy, Pepper Johnson, is one of his major stockholders."

"So what? That isn't our business. And remember we're on a cell phone, somebody might overhear this."

"Pepper's a friend. He was a grunt like us, lost his left hand in Vietnam."

"Vietnam was before our time, buddy."

"He was a grunt like us. He's a friend of mine. And he's being hassled by Izzy. What else do you have to know?"

When Sam gave one of his deeply tortured sighs, the cell phone made it sound like he was talking from the bottom of a well. "Okay…okay…I understand. What'cha want from me?"

"Pure John's on his way to the Kinko's in Palo Alto. Do you know where it is?"

"Sure."

"Meet me there. Don't let Pure John see you. I'll be there as fast as I can, we'll follow him to wherever Pepper's being held. By any chance do you have Betty with you?"

Betty was a palm-sized .25 caliber Beretta Sam used to carry under his ammo belt. A popgun, the other guys in the platoon called it. They ribbed Sam because he was hauling around an M-16 that'd kill a slew of people at five hundred yards, plus three hundred rounds of ammo, plus five hand grenades, plus a K-bar. And still he felt the need to carry little Betty with an effective range of only about fifteen yards. Sam only had occasion to use Betty once that I know of, but in that case it saved his life.

Sam groaned. "I don't have a need for Betty now that I'm a well-loved businessman and philanthropist."

"Okay, just meet me at Kinko's."

"What are you drivin'?"

"Same as always, my Karmann Ghia."

"Pure John might come and go by the time you can get here in that old piece of junk. If he does, I'll follow him. You call me on the cell phone if I'm gone."

"What are you driving?"

"I'm still in the Rolls."

"He'll spot you in that car."

"Not to worry, I'll pick up somethin' less flashy on the street."

"Isn't that a little risky, considering your current legal troubles?"

"Busman's holiday," Sam said. "Get humpin'."

CHAPTER 24

"This can't be the right place, there's some mistake."

"I followed Pure John here from Kinko's like you asked."

"Can't be."

"What's the matter with you, Mister Whitebread?" Sam eyed me nervously. "You look confused."

Yes, I was confused. And flustered. Not to mention bewitched, bothered and bewildered. We were standing on a bluff overlooking the quietly fastidious grounds of the Childrens Bayside Shelter in Palo Alto.

"There's his car. Pure John pulled up to that little bungalow behind the main buildin' and went inside. What is it? You've been here before?"

Sam had been right about my Karmann Ghia. By the time I arrived at Kinko's, Pure John already had left. Sam, in a green Camry "borrowed" off the street, followed. I contacted Sam on his cell phone and took his directions to the Bayside Childrens Shelter, even though I thought he must have made a mistake. Now that I was standing next to Sam, looking at the shelter, I still thought he'd made a mistake. "I was here just yesterday for a meeting with Amelia Valentine. She wants me to do a poster for the shelter."

"Well, that cinches it. The Valentines got a connection to this place, so they're able to use that little bungalow. It's quiet. Isolated. Part of a legitimate organization. Perfect place to bring your friend Pepper, work him over until he agrees to whatever Izzy wants."

"Izzy doesn't have any connection here, it's Amelia who's a volunteer here."

"If the wife is connected, so is Izzy."

"Doesn't track. Izzy wouldn't involve his wife in something as hard as a kidnapping. I've seen them together, he loves her."

Sam looked at me as if I'd told him Izzy Valentine knitted his own socks. "The guy's a creep, he'd let his dog fuck his cat."

There was something wildly wrong with Sam's metaphor. I was too preoccupied to pin it down. "Maybe Izzy sent Pure John here on some innocent errand."

"You tellin' me that stoppin' to buy Last Will and Testament forms is an *innocent errand*? Come on, Kevin." There was movement down by the bungalow. "And who's that guy? Another man on an *innocent errand*? The Archbishop of San Francisco maybe?"

The bungalow was about two hundred yards downhill from us. A man, not Pure John, had come outside in his shirtsleeves for a cigarette. Sleeves rolled up as if he'd been doing hard physical labor. Though his face was indistinct, we could see him well enough to tell he was not the Archbishop of San Francisco.

"That's probably the muscleman who helped Pure John force Pepper into the car. You're right, he doesn't look very innocent. On the other hand, he doesn't seem to be carrying a gun either."

"Can't tell for sure, not from here."

"Wish we had some firepower."

Sam looked at his watch. "We'll have some any minute."

"How?"

"Got a delivery comin' from UPS." Sam enjoyed my blank stare. "United Pistol Service."

Sam has this tendency to say smartass things that turn out to be true, so I didn't dismiss the remark out of hand. Once, when we were in the army, he told me in an offhand way that he was going AWOL to see his new girlfriend in Kansas City. "Gonna buy her a red Corvette for her birthday. Buy it, I said. Not steal it." I didn't believe Sam would pay hard cash for an automobile, or that he'd go AWOL just to see a girl. The next morning Sam missed reveille. He stayed AWOL for three days, came back riding in the passenger seat of a new red Corvette driven by a stunning girl named Esmerelda who was part Asian, part Latino. Yes, Sam had bought her the Corvette. Going AWOL cost him thirty days in the stockade. I never did find out what he paid for the Corvette. While Sam was in the stockade, Esmerelda drove the Corvette to L.A. and married a heart surgeon. Ever since, Sam has been an advocate of socialized medicine.

So while his UPS remark was strange, I didn't kiss it off. Especially when he showed no surprise at the ten-year-old BMW that came up the hill and parked between my Karmann Ghia and the borrowed Camry.

"Who's that?"

"Like I said, United Pistol Service. I called him from my cell phone, said I'd need a delivery here."

The driver of the old BMW stepped out and leaned back against his car. He looked like he'd spent last night sleeping at the bottom of an ash tray. His skin, clothes, hair all had a dirty gray pallor. Somewhere along the way he'd lost the ability to smile. He just nodded and said, "Hello, Sam."

"Freddie, this is my pal Kevin. Let's see what you've brought."

The man from the bottom of the ash tray opened his car trunk. He threw back a folded blanket to reveal an assortment of handguns: couple of S&W .38s, a Beretta 92FS, a Phillips and Rodgers Model 47, a big old-fashioned army-issue Colt .45, a Russian Makarov equipped with a silencer, a 9 millimeter Glock, an over-and-under .22 caliber Derringer, two standard police .38s with three-inch barrels. There were boxes of ammo, holsters, speed-loaders, cleaning kits, other paraphernalia.

"What's the pedigree on these pieces?" Sam asked.

"Nobody's been killed with any of them," Freddie replied. "No liquor stores held up. No straying husbands shot in the ass. No gang members blasted in drive-bys. I'm not saying these pieces are virgins, but they won't get you sent away either."

"What's your price?"

"A thousand for any piece except the Derringer, you can have that for a hundred bucks. I know that's above market, but the pieces are reasonably clean and you asked for UPS delivery." He looked around at the hills and the peacefully secluded Bayside Childrens Shelter. "What are you guys up to? Gonna stick up a children's shelter? Don't seem worthwhile."

"The NRA sent us to give marksmanship lessons to the little tikes," Sam said.

"Wouldn't surprise me. So you want a couple of pieces? I'll throw in box of ammo and an extra clip for each."

From the trunk I selected the army-issue Colt .45 because the weapon was familiar to me. Sam picked up the Beretta 92FS, he has a thing for Berettas.

I was still carrying around the money I'd won from Bobby so I took out the roll of cash and casually peeled off two thousand dollars in hundred dollar bills. Sam's eyes bugged. Once the money was paid and we had our guns and ammo, Freddie took off. Back to the bottom of his ash tray, I suppose.

"Has that guy ever taken a bath?"

"Not since I've known him. Where'd you get all that dough?" Sam began loading the clips. "You've never carried more than fifty bucks in your pocket since I've known you."

"I won a five thousand dollar bet from Bobby Race."

"Your lifestyle's gone through some radical changes the last few days." Sam carefully ran the slide forward and checked to make sure the safety was on. Then he tucked the pistol underneath the waistband at the small of his back.

"You'll have a hard time getting to it there."

"This is an eighteen hundred dollar suit. I'm not about to put a heavy piece in one of the pockets, fuck up all the tailor's good work. Your clothes, it don't matter if the pockets sag."

"You've gotten to be a terrible snob."

"I'm just stylish, is all."

We worked our way carefully down the hill, staying just inside the tree line to avoid being seen by anyone in the shelter. When a dozen children poured out of the main building into the playground, we retreated into the trees. Susan Wells, the director of the center, came outside with the kids. Even at a distance, her concern for her temporary wards was evident. Two of the children just slumped to the ground and another stood apart from the others, still too distressed by their troubles and fears to play the usual childhood games. Susan Wells went to each of those three, talked with them patiently, stroked their backs or arms, got them on their feet to join the other kids in a game.

I still doubted Pepper was being held prisoner on this property.

Walking deeper inside the treeline meant slogging through knee-high brush. Sam cursed all the burrs and weeds caught in his pants legs, tried to keep them brushed away to little avail. I couldn't fault his irritation. If the suit cost eighteen hundred dollars, the pant legs alone were worth six hundred. Or was that even a sensible calculation?

Didn't matter. We soon emerged from the woods behind the shelter's main building. No one in sight. The kids were still playing in the field out front. The small structure we headed for had its own small parking lot, which could accommodate half a dozen cars. The structure was about thirty by thirty, single story, no windows at the front, three windows on each side. A classroom, storage building or ancillary office space, I guessed.

Sam tested the door handle. He used infantry hand signals to let me know the door was unlocked. With his right hand, he signaled that once inside he'd go left and I'd go right.

I moved the Colt off safety. Sam drew the Beretta and likewise took off the safety. Neither of us cocked the hammers. Too easy to trip going fast through a door and accidentally discharge a weapon.

Sam threw open the door and dodged inside and to the left. I charged in right behind him, skip jumping to the right. The fellow who'd been having a smoke outside was rolling down his sleeves just inside the door. His forearms looked as big as Louisville sluggers. He saw a huge, scowling black man coming at him with an upraised pistol and froze like a deer caught in headlights.

Sam smashed the heavy Beretta across his face and the fellow went down in a sort of skidding motion.

"No gun!" Sam roared. "No gun, John! I'll drop you!"

I came up shoulder to shoulder with Sam. "Don't pull it! One of us will nail you!"

For once Pure John looked anything but insolent. His right hand was inside his jacket, but he looked unsure what to do with it. While he was thinking it over, I walked briskly across the fifteen yards separating us. His bald pate had broken out with huge beads of sweat. I took care not to put myself between Sam and Pure John. When I reached him, I pushed the barrel of my Colt against throat right under his chin. Pure John stiffened and drew a labored breath. I put my free hand inside his coat and removed the heavy Browning 9 millimeter.

"Might have a backup," Sam said.

My eyes asked the question.

"Ankle gun," Pure John said.

I moved around to his rear and placed the barrel against his kidney. That's a killing shot and Pure John knew it. "Bend down slowly. Get the ankle gun slowly. Leave it on the floor."

He did exactly as told. As I turned Pure John around to face me, the anger I'd been repressing since his attempt to toss me off a cliff got the better of me. With a flick of my thumb, I reset the safety on the Colt so it wouldn't go off accidentally and slashed Pure John across the face. He crumpled as the bridge of his nose broke with a twiggy snap. He didn't fall though, so I put my right foot against his chest and sent him cartwheeling back into the nearest wall.

This time he did go down, his face badly cut. I hoped the scar would be permanent.

"Stay on the floor," I ordered.

"If he moves," Sam said, "can I shoot him?"

"Help yourself."

We were in a classroom obviously not in use. Childrens' school desks and chairs had been stacked in one corner and the traditional blackboard mounted on the far wall. Childrens' crayon drawings ringed the blackboard; they were tattered enough to have been there a long time. Everything had a layer of dust except a table that had been moved to the center of the room.

Pepper Johnson sat at one of the school desks handcuffed to a steel ring set into the wall. He was dressed in his blue work clothes with the Race Software logo on the pocket. Pepper appeared unhurt, though the hook had been removed from his left hand and lay on the floor several yards away. The bare stump of his left arm was covered with old healed-over sores.

"Kevin!" Pepper yanked at the handcuff and ring in wild frustration. "Get me loose from this thing, will ya. I want to bash that son of a bitch myself. No, wait, I want my hook back so I can rip it through his gut."

"Where's the key to the cuffs?"

"He's got it." Indicating Pure John. "Left hand coat pocket."

I went back to Pure John, still careful not to put myself in Sam's line of fire, and retrieved the key. While I knelt there, I told him, "By the way, I never did care for salmon."

He raised an eyebrow in mock disappointment.

With the cuff unlocked, Pepper instantly scooped up his hook. He reset it against the stump of his arm with his back turned against curious eyes. When he swung around, he headed straight for Pure John.

"Stay back." Pure John's eyes shifted from Pepper to me. "Mr. Pierce, keep him away and I'll tell what's behind this. You'll get the surprise of your life."

"I already know Pepper is really Clarence Wells."

Pure John was the one who got the surprise. "You do? You're smarter than people think. Everybody's underestimated you, Mr. Pierce. Right down the line." He recovered some of his aplomb. "But you don't know who's behind this."

"You talk too much." Pepper stepped forward, sliced his hook through the lapel of Pure John's jacket, and pulled him to his feet.

"Let go." John struggled, but Pepper was too strong and angry. He raised Pure John completely off his feet and shook the man as if he were a rag doll. "Make him let go!"

Sam laughed and I couldn't find it in my heart to spoil Pepper's fun.

"Kill him if you want," I said. I didn't believe Pepper would do that. On the other hand, I didn't really care if Pepper made good on the threat.

"Stop that! Put my driver down right now!"

The voice that barked the order bore such cultured authority Pepper did stop shaking Pure John, though he didn't set him back on the floor.

"Put him down, I said! Immediately!"

Amelia Valentine had entered the abandoned classroom in her motorized wheelchair. She came gliding toward Pepper and me, ignoring Sam and his big Beretta as she rolled past him, her eyes crescents of fire and back stiff with outrage. "John is my employee. You'll oblige me by treating him with more respect."

Pepper didn't exactly put him down. He threw Pure John against the wall, then pointed at Amelia. "That's the bitch who had me snatched off the street!"

Amelia came to a halt about two feet away and glared up at me from her wheelchair. I'd never seen her as anything but an angel on wheels and was having a hard time accepting her in a different light.

"I'm disappointed in you, Kevin," she said. "Extremely disappointed."

CHAPTER 25

"Amelia, what are you doing here?"

"She had me snatched," Pepper insisted. "Wanted me to sign my stock proxies over to her husband, then sign a will leaving all my Race Software stock to him. They've been slapping me around. The old bitch talked about arranging an *accident* for me after I signed the proxies and the will. Ya got here just in time. They were about to crush my balls or do some other mischief to get me to sign."

I was into basic head-shaking denial. "That's not possible, Pepper. This is a fine lady."

"Ya wanna bet?"

Sam had moved around picking up guns and motioning Pure John to stay put against the wall.

"Who is that man?" Amelia demanded to know.

"Sam Cody," I said. "Friend of mine."

Her mouth tightened. "I know the name. Another enemy of Isadore's. Kevin, you have ruined all my plans. I'm never in my life been so furious with anyone. I told Isadore you were a serious threat, he wouldn't listen. I told John to deal with you decisively. He failed to eliminate you and now look at the mess you've caused."

"You sent Pure John to throw me off the cliff?"

"I didn't care if he threw you from a cliff or a bridge, so long as we were rid of you."

"But...I thought...you wanted me to do a poster for the shelter."

"Oh, that was just to lull you into complacency. Distract you. I wouldn't hire you to paint my bathroom."

I felt much the same as I did at the age of eight when mom let slip that terrible secret about Santa Claus. "Amelia, I just don't understand why you'd want to do me any harm."

The set of her chin was concrete. "You and your trashy friends are attempting to deny Isadore his rightful place in the community. It's my…my duty…as Isadore's wife to help him achieve his goals."

"Your husband's nothin' but a thug," Sam snapped.

"He's the finest, bravest, most intelligent man you'll ever meet!"

"I don't get it." I tried to maintain an even tone though something inside me had soured. "Does Izzy know what you've been up to?"

"Of course not." Amelia had the contemptuous expression Nazi war criminals used when they explained why nine million Jews had to be put to death. "I've done this on my own because it needed doing. Isadore has always been protective of me. Unnecessarily so, I'm quite strong except for my legs. He's such a gentleman…" She flicked a hand at me dismissively. "A person like you wouldn't understand Isadore. Nothing changed when I became crippled. Isadore continue to love me, support me, understand and cater to my needs. He moved us from Buffalo to San Francisco when the cold winters became too much for me. He had to start all over again. Of course, he was even more successful here than he'd been in New York. I won't let anything or anyone interfere with his plans."

"This is crazy." I looked at Pure John, who had propped himself up against the wall. He sat absolutely still with Sam's Beretta aimed at his midsection and Pepper still swinging his hook. "Who hired you to kill me and to bring Pepper here? Izzy or Amelia?"

Pure John's face had glazed over like a Thanksgiving turkey. "Mr. Valentine is my employer. I have a side arrangement with Mrs. Valentine to perform confidential services for her. Mr. Valentine is unaware of that arrangement."

"Confidential services? Like kidnapping and murder?"

A shrug of indifference. "You don't make the kind of money she's paid me without risk."

Sam could hardly contain his self-satisfaction. "I told you both the Valentines were in on it. I'll bet she even sent those three apes who beat you up in the alley next to Cynthia Gooding's apartment."

"Did you send them, Amelia?"

"Of course I did. They were associates of John's, he found them for me and gave them their instructions." Amelia regarded Pure John with distaste. "In retrospect I see my confidence in John was misplaced. If my legs were still good, I would have put a stop to your meddling myself!"

Her manic intensity made me realize Amelia wasn't playing with all fifty-two cards. The aces were gone, maybe all the face cards, too.

"Isadore knew you were employed by Bobby Race to dig up dirt on him. Doing a portrait of Race was just a cover story. You're trying to stop Isadore from winning a seat on the Race board of directors. Isadore wants to be a major force in the Silicon Valley and you were in the way. That's all I needed to know."

Pepper cleared his throat. "How'd ya find out my real name? I've kept that quiet for ten years."

"You can change your name, not your social security number. Isadore tracked Clarence Wells to an address in Maryland. He bribed someone from the IRS to give him a copy of your last tax return, including your home address in some squalid part of Milpitas. You amazed him, Mr. Wells. A person of your net worth working as a maintenance man. He intended to make you a cash offer of fifteen million dollars for the privilege of voting your proxies just once. He's also borrowed heavily to buy Race Software stock. This deal has strapped him for cash so I decided to step in on my own."

Sam had tired of standing. He separated one of the school desks from a stack and sat down. "And you're tellin' us Izzy don't have a clue what you're up to?"

"I detest hearing my husband referred to as Izzy. Do not make that mistake again."

"Or what?" Sam challenged.

They exchanged malevolent stares. I was surprised when Sam's eyes shifted first. Amelia may have been crazy and wheelchair bound, but she was as formidable as some of the first sergeants I've served under. "Sam, I need to borrow your cell phone." He gave it to me.

"Where can I reach Izzy right this minute?" I asked Pure John.

"Don't you dare tell him!" Amelia snapped.

Pepper put the point of his hook down between Pure John's legs. He pulled the point slowly upward until it went through his pants and hooked lightly on Pure John's testicles. Pure John sucked in his breath and spit out Izzy's cell number faster than I could write it down.

"Tell him to take away the hook," Pure John said in a hoarse voice.

Pepper removed the hook, ripping the crotch out of Pure John's pants.

I dialed the number Pure John gave me and listened until Izzy Valentine's voice came on. "Izzy? This is Kevin Pierce."

"Pierce?" Izzy's guttural tones were instantly combative. "I've got nothing more to say to you. Wait, I do have something to say. You chose up sides with Sam Cody and Bobby Race, you live with that. I could've done things for you, pushed your art with important people. You didn't want that, so go to hell."

"I'm at the Bayside Childrens Center. Amelia is here, so is Pure John. This morning they kidnapped Clarence Wells, also known as Pepper Johnson. They were going to make him sign some proxies and a last will before leaving you his Race Software stock. And then they were proba-bly going to kill him."

"You're nuts! You're a lunatic! Amelia would never do such a thing!"

"She's in big trouble, Izzy. And so are you. Where are you now?"

"On Route 280, headed home. I'm told there are police helicopters circling over my estate and I want to know why."

Before I realized what was happening, Amelia rolled her motorized wheelchair onto my toes and was grappled with me for the cell phone. "Give...me...that!" she panted. "I won't..." She struck at me with the purse that had been lying on her lap "... let you involve..." The purse whopped me across the face and I almost lost the phone. "...my husband in this."

"Who's that?" Izzy said. "Amelia? Is Amelia really there?"

I got my toes out from under the wheelchair and hustled out of Amelia's attack zone. "Yes, Izzy. That was your wife. Your crazy wife. She's gone bananas and I'm about to call the cops on her unless you get over here."

"I'm approaching the Page Mill Road turnoff," Izzy said grimly. "I can be there in five minutes."

"We're in a small building behind the shelter. An unused classroom."

"Don't you dare lay a hand on Amelia." He broke the connection.

Amelia revved up her wheelchair and made another run at me. I danced aside like a bullfighter and almost shouted "Ole!" I hoped Izzy could get here in under five minutes, I didn't have too many more moves like that in me.

While waiting for Izzy, we decided the handcuff bolted to the wall ought to get more use. Pepper locked Pure John's wrist into the cuff. Then, I suppose out of residual anger, Pepper used his hook to make long vertical cuts in Pure John's conservative black suit. When he finished, Pure John resembled a bald scarecrow in a parched field.

Dealing with Amelia was more difficult. She continued to run her wheelchair at us and swing her purse like a mace until Sam found a broom that he stuck through both rear wheels, immobilizing her. "Take that out!" she screamed. "You'll pay for this! Isadore will have you torn apart by wild dogs! Put into cement! He'll never forgive your treatment of me!"

Finally we dragged Pure John's unconscious partner into a corner. His condition worried me. He was still out cold and seemed to be breathing even more shallowly. His complexion had gone slate gray, the bump on his forehead was enormous and had become an ugly red/blue. "Don't worry so much about this dude," Sam advised. "Day or two, he'll come around. They almost always do. If not..." Sam shrugged. "No big loss. Guy's a kidnapper, right?"

"We have to get him to a hospital," I insisted.

"Son of a bitch shoved me into a car, hit me with a pipe." Pepper showed us a lump behind his right ear. It must have bled freely at first. The blood now coagulated into a scabby mess. "He was the one ready to play ping pong with my balls to make me sign those papers. I don't really care if he croaks, ya wanta know the truth."

Pepper and Sam were both thinking like infantrymen. Wounded enemy? Fuck him, let him lie there and die. I'm ex-infantry too, but I never had Pepper's or Sam's cold attitude toward the enemy. "I do care. After we've talked with Izzy, we'll take this man to the nearest emergency room."

A few minutes later Izzy Valentine threw open the double doors and came striding in like Patton invading Sicily. His heavy features were crimson. His hands balled into fists. All that combative energy collapsed when he saw his wife sitting forlorn and immobile. "Amelia, what have they done to you?"

"Isadore...I'm so sorry." She raised her arms, which Izzy rushed into. "I meant well, darling. I've made a proper balls up of everything, but I meant well. Truly I did." And then Amelia burst into tears.

"Now...now...don't cry." Izzy attempted to comfort his weeping wife, but Amelia's toughness had crumbled at the sight of her husband. Izzy kept murmuring, "Now...now..." and patting Amelia's shoulders while kissing the back of her neck. He kept one arm tightly around her at all times. Their voices slowly dropped until they were holding a whispered conversation during which Izzy appeared to be absorbing a number of unpleasant shocks.

Now and then his voice would rise. He could be heard saying things like: "No, you didn't! What? Why the hell…God, no!"

By the end of the conversation, Amelia sat slumped in her wheelchair. Despite Izzy's efforts to raise her spirits, she continued to sob into her handkerchief. The only changes in her attitude came when she looked at me. Then her air of defeat was fleetingly replaced by a sizzling glare of pure hatred.

Izzy gave Amelia one final hug and removed the broom handle from her wheels. He walked slowly toward me, a contemplative expression giving his unpleasant features the statesmanlike image he craved so much. "Can I talk to John for a minute?"

"Go ahead," I said.

He walked over and unleashed a backhanded slap to Pure John's face, which was beginning to look as rutted as a dirt road.

"You greedy fool, I should have left you in Philly."

Pure John accepted the slap as something he had coming. "She offered me too much money. I couldn't turn it down."

"You could have come to me, told me what Amelia was up to."

"Then I wouldn't have gotten the money."

Pure John's thinking sounded logical to me.

"How much has she paid you?"

"Sixty-five thousand, so far."

"Don't say 'so far.' You've milked my wife for every dollar you're going to get."

Izzy stopped to light a cigarette. As soon as the cigarette was burning, he ground it out on Pure John's bald head. Pure John winced and brushed the cigarette away. Though I thought Izzy was unnecessarily nasty in the way he made his point, I didn't do anything to stop him. My sympathies for Pure John were a mile wide and an inch deep.

"I want you to use that money to haul your ass out of town tonight." Izzy spoke with extraordinary calm, the voice of a judge handing down a sentence. "If you ever set your foot west of the Mississippi, you're dead."

I had a glimpse of what Izzy must have been like before he moved from Buffalo to San Francisco and began impersonating a solid citizen.

"I'll go, Mr. Valentine, fast as a scalded cat." Pure John waved a hand at me and Pepper and Sam. "If those people will let me leave."

"That's something I'll have to negotiate." Izzy approached me pensively, his corporate chieftain face firmly back in place. He paused for a cursory glance at the unconscious character lying nearby. "That guy doesn't look too good," was his only comment. "Can we talk outside? I'd like to give Amelia a few minutes to pull herself together."

"Sam, watch the lady. She might try to set Pure John loose, she might even try to hurt herself. Pepper, will you join us outside?"

"Amelia," Izzy said, "just sit there, please. Do nothing. I'll be right back to take you home."

When we were outside, I said, "I wouldn't be so sure you're going to take Amelia home or that Pure John is going to leave town today. We've got charges of kidnapping and attempted murder to file against both of them."

Izzy looked Pepper up and down. "You're Clarence Wells? Pepper Johnson? Whatever you call yourself, I've gotta hand it to you, getting in on the ground floor at Race Software."

"I was lucky," Pepper said.

"You've got my apology for what happened today," Izzy told him.

"That ain't enough," Pepper shot back.

"Look..." Izzy couldn't quite meet our eyes. He looked at my chin, at Pepper's chest, finally into the empty space between us. "Amelia is ill. Several years ago, back in New York, she had to be hospitalized in a private institution. She's been fine the past few years. Or so I thought. I see now it was a mistake to let her visits with the psychiatrist tail off. Way the doctors put it, without the five-syllable bullshit, when Amelia lost the use of her legs she also lost her own ambitions. She compensated by fixating on my career. I swear I didn't know she'd gone over the edge."

I tended to believe that. Amelia had fooled the hell out of me and it would have been even easier for her to manipulate Izzy. The bum really did love her.

"You expect us to let your wife and that bald killer just walk away?" Pepper asked. "They were ready to shred me."

"And Amelia sent Pure John and two others to kill me," I informed him. "How can I overlook that?"

Izzy's shifty side took over. "Amelia told me she sent John and two others to drop you off a cliff over there in Half Moon Bay. Instead, you and Sam Cody aced John's buddies. Did you guys report that little incident to the cops?"

I said nothing to that question.

"Hey, I don't give a shit they're dead. They weren't my guys, they were hired by John ."

"And Amelia," I quickly added.

"Yes, and my wife," Izzy conceded. "However, I can produce medical records on Amelia's psychiatric history. She'd get a sympathetic court hearing and probably have to go back into a private institution for a while. Which, incidentally, is something she'll have to do anyway. Get her back in the hands of a good doctor. You and Sam, on the other hand, would have to explain why you killed two people, then forgot to tell the police. Maybe the cops'll buy self-defense, but you've already turned yourselves into murder suspects."

I hate it when guys like Izzy are right.

Pepper's agitation was growing. "That Pure John gumbo tried to kill you too, Kevin?"

"He did. Izzy's right, it won't look good that Sam and I didn't go to the police."

"Why didn't you?"

Izzy took pleasure in answering for me. "Sam Cody is a car thief who's already under indictment. He can't afford to go to the police. Kevin has a problem working within the system."

This negotiation was becoming as complicated as the Mideast peace process. For example, Pepper could probably have Izzy thrown in jail for kidnapping. But if that happened, Izzy and Pure John would surely rat out Sam and me for tossing Pure John's two friends off the cliff at Half Moon Bay. Pepper would then feel guilty for getting Sam and me in trouble after we'd saved his life, not to mention his testicles. On the other hand, Izzy would owe us big time if we kept Amelia's fondness for homicide to ourselves. Though Pure John probably had enough on both Izzy and Amelia to send them away for life, he'd lose his own freedom and maybe his life if he talked to the police. And all of us might be legally liable if the nameless man lying on the classroom floor took a turn for the worse and died.

My ace-in-the-hole was that Izzy didn't know disaster was about to befall him at his beautiful Hillsborough estate.

"We've got what looks like a Mexican standoff," I said. "So my solution is we all just walk away from today's misadventure. Just make sure Pure John leaves California today."

"Agreed," Izzy said immediately.

"I don't like that deal," Pepper complained.

"It's a good deal," I assured him. "I'll explain why later. Izzy, you've also got to get medical treatment for Pure John's buddy right away, the one lying on the floor back there."

"You and Sam busted his head!" Izzy was indignant. "He's your mess to clean up."

"No, Mister Anonymous is lying there because Amelia hired him to kidnap, torture and maybe kill Pepper. You call 911 and have him treated right away or the agreement is off, we call the cops and let them sort it out. Yes, Sam and I would be in some trouble. But Bobby Race has deep pockets and he'll owe us on this one."

From out of nowhere, Pepper let out a booming laugh. "Hey, fellas, I've got deep pockets, too. Sometimes I forget how rich I am. Fact is, I'm a billionaire! Ain't nobody sending Kevin and his car-thief buddy to jail.

I'll hire O.J.'s Dream Team to defend them." A second thought hit Pepper, you could see it in his smile. "Yeah, and then I'll turn The Dream Team loose on you, Mr. Valentine. I'll get your ass thrown in San Quentin for...for..."

"Kidnapping," I suggested. "False imprisonment. Reckless endangerment. Assault and battery. Extortion. Home invasion. Theft of securities and other business documents. Having a big nose."

"What he said," Pepper confirmed.

Izzy stared wearily into the distance. He'd thought he was rich until he met Pepper. He hated being reminded there are other people with more money, more clout, more respect than he could ever muster. Especially when the guy with the upper hand, no joke intended, was a black maintenance man with only one hand.

Presently Izzy said, "Mister Wells...I should say Mister Johnson if that's the name you prefer...all I've been after is the opportunity to claim a seat on the Race Software board of directors. I was prepared to offer you fifteen million dollars just to let me vote your proxies at the next annual meeting of Race Software. A legitimate business offer. That offer is still open."

"Don't insult me with your little pissant offers," Pepper sneered. "I use that kind of dough for pocket change."

The words must have gone through Izzy like a sword because he took hold of my arm to maintain his balance.

"You'll get medical attention for that man?" I pressed.

Izzy nodded wordlessly. His lips were gray and trembly. With immense effort, he pulled himself together. "Tell Bobby he hasn't heard the last from me. I want a piece of Race Software and I'll have it."

"Please don't make me tell him that," I said. "He might get hysterical."

Izzy didn't think that was funny, but Pepper laughed so hard his hook almost came loose.

CHAPTER 26

"Carta Blanca…boilermaker…Jameson's on the rocks."

"Got it." Billy Jack extended his hand to Sam. "Yew must be the Jameson's. Glad to meet yew, I'm Billy Jack Henderson. Me and Kevin was in high school together, y'know."

"Sam Cody." He shook Billy Jack's hand. "I was in the army with Kevin. Was he a complete fuck-up in high school, too?"

"Naw, he was pretty normal back then. Chased girls, raced cars, set fires, shoplifted from Woolworth's, discovered beer, din't like to study. I was a damned good student myself, C minus average though I don't like to brag. Would've graduated, I hadn't stuck up the Seven Eleven. Yew fellas want any ribs?"

"Mountains of ribs," Sam said. "I haven't had a real meal since last night."

"Then yew want the Mother Lode platter. Excuse me, I gotta go kick the crap outta my cook, he come in drunk again." Billy Jack hustled off to fix our drinks and force his cook to put some ribs on the fire.

"This'll sound funny," Pepper said. "But after the day I've had, Billy Jack's seems a nice, quiet, run-of-the-mill place."

"We can all bask in the light of Billy Jack's sanity another time," I said. "Right now we have to decide what we're going to tell Bobby."

Pepper disagreed. "No, first I have to thank ya for getting me out of that fix. You guys really put yourselves on the line for me, I'll never forget that. I was more than a little pissed when ya let that woman and old baldy walk, even though I take your word there was a good reason."

"Izzy's not really walkin' away." Sam launched into the full story of how he'd covertly had an acre of land on Izzy's estate planted in marijuana, then tipped the DEA in return for a payment from Bobby to defer his legal expenses. He consulted his watch. Three-thirty. "Izzy's day is only gonna get worse, Pepper. I guarantee it. By now the DEA should be at his gate with a search warrant. That's why Kevin let Izzy and Amelia go, he wanted them at home when the DEA showed up."

"I feel better." Pepper leaned back to give Billy Jack room to put the drinks on the table. "In fact, I feel good." Pepper's boilermaker consisted of a large schooner of beer and a double shot of Wild Turkey. He lifted his oversized shot of whiskey, dropped it...shot glass and all...into his beer, and said "Bombs away." Then he drank off a healthy portion of the boilermaker.

"So you're a billionaire." Sam sat back. "I never before had a drink with a billionaire."

"Don't make your Jameson's taste any better, I'll bet." Pepper looked into his glass to seek perspective on the past. "It was pure luck I bought into Race when the stock was at its bottom. Looked to me like Bobby knew what he was doing, and he did. Other things in my life haven't worked out so well. Lost my left hand. Did Ernesto tell you how I also lost my family to a truck driver with a nose full of cocaine? I thought so. The money to invest in Race came from the wrongful death settlement. You know what? I'd trade the whole billion to have my wife and boy back." His eyes moistened and he cleared his throat. "They were my heart and soul, those two."

Pepper brooded in silence for much too long. A change of subject was called for. "I've got a favor to ask."

"Name it," Pepper said.

"I want to be the one to tell Bobby that you and Clarence Wells are one in the same."

"Why does anybody have to tell him? I been happy just working there as a maintenance man."

"Now that Izzy and Amelia know you're Clarence Wells, others are bound to find out."

"I suppose that's true. Okay, live it up. Go ahead and tell Bobby." Some light came back into Pepper's eyes. "Lots of times I've come close to telling Bobby myself, just to let him know I've been in his corner all along. Some of the execs get mighty self-important, I've wanted more than once to rub their noses in my money. That Greg Tillotson sometimes looks at me like he wished lynchings were still in fashion."

Sam finished his Jameson's and ordered another. He kept glancing at his watch. "Couple of hours yet till the six o'clock news. Meanwhile, you boys've got an even bigger question. Was Izzy connected with your ghost at Race Software? Or is the ghost what you might call an independent operator?"

"I don't think Izzy Valentine and the red thing have any connection," Pepper responded. "He knew Cynthia, that's all. Lots of people knew Cynthia."

"I'm leaning that way myself." There was a tickle at the back of my mind telling me to look elsewhere for the key to Cynthia's appearances. My memory's a funny thing. The harder I try to make it work, the less it'll do. I've been wanting to take one of those memory courses, I even got the application from the school, but I keep forgetting to send it in. Anyway, somebody other than Izzy had done or said something incriminating that was rattling around in my leaky brainpan. No way I could dredge up that particular memory right now. I'd have to wait for it to percolate to the surface. "There's a reason Cynthia Gooding won't leave Race Software alone. I just can't figure out what it is."

"Let's go see Joe Patterson in the hospital," Sam suggested. "That guy was one smart cop. Now that you have more info about Cynthia, maybe Joe can figure out why she's comin' around and what she wants."

Pepper let out a belch that would've cleared an ordinary bar. It was hardly noticed in Billy Jack's. "That's a good idea. Let's eat a few ribs and then go see Joe Patterson."

"Let's eat a *lot* of ribs," Sam said.

The Mother Load platter arrived, stacked a foot high with ribs, mounds of onion rings on top, garnished with french fries as sticky as a Hyundai's transmission, pots of extra barbecue sauce on the side. "Sing out when yew want seconds," Billy Jack advised.

We arrived at the hospital a little before five o'clock, leaving a trail of gargantuan burps in our wake. Joe Patterson was sitting up in bed with the tv remote in his hand watching a rerun of *NYPD Blue*. He quickly switched to the education channel, then turned off the set. "Hey, good to see you guys. Kevin, get a haircut. Pepper, you look tired. And who's that with you, Sam Cody? Jesus, step outside a minute while I hide my car keys."

Sam took the remark with a smile. "Good to see you too, Joe."

Joe's hospital room was much less depressing than my last visit. It overflowed with books, CDs, a compact Sony sound system, balloons, boxes of candy, new videotapes, a combination tv/vcr, a Gameboy and several new cartridges, plus other entertainments.

"See if you can clear a place to sit down. All these goodies were delivered from out of nowhere, the nurses hardly have room to empty my bedpan." Joe's usual gritty personality softened around the edges. "I made a few phone calls, learned this stuff came from an S. Cody in San Francisco. If I was still on the force, I'd have to send it all back. Good thing I'm retired. Thanks, Sam. I really like the Gameboy, you should see me shoot baskets against those NBA stars."

Sam winked.

"You'll never be retired," Pepper said. "And ya look okay, Joe. Considering what'cha been through."

Actually, Joe Patterson still looked horrible. His face now bore a rather amazing resemblance to the platter of ribs we'd just eaten. The amputations of his fingers seemed to be healing, though they were also the reddish color of the little pots of barbecue sauce we'd had at dinner.

All the skin I could see had been smeared with a disgusting yellow lubricating goo.

On the plus side, Joe's eyes were brighter, his voice stronger, he'd waved his bad hand to us when we came in. Joe immediately proved he was on the road to recovery by acting like a cop.

"I'm glad you guys came," Joe said. "I've been picking up a lot of strange stuff off tv and from the newspapers. Like the ghost at Race Software made a major appearance yesterday, scared all the executives out of their Ralph Lauren underwear. What's the story on that? Also, I read in the *Chronicle* where two guys I happen to know, habitual perps with long sheets, were found dead in Half Moon Bay. One of them at the bottom of the cliff. The other stabbed to death up above, thrown down to the rocks. Happened about two miles from your house, Kevin. Don't try to tell me you don't know anything about that. You got a look on your face like the little boy who just stole two dollars from his mom's purse."

The bright blue eyes moved between Pepper and Sam and me.

"Oh yeah, there's things I should know. Sam Cody, you have things to tell me, too? Pepper, have you fallen in with bad company?" Joe Patterson grinned. "*The Three Stooges At Play*, that's the title of this movie." He settled himself more comfortably against his pillows. "I've got nothing but time, so start talking."

Before filling in Joe on the events of the past few days, I asked Sam to switch the tv back on for the six o'clock news. Sam explained the joke...his word...he'd played on Izzy, breaking off the narrative when the hot new girl on Channel Seven appeared at the front gates of the Valentine estate. She wore an orange dress and her mass of hair was groomed to depressing perfection. She was talking with breathless excitement. "Agents from the Drug Enforcement Agency this afternoon raided the Hillsborough estate of millionaire businessman and philanthropist Isadore Valentine. Discovered on his property were four acres of marijuana plants said to be ripe for processing."

"Four acres!" Sam was intoxicated by the success of his joke. "Lyin' bitch just had to goose up the story for one acre to four, didn't she."

"Despite his many successes in the San Francisco business world, Isadore Valentine has never quite shaken rumors of a mob-connected past," the Channel Seven reporter continued. "This week, in a well-publicized bid to gain a seat on the Race Software board of directors, Valentine appeared close to achieving a prominent place among Silicon Valley's most elite players. This new scandal will probably spell a tragic end to those ambitions. We can only speculate why a man of his wealth and position would allow…wait…Isadore Valentine is being brought out!"

The cameraman hastily switched to a long lens which picked up a rather soft image of Izzy being hustled out the front door of his estate by three grim cops wearing black jackets bearing the initials DEA in foot-high yellow letters. Izzy's face was florid. He screamed curses at the men who had his arms pinned and struggled impotently as they grabbed the top of his head to maneuver him into a police car without injury. The DEA agents jumped into the car and drove Izzy out the front gates.

In the next shot, the Channel Seven reporter was interviewing Izzy's lawyer, who of course was "outraged by this malicious persecution of a valued member of the Bay Area's business community." His further take on the matter seemed to be that his client should be accepting a Nobel Peace Prize instead of an arrest warrant.

"Turn it off." Joe Patterson rubbed his eyes. "I can't believe Bobby Race, the man I work for and respect, is paying you to frame somebody for a major felony, I don't care that it's Izzy Valentine, a born scumbag." He shook his head. "I was a cop for too many years, guys. I can't let this happen."

"Wait a minute." I pulled my chair closer to Joe. "Let me tell you everything else that's been going on this week."

It took me a solid thirty minutes to go through all the twists and turns of the past few days. I think I got it all in. Izzy's connection with Cynthia Gooding. My invitation to Izzy's house by Amelia. Being mugged in the alley near Cynthia Gooding's apartment. Izzy setting up Sam for a grand theft auto arrest. The attempt on my life by Izzy's chauffeur, Pure John Braggia, and the unfortunate deaths of his two colleagues. Amelia Valentine's homicidal tendencies. The latest appearance of Cynthia Gooding's ghost and the resulting havoc at Race headquarters. And the kicker: Pepper kidnapped because his name was really Clarence Wells.

"What?" That's the one that made Joe's eyes bug out. "Pepper, you're Clarence Wells? You're the major stockholder everybody's been courting? How the hell can that be?"

"You know I lost my wife and son a long time ago," Pepper said.

"Yes, I do."

"I got a settlement at the time," Pepper explained. "Invested a big part of it in Race Software shares back when Bobby was just getting started."

"Holy shit!" Joe's head fell back against his pillow. "If you don't mind my asking, how much are you worth?"

"A billion dollars, give or take fifty mill."

"Holy shit!"

"You're repeating yourself," I pointed out.

"Holy shit!"

"Call the nurse," Sam suggested. "He's delirious."

"You're right," Joe agreed. "I am delirious. That's 'cause you guys have fucked up my life beyond belief! I used to know exactly what I stood for. The law. Somebody broke the law, I'd arrest him or her. Let the D.A. sort out the charges. This is different, confusing, I don't know what to do." He looked like Winnie the Pooh trying to figure out how to deal with a hive full of bees.

"You're a corporate animal now," I reminded him. "This is my first experience working for a corporation and you haven't been at it much longer than I have. What I've learned, Joe, is money makes its own rules. I don't like it. I'm an artist and that's not a pretty picture. But that's the way it is. You can't have us tossed in prison for protecting your boss. Our boss. It just isn't done."

"You're telling me I'm Dilbert," Joe croaked.

"With a real big cubicle."

"Why are you telling me all this?" He pulled the starched hospital sheet up to his chin. "Why couldn't you keep all that information to yourselves? I think you've set my recovery back six months."

"You're a detective," I said. "Or you were, for a lot of years. The idea is, maybe you can figure out what our ghost is after. I don't think Izzy Valentine has anything to do with Cynthia Gooding's ghost. All he did was send her to a DMV clerk who helped Cynthia set up a new identity. So what does she want?"

Joe looked at each of us in turn. "A car thief...a billionaire...and a penniless artist want me to figure what's in the head of a ghost. Is this the bad dream of the century?" He closed his eyes and lay back in mental exhaustion. I thought we'd lost him. But after a few seconds Joe's eyes opened and he told Sam, "Crank up the bed to a sitting position. I can't think lying on my back." When the bed was cranked up to his satisfaction, he said, "Kevin, tell me in detail what happened when the red thing came into the building yesterday. Don't leave out a single detail. Pepper, you add any details Kevin might leave out."

So I talked while Joe Patterson listened intently. He asked a number of crisp questions and often turned to Pepper for his perspective on specifics. "You call the red thing Cynthia like it was alive," Joe noted.

"This is a thinking entity, Joe. Cynthia Gooding wants something. I thought I had an angle on what she wants because she always appeared in places where there's a lot of red, like the Coke machines in the break room. But there's no red in Bobby's office, just the cool blues and grays from the Race Software logo."

Joe shook his head. "That's where you're wrong, Kevin. There's a lot of red in Bobby's office. Think about what's on the wall across from his desk."

"Bobby's collection of antique baseball cards." I visualized the wall. "Plus his collection of Pete Rose cards. Rose is Bobby's hero."

"Who did Pete Rose play for?" Joe prompted.

Sam exploded out of his chair. "The Cincinnati Reds!"

I could have kicked myself. "That's it."

"They're just baseball cards," Pepper said. "What do they have to do with anything?"

"The Cincinnati Reds. Right in front of us. Pepper's right, what do they have to do with Cynthia?" I wondered.

"Take the frames off the wall," Joe suggested. "See what's behind them."

CHAPTER 27

Many events are better in anticipation than in reality. The Super Bowl. That dinner date I had with a girl named Trixie. Those wonderful tax cuts our Congressmen always promise. One thing that did live up to my high expectations was Bobby Race's reaction when he found out Pepper Johnson and Clarence Wells were one in the same.

When I gave him the news, Bobby rose shakily from his chair. "You're Clarence Wells? I don't believe it."

"That's my legal name," Pepper said. "I was born Clarence E. Wells in Baltimore fifty-nine years ago. My mother's still alive, ask her yourself. Spent most of my life as Clarence Wells, though my friends always called me Pepper. Pepper Wells. 'Cause I never liked the name Clarence. I started calling myself Pepper Johnson about ten years ago. Ya want proof? Here's my proxies."

When Pepper showed Bobby the stock proxies he'd taken back from Amelia Valentine, Bobby went pale. His mouth moved but no sounds that could legitimately be called words emerged. For the first time in my experience with him, Bobby seemed unable to speak coherently, much less employ his trademark decisiveness. He sank back into the chair and, after a lot of lip smacking, regained his voice. "This is...I don't know how to put it...I'm amazed...though if you are Clarence Wells, it makes so many things clear."

Bobby finally composed himself, aware I'm sure that he was at a disadvantage sitting there in Pepper's cluttered basement office rather than behind his own impressive desk in the executive suite. "Sorry. I'm not making sense. Pepper, seven years ago a man named Clarence Wells invested about a million dollars in this company. A million dollars! Where would you get kind of money?"

Pepper didn't need to again explain that his wife and son had been killed in an accident, Bobby already knew that. What he'd never told Bobby was that he'd won a large settlement from the trucking company's insurer or how he'd used the settlement. "I started a scholarship fund at Stanford in Joey's name . Loaned some bucks to friends. Bought my mom a little house in a neighborhood she likes back in Baltimore. Still had a million or so left in the bank. The salesmen were on me like bees on honey, so I started using my mom's maiden name. Johnson. Started working for your company about that same time. Ya treated me right, Bobby. And ya seemed to know what the software business is all about, so I took a gamble." Pepper grinned. "Paid off big."

"Why did you never tell me?" Bobby couldn't comprehend Pepper's thinking. "Why are you still changing light bulbs and sweeping floors? You can do whatever you want. You saved this company. I'd have gone under if you hadn't put up that money when you did." Bobby swallowed so hard I thought he'd crack his adam's apple. "You saved *me*. A thank you isn't enough. There must be *something* I can do for you."

"What I want," Pepper said, "is to keep on doing my job, talk sports with ya when you're not too busy, poke my nose in here and there around the headquarters, grab a nap at my desk from about two o'clock to two thirty most afternoons. That's a good life for me."

Bobby suddenly realized this cramped, untidy cubbyhole was the working space of the biggest individual stockholder in Race Software, with the exception of himself. "You ought to at least have a real office up on the sixth floor. I mean, look at this place, it's the size of a closet! Hey, right down the hall from me is Arthur Forest's old office. Corner suite, nice view of the bay. He's still out recovering from his nervous breakdown. Why don't you move in there for the time being?"

"Maybe Pepper doesn't want a nervous breakdown," I said.

The level of irritation in Bobby's glare signaled his return to normalcy. "How long have you known about this?"

"Just found out this morning. Let's tell him the rest of it, Pepper."

Between us, we pretty much reprised the story we'd told Joe Patterson. Bobby already knew about Izzy's arrest, he'd watched the five o'clock news avidly. Sam was with Hugh Wilson right now arranging payment for his little "joke" on Izzy.

"Joe's opinion," I said, "is that your visitor is after something connected with your collection of Pete Rose baseball cards, the ones on your office wall."

"That's ridiculous."

"Pete Rose played for the Cincinnati Reds," Pepper reminded him. "The Reds," I said. "The Redleaf project. Our red visitor. Get it?"

Bobby could only frown. "No, I don't understand."

"Take the frames off the wall, Joe said. Let's see what's on the backs of the frames."

"This is crazy." Bobby dismissed the possibility with one of his impatient waves. "The notion that my baseball cards have any connection to my business problems is ludicrous."

"Hey…" Pepper spread his hands. "I'm a major stockholder in this corporation. Right, Bobby?"

"Yes, apparently you are." Bobby's crinkly smile flashed on and off at a nervous beat.

"As a guy who respects Joe Patterson's view on things," Pepper said, "*and* as one big fucking stockholder, I'd like to see for myself what's behind those framed baseball cards."

A sardonic grin flitted across Bobby's face. "I'm not sure I wasn't better off when you were my maintenance man."

"I'm still that. But I'm a *curious* maintenance man."

Bobby's decision-making ability rebounded. "Okay, if you think Joe might be right, let's check it out." He came out of the chair like a shot and a moment later Pepper and I were half jogging down the sixth-floor corridor to match his brisk pace. I'm a stroller myself, which I believe to be a more civilized way of walking, so Bobby's relentless energy was often annoying.

The sixth floor was still closed down, as Bobby had ordered. As we hurried towards Bobby's office, the lights automatically came on at their programmed time. Pepper checked his watch to make sure the program was accurate. Twilight. Darkness soon. The witching hour after that. Our footsteps sounded hollow in the deserted corridor.

We entered Bobby's office and went straight to the three frames that held his collection of antique and Pete Rose cards and other memorabilia.

"I mounted them frames myself," Pepper recalled. "Wasn't anything behind them then."

"Probably nothing there now," Bobby said.

Pepper slipped his hook behind the first frame and nimbly picked if off the wall. Nothing on the back of that frame or on the wall either. The second frame also held nothing of interest on its reverse side. The third frame was the largest and Pepper had trouble removing it from the wall. "Shouldn't be stuck to the plaster like this, it's only mounted with two hangars and regular picture wire."

Finally the frame came loose. Nothing on the back. However, a flat black electronic instrument that might have been a smaller version of the monolith from *Space Odyssey* had been set into the wall behind the frame.

"Spooky." Pepper put out his good hand to touch the thing, then drew back. "Puts me in mind of a little tombstone."

Bobby had no such fear. He reached out and flipped up a small panel built into the front of the instrument, revealing a set of perhaps two dozen keys labeled with numbers and symbols. "I've seen one of these. It's a Helstrom ADC."

"Must everything in this building have an acronym?" I hate acronyms. "What does ADC mean in English?"

"Advanced Data Client." Bobby ran his hand over the smooth surface of the black box with something like a caress. "It's a specialized computer still under development by a company called Helstrom Information Source. This little box has almost two hundred gigabytes of memory. It's designed to capture and encode a vast amount of data under a variety of protocols."

When Pepper and I gave him blank and probably open-mouthed stares, Bobby broke down his explanation into simpler terms.

"Let me put it this way. Data processing hardware consists of servers and clients. The servers are large computers that run…or serve…a lot of clients, or smaller computers. Here's an example: the ATM that gives you money from your bank account is a computer in itself. It's a client attached electronically to a large computer, or server, located somewhere else, maybe in another city, state or country. A really big server might run a network of hundreds or thousands of clients. Got it?"

I sort of got it. "Big computers called servers run small computers called clients."

Bobby looked uncomfortable with my simplistic summary. "When it finally comes to market, the Helstrom ADC will be used to automatically capture vast amounts of data from other computers no matter what protocols they're using."

"A waste basket for data," Pepper put in.

Bobby resigned himself to simplistic terms. "I suppose that's one way to put it. You can throw paper or rags or Coke bottles or anything else into a waste basket. Likewise, this little computer will retrieve and store information no matter what form it comes in. Lotus spreadsheets. Word documents. Object-oriented programs. Cryptolopes. Whatever."

I asked Bobby how he'd come to see this computer if it was still under development.

"Helstrom loaned some prototypes to companies in the industry, including Race Software. That's a standard development technique. We get a chance to try out new hardware before it hits the market, Helstrom gets our feedback on how well its new system works." Bobby's face darkened. "As far as I know, Helstrom loaned us only one of these. I believe it's being used by Greg Tillotson."

"What's it doing here?" Pepper said. "Somebody went to a lot of trouble to install this thing in the wall. Would've taken three or four hours to cut a neat hole into the plasterboard, saw through that one stud, attach cables, remount the baseball card frame."

"No cables necessary, this is a wireless computer," Bobby pointed to a battery compartment. "I suspect it's set to capture whatever goes through my computer. Since I personally review all the Redleaf code and other material, that's probably what this system is programmed to retrieve and store." He frowned. "Almost daily someone would have to insert new batteries, take out the disk that had picked up the day's activity on my computer, and put in a fresh disk. Meanwhile this box is soaking up Redleaf data from my computer. Dammit!"

I followed his thinking. "A person who has daily access to your office."

Pepper scratched his chin with the tip of his hook. "Somebody who can come and go on the sixth floor at any hour. I never liked Greg Tillotson, but I can't see him selling you out."

"I wouldn't have thought so, either." Bobby began punching the keys of the box. "I confirmed today that Zebulon-Perry is definitely coming to market with a networking package that'll compete directly against Redleaf. Greg's made some sort of deal with them. He's feeding ZP not only the Redleaf code, but financial projections, marketing plans, everything they need to go to market. After they announce their product, he'll quit me and go to work for ZP for a bigger salary and better title, a huge signing bonus, stock options. You see that happening in Silicon Valley every day." He grimaced. "This is the first time it's happened to me."

His scenario didn't sound right. "It was Greg who told you what Zebulon-Perry is up to."

Bobby gave me a sharp look.

"All right, I've been eavesdropping on some of your conversations. Why would Greg warn you about Zebulon-Perry if he was about to jump ship? And why would he need to put this weird box in your office to spy on you? As the Redleaf project leader, he already knows all about the product."

"Greg told me about ZP to put me off guard. Yes, he's got the Redleaf code. But he's a technical guy, a propeller-head. The financial data and marketing plans are just as important. Greg also needs to know who our independent software vendors are going to be, how much they'll charge for customizing Redleaf for our customers, a lot more. No single person except me sees the entire Redleaf picture. It's very complicated, Kevin."

A simpleton like me wouldn't understand, Bobby was saying. I wasn't offended, he was right.

"So what do we do now?" Pepper asked.

"I'm going to play with this system," Bobby said. "Find out whether my thinking is correct, that it's electronically capturing everything that goes through my computer. Remember when Greg left Billy Jack's ahead of everyone else last night? I'll bet he came straight back here to my office."

"No wonder Greg looks tired and nervous all the time," Pepper said. "Lot of pressure on a thief."

I still didn't buy it. "Greg Tillotson strikes me as a workaholic, not a thief."

"I hope you're right." Bobby looked tired and old. "Maybe somebody else got hold of a Helstrom ADC. Kevin, why don't you go to Greg's office and see if his ADC is still there. No one else is on the floor, you'll be free to make a thorough search of his office. Don't break open his desk or anything like that, just look around. If the ADC isn't there, check some of the other offices. Maybe Greg loaned the Helstrom to someone else. I'd like to be convinced Greg is innocent."

"All right."

"Pepper, go downstairs and find Jenny." Bobby checked his watch. "It's almost seven o'clock. Tell Jenny I'm holding a meeting of the management team in my office at nine o'clock sharp. Most of the team's still in the building, some are working at home. Attendance is mandatory. Jenny should let the team know that anyone who misses tonight's meeting is fired. Tell her the sixth floor will be reopened at seven thirty and give those instructions to the security staff. Got all that?"

"On my way, Bobby." Pepper took off like a hot rocket.

"Pepper!" Bobby called him back to the office. "I want you in that meeting. You two guys have had all the excitement today. I need some recreation too, so I'll be introducing the team to Clarence Wells."

Bobby turned back to the box and began manipulating its keyboard. The system had a small screen on which a jumble of data that was gibberish to me, but mother's milk to Bobby, flashed by.

Before going to look into Greg Tillotson's desk, I sneaked a quick look at my unfinished portrait of Bobby, which languished on the easel in the corner of his office. It still looked good to me even though the events of the past few days had wrought some changes in Bobby's boyish features. He had a couple of new lines across his forehead and the hint of crow's feet under his eyes that I'd have to work into the portrait. I decided to darken the shades of most every color, hoping to suggest the new maturity these travails were producing in Bobby.

Tillotson's office looked as if someone else already had ransacked it. Strewn everywhere were memos, empty Styrofoam coffee cups, messages, notes Tillotson had made to himself, mathematical equations, ads for computer equipment, Internet site addresses, photos of his family in cheap frames, stacks of printouts leaning perilously to starboard, half-consumed cans of Diet Pepsi. I'd seen his cluttered office before, but the mess was worse than ever.

Everything under the sun could be found here except the black box.

I went from one office to another looking for the box. All right I'll use its stupid name, the Helstrom ADC . No sign of it.

In Dorothy's office I did find something unexpected. Dorothy herself working at her computer, the only light in the office coming from the screen. "What are you doing here? The floor is closed, Bobby's the only one the security guards will let onto the sixth floor."

"I sneaked up. Nobody knows this building better than I do." She raised an eyebrow. "How did you get onto the sixth floor?"

"I came up with Bobby. He's re-opening the floor at seven-thirty and there's a management team meeting at nine."

Dorothy seemed unconcerned with Bobby's agenda. "I suppose I'll be there." She became more animated as she drew me toward her computer. "The Internet has the story of Daniel Dunglas Home, born in Scotland in 1833. He was the preeminent psychic of the nineteenth century. There's no question he was visited by spirits throughout his life, there were too many eyewitness accounts by skeptics to dismiss his gift. For one example, on August 8, 1852, sitting in a circle of people, Home was lifted up by a spirit until his head touched the ceiling. There were disbelievers who considered Home a charlatan, of course. Charles Dickens called him 'that scoundrel Home.' Still, his documented experiences are impressive."

"Uh-huh," I said.

"Home had a personal spirit guide, just as you have Sport Sullivan."

"I don't 'have' Sport Sullivan. He comes and goes at his own pleasure."

Dorothy continued with her enthusiastic description of Daniel Dunglas Home's exploits. She could not be, shall I say, dispirited. "When he lived in Florence, he was visited often by the ghost of an Italian murderer who had been present for several hundred years in the villa Home rented. Here's the interesting part. The temperature either plunged or rose when the ghost appeared, just as it does when Cynthia Gooding appears here at Race. Did you know that many spirits are people who died in tragic accidents or had been murdered or committed murder themselves? Just like Sport Sullivan?"

"Yes, I've read that."

"And ghosts have been known to appear when people are having sex, the way Sport Sullivan showed up while we were in bed." Dorothy giggled and tossed her curls. "The ghost of Cagliostro, the famous Italian medium who died in prison about sixty years before Home moved to Italy, appeared one night when Home and his wife Sacha were in bed. Maybe we should have sex right now just to see whether Sport shows up." Her eyes flashed. "I'm game if you are."

"Probably not the best reason to have sex."

"You've become awfully stuffy since you went to work for Bobby."

This new light-hearted Dorothy could be more aggravating than the old up-tight Dorothy. "I'm not working for Bobby, I'm just painting his portrait."

"And doing his ghost hunting." Dorothy leaned forward and gripped my arm tightly. "Kevin, you should be happy you're a natural medium like Daniel Dunglas Home. Why do you fight it? I envy you that power. You must let Maximilian help you channel your power."

I tried to disengage, but Dorothy now possessed a fanatic's strength. Why do I always fall for women who either go crazy or think I'm crazy or eventually want to turn me into something I'm not?

"Sport Sullivan is my one link to whatever's out there in the netherworld, and I'm trying to get rid of him. I don't know any more about ghosts or spirits than Maximilian does. We're both just people, we have limited 'powers.' Ghosts are like UFOs. If they do exist, they're too disconnected from human experience for any of us to understand."

"You just don't *want* to understand. And you're jealous of Maximilian."

"Dorothy, you've lost your sense of balance."

"You're wasting a great gift." Dorothy withdrew from me, physically and emotionally. "I'm busy, Kevin. I'll see you at the nine o'clock meeting." She turned back to her computer.

As I left Dorothy, the executives and some of their support staff were beginning to return to the sixth floor. Office lights and computers were switched on. Files opened. Phone calls made. But no one I saw looked very happy to be back in their comfortable executive suites.

CHAPTER 28

Most of the execs ventured cautiously into Bobby's office. Those who hadn't seen last night's spook show had heard about it and didn't want to be around for a replay. Neither did they want to risk losing their jobs, so they turned out for the meeting in force. About twenty people made up the full management team, including some I'd seen only in the meeting where they tried to take my portrait away from me.

Pepper had remounted the center frame of Pete Rose cards on the wall to cover the black box so expertly that I doubted anyone would be able to tell the frame had been disturbed.

Chairs were pulled in from other offices and arranged theater-style in front of Bobby's immense desk. Jenny flitted in and out making sure all the execs were present and that everyone had note pads, fresh coffee and were otherwise comfortable and prepared. Though her relentless efficiency remained intact, Jenny's perkiness had been replaced by a grim determination to get through the day without any additional disasters.

I patted Jenny's shoulder. "Try to relax, everything's going to be all right."

"No." Her chin was jittery and her eyes had become as sharp as the tips of ice picks. "Nothing will ever be all right again."

"Sure it will." Hugh Wilson came over to us. "Jenny, you've been running around this place like a mad woman since dawn. Kevin's right, you need to sit and relax. Come over here by me, there's an empty chair."

Before getting Jenny settled, Hugh leaned close and whispered in my ear, "On Bobby's direction I've transferred money into the offshore

346

account of your friend Sam Cody. Though I'm still uncomfortable with the legality of what was done to Izzy Valentine, I'll admit Mister Cody's efforts were…well…effective."

"Today was nothing, you should see him break into a Mercedes."

Hugh gave a lawyer's censorious sniff and went off to comfort Jenny. Now that I thought about it, he'd been comforting Jenny a lot lately. I recalled how he'd leaped to protect Jenny when the ghost of Cynthia Gooding put in its appearance. Then he ducked out on drinks at Billy Jack's to drive Jenny home because Cynthia's apparition had upset her so much.

I might've come up with a derisive comment about office romances if I hadn't slept with both Jenny and Dorothy myself.

A few of the execs stared or looked puzzled when Pepper came in and took a chair next to me. I drew a few stares, too. Nobody sat near us. We were lepers in this elite group because neither of us could write a computer program, or use one for that matter.

"All right, let's get going," Bobby said. "We have a lot to accomplish and I don't want to keep you here too late. This has been a rough enough day already. The roughest day Race Software has ever experienced." His eyes rested almost imperceptibly on Greg Tillotson, who was employing his usual combination scowl and sneer, then moved on. "The good news is that the reporters and tv units have packed up their hatchets and decamped." He extended an approving smile to Ray Waters. "Ray, you did a good job of keeping the media vultures circling overhead where they belong. Not one of them got onto the property. Only a few employees broke the cover story you passed out. The media chewed us up anyway. But you got our version of the 'power failure' story out there and so our stock took only a two and three-quarter point hit today. That could have been much worse. Nice work."

"Thanks, Bobby." Waters had dragged himself into the meeting like a dying pachyderm looking for the elephant's graveyard. The compliment affected him like a shot of B-12.

Bobby addressed Pam Solter. "How's the HR situation?"

"My staff's been conducting interviews all day." Pam flipped through her notes. "A hundred and twenty-two employees have resigned. I've been able to backfill about a third of those people today. By this time next week I expect most of the key positions will be filled. We were lucky to find some good resources because the employment market's a bit soft right now."

"My division lost the most people," Tillotson growled. "We'll definitely have to postpone the Redleaf announcement."

"Till when?" Bobby asked calmly.

Tillotson threw up his hands. "I don't know yet. I'll have a date for you tomorrow."

"Tomorrow isn't good enough." Bobby shifted his attention to Dorothy. "You should all know that Dorothy Lake has submitted her resignation effective the day Redleaf is announced." There was a nervous stir which Bobby quickly moved to dampen. "Her resignation has nothing to do with yesterday's rather puzzling events. Dorothy simply wants to follow an area of independent study. Since we don't have Dorothy for very much longer, we're going to use her talents to the fullest. Dorothy, you're now director of the Redleaf project. You'll do whatever it takes to bring in a quality product on time and on budget. Greg, I'm putting you in charge of the upgrades to our current products. We'll discuss your new title later."

Tillotson acted like he'd been hit by about twenty thousand volts of electricity. I swear his hair even stood up. "You can't do this!" He jumped to his feet. "You people can't *let him* do it!" Tillotson looked around like a seaman trying to organize a mutiny. I guess nobody wanted to walk the plank with him because the execs began to study their shoetops or the light fixtures on the ceiling. "Fuck you, Bobby. And fuck your new title. I quit!"

When Tillotson stormed out, everyone breathed a collective sigh that encompassed shock, regret and sadness.

"Greg will be missed." Those were Bobby's words. His tone indicated Greg was about as important to him as his toenail clippings. "On a more upbeat note, I have the pleasure to at last introduce you to the Race Software Corporation's largest individual stockholder, Mr. Clarence E. Wells." Bobby stood up behind his desk. "You've all heard his name over the past years, though none of you has ever met Clarence Wells. About seven years ago Mr. Wells saved this company by making a large investment in our stock at a critical time. We all owe him a great deal. This will surprise you, amaze you, as it did me. Clarence Wells is a longtime employee who's been going by the name of Pepper Johnson in order to guard his privacy. Today he 'comes out' as Clarence Wells. Pepper, I refuse to call you Clarence, please stand and accept our gratitude."

Pepper slowly came to his feet with a bashful grin. He sort of saluted with his hook as Bobby began to applaud. At first no one else joined in. This was a joke, right? Had to be a joke. I began clapping. Dorothy, bless her, realized Bobby was serious. She enthusiastically joined in. Others began to clap because they were afraid to sit on their hands while Bobby applauded and grinned at Pepper with considerably more warmth than they were accustomed to seeing in him.

Dorothy came over to shake Pepper's hand and impulsively kissed him on the cheek. "Good old, Pepper! You fooled us and everybody else. Congratulations!"

As the truth about Pepper sank in, everyone suddenly became terribly jolly. Congratulations, handshakes, kisses on the cheek, slaps on the back flowed like wine. I heard invitations to lunch and offers to team up on the golf course. Pepper, in his workman's clothes with his name labeled on the shirt pocket, accepted the extravagant attention as routine. I think Pepper was beginning to realize what he'd passed up all these years.

When everyone had returned to their chairs, Bobby announced that Zebulon-Perry Software would soon be announcing a product similar to Redleaf. Consternation in the ranks. Bobby asked for ideas to combat this competitive threat. Everyone had something to say and the discussion droned on in a way I didn't care to follow.

I looked at the half-finished portrait of Bobby and decided to take it home and work out on my deck in the morning. Race Software was beginning to wear me down. I longed for the peace and quiet of my own tumble-down house, watching the hummingbirds zip from one wild flower to another while I worked out on the deck, knocking off now and then for a sip of Mexican nectar and a short nap.

I happened to glance toward Hugh Wilson as he was conferring in whispers with Jenny. When they noticed me looking at them, Jenny blanched. Hugh covered Jenny's nervous hands with his own and whispered soothingly in her ear.

I stared at the frames holding the baseball cards and then looked pointedly at Hugh and Jenny. She became even more agitated. Hugh had to forcibly restrain Jenny from getting up and leaving in the middle of the meeting.

Bingo! A lot of loose ends quickly came into focus.

"Bobby, can I say something?" I stood and went right on without waiting for his permission. "Looks to me like the answer to your problem is to beat Zebulon-Perry to market. Also, you have to prove this other company has actually stolen your trade secrets. Am I right?"

"That's rather obvious." Bobby's sarcasm had a question mark at the end.

"I just thought of a really simple way to prove who's been feeding your company secrets to Zebulon-Perry. If I were a good cop like Joe Patterson, I would have thought of it right away." I went to the wall and yanked the center frame from its mounts to reveal the black box. "Fingerprints, Bobby. Whoever's been stealing your secrets must have left his or her prints all over this thing. You probably messed up some of them when you played around with the keyboard, but there'll still be prints on the box itself."

"What is that?" Pam Solter said.

"It's a Helstrom ADC. A very sophisticated client platform equipped with Java-based applets and other leading edge software." Bobby was furious with me for revealing how badly he'd been conned. Now that I'd done so, he explained its purpose to his execs. "The Helstrom development people loaned this prototype to us. Someone hid it inside the wall of my office to strip Redleaf data out of my computer. I think ZP's behind this, but I have no proof. "

Everyone in the room, except me, seemed to instantly grasp all the ramifications behind Bobby's revelation.

Bobby smiled. "Fingerprints. You're right, Kevin. That's so obvious I didn't even consider it."

"Actually, I already know who planted this thing inside your wall." I summoned up my best Perry Mason impersonation as I pointed dramatically at the culprits. "Hugh and Jenny. I think they were behind Cynthia Gooding's death, too."

"That's a lie!" Hugh came slowly to his feet with a quite convincing expression of outrage. "You've just bought yourself a major lawsuit for slander. I've got twenty witnesses to your wild accusations."

"And I've got one witness who'll put your crooked ass in jail, counselor." I was referring, of course, to Jenny, who was now sobbing behind her hands. "Sending one lawyer to jail isn't much, but it's a start."

Hugh's already lean face became as sharp as an ax. "Bobby, you're not buying this bullshit, are you?"

For an extended period, Bobby examined Hugh and Jenny as if they were specimens in a petrie dish. "Give me some solid data, Kevin."

"Data? Ah…I get it…factual stuff. Well, the first time I met Hugh he complained that the old timers at Race Software had soaked up all the stock option gravy. Hugh only recently joined the company. He has a good salary, he said, but the stock price was now so high his options weren't worth a bundle. Also, Jenny has big plans for a sort of health clinic specializing in geriatric care. She told me she'd soon have enough money for that.

"Here's some more data. Last night, when Cynthia's ghost came gliding into your office, Jenny let out a yelp and Hugh told her, *Shut up. Just keep quiet for once.* What was Hugh afraid Jenny might say? Maybe you noticed, too, that Hugh looked past Cynthia's ghost at the wall where that gizmo is hidden. You want more data? Who has better access to your office than Jenny?"

"Nobody," Bobby admitted. "She's usually the first one in every morning, the last to leave at night. Jenny, look at me."

Jenny took her hands down from her face because, I suppose, she was accustomed to doing whatever Bobby said. Her face was tear-stained and in a state of collapse.

"Don't say a thing," Hugh warned her. "We'll let our attorney speak for us."

"I'm so sorry, Bobby." The words came gushing from Jenny in a torrent. "In the beginning, Hugh told me there was no real harm in what he wanted to do. Industrial espionage is a game in Silicon Valley, he said. Like bridge is a game other places. I was greedy, I'll admit. I have my cherished dreams too." Jenny clumsily wiped away tears. "I wasn't going to do it, I really admire you. But after a while I became one of *Bobby's Harem*, like Dorothy and Cynthia and lots of others. When you stopped fucking me, when you moved on to a different girl, I decided to go along with Hugh's plan. Hugh borrowed the Helstrom from Greg Tillotson, who wasn't using it for much. I was the one who put it behind the display of your Pete Rose cards, but all the data went to Zebulon-Perry through Hugh. We were expecting a ten million dollar payoff, at least that was Hugh's story and I believed him."

If Jenny's motivation embarrassed Bobby, he didn't show it.

She gulped down a deep breath. "I was devastated when Hugh told me he'd killed Cynthia."

When Hugh raised his hand to slap Jenny, Pepper yanked him back into his chair.

"Why did he kill Cynthia?" I had a second question. "And how?"

Jenny seemed relieved to be getting the poison out of her system.

"Cynthia came to work here simply to meet Bobby. She was a terrible girl, you know. Vain. Ambitious. Conniving. Greedy." Jenny let loose a corrosive laugh directed at herself. "Not that I should talk. Anyway, Cynthia was a supremely confident person. She thought she could do what no other girl had accomplished, snare Bobby into marrying her. Or at least get him to keep her in grand style. Cynthia was beautiful and sexy, I'll give her that. She came into the office late one night, looking for Bobby. I was changing the batteries on the Helstrom ADC. She asked what I was doing. I made up a story but over the next few days Cynthia figured out what Hugh and I were up to. She took one of the disks from the Helstrom and printed out everything that was on it. The stuff Kevin found at her apartment. She was going to use it to prove to Bobby that we were stealing Redleaf data. She figured either Bobby or Hugh would give her a big payoff."

When she lapsed into forlorn silence, Bobby prompted her. "That's why Hugh killed Cynthia?"

The other execs had edged away from Hugh, who was now an official plague carrier.

"Yes." Jenny gave a single ferocious nod that ought to have torn her head from her shoulders. "He followed Cynthia into the library, found her alone, hit her over the head with a fire extinguisher, threw her off the top level of the library so it would look like she died in an accidental fall. He told me about this days later. He also said I'd have to keep my mouth shut because I was an accessory to murder. Hugh's way of controlling me, I see that now." Her face flushed. "For a while, I thought he loved me."

Hugh responded with cool authority. "Jenny's lying. Cynthia's death has already been ruled accidental and there isn't a single point of evidence to corroborate her story that I killed Cynthia. Go ahead, take fingerprints off the Helstrom. You won't find my prints on that machine. Only Jenny's. She's the industrial spy, not me."

"Your friends at ZP aren't going to be happy with you," Bobby said. "Sounds like Jenny can prove your involvement in selling our company secrets to ZP, if not Cynthia's murder. I'm going to slam ZP with a restraining order on their new product and sue the corporation for a tremendous sum. You're going to prison for industrial espionage, Hugh. That's a federal offense."

"Better than a murder charge."

Hugh had regained a large measure of confidence. As a lawyer, he saw a weak case against himself for murder. Nothing but Jenny's hearsay, in fact. He stood up, half expecting Pepper to push him down again. So did I. Pepper looked to Bobby, who shook his head.

"I hereby submit my resignation as Race Software's corporate counsel." Hugh smiled around arrogantly at his ex-colleagues. "See you folks on the golf course."

It took him a minute to work his way to an aisle as no one seemed inclined to move knees or feet out of his path. As Hugh made his way, the room became gradually brighter with various pulsing shades. A burst of color by the door stopped Hugh in his tracks. The execs scrambled backwards, knocking Hugh to the floor and jostling each other like frightened cattle coming down the slaughterhouse chute.

"It's back!" Pam Solter screamed.

Someone else yelled, "Let's get out of here!" but nobody dared rush the door because that's where the light storm was centered. Instead the execs pushed each other backwards amid a chorus of whines and what-is-its. Pepper caught someone from falling and tried to separate those who'd become entangled.

I rose and spread my arms with, I would like to think, magisterial calm. "This isn't Cynthia! It's somebody else and he won't hurt you unless you let him talk you to death."

The fireworks built to a crescendo and fell away to reveal the customarily grotesque image of Sport Sullivan.

"…the fuck's going on this time? What am I, Kevin? Your personal scut boy?"

Sport's eyes were a ghastly black all the way through, no pupils at all. His teeth were likewise black and his tongue an unworldly shade of green. The blood from the bullet holes in his suit front was also black, which somehow made the wounds all the more terrible. Sport's long outdated suit and tilted derby lent him a strangely jaunty air.

"…think I got nothing else to do except…hey…the fuck are all these people?" He spotted Dorothy. "Hey, the Gibson Girl. Hiya, Dorothy."

Somebody on the executive team fainted. Not one of the women. A man. Nobody moved to pick him up.

"Don't be afraid, this is Sport Sullivan." I considered how I might describe him. "He's in limbo."

"Arnold Rothstein had me bumped off."

Sport had a brand new audience, so of course he launched into the story of how he'd helped Arnold Rothstein fix the 1919 World Series. Though he strutted up and down while he talked, he continued to block the door. Otherwise there would have been a stampede. Sport hardly noticed as I moved slowly around the office trying to allay fears by patting this person on the shoulder, moving a man with shaky legs into a chair, stopping a woman from biting hard enough on her fist to draw blood. Pepper saw what I was doing and did his best to help. Over a couple of minutes the two of us managed to damp down the hysteria.

Bobby was another story. At first he was as frightened as the others, but soon he began watching and listening with hard concentration. His curious eyes roamed here and there looking for some trick. The pulse of a laser or a light beam from a conventional source. Bobby searched for what he liked best. Clear data. The problem is creatures like Sport Sullivan don't generate clear data.

Equally fascinated was Dorothy, who slowly edged toward Sport in an attitude of abject worship. The girl had gone bananas over a ghost.

Excuse me, Sport. Over a spirit in limbo. I put a restraining hand on her arm. She pulled away.

"Arnold never could've fixed the Series without me," Sport was saying. "That's the thanks I got, shot down in a cheap New York bar." Sport abruptly changed the subject. "I wasn't always a gambler and a fixer y'know. I started out in burlesque as a soft shoe dancer. Did I ever tell you that, Kevin?"

"Never heard that one," I said.

Sport went into a little dance on Bobby's carpet, singing in a loud and particularly obnoxious voice, "Give me that old...soft...shoe...I said that old...soft...shoe. Uh-one...Uh-two...Uh-doodely-doodely-do. Give me that old...soft...shoe...'cause nothing else will do. It's the dance I always danced for you."

His dance carried him away from the door, which gave a dozen scared execs the opportunity to bolt into the corridor. When Hugh Wilson tried to run, Pepper and I grabbed him from each side and forced him into a chair.

"Let me go." Hugh struggled. "You have no right to keep me here."

"Stick around," I told him. "Sport hasn't finished his song."

"Hey, where's everybody going? My dancing ain't that bad." Sport's dance came to a jerky halt. "Is it my singing? For shit's sake, gimmee a break. I haven't had time to rehearse."

Dorothy began to applaud. "You were wonderful."

Sport grinned and bowed. "Don't applaud, just throw money. That's what we used to say in burlesque. Of course, I don't have much need for money these days, so keep up the applause, Dorothy. I love it."

"Who are you?" Bobby asked.

The question vexed Sport, who showed his irritation by flashing himself in different colors. "Weren't you listening? I'm Sport Sullivan! I helped fix the 1919 World Series! Kevin, what kind of dumb bastard is this? He never heard of Arnold Rothstein? Never heard of Shoeless Joe Jackson? What do people talk about these days?"

"They talk about computers," I said.

"What's a computer?"

I jerked a thumb at Bobby. "He'll have to explain."

Bobby stirred, wondering if he could make a man who had been shot to death in 1920 understand what a computer is.

Turned out he didn't have to do that. The temperature dropped so suddenly and so far down that my teeth began to chatter. The room temperature must have gone from forty to twenty in the space of a few seconds. The eight or ten of us still in the office doubled up in agony when the dry, icy air hit our lungs. Sport, being out there somewhere in limbo, was the only one not affected.

"What's going on?" Sport squinted at us. "You people drunk? Hope you saved some of the good stuff for me. Lotta bad booze around since Prohibition came in."

The vividly red form of Cynthia Gooding came floating through the door. This time there was nothing indistinct about the apparition. Her features, clothes, hair, were much clearer than any other of her appearances.

"...the fuck is that?" Sport recoiled from Cynthia's specter. His mouth gaped. "It's a fucking ghost!"

Sport disappeared with a popping noise.

"No!" Hugh Wilson lurched to his feet and this time Pepper and I did nothing to restrain him. "Get away from me!"

Pepper grabbed my arm and pulled me aside as Cynthia glided toward Hugh. Bobby jumped out of his chair and scrambled away, knocking his beloved desktop computer to the floor. Ray Waters tried to run and tripped over the guy who'd fainted. Jenny vomited on Bobby's desk. Others tripped over themselves making tracks away from Hugh.

The temperature dropped still lower. Below zero. Way below zero. I could hardly breathe. My movements became jerky and my thoughts confused. I sank to my knees and put my head down to keep the blood flowing through my brain.

Hugh stumbled and fell along with everyone else. He crawled away from Cynthia crying and begging. Dorothy collapsed a yard or so from me and I threw myself on top of her, hoping to share whatever warmth I still possessed.

A second later Cynthia's specter enveloped Hugh Wilson. He gripped his throat and gagged. His skin went blue and turned to parchment. I have no idea how cold it was inside that terrible presence, but Hugh's body shook so hard his bones rattled. I'm sure I saw Cynthia smile. Moments later her presence dissolved and the temperature shot back up as dramatically as it had dropped.

Precious warm air flowed into my lungs. My skin stopped aching and I began to be able to move some of my body parts without severe pain. I lay there waiting to feel normal. Beneath me, Dorothy was stirring. I rolled onto my side and managed to get up onto my knees.

After a time I crawled painfully toward Hugh. His skin had gone an ugly blue/white and his body looked as stiff as a Thanksgiving turkey just taken from the freezer. I touched him and quickly drew back my hand. Hugh was frozen solid. His eyes stared into deep space. The arm he had put out to ward off Cynthia was still upraised and sticking straight out from his body. One leg stretched far out to the side. I tried to shift him and he made that clunky sound you get when you drop frozen food into the sink.

Bobby stood up, rubbing himself all over to get his circulation going. "Is Hugh dead? Shall I call the police? Shall I tell them to send an ambulance?"

"Yes, he's dead," I said. "You'd better call the cops and the EMS." I got to my feet as if climbing out of a grave and helped Dorothy up. Her shoulders were covered with frost. "While you're at it, tell them to bring a hair dryer or they'll never get Hugh into the ambulance."

CHAPTER 29

One evening several weeks later I found myself in the north end of the Napa Valley in the small town of Calistoga. Eight p.m. on a crisp night and I was sitting at a picnic bench in the park across the street from David Maximilian's Institute For Psychic and Paranormal Research. There were four or five wineries nearby and you could smell the wine fermenting in huge oak casks. I was eating a ham and cheese sandwich from a local deli and drinking a Carta Blanca. At my feet a cooler held five more beers on a bed of ice. The unusual part of the picture is that I didn't bring the beers for myself.

A police patrol car had twice driven by the park and the officer behind the wheel eyeballed me both times. The third time he parked and walked across the grass to check me out. He slapped the leather on his holster a couple of times to remind me that he was armed.

"Good evening, sir." He was almost too short for police work. I didn't get the sense he was out to hassle me, he was just curious. He had the only crew cut in the Napa Valley.

"Hello." I held up my sandwich. "Want part of this? It's too much for me."

The cop cocked his head. "You got that from Mario's deli. He makes those mothers big, you ought to have ordered a half-sandwich. Mario sells them that way too, y'know."

"I'll remember next time."

He rapped his toe against my cooler. "You got more beer in there, I'll bet."

"Five bottles. Don't worry, I'm only drinking this one. The others are for a friend I'm expecting."

The cop nodded. "That your Karmann Ghia?"

"Yep."

"Don't see many Ghias these days. This one's in nice condition."

"I just put six thousand dollars into it."

"Lot of money to put into an old, underpowered automobile."

"I find it hard to part with old things I like. I recently collected a pretty good paycheck from a software company in Silicon Valley. Used the money to fix up my house and the Ghia."

"You live around here?"

"No, I'm from down the coast. Half Moon Bay."

"Mind if I ask what you're doing in Calistoga? I mean, in this little park...at night...a hundred miles from home...with a sandwich and a beer?"

He asked me that question at just the right time. I'd been brooding all night and was in a mood to unload my frustrations on someone. "Do you have time for a story?"

"I guess." The cop sat down and picked up the other half of my sandwich. "You sure you don't want this?"

"Positive."

He took a bite and smiled. "So what's your story?"

I pointed at the Victorian house across the street that housed the Institute for Psychic and Paranormal Research. "I'm here because of the guy who runs that place. You know him? Calls himself Maximilian?"

The cop nodded between bites. "I know Maximilian. Con man, you ask my opinion."

"Exactly. My problem is, I fell for a girl named Dorothy. She's gorgeous. Little slip of a girl, honey blonde hair, wonderful figure, bright as hell, warm, a little mixed up but delightful. We were getting along pretty well until Maximilian showed up. She bought his whole line. I've had dinner with her twice this month trying to convince her of what a phony he is. She can't see it. Now she's engaged to him. Dorothy's got some money, I'm sure that's what Maximilian's after."

"Maximilian is slick, I'll give him that." The cop had already finished the half-sandwich. He produced a toothpick and stuck it in the corner of his mouth. "I've been on the force here for eight years. During that time Calistoga's had its share of phonies, con men, hustlers, deadbeats, big talkers. We had a minister who sold shares in his church, raised almost two hundred thousand bucks and left town overnight. He was good. Maximilian's better. Everybody wants to believe they can talk to spirits, 'pierce the veil' I've heard Maximilian say. He preys on the gullible, and there are plenty of those. Including, I guess, your girl Dorothy."

"Including her," I agreed.

"Good thing is, most of his marks get wise to him sooner or later. Maybe this Dorothy will kiss him off. Is that what you're sticking around for?"

"Maximilian's holding a seance tonight. Dorothy's over there trying to chat up some spirit or other. I told her she's got about as much chance of talking to a spirit as I do of batting .400 for the Giants."

"Hey, the Giants could use you if you only batted .275." The cop squinted at me. "You don't have any ideas about beating up on Maximilian, do you? Not that I'd care a whole hell of a lot, but I wouldn't want you doing it on my shift."

"I wouldn't touch Maximilian with a long stick."

"Glad to hear it."

During our conversation, the cop had unobtrusively looked me up and down for signs of a weapon. He opened the cooler with the toe of a spit-shined shoe. "All Carta Blancas. I hear that's a good beer. I'm a Coors man myself."

"Take one for later," I offered. "Might change your life."

"No, thanks. Have to get back on patrol. I appreciate the sandwich. Mind you don't try to finish off all those beers yourself and then take the Ghia on the road. I'd bust you real fast."

"Message received and understood."

He waved good-bye as he got into his car and drove off. Nice guy. He'd checked out me and my cooler in a nice way, satisfied himself I wasn't going to do anything stupid, couched his warning in a friendly way.

The lights in the Institute for Psychic and Paranormal Research suddenly dimmed, which meant the seance was getting underway. Dorothy told me Maximilian charged each participant five hundred dollars to take part in one of his "spirit guide evenings." Ten people. Five thousand dollars. Not a bad payday. Even though Dorothy was now Maximilian's fiancee, I'll bet she had to come up with five hundred bucks like all the rest.

I closed my eyes and tried to concentrate on Sport Sullivan. The asshole always said I had the power to summon him up and that's what I intended to do.

Now that I actually wanted him to appear, I doubted he'd do it. I concentrated on Sport's ugly countenance for maybe fifteen minutes. Put everything else out of my mind, even beer. Okay, I did think of beer a few times. Only as fleeting images. I really did try to coax Sport out of his famous nest in limbo. As usual, he wouldn't cooperate. All I got for all my concentration was a migraine.

I left the picnic table and walked around the park hoping to clear my mind by thinking about people other than Sport.

Big Sam's attorneys had gotten another continuance; the strategy was to delay any kind of court action on the auto theft charge for at least a year when evidence would be harder to come by and details of the event would be hazy in the minds of the arresting officers. Izzy Valentine had already beaten the DEA's charge of cultivating marijuana, his lawyers were even better than Sam's. But Izzy's reputation was permanently damaged. Sam read in the *Chronicle* that Izzy was moving his home and business operations to Phoenix where Amelia was "recuperating from asthma attacks" in a private hospital.

Bobby Race stayed in the news. Thanks to Dorothy, the Redleaf project got out the door to rave reviews from the trade press. Redleaf was selling briskly and *Business Week* used my portrait of Bobby on the cover to illustrate its story. As a result, the price for my oils had gone up by about a thousand dollars and they were selling slightly better. I wasn't getting rich, but my credit rating had marginally improved.

Though the police were awfully curious about how Hugh Wilson got himself been turned into a popsicle, their investigation hit a brick wall and was finally dropped. Nobody took the ghost rumors seriously and Cynthia Gooding's image has not been seen again.

Pepper continued to change light bulbs and sweep floors at Race headquarters. Every couple of weeks we'd meet at Billy Jack's for ribs. Last time Pepper told me he was being kept busier than ever. Now that the execs knew he was a big stockholder, they were always calling him to their offices to fix the lights or air-conditioning just so they could chat him up.

I went back to the picnic table and sat down again with my eyes closed. Sport's out there somewhere, I told myself. Here Sport! Here Sport! No, that's a bad attitude, I have to take this more seriously. I cleared my throat and scrunched up my eyes. Sport? Come out…come out…wherever you are!

Wait! Is that Sport? No, it's the Mother Ship!

When I began to giggle I knew this wasn't going to work.

"Sport, you old bastard. You could've gotten gloriously drunk tonight. Your loss, pal."

From behind me, Sport said, "You brought some of that good Mexican beer, Kevin?"

I almost jumped out of my skin. I turned and there Sport was, flashing green and red and violet and yellow and blue and ochre and more damned colors than I could follow. "Where did you come from? I didn't see any flashing lights or hear any static."

"Hey, I came in quiet because I wanted to make sure there weren't any more of them fucking ghosts around." Sport shivered. "That was spooky last time, wasn't it?"

"Spooky," I agreed.

Sport looked a bit more conventional tonight. His teeth and tongue weren't black and the bullet holes in his sack suit were only mildly disgusting. My usual bad luck. Just when I want Sport at his worst, he shows up looking less scary than usual. "I've always wondered, Sport. Where did you get the suit?"

"Like it?" Sport did a turn to show himself off. "Special order from the Sears Roebuck catalogue. Peg top pants. Rolled lapels. Watch pocket. Five button vest and the buttons are real ivory. Strap and buckle in the back of the coat. Padded shoulders. The latest style and only eight bucks including the vest. Classy, huh?"

"Knocks me out." I opened the cooler. "I brought you a few beers."

When Sport frowned, his eyebrows turned electric blue. "You wanted to see me? You're buying me beers? The fuck's going on here?"

"Hey, you said it yourself. Last time was spooky, I wanted to make it up to you."

Sport's suspicions eroded slightly when I opened the cooler and popped the cap on a Carta Blanca. "Come on, have a brew."

"You ain't gonna poison me or something?"

"How can I poison somebody who's already in limbo." I raised the bottle to the level of his mouth and began to pour. It worked for Dorothy and it worked for me. The beer cascaded through Sport, most of it splattering on the ground but some of it dissolving inside of him.

He smacked his lips. "Damned good." Sport burped behind the back of his hand. "I could use another."

I poured another into his mouth and Sport gave me a silly grin. "Limbo don't look so bad right now."

A man walking a terrier came down the path next to the picnic bench. The terrier's tail went up and it growled. "Quiet, Teddy," the dog walker said. "What's wrong?" The terrier yelped and strained on its leash to avoid me and Sport. It began barking and digging its paws into the pathway. "Teddy?" The dog walker finally noticed Sport. "My God! What is that?" The leash fell from his hand. "Oh no, it can't be!" The dog walker turned and sprinted away with the terrier on his heels.

Sport threw back his head and laughed. His tongue came flicking out of his mouth. Each time it emerged bigger and in a different color. My stomach heaved. This was more like it.

"See that old fart run?" Sport put his hands on his knees and bent over, laughing so hard he could barely stand. "Dogs! I hate dogs! Most of 'em eat better than I did when I was a kid in Hell's Kitchen. Fuck all dogs. I used to kick every dog crossed my path." The laughter wound down and Sport said, "How about another beer? Ain'tcha drinking tonight, Kevin?"

"I already had mine, Sport. Come on, drink up."

By the time I got all five Carta Blancas into Sport, he was singing again and dancing, too. "East side...west side...all around the town. Me and Rosie O'Grady...on the sidewalks of New York!" The ground beneath him was soaked with beer, but he'd absorbed enough to alcohol to do him some damage. I wondered if Maximilian's research had turned up the fact that ghosts can't hold their liquor.

I knew sooner or later Sport would begin his harangue about Arnold Rothstein. That's the one thing in the universe I can depend on.

"...couldn't have fixed the World Series without me, Kevin. I mean...I carried...big money...paid off the ball players. Then Arnold Rothstein had me rubbed out. Me! Sport Sullivan!"

"What was that name again?" As if I didn't know.

"Arnold...Fucking...Rothstein. The Big Fixer." Sport, drunk as he was, vibrated with rage.

"You know something, Sport? There's a descendant of Arnold Rothstein right across the street."

"What? Where is he? Who is he?"

"Arnold Rothstein's great grandson is right across the street in that building." I pointed at the Institute for Psychic and Paranormal Research.

"Arnold's great grandson?" Sport shook his head. "Here?"

"A direct descendant of your old boss Arnold. He brags about that."

"Son of a bitch." Sport clenched his teeth, which had become as sharp as a tiger's. "What's the bastard look like?"

I described Maximilian right down to his ponytail. Sport didn't know the phrase ponytail so I explained, "He has long hair tied back behind his head."

"I'll teach those Rothsteins not to...not to...fuck with Sport Sullivan." He staggered towards the institute yelling obscenities and gesturing wildly. When Sport reached the building, he walked right through the wall and into the institute.

When Sport disappeared into the building, I settled down at the picnic table and waited. Maximilian wanted to commune with spirits? This was his big chance.

I didn't have long to wait. Hysterical screams. Frightened cries. The crash of furniture being smashed or overturned. Potent profanity. Those sweet and satisfying sounds mingled as the participants in the seance came pouring out of the institute. At least they'd gotten their money's worth. Maximilian exploded through the front door with Sport close on his heels. Others fled the building with him and ran off in all directions. Maximilian's face was washed in horror. Even from across the street I could see the foamy spittle running down his chin. He stumbled and fell, scrambled up and ran. Though Sport was still staggering, he had the ability to cover lots of ground in one stride. Sort of like an astronaut walking on the surface of the moon.

"Hey, Max!" I called. "Give him your tests!"

The last I saw of them, Maximilian was pulling ahead of Sport. Dorothy stood on the front steps of the institute crying. She heard me call out to Maximilian, saw me at the picnic bench. Dorothy's face hardened. I saw contempt there. She went back into the institute and slammed the door behind her.

It occurred to me that sending Sport after Maximilian might not have been such a great idea.

ABOUT THE AUTHOR

William D. Blankenship is the author of nine other novels. His work has been published throughout the world in ten languages. He has been at various times a newspaper reporter, soldier, advertising copywriter, and corporate speech writer. His novel *Brotherly Love* became a CBS Movie Of The Week. Mr. Blankenship lives in Northern California.